UNDER DARKENING SKIES

RAY KINGFISHER

Text copyright © 2020 by Ray Kingfisher

Published by Lake Union Publishing, Seattle
www.apub.com

Amazon, the Amazon logo, and Lake Union Publishing are trademarks of Amazon.com, Inc., or its affiliates.

ISBN-13: 9781542040419
ISBN-10: 1542040418

Cover design by Sarah Whittaker

Printed in the United States of America

To my mother and father

Prologue

National Socialist German Workers' Party Headquarters, Munich,
1933

The slender man of studious appearance held himself upright, making the most of his modest height, as he entered the building. A servant greeted him and politely asked him to follow. They walked without another word along a wide corridor, past a large photograph of a row of SS soldiers saluting the German flag, past a portrait of the Führer, and stopped next to an eagle of gold, its wings spread, its talons clutching an ornate gold ring around a swastika.

The servant knocked on the door, was told to enter, and opened the door to reveal a small wood-paneled room with four large upholstered armchairs, two of them set on either side of a roaring log fire. The only man in the room immediately got to his feet.

"Herr Himmler to see you, sir," the servant announced, stepping aside to allow the visitor to enter.

The two men exchanged a vigorous handshake and settled into the armchairs on either side of the fire. By the time they'd exchanged pleasantries about the journey and the weather, the servant had returned with a tray of two drinks and was handing one to each man. No more words were exchanged until the servant had left the room, shutting the door behind him.

"I do like chilled lemonade," the slim, studious-looking man said, taking a sip.

The other, larger man took a gulp of beer. "You don't know what you're missing, Heinrich."

They put their glasses down on small wooden tables next to their chairs.

"So it would appear the future is assured," the larger man said.

"Yes, the negative types who stand in the way of progress have finally given in. The party can now concentrate on the job in hand: making our country one to be proud of."

"Have you thought how this affects you, Heinrich?"

"You think I have ambitions on power? That sort of power? I'm merely a humble chicken farmer."

The larger man laughed. "Not that sort of power. But you've exceeded expectations in your political duties. You took the party to the people and convinced them we are right, and you've taken the SS from a club of a few hundred to a potent force of fifty thousand. We all know how you rise to every challenge and how popular you are with the Führer."

"I try my best for Germany and for mankind."

"Which leads me to our talk. I have a proposal for you."

"Another challenge, perhaps?"

The man paused, and Himmler stilled himself to listen. "It's not official, but I've been asked to suggest if you . . . well, yes, to ask whether you'd be interested in a new challenge."

"Go on," Himmler said.

"We're looking for someone to manage the creation of a new camp."

"A camp?"

"A prison camp, one unlike any other."

"In what way?"

"One to keep all the Jews and other undesirables separate from the rest of the population—a place where they pay their way by working, where they are punished if they disobey."

Heinrich nodded. "Yes, of course. Anything for the fatherland."

"And perhaps there will be more camps if you make a success of it, which I have no doubt you will."

"Please let the Führer know how honored I am to be asked. But . . ." His eyes scanned the room, eventually settling on his glass, and he took a few moments to sip slowly and savor the rare tang of fresh lemon. "I do have another idea—a project I've been thinking about for some time—something I want to discuss with you."

"Of course. We are all as one. If I can help a fellow patriot, I will."

Himmler cleared his throat and took another sip of lemonade. "And I was wondering whether you could talk to our glorious leader about it: sow the seed, suggest it to him, let me know how he reacts."

"You're sneaky, Heinrich. Do you know that?"

Himmler's lip curled. "Don't call me that. There's nothing sneaky about me. I'm deadly serious and proud of my scientific skills; I just want to put them to the best use."

"Of course. Please accept my apologies. For you, I would be honored to help. Carry on. Tell me what you have in mind, and I'll talk to him."

"Well, no doubt you know that the birth rate of Aryans—of pure Germanic people—has been falling lately."

"Aren't we all aware of the statistics. Very worrying."

"And that if we relieve ourselves of the undesirables in our society, we create more room for Aryan children."

"I suppose so."

Heinrich leaned forward, his eyes twinkling with enthusiasm. "My plan is for a program to regenerate our Aryan genes, to radically improve the physical makeup of the next generation, to provide a pure and noble German society that will ensure the Third Reich lasts for a thousand years or more."

"It sounds interesting. Go on."

"I'm proposing a program to encourage Aryan men and women to procreate."

"But . . . doesn't that already happen?"

"No, no. I mean regardless of whether they're married to each other, and on a more organized, efficient scale."

The man smirked. "To . . . boost productivity, as it were?"

Himmler nodded. "And we could use SS officers. After all, we go to great trouble to ensure they are racially pure."

"They're barred if they're not."

"Quite. And I'm sure none of them would object. Don't you see? Half of the solution to our breeding problem is already in front of us."

"But what about the women?"

"That's the part I've been thinking about. We could actively seek out women of the correct hereditary features and offer incentives for the reluctant ones. I propose setting up a network of clinics to look after mothers and babies to ensure both are well nourished and cared for, then handing the child—who should be of good, virtuous Gentile stock—to a deserving German family to bring him or her up."

"You really have thought this through, haven't you?"

"Oh, I've thought a lot further than that. In time, if we get the opportunity, we could even expand the scheme to other countries."

"Would other countries agree to such a thing?"

"Mmm . . . we'd have to wait and see. Who knows what the future may bring? Some races are more suitable than others, of course. But I hope to concentrate on Germany first."

"You'd be taking on a lot, Heinrich. You're still running the SS, you head the Munich police force, you control the political police for the whole of Bavaria, you're managing the creation of these new Jew camps, and now you'll be organizing this breeding program—that is, if the Führer agrees to it. And you still have the farm. How will you manage it all?"

"Oh, I've already decided about the farm. I've talked it over with Margarete. We're going to sell it."

"Really?"

"I have much more important issues to contend with. I see rapid progress ahead now that the Führer has a clear run to implement our policies, and I intend to play a big part in that progress."

"I'll drink to that, Heinrich."

"Mark my words," Himmler said. "History will remember me."

Chapter 1

In the intensive care unit of Toronto Western Hospital, Arnold Jacobsen sat at his mother's bedside, silent and motionless apart from his fidgeting fingers. The only noise was the regular bleeping of the monitoring equipment attached to his mother; the only movement from her was the slow rhythmic rising and falling of her chest. Arnold's senses were tuned in to that sound and that movement, the symbols of his hope, his mind willing on the next bleep, urging her to push for that next hard-fought breath.

He felt powerless—redundant, even—but then realized there *was* something he could do: he could talk. So he started reminding her of the happy days spent playing with his two girls, now grown up. The girls owed a lot to their grandmother, particularly during that dark period when their mother had walked out, leaving Arnold to care for them in those most difficult teenage years. And if his daughters didn't appreciate what they owed to the recumbent, softly sleeping form now laid out in front of him, then he sure did. Talking to her was hard at first—there was the sense that he was really talking only to himself, but soon he'd said all those things he'd meant to say to her over the years but had never plucked up the courage to, thinking he could tell her another day—thinking that there always would be another day.

And then, just when he realized that talking to himself had probably been for his own benefit rather than hers, she woke up; almost smiled at him; said his name in the gentlest of tones, which seemed at odds with the sharpness of her accent; and shut her eyes again. He leaned closer and asked her if she was in pain. She replied with a wonderful smile and a brief sideways movement of her head before she drifted back to sleep or wherever the cocktail of sedatives was taking her.

Arnold spent twenty minutes just watching her quietly battling with her natural life span; then the door behind him opened, and he heard that distinctive and reassuring rustle of a nurse's starchy uniform.

"Hey, Merlene," he said as she moved a chair next to him and eased herself onto it.

"Just finished my shift," she said. "Thought I'd see how she's doing."

He shook his head. "Same as yesterday. She wakes up now and then. I managed to ask her if she was in pain, and she's not."

"Good," Merlene said, laying a hand on his shoulder and patting it gently before withdrawing.

He turned and looked into her dark eyes, noticing how they tilted up at the corners when she gave that big warm smile. "And I guess I owe you a special thanks," he said.

"I'm a nurse, Arnold."

"Hey, we all know you did more than nurse her while she was living at her apartment. You bought groceries for her whenever I couldn't. You were her friend."

"*She* was a good friend to *me*."

"I know you two got along well. She always said your accent was like a lime-and-coconut cocktail. And I'm sure without you . . . well, I guess I should have done more, and without you she'd have ended up here much sooner."

"Don't be putting yourself down, Arnold. In the end you gave up your job to care for her. And it was my pleasure to help. Ingrid was good to me. She was my first regular home visit after . . ."

"After Herbie died. She told me. Uh, you don't mind, do you?"

Merlene gave her head a dismissive shake. "She might have told you what happened to me. But she'll never know how much she helped me."

Arnold pointed to his mother. "You could tell her now."

Merlene hesitated, opening her mouth to speak, then halting.

"Or just tell me if it's easier. Either way, she'll know."

Merlene's broad smile hit him again, this time with a coy twist of the head. "Well, you know what happened to my Herbie. It was almost two years ago now. My mind was a swirling mess. I wasn't really in a fit state to work, but I forced myself to do it because I didn't know what else to do. I went to her place to take a blood test, check up on her breathing, make sure she was eating a balanced diet. And you know what? She knew something was wrong with me. She sensed it. I don't know how, but she sensed it. I almost told her to mind her own business, but she . . . she told me to make myself a coffee and sit down, to forget about taking a blood sample and checking her blood pressure and worrying if she was eating properly and the rest of it. She said she'd like to hear what was troubling me."

Arnold allowed himself a wry half grin. "I can just imagine her doing that. You go to check she's well, and she starts ordering you around like *you're* the patient, eh?"

"Well, I guess that's what I was until I'd poured my heart out to her, and she, uh, gave me the benefit of my experience. Then I felt a whole lot better."

"And did she tell you about my dad?"

"She did. She said he died a long time ago, but that was why she knew how I felt. She told me not to fight that kind of pain, because your precious memories are mixed in with it all. She told me to hold the pain, to caress it, and then to slowly strangle it, to help it wither and die while it's close to you. She said if you push the pain away, you lose those memories too. I didn't completely understand what she meant at the time."

"It hit her hard, losing Dad. It happened a long time ago now, but I remember it well. One day he seemed fit and well. The next day a brain aneurysm felled him just like a . . . like a Scotch pine taken down with a chainsaw. It hit me and Barbara hard too."

"Your sister, right?"

Arnold nodded. "It affected Mom the most, obviously. She and Dad came over to Canada from Norway when they were in their twenties. They brought across her own mother—my grandma—but for most of her life there was just the two of them trying to cope in a foreign land. You forget how dealing with that sort of stuff is so much easier when you're in the city you were born and bred in, when you have friends and relatives. She never had those. She had nobody here apart from me and Barbara. And I'm not sure how much help we were to her back then."

"Guess that was like a common bond between us." Merlene gazed at Arnold's mother. "Just like Herbie and me coming over from Jamaica all those years ago. It was just the two of us on our own for so long, and then, on that horrible day I've tried my hardest to forget, it became just the one."

"You have two boys, though, don't you? Is it two?"

"Uh-huh. Teenage boys. Well, more like young men in their minds, but at the time *they* needed *my* help, and I didn't want them to worry about helping me. But Ingrid, well, you see, she . . . she knew exactly what I was going through because she'd lost her rock too. And back then I visited her twice a week, and each time she managed to wheedle a little more out of me. She kept telling me how to deal with the pain—those words about not fighting it but holding it close and then strangling it—and eventually she got me out of that . . . that blue fog of depression. You know, I could easily have been a different person if it wasn't for her."

Arnold smiled proudly at his mother. He put a hand out and caressed the side of her face. "I got the same treatment when my marriage fell apart; she said pretty much the same words to me back then. Thing is, and she might not have told you this, but . . . well, those words of advice she gave you—they weren't exactly her own."

"Meaning?"

"I guess she didn't tell you what happened to her in 1940."

"1940? No. No, she didn't."

Arnold gave a short chuckle. "1940. Doesn't it seem a hell of a long time ago?"

"Like it's another world."

"You see, my dad told me a little of what happened back then—just a little because Mom never spoke about it—too painful, I guess. My mom was an incredibly resilient woman, and I think she took that from watching how her own mother coped with being widowed at about the same age as you—just in her early forties. I guess that process of coping stuck with her, like it was inherited or something."

Merlene was stifling a laugh. "Did you just suggest I'm in my *early forties*?"

"What? Aren't you? Ah, your raised eyebrows would indicate I've got it horribly wrong. I'm sorry."

"Hey, you're a full ten years out, buddy, but, uh, in a *good* way, so please, please don't apologize. Now, tell me about Ingrid and your grandma."

"Well, I don't know everything—only what Dad told me. It happened at the start of the war. At least, at the start of the war where Norway was concerned."

Chapter 2

Ingrid Solberg liked to think Ostergaten 41 was a nicer-than-average Oslo house. It was dominated by one main room with a kitchen area on one side and a large fireplace on the other, with a table and chairs near the kitchen sink and cupboards, and three armchairs gathered around the fireplace. Two bedrooms—one for Ingrid and one for her mamma and pappa—were nestled at the far end, next to the back door. All the floors were tiled but mostly covered with rugs, and the brick walls were so clean they looked freshly whitewashed. In fact, unlike many neighboring dwellings, the whole place was always clean and tidy; Ingrid's mamma insisted on that.

But lately the pleasantness of the house seemed unimportant. Most people were much more concerned with happenings abroad; some people carried on as normal, saying it would come to nothing or there was no point worrying until you were forced to. Ingrid was as confused as anyone by the government reassurances that were regularly wheeled out, while at the same time stories circulated of battles being fought not too far from Norway's doorstep.

It was public knowledge that the government had lately been bolstering defenses, but people hoped and prayed that the measures were nothing more than precautionary. It was also strongly rumored that they had been negotiating with the British government. And then there were the rumors of opposition politicians negotiating with the German government. More worryingly, there were stories of German U-boats sinking British ships in Norwegian waters and incursions by both sides into Norwegian airspace, not to mention the maneuvers of the Soviet Union. But despite all the rumors of threats and hidden intentions, day-to-day life carried on as it had for decades. The government assured citizens that Norway had no quarrel with Germany or Great Britain or the Soviet Union and had no reason to believe any of those other countries felt any differently about Norway. Above all else, the government insisted that Norway would remain resolutely neutral and independent.

Even by April there was still no panic, which suited Ingrid and her parents because they wanted nothing more than to be allowed to work, to buy food and one or two luxuries, and to be left in peace.

At eighteen, Ingrid thought perhaps she should know more about the war, but many people—including her pappa—said it wouldn't directly affect Norway, so she shouldn't worry. The closest she'd come to understanding what was happening was when a new neighbor had come to the door only weeks before and had been arguing with her pappa.

"I want to stay out of it," Ingrid's pappa had insisted.

"You should listen to the radio reports," came the gruff reply. "You need to know the truth."

"The truth? Who knows the truth?"

"If you knew the truth, you'd know that the time for staying out of it has passed. Europe is in turmoil since the Germans and Soviets invaded Poland. And with the Soviets taking over Finland, too, we can't pretend it doesn't affect us."

"But it doesn't. There's lots of bluster and strong words from all governments of Europe but no genuine hardship for anyone."

"Not even the Poles?"

"Well, yes," Ingrid's pappa conceded. "But Poland is a long way away."

"And did you hear how easy the Germans rolled into Poland? And *that* was because they've been building up their forces for such a long time."

"And so what? That's up to them. I agree with our government. We should stay neutral."

"And what do you think the Germans are going to do next with those forces? Organize a street party? No. We should join the British in declaring war on Germany at the very least."

"I disagree. They're more likely to cause us trouble if we provoke them."

Ingrid glanced over to the doorway and saw the man, a young, stocky sort with unkempt strawberry-blond hair and a straggly beard, shake his head angrily. "But we need to be able to defend ourselves," he insisted. "You only need to look at the geography of our country. Britain and Germany will soon be at each other's throats, and we're stuck in the middle. Just think what they would do to be able to control shipments of raw materials for their industries, to use our ports as naval bases, to control the skies above us. We need action, particularly against Germany. Mark my words; that country is nothing but a fighting machine."

Ingrid's pappa sighed. "Well, now *I* need action. I need to get ready to go to work, to earn for my wife and daughter. Would you mind that?"

"Just promise me you'll think about it. We need to pressure our government to act; we need to form action groups to—"

"Yes, yes, yes. Look, Olav, I know you mean well. I know there's concern, but I really do have to go, and I promise you I'll give it some thought."

"Thank you for your time, Anders."

It was late one night very soon after that conversation that Ingrid heard her parents arguing. But unlike Pappa's talk with young Olav, there was little politeness. Ingrid knew Pappa had to go out on the trawlers very early the next morning. It was what he did most days. But this time things were different; this time there was a raw and uncharacteristic fear in Mamma's voice.

"Please!" she said. "Do I need to beg? To cry? To hold you and not let go?"

"Listen to me, Helga," Pappa said. "This is my job. What else do we have to live on?"

"Ingrid brings in a little money. And she and I can darn clothes for food or money."

"That's not enough. I wish it were, but it isn't."

"I'd rather you be alive and we struggle. You know what the government said. German troops are building up on the Danish border. British and German warships patrol the seas."

"When foreign troops arrive in Oslo, I'll do as I'm told by the government. Until then I have a skipper to answer to, and he expects me on that quayside before dawn."

Ingrid heard her mamma crying, then her pappa adopting a gentler tone.

"Helga, I have to go. Please don't make it harder for me. I'll miss you as it is. But we need to eat."

"But it's dangerous, Anders. Please, just for a few days. I won't ask again. Please wait and see what happens."

"We both know it's dangerous. It always has been, and we've always accepted the risk. You think the Germans or the British will add to that danger? You think they have good reason to blow up a trawler?"

"Don't say that, Anders. You're tempting God."

"I'm sorry. But a fishing vessel is no threat to anyone. I have to go, Helga. I'm sorry, but . . . I *have* to."

Before dawn the next morning, warm in her bed, Ingrid heard Pappa getting ready to go to work: his heavy boots clonking around, the distinctive whistle his thick oilskin coat made as he moved. She heard no words from Mamma, which was only to be expected hours before dawn, but something urged her to leave the warmth of her bed and see her pappa. Perhaps it was all the stories of war circulating—perhaps it was the poor weather forecast—but whatever it was, she had to say goodbye. She jumped out and ran out of her bedroom, her feet cold on the tiled floor, and flung her arms around him as he stepped over to the front door.

"What's this all about?" he whispered in her ear.

"Just take care, Pappa. Promise me you'll come back. Tell me you'll be safe."

His hand—all thick fingers of dark cracked skin—reached up and moved a stray lock of hair away from her eyes. "Oh, Ingrid. You know I'll be safe. Just look after your mamma while I'm away. She's . . . very upset. But I'll see you both in a couple of days. I promise." Ingrid felt the heat of his lips on her forehead. "Now go back to bed," he said, the wetness of his kiss quickly turning cold in the chilly air.

Ingrid squeezed him tightly, inhaling the smell of greasy cotton, of fish, of salty air. Of Pappa.

"You'll get cold," he whispered, gently easing her arms off him. "Go on. Bed."

Ingrid turned and ran, jumping into bed, pulling the woolen blanket up to her neck, waiting to hear the front door open, the front door close, then silence. Only then did she shut her eyes and go back to sleep.

By late morning Ingrid's mamma seemed to have overcome what worries she'd had. That was Mamma: put trouble and worries to one side, concentrate on the job in hand, don't look back, never assume the worst. Just as Ingrid thought, her argument with Pappa the previous night had been a rare lapse in her usual fortitude. They ate together, washed clothes together, darned socks and gloves together, and found time to sit by the fireside and talk. Ingrid asked her mamma about the war going on in the rest of Europe. Mamma said she was worried, but the rituals and habits of life had to continue. She said that the politics should be left to the politicians, and the pointless arguing should be the domain of men, leaving the women to get on with the real work.

By the next morning, Ingrid's mamma seemed to have buried every trace of worry about Pappa. They ate their usual breakfast of pickled herring and rye bread with some yogurt, accompanied by conversation that was only slightly stilted, and as they were washing up together there was a knock at the door.

Mamma went to see who it was, showing absolutely no sense of foreboding. Ingrid spied Laila, a neighbor, outside, then saw Mamma step out and close the door behind her. Ingrid strained to hear through the door but could only make out a short but frightened exchange between the two women.

When Mamma returned, she shut the door firmly behind her and leaned back against it, a palm covering her chest, her breathing labored.

"What is it?" Ingrid asked, running toward her, holding her, feeling a tremble in her whole body. "It's not . . . Pappa. Tell me it's not Pappa."

Her mamma sighed as if relieved herself and shook her head. "Thanks be to God, no. But . . . there are rumors."

"Oh, Mamma, there are always rumors."

Mamma shook her head again, this time more forcefully, so much so that strands of graying hair fell down to frame her face. "Ingrid, please put my mind at rest. You need to go into the city center to check."

"Check what, Mamma? Check what?"

A weary hand pointed to Ingrid's coat. "Just go," she said. "But just look; tell me you'll do no more than just look."

Ingrid nodded, grabbed her coat, and made her way to the city center.

As she got closer, it was clear something was wrong—or at least different. She heard music—unfamiliar music—but more importantly the streets were busier than she'd ever known. It was as if every movie star, every sports champion, and every famous Norwegian had arrived, promising to hand out free beer to the men, free stockings to the women, and free candy to the children. At least, the *quantity* of people nudging each other, all vying for the best viewing point, would have implied good news.

Yes, the big crowds of city dwellers might well have implied good news under other circumstances, but the faces of those people told a very different tale. Nobody smiled. Frowns competed with frowns. Very few words were exchanged. And such behavior against the backdrop of that stirring, almost jolly music was as unsettling as it was strange.

Ingrid leaned out from the crowd lining the street and saw perfectly coordinated rows of field-gray uniforms gradually moving along like drifting clouds. But clouds weren't regimented; they weren't topped by a perfect array of steel helmets; they weren't accompanied by the clattering of boots, perfectly synchronized with the brass band that was playing. And clouds definitely didn't carry rifles. The soldiers marched past, wave after wave, thousands upon thousands of them. And as yet more approached and passed by, Ingrid saw nothing but resolve in their eyes. This display was a warning to the natives: Oslo is ours. Accept the new power, because there will be no alternative.

And the message got through. The shock of seeing so many German soldiers strutting down streets more used to cars or horse-drawn carts was doing its job.

Other soldiers were working their way along the crowds, handing out leaflets. Before Ingrid knew it, one was thrust into her hand, and the soldier moved along. A few people crowded around her to read. It was printed in badly translated Norwegian, but, like the military display, the message was clear. Norway would soon be completely under German control, with the agreement of a new national and local government structure and the support of the local police. There was no need to be afraid. The German troops weren't *invading* but merely being stationed here to protect Norway from a *British* invasion, and everything—jobs, laws, education, food provision—would be unchanged. Yes, the message was clear, even if hard to believe.

Ingrid had seen and heard enough. She let someone pull the leaflet out of her hand and turned, forcing her shoulder between the bodies, threading her way through the crowds, running away from the city center, heading for the main road leading to the side street of Ostergaten, to house 41, where she knew she would have to break the news to her mamma, to tell her that the stories she'd heard were more than mere rumors.

She stopped running as she turned the corner into Ostergaten, conscious that she would need all her breath to talk to Mamma to stop her from getting upset. But the street was busy. Olav, the neighbor who'd been arguing with Pappa only weeks before, was now gesticulating wildly as he spoke with two other men. Ingrid caught a few words spoken with disgust, of ships being sunk not far from the coast, of German planes circling above, of German soldiers falling from the skies like the devil's raindrops, of naked fear and the demise of all hope.

She hurried on to house 41, her steps faltering as the door opened, and a well-dressed man in spectacles appeared. She vaguely recognized him but couldn't remember from where. She stared at him as he walked past, head down, sullen faced, not even trying to return her stare.

She pulled her gaze away from the man and ran to the door.

"Mamma! Mamma!" she cried as she entered. "It's true, Mamma. It's all true. German troops are . . ." Her words trailed off as she saw her mamma kneeling by the fire, crying, head in hands.

Ingrid knelt down next to her, put an arm around her, and started rocking her gently back and forth. "It's not so bad, Mamma. We'll survive. Whatever it takes, we'll eat and stay warm. I promise."

Then her mamma looked up, and Ingrid knew from the redness of her eyes what was wrong before she uttered a word. "It's . . . it's your pappa," she said.

The man. The morose-looking man who had just left the house. Now Ingrid knew who he was. She'd seen him once or twice over the years. He was from the trawler company Pappa worked for.

"Early this morning . . . ," Mamma continued. "The trawler ship. A stray mine."

Ingrid felt a foggy heat engulf her body and mind. She could do nothing more than burst into tears and throw her arms round her mamma.

Chapter 3

Oslo, April 1940

Within a few days of the German invasion, Vidkun Quisling—a Norwegian politician who had for many years supported the aims of the German National Socialists—was installed as prime minister and immediately took control of the press and banned Norwegians from listening to foreign radio broadcasts.

Nevertheless, people *did* listen, their appetites for news bigger than ever, and the news quickly spread. Within a matter of days German troops had advanced well beyond the capital. But the terrain to the north and west was vast and wild and sporadically defended by what remained of the army and locals who knew that terrain all too well, so this proved more troublesome to capture than the main cities.

The Norwegian royal family and top government officials had relinquished those main cities to the rampant German forces but refused to capitulate entirely. They retreated to the sparsely populated areas, where Norwegian, British, French, and Polish troops courageously fought on. Some people had faith that those forces would halt the progress of their German counterparts; some had faith in higher powers. Both were wrong. The defending troops were vastly outnumbered and outgunned, so the Norwegian royal family and government officials were finally forced to flee the country in June, leaving their citizens at the mercy of the German machine.

By then, citizens of Oslo had come to terms with their new rulers. The troops kept coming, so much so that within months it was hard to find one park, one square, or even one street free from the sight of those uniforms. This made it dangerous to talk or act freely. Locals spoke in fearful whispers, their eyes scanning the surroundings, for the city was alive with German oppression.

Ingrid and her mamma must have been the only two people in the whole of Oslo who hardly cared. Pappa's funeral had been a rushed affair, and the shadow of more momentous events encroached on their grief, almost denying them the chance to mourn or honor the man they both loved. Or so it seemed, with friends and neighbors talking of little else but resistance, rebellion, and civil disobedience to make a stand against the new rulers. But talking was all they seemed to do; there was no clear sign that anything would wrestle the iron fist of the Führer from the country.

Ingrid and her mamma busied themselves with household chores, repairing neighbors' clothes in return for food or firewood, shopping around for food to make the meager savings Pappa had left for them go as far as possible. But there was little talk of Pappa between them. Yes, there had been tears for the first few days and then a tight and inward stoicism from Ingrid's mamma that Ingrid seemed to feed off. Occasionally Ingrid felt the urge to ask her mamma why she was no longer upset, but each time her thoughts inevitably came to her pappa and stumbled there. She imagined how he, in his no-nonsense manner, would surely have wanted them both to live the rest of their lives for themselves, not for their memories of him. So she held her tongue.

But the clear light of midsummer brought with it an event that would change them, even break them, where confronting their loss was concerned.

Ingrid and her mamma were sitting at the table, halfway through their midday meal—some white bread, a little cold pork they'd gotten from Peder Munsen three doors down in return for repairing his torn pants, and a rare tomato each—when they heard a commotion outside.

Mamma frowned and shook her head. *Ignore it,* was what Ingrid knew she was saying.

They continued eating, but the commotion continued too. Soon it became more intense, the shouts louder, the noise of a revving engine of some sort joining in.

This was now different, and Ingrid could no longer contain her curiosity. She gave her mamma a sideways glance and ran to the door. She opened it and saw two separate scenes being played out in front of her and the rest of the neighbors. Her mamma was soon at her side to see too.

Halfway across the street a middle-aged couple was being forced into a truck by German soldiers, shoved by hands and the muzzles of rifles where that hardly seemed necessary. Both the man and the woman had head wounds—the man with blood streaming from his nostrils all over his shirt, the woman with a cut above her eye, turning the socket below a glistening scarlet. Ingrid recognized them as neighbors but didn't know them by name. But she saw other doors opening and recognized heads popping out: Egil Hauger, the boatbuilder; Olga Bakker, the postman's wife; and others. They quickly returned inside, no doubt barricading themselves in.

"Shut the door," Ingrid's mamma said to her. "We shouldn't be watching; it's dangerous."

Ingrid knew her mamma was right, but her instinct was to keep watching the spectacle.

Some distance away from the truck, just outside the door to a house, four more soldiers were beating a man with their boots and the butts of rifles, each jockeying for position to get another blow in.

One of the soldiers took a break from beating and turned to face Ingrid and her mamma. Ingrid gasped; her mamma pulled them both in and slammed the door shut. Ingrid's throat was dry, her heart was thumping, but it was no good. However dangerous, she had to look— if only through the crack of a barely open door—while her mamma backed away.

Shouts from the truck told the soldiers their job in Ostergaten was done, and they all returned to the truck, which drove off. Now Ingrid felt safe enough to open the door wider. The man lying on the street managed to lift his bloodied head and shoulders, supporting himself on one hand, and shouted abuse at the truck. Ingrid thought this was very unwise, that the truck might stop, and the soldiers might revisit what had seemed like a punching bag. But they didn't, and the man cursed again, now more to himself, and started crawling along the edge of the street.

More neighbors opened their doors to check whether the soldiers had gone. Most of them immediately slammed their doors shut again, but three tentatively approached the bloodied form as it crawled toward a nearby front door. Ingrid's mamma told her to come in, too, and to shut the door, but she felt compelled to continue watching. The man was helped up but shrugged the helpers off once he was on his feet, cursing indiscriminately. He spied Ingrid, his battered face pointing directly at her, and then he shouted at her, his crooked mouth distorting the words, giving them a more sinister edge.

"This is your fault!" he yelled. "This is because of you and your coward of a pappa!"

Ingrid shut the door and started to cry, holding her head in her hands. Then she felt her mamma's gentle embrace, heard her soft voice, felt a cloth pat her cheeks.

A few minutes later she was looking at her mamma, noticing her dry eyes.

"How do you do it, Mamma?" she asked. "How do you not cry over Pappa?"

"One day I'll tell you," she said. "When you need to know."

For the next two days Ingrid and her mamma stayed indoors, too scared to go out in case they bumped into the man who had said such a horrible thing about Pappa. By now Ingrid had realized who the man was. Beneath the blood this was the man who had been arguing with Pappa about politics just before the invasion, trying to persuade him to lend his support to the cause. She remembered Pappa talking about him. Olav was his name.

And when, after those two days, a knock came on the door, it was slow and quiet, almost reluctant.

"Who is it?" Ingrid said firmly.

"It's safe to open your door," was the mild reply. "I just need to talk to you."

Ingrid opened the door just a crack at first, then wider, and stepped back, gasping and covering her mouth with the palm of her hand. It was Olav.

He, too, took a step away. "I'm sorry. Excuse me. I don't mean any harm."

Ingrid said nothing but noticed the dried blood in his long hair and straggly beard, the purple-skinned and slightly drooping eye, the grazes and bruises on both cheeks, the lips split and swollen on one side.

He held a bundle of wood in the crook of his arm. "For your fire," he said. "I know it's not very cold at the moment, but . . ."

"Who is it?" Ingrid heard her mamma call from far behind her.

Ingrid was still too shocked to speak and soon felt her mamma's presence at her shoulder.

"Oh, it's you," Mamma said on seeing Olav, her tone low and accusative. "What do you want?"

"I . . . uh . . . I want to apologize."

Mamma thought for a moment, then sighed. "You'd better come in."

Ingrid was speechless, memories of what this man had said about Pappa careering through her mind. But Mamma stepped aside, and Ingrid instinctively did the same, giving her mamma a scowl as Olav sidled past them. Her mamma shrugged. "Look at him," she whispered. "The man's suffered enough."

The smell of stale sweat and fresh sawdust that lingered in Olav's wake took Ingrid's mind away from any thoughts of arguing with her mamma. Olav let the wood down by the fireplace, and Mamma asked him whether he would like some apple juice.

"No, no," he said, shaking his head. "You keep that for yourself."

"I'll get you some," she said, intoned as if she were talking to a child.

A few minutes later they were all sitting at the table, holding cups of juice.

"I'm sorry for what I said to you," Olav said, his battered face now looking even more pitiful. "And I'm sorry for your loss."

"We accept your apology," Mamma said. "All of us Norwegians will need to stick together, so we'll hear no more about it."

"Thank you," Olav said.

"And we accept your firewood too. We're going to need it."

"You're welcome," Olav replied. "Your husband and I had our differences of opinion, but I know he was a good man and didn't deserve what I said about him." He lifted the cup and grimaced slightly as he rested it on his swollen lips.

"He only wanted to look after us," Ingrid said.

"Of course. It's not his fault. None of what is happening is his fault. People just want to get on with their lives. I understand that."

"Were they your parents?" Ingrid asked. "The couple taken away by the Germans?"

"They were," Olav said, his head bowed, his gaze fixed on the apple juice he was swirling around in the cup.

Ingrid looked at her mamma, who glared back and gave her head the briefest of shakes. Neither woman spoke.

"Well I . . . ," Olav started, huffing and wiping a hand over his beard. "I'm not sure what to say."

Still, Ingrid and her mamma just waited.

He quieted his voice. "The soldiers wouldn't tell me what it was all about, just that they were arresting them and taking them away. I think it was just to show us how much power they have over us. All I could do was ask where they were taking them, tell them that I was their son and had a right to know what was happening. All the soldiers said was that I . . . I would never see them again."

"Oh, Olav," Ingrid said. "That's terrible."

"And although I fought them, they . . . well, you saw what happened. I stood no chance."

"I see," Mamma said. "It must be hard for you, and I can understand why you were angry with my husband."

Olav shook his head dismissively. "I wasn't angry with your husband; I was just angry, and even more so now, but what can I do?"

There was a long silence; then Mamma asked, "What do you do for a living, Olav?"

Olav's battered face took its time to react but eventually perked up just a little. "I mainly work with wood. But I do other work, too—whatever brings in money or food or materials for me to work with. I manage to go on the trawlers occasionally too. That's how I knew your pappa. What about you, Ingrid? Do you work?"

"I wanted to be a seamstress. Well, I *was* a seamstress. I felt unable to go back to it once Pappa . . ."

"Of course," Olav said. "You don't want to leave your mamma alone."

"We'll have to do something soon, though," Mamma said. "Our savings won't last much longer."

"Oh, people will look after you," Olav said.

"That's easy to say when you can fend for yourself," Mamma replied.

"I'll look after you if nobody else will."

"That's very kind of you, Olav, but we won't need your help."

"Please," he replied. "I'd like to. I still feel bad for what I said about your husband . . . and . . . and, well, I have nobody else."

Mamma nodded. "Thank you, but let's see how we manage."

Olav fidgeted for a few moments, embarrassed like a schoolboy caught cheating, Ingrid thought. "Mrs. Solberg," he said, "if you don't mind me asking . . ."

"What is it, Olav?"

"Well . . . this is hard for me to explain."

"Just speak. You're a big enough man. Say it, and I'll listen."

"My mamma and pappa have been gone only two days. I have no idea where they've been taken—even whether they're still alive. It's . . . it's driving me mad. I can't sleep, I don't feel like eating, I—"

"It will get better," Mamma said. She leaned over and covered his hand. "We all hope to God your parents return safe one day, but in the meantime you just have to carry on, to do what they would have wanted."

"That's easy to say."

"I know it is, Olav."

"But you, Mrs. Solberg. You seem very strong. After . . . after your husband didn't come back from the trawler. How do you cope with being alone?"

"I'm not alone." She glanced to her side. "I have Ingrid."

"Yes, I know. But don't you miss Anders?"

"Do I miss him?" Mamma said. *"Do I miss him?"* She thought for a while, her face showing no sign of emotion. Eventually she took a breath. "I miss my husband like I would miss my sight or my hearing, as if nothing I do has any point. I miss his gravel voice; I miss the smell of the trawler that I used to detest. I hear him in every sound in the house. Every time I wake up, for one moment I still think he's by my side—and I treasure that moment. In my dreams I feel his hand as rough as rock yet so gentle with it. When I'm outside I hear some news and say to myself, 'Wait until I tell . . . ,' and I have to stop myself because I realize I'll never be able to tell him anything ever again." She paused, gathering herself together before continuing. She laid a hand on Olav's arm. "But my pain holds all the good memories too. You have to hold the pain, not fight it or shove it away so that it makes you feel bitter inside. You have to hold it close, keep it to your chest, and that way you can eventually strangle it, help it wither away and die."

Olav's face showed an unnatural fixed frown. "I . . . I'm not sure I understand."

"Think it through, and it will come, Olav. It will come. And then you will know in your heart that your pain has died, even though your memories will stay close and live forever."

He nodded. "I'll think about that. And thank you."

Chapter 4

Toronto, 2011

At Toronto Western Hospital, Arnold took a break from being at his mother's bedside to call his two daughters, Rebecca and Natasha.

Both had been expecting the call. They were fully aware that their grandma had been fighting a losing battle with her health for months. The stents fitted to her arteries many years before were now starting to fail. The pacemaker was doing its job, but it was clearly not enough. Her pulse was getting lower by the day. There had been an assumption by all that she would somehow struggle through and reach her ninetieth birthday in August, but words to that effect were only ever expressed to Grandma herself, meaning that it was little more than encouragement in a time of adversity. They all knew she was unlikely to last the week, let alone a couple of months.

As usual, Rebecca was the most talkative of the two.

"How is she?" she asked.

"Not much change," he replied.

"Should I come over, or . . ."

"It's up to you, Rebecca."

"I mean, how . . . uh . . . how long, do you think?"

He tried to disguise the tremble in his voice, coughing and for a brief moment almost asking her how her day at work had been.

"Nobody can really tell us for sure, but I'd say it's worth you coming over tonight."

"Right," Rebecca said weakly, her attempt to take a calming breath coming through the phone. "I was thinking," she continued, "did you tell Mom?"

"I called her last night. She said she was sorry for me, that her thoughts were with us all."

"Was that it?"

"No. She asked me if she could do anything to help, that she hoped to come to see her before, uh . . ."

"She always liked Grandma."

"She did. Listen, you should get moving, eh?"

"Oh."

"No, no, Rebecca. I didn't mean it like that. Don't rush over here; she's . . . stable."

"Just stable?"

"Also a little . . ." Arnold paused, immediately regretting what he intended to say. "Well, don't expect too much talking from her."

"I know, Dad. I've noticed, and so has Natasha. Everybody knows."

Arnold said nothing further on that subject. They all knew by now, so there was no point. All he could manage to say was, "Drive carefully, Rebecca."

Rebecca arrived within five minutes of her sister, by which time their grandma was sitting up and looking at Arnold and Natasha between lengthy blinks. And probably listening too. It was hard to tell. A framed black-and-white photo of Rebecca's grandma and grandpa lay in the bed with her, the sight of which made Rebecca pause for a moment and visibly rein in her emotions. She recovered, then leaned over and kissed her. "Hello, Grandma."

A weak smile from Grandma prompted a bigger one from Rebecca, as well as a watering of her eyes that she struggled to contain.

"Ah, Mamma," Grandma said in slurred words. "Good to . . . see you."

The mistake wasn't unexpected by anyone. Like Rebecca had said on the phone, they knew; they all knew. Grandma had been confused for a week or more and delirious for a couple of days. According to the nurses, lack of oxygen to the brain was probably responsible, imbuing her thoughts with a dreamlike quality, so her words reflected a curated selection of memories, new and old, slipping in and out of her mind like casual acquaintances. The advice from the nurses was to gently correct as much or as little as they felt appropriate but never to upset her. So that was what happened.

"This is Rebecca," Arnold told his mother. "You know, your granddaughter."

The words came as a revelation to her at first, but then there was a slow-motion nod. "Ah, yes."

There had been a time, mere days before, when Grandma would try to make excuses to cover up her mistakes: "It was just a slip of the tongue," "My mind was wandering," "I'm a little tired," "That's what I meant to say." But not now.

"Rebecca," she continued breathlessly, "did you have a good day at school today?"

A tension of held breaths filled the small room, the weight of all eyes on Rebecca for a moment. This time she obliged, nodding and saying, "Yeah, Grandma. I had an awesome day; thank you."

Her grandma went to speak again, but only a faint dry cough emerged.

"Are you thirsty, Mom?" Arnold said, leaning over the bed toward her.

She replied with nothing more than a weak nod and a slight grimace.

"Natasha," Arnold called over, pointing at a plastic beaker of drink on the table at the bottom of the bed.

It was a baby beaker, a handle on each side for an easy grip, the top covered to prevent spillage. The beaker was soon in Grandma's hands, with her son holding on, tilting it so that the spout allowed just a little fluid to wet her tongue.

She nodded, satiated, and pushed the cup away.

"Thank you, Olav," she said.

"No, Mom." He picked up the framed photo and pointed to his father. "This is Olav; I'm Arnold."

"Oh, yes. I'm sorry, Arnold." She shifted in the bed, an attempt to reposition her body, a futile effort due to weakness. "Tell me, Arnold. When am I going home?"

He took a breath to reply, then merely exhaled, swallowing hard and drawing breath again. He was saved when the door opened. They all turned to see Merlene enter.

"Oh, I'm sorry," she said to Rebecca and Natasha. "I didn't realize—"

"Hi, Merlene," Rebecca said. "It's fine."

"Come on in," Natasha added. "She was just asking when she's going home."

Merlene approached the bed and gave their grandma's arm the briefest of squeezes. "Hello again, Ingrid," she said. "Just you concentrate on getting yourself better. You can go home when the doctors say you're well enough."

"Grandma, you need to eat," Natasha added. "You have to build your strength up so you can look after yourself."

"Not hungry," was the drawled reply. "I'll make some soup when I get back to Ostergaten."

There was a pause, nobody making eye contact with anybody else; then Arnold nodded agreement, and the others followed suit.

"Where's that?" Rebecca whispered to nobody in particular. "What's she talking about?"

Everyone knew that only Arnold might have any clue what Grandma was referring to, but he could only shrug and shake his head.

Then Grandma's head lolled back onto the pillow, her mouth gaped, and her gurgling breaths filled the pregnant air.

"She's probably talking about somewhere back in Oslo," Arnold said. "She's been talking all day about places and people I just don't know. She's confused."

"Mmm . . . but she makes sense now and then," Merlene said. "She seems confused about what went on last week or even a couple of days ago, but if you get her talking about the old days . . ." A series of knowing nods completed the sentence.

"You mean, growing up in Oslo?" Rebecca asked.

Arnold turned to her and Natasha. "I guess so. She's been talking about digging at the gardens, about visiting her mother, how much she misses her baby."

"When I was alone with her," Merlene said, "she talked about the day her . . . the day her father didn't come home from the trawler ship."

"That happened, for sure. She never even mentioned it before, but my dad told me a little about it when I was in my teens."

"I guess it all makes sense in a way," Merlene said. "All those memories—a lifetime of them—all jumbled up like a shuffled pack of cards."

As Grandma slept for a few minutes, they all caught up on what they'd been doing that day—Rebecca, Natasha, and Merlene at work, Arnold staying at his mother's bedside bar the occasional half-hour break. But conversation was muted and soon fizzled out to leave another long silence.

"You don't all need to stay here," Arnold said. "You must all be pretty tired."

"I'll stay only as long as you want me to," Merlene replied. "I'm off duty. You say the word, and I'll leave you in peace."

"I'd like to stay with her as long as possible," Natasha added. "And I don't mind how long you stay, Merlene."

Rebecca nodded agreement. "That goes for me too."

"Thank you," Merlene said.

"Have you eaten?" Arnold asked. But before anyone could reply, Grandma's gurgling turned to a long gasp, and she awoke, blinking slowly and scanning the room through stubbornly half-closed eyes.

"Who are these people, Pappa?" she said to her son, her face suddenly dark with fear.

Arnold tried to smile away his embarrassment, while Merlene tried to explain. "This isn't Pappa," she said. "It's Arnold, your son."

"Arne?" Grandma said, her fear refusing to go away, her face distorting with pain. "My Arne?"

Merlene nodded. "Your son." Her mouth opened again to say more, but any words were lost as they all saw Grandma grasp out at her son, eventually hitting the target and holding his shirtsleeve, pulling him closer.

"What?" he said to her, his face tinged with pain. "What is it, Mother?"

"I'm so worried about my Arne," she said.

Arnold's face twitched briefly, and he suppressed a sad smile, replacing it with a calming sigh. "You don't need to be worried about him, Mother."

"Olav, please promise me something."

Arnold glanced down at his mother's hand, now as weak as a baby's but also as desperate, clinging onto his shirtsleeve as if it might somehow rejuvenate her. "What is it?" he said softly. "What's wrong, Mother?"

"Don't laugh at me. This is important."

"I'm sorry. I'm not laughing. Really. Tell me what's so important. Tell me."

"Listen to me carefully," Grandma said; her words were now intense but as clear as they had been in her younger days, and she spoke with a reverence Rebecca had seldom heard from her, the sharp edge of her Scandinavian accent more prominent than ever. "You need to promise me something. This is important. Arne must never know about his father. Do you hear me? *Never!*"

Arnold, his mouth slightly agape, wanted to glance at his daughters or Merlene, thinking somehow that might help, but he was unable to pull his gaze away from his mother's gaunt face, his focus some distance beyond her, his form still, as if not breathing.

"Do you understand me?" Grandma insisted, this time speaking even more forcefully, as though she were fighting for oxygen.

It was so quiet that the breath of air that escaped from between Arnold's lips might just as well have been a word. Then he started to nod, but very slowly, and fumbled for words. "Uh, yes, I . . . I understand."

"You know it's for the best," Grandma added. "Promise me you'll never tell him. Promise me."

"I understand," he said, the words utterly at odds with his stillness, his frown, his stilted speech. "And I . . . I promise."

"That's good," she said. Only then did she let go of his shirt, leaning back onto the pillow and closing her eyes. "You've been a good husband to me," she added weakly. There was now some serenity to her appearance there hadn't been in a long time, and within minutes that calmness had taken over her face.

Nobody spoke during those few minutes. Indeed, by the time any of them mentioned Ingrid's final wish again, it would be too late to ask her for any kind of explanation.

Chapter 5

More than two years had passed since the German invasion of Norway. For their first few months in charge, the Germans had changed very little. But new laws had been gradually and quietly introduced—some outlawing certain newspapers and periodicals, some preventing Jews from owning businesses and properties, some introducing a food-rationing system. The last of these affected Ingrid the most, meaning she and her mamma had to grow vegetables to support themselves. Of course, the rest of the neighborhood had the same problem, so Lyngstad Park—a small patch of greenery behind the row of houses—had been turned into a community garden for them all, referred to as "the park gardens" or simply "the gardens." So, as well as being boatbuilders, fishermen, nurses, plumbers, housekeepers, and engineers, everyone was now also a farmer.

The arrangement caused widespread resentment because the people knew the reasons for the food shortages; the Germans had confiscated all farm livestock and continued to seize a large part of crop production to feed the ever-increasing number of German troops stationed in Norway. But people also knew they had little choice, so they knuckled down and got on with the tasks of clearing weeds, fertilizing the ground the best they could, and planting seeds. Insects and drought were minor problems; frost and mold were major ones.

When the park gardens were first cultivated, some people joked that the biggest pests were those in foreign uniforms standing on street corners. And some of the people who made those jokes subsequently disappeared, so jokes at the expense of what the Norwegians politely referred to as "our German guests" were few and far between and only spoken in the most trusted of company.

There had always been suggestions from some people that they should keep chickens if the occupation was to continue, and by 1942 it was clearly not going to end anytime soon, so the decision was made. But chickens needed enclosures, and there also came the realization that the thirty or forty people who regularly tended the gardens could do with some sort of storage area for tools and seeds.

That was where Olav's skills came in. A self-taught carpenter, he could seemingly make anything out of wood. He was also taller than average and broad backed with solid limbs and hands that looked swollen at first glance. The joke was that you could give Olav a saw and point at a tree, and the next day he would give you a house. Whenever he heard such jokes, he would shrug shoulders that had grown bulky from hard work and say, "Yes, so what?" as if everyone could do the same if they tried. But he would say it with what Ingrid always considered a sweet smile, his dimples just about peeking through an undergrowth of bushy beard that was, if anything, more unkempt than it had been the first time she'd seen him.

By now Ingrid and Olav had become regular acquaintances, if not firm friends. He kept his promise of looking after her and her mamma, bringing firewood and making repairs around their house, occasionally joining them for meals. It was the least they could do, because Olav told them he still had no idea where his parents had been taken. Ingrid found out that Olav was now twenty-four, four years older than her, although he seemed even older, carrying an air of someone with a lifetime of wisdom. Or perhaps only Ingrid thought so—she was never completely sure. There were times when he wanted to stay alone in the house, saying he had work to do. At first, she wondered what the work was, but she soon left her curiosity behind and accepted that he was a good friend—no more and no less—who had his own private affairs to deal with. For this reason, as much as any, she kept friendship at arm's length despite their regular contact.

Olav was quiet and reserved and so cheerily got on with the task of sawing wood and nailing the planks together to form the gardeners' toolshed. Toward the end of the project, as the walls were taking shape, one of the other gardeners from another street felt the need to crack a joke.

"My God, the man's a human sawmill," he said. "With skills like that and his appetite for hard work, his parents will never be without a roof over their heads, that's for sure."

The man let out a hearty laugh to support his joke, but it quickly stalled when he noticed most onlookers had adopted grim expressions. More importantly, Olav's saw was silenced, left lodged halfway through a plank. He stared at the ground for a few seconds while everyone stilled themselves, a few taking a pace back. Then Olav yanked the saw out, threw it to the ground, and strode away, his eyes looking straight ahead, ignoring the stares of the other gardeners. Ingrid just watched him, too, now thinking that it wasn't so much a lifetime of experience Olav carried with him but the bitter memories of what had happened to his parents two years before.

"What did I say wrong?" the gardener who'd cracked the joke said—although he spoke only once Olav was out of earshot. "I was only joking. If anything, I was paying him a compliment."

Nobody answered at first. Then one of the old men from Ostergaten, a few doors down from Ingrid, told him about Olav's parents.

"Oh," he said. "I didn't know. Perhaps I should apologize to him."

"No," Ingrid said. "I'll talk to him. We all know you meant no harm."

The next morning, Ingrid was the first person working at the park gardens. She often was. She loved the camaraderie of fellow gardeners, the exchange of tips on how to best sow seeds and keep pests away, and even the simple passing of the time of day, but there was a certain primeval feeling to being alone in the morning, to digging up carrots and potatoes in the dawn half light while the birds and the occasional rabbit or squirrel still rejoiced in the new day. The fact that there were few German troops hanging around street corners in the early hours helped make for a calmer atmosphere too.

She'd dug up enough potatoes to last her and her mamma a few days, when she heard the gate at the far end squeal open. She looked up to see Olav, and he wished her a good morning and smiled his usual cheery smile, showing no hint of his moodiness from the previous day. He carried on where he'd left off, sawing a length of timber in half. The loud rasping noise put an end to Ingrid's solitary peace and caused the birds resting on the nearby trees to scatter wildly in all directions. But this was Olav, so she wasn't going to complain; she just gave him a wry smirk as she caught his glance during one particularly noisy bout of sawing.

He suddenly stopped. "I'm sorry," he said. "This is too noisy for so early in the morning, isn't it?"

Ingrid tilted her head to one side, then the other, trying to show agreement with his suggestion without speaking.

He laid the saw down with a gentleness at odds with its purpose. "Do you need help with that digging?" he said.

"I've just about finished," she said. She hadn't—there were carrots to dig—but she wanted to do all her own work; she owed Olav enough for the shed he was in the middle of constructing, not to mention helping her and Mamma out with firewood and household repairs.

"Oh," he said, as though disappointed he couldn't punish his muscles even more.

They both stood, smiling and nodding, each waiting for the other to speak. Their eyes, too, seemed to be teasing each other, she catching his stare every so often as she scanned the greenery, then he doing the same.

But then Ingrid's eyes took on a life of their own, settling on him and somehow locking there, unable to look elsewhere. She'd had the nerve to look before—particularly noticing those dimples—but not the self-indulgent audacity for the long and wishful look she was now taking. It was unlike her—which gave her a strange excitement—and she was unable to pull her gaze away. Olav was a brute of a man, built for physical grunt work and little else. He wasn't only taller than average but also had forearms, hands, and thighs as bulky and well built as those big wide shoulders. And it was a straight fight between his straggly mop of strawberry-blond hair and that bushy beard for the title of the unruliest aspect of his appearance.

While she couldn't stop staring at him no matter how rude she realized she was being, he appeared embarrassed at the attention, his hands fiddling with the corners of his ripped black jacket, his head looking left and right, his body, if not his mouth, clearly asking Ingrid to stop staring.

"He was only joking, you know," Ingrid said.

The words creased up his forehead in confusion.

"The man yesterday," she said. "When he talked about you building a house for your parents."

"Oh, I see." The frown fell away, and the dimples reappeared as he smiled politely. "I'm sorry about that. Not his fault. Not at all. I get upset when people talk about my parents."

"We all noticed."

"I already decided to apologize when I see him."

Ingrid let go of the garden fork she'd been leaning on and walked over to him. She'd been slightly in awe of the man, but now he was behaving like a nervous schoolboy, and any apprehensiveness she might have had about talking to him faded away. He was no monster; he just looked like one. And there was much more to him than his unwavering appetite for toil. That much had been clear the previous day.

"You still haven't heard any more about your parents?" she said, now quietly as they were almost within touching distance.

He looked down and shook his head, his shaggy locks taking time to catch up. "Nothing."

Ingrid sensed that there was something more. His reaction to the question had been awkward—guarded, even. *Was there something else— something he wasn't telling her?* He said nothing more, but Ingrid kept still, staring at him, willing him to explain.

Eventually she gave in and said, "It's terrible that they got taken away like that for no reason."

He let out a long breath, then looked left, right, and behind him. "It's a long story," he said.

She stared a little more before coming to her senses. "Mmm . . . well, it's obviously private. I shouldn't pry."

"No, no." He held his hands up, and every feature of his face entertained a troubled expression. He glanced behind him. "We've known each other for some time now, haven't we, Ingrid?"

"You've helped Mamma and me a lot. I like to think you're a good friend."

"And you deserve a friend after what happened to your pappa."

Ingrid felt her heart twinge. "My pappa?"

"Yes. I often think about him—the time I talked to him before he went out on the trawler that terrible morning."

A ripple of nausea threatened to engulf Ingrid. It was something she couldn't even attempt to disguise.

"I'm sorry," Olav said. "I didn't mean to upset you. But I know, like me and my parents, you must have times every day you miss him."

Ingrid nodded. "Mamma more so, but she hides it well."

"You're a good daughter for looking after her. That must be hard."

"Not having Pappa around, that's hard."

Olav looked around again, narrowing his eyes to scan the neat rows of crops and beyond. "I'm not sure whether to tell you, but somehow, because of all that's happened with your pappa and how you still manage to hold that lovely smile, it leads me to think I can trust you." He paused, waiting.

"You're right, Olav. You *can* trust me."

A few nervous breaths escaped from his mouth and caught the sun's rays.

"Don't feel you have to tell me," she said. "But I promise I won't tell anyone else."

He glanced all around them, then fixed his eyes on Ingrid, then on his boots. "Well . . . together with a few friends, my uncle started up a newspaper—the *Norway Light.*"

Ingrid felt her mouth go a little dry. She hadn't heard of the title but knew. "Resistance?" she whispered.

He nodded. "And very illegal. The Germans found the printing press, destroyed everything. My mamma and pappa thought my uncle going to prison was the end of the matter. They were wrong."

"So, you lied when you said you didn't know why they were taken away?"

"Ingrid, nobody knows who they can trust these days. I'm sorry I lied to you and your mamma. I feel bad. But the whole thing was over so quickly. One day I went to chop some wood. I came back to find the soldiers arresting them. I . . ." He took a gulp and a long breath. "I argued with them—for a few seconds only—and they said my parents had been dealing in illegal publications and that I should be thankful

I wasn't going with them. I . . . uh . . . well, you know what happened in the street."

"I remember how hard you fought."

"And you understand that I'd rather people didn't know. There are informers around. They might think that I was involved."

Olav fell silent as Ingrid threw her arms around his barrel torso. She wasn't a short woman, but even her hands had a problem meeting behind his back, so she squeezed him as best she could.

"I'll have to confide in you more often," he said, the laughter in his voice lifting Ingrid's heart.

She released him and stood back. "I'm sorry," she said.

"I'm not," he muttered, a hint of the laughter remaining.

"I mean, I'm sorry about your parents."

"Ah, yes." His cheeks blushed; the flesh around his eyes crinkled with an embarrassed grimace. "Of course. I'm sorry. I'm being too forward."

Ingrid couldn't help a little giggle escaping from her lips. "There's enough misery around here already, Olav. Let's both agree not to be sorry anymore."

"You know, that's such a good idea."

"And your secret's safe with me."

"Thank you."

Throughout the summer and autumn months, Ingrid and Olav talked almost every day at the park gardens—of their parents, of how they were going to prepare the vegetables they'd grown, and occasionally of their hopes and fears for their country, their city. When they were alone, Olav spoke more of the night his parents were taken away and of his fruitless attempts to find out where the authorities had taken them. Not long after that, Ingrid told him of the time she'd kissed her pappa goodbye early that morning, knowing he would be going out on the trawler but not knowing she was seeing, hearing, smelling, and touching him for the last time.

In the harsh winter that followed, when Ingrid and her mamma had both been laid low with a particularly heavy cold, Olav made sure that the fire was always stacked with chunks of wood and that potatoes, carrots, and onions always appeared in their kitchen. He also took their ration books to get their bread and milk and even shared with them the occasional piece of fish or few rashers of bacon he'd managed to buy on the black market.

A good friend is someone who always shines a light in dark times. Olav was a good friend.

Chapter 6

Ingrid peered along the line of fellow Norwegians that led to the shop doorway, then pulled the lapels of her coat closer to her neck and stamped her feet. But that seemed so pointless. How would thumping her frozen feet down onto frozen paving slabs produce heat? It only ever seemed to hurt her bones. In the foggy corners of her mind, she knew it wasn't completely pointless; the pain would shoot up her bones and so enliven her, taking her mind off the cold and the boredom. The boredom. Yes, the boredom. She was used to lining up for food in cold weather. That wasn't the problem; it was the boredom that seemed to hurt more.

And it was a curious sort of boredom.

There had been a time when every footstep along familiar roads was trodden with an all-encompassing fear—fear of the German soldiers who seemed to gather in groups on absolutely every street corner and square in the city. The soldiers watched local people going about their business, but it was a brave person who returned the stare. They called out insults, but only a fool dared answer back. Whenever they asked for identification papers—which appeared to be whenever they felt like it—anybody who argued was more often than not taken away, never to return.

But now it was different. The soldiers were still here. The fear of them was still here. But now the tension had become accepted; heightened senses had become the norm. These were merely part of everyday life, even contributing to the sense of boredom.

Ingrid stamped some more and looked at the line again, this time totting up the people between her and the counter of the bakery. Perhaps only fifteen or twenty now.

All the eyes of those fifteen or twenty followed a woman emerging from the bakery, clutching a small loaf of bread. She halted for a moment at the group of four German soldiers who were smoking and laughing there, although it should not have come as a surprise; a street corner with *no* German soldiers—that should be a surprise. Then she scurried around the corner and away, and yes, it meant everyone could shuffle along one more place. So, the fifteen or twenty became fourteen or nineteen. And perhaps, Ingrid thought, some of them might have forgotten or mislaid their rations books. That would help.

She told herself off for wishing misfortune on others for her own benefit. After all, that was exactly what her mamma would do if she was party to Ingrid's thoughts.

She whiled away a few more moments, flinging her arms around her torso to create some warmth. That was just as pointless as stamping her feet, but it made the time pass. Then an awful thought hit her. She quickly opened her handbag, holding her breath, and rooted around inside for the two ration books—her own and her mamma's. A sigh of relief, an absentminded glance toward the soldiers standing at the bakery entrance, a frisson of fear at the prospect of one of them noticing; then she pulled her gaze away. Perhaps the near miss was poetic justice for wishing misfortune on others, but the ration books were safely tucked away. She closed her handbag and blew hot air into her cupped hands, letting some of the heat deflect back onto her nose and cheeks. It was ecstasy, so she summoned up another gasp from deep within her lungs, and the sensation was every bit as pleasurable as the first time.

She inhaled again, holding the air in her lungs to give more warmth to it, and readied herself to experience the decadence of yet more heat on her hands and face. Others were pulling the same trick, but a loud screech from behind took their minds off their discomfort for a moment. Every head in the line turned to see the truck careering around the corner. It slid on a patch of ice, momentarily heading straight for them before regaining traction and accelerating along the street.

Four German soldiers cast glances all around, clearly searching among the passersby. Then one of them pointed and shouted, and the truck headed in that direction, skidding as it came to a crooked halt.

As a sideshow to this event, an elderly man came out of the bakery, holding a loaf, and the people shuffled along one more space. The action was automatic, their eyes never moving from the more dramatic scene developing across the road. Well, it was dramatic but hardly rare.

The soldiers singled out one man from the many poor souls trudging along and shouted at him as they forced him at gunpoint against the wall. One talked to him, barking the words out, while the others stood back, keeping their rifles at the ready, holding them casually but with the threat loud and imminent.

The man, his cloth cap having been thrown onto the ground in the scuffle, turned the lapels of his long overcoat tightly around his neck, shrugged his shoulders, and held his arms out. "What?" he was heard to shout back. "What is it?"

The soldier started patting him down and searching his pockets. "Turn around," he said in broken Norwegian.

"Why?" the man replied. "What have I done?"

The soldier slapped his face and grabbed his shoulder, forcing him to turn to the side. A lift of the man's overcoat, and the soldier launched into a tirade in his native language. He pulled a folded newspaper from under the back of the man's belt and started batting him around the head with it. Another soldier approached, took a glance at the newspaper, and in a flash thrust the butt of his rifle into the man's belly.

Moments later the man, now almost doubled in pain, was dragged into the truck, which then left the street in a more restrained manner than it had entered.

None of the people lining up outside the bakery spoke. They all knew. The newspaper in question had been one of many spreading news of the Norwegian government in exile or details of the war elsewhere in Europe or stories of success from the Norwegian Resistance movement and hence was one of those publications banned by the Germans. Anyone caught in possession risked immediate arrest.

For a moment the episode made Ingrid think back three years to that day it had all started, when she'd gone to the center of Oslo to find it swarming with German troops and found out that the country was being overrun just like Poland had been months before or like Denmark had been only days before.

But no. Ingrid quickly put these desperate memories to the back of her mind and smiled inside as vivid recollections of a warmer nature replaced them. Her life had taken a turn for the better, and during times like these, that was something to rejoice at, to thank the heavens for. And this turn for the better had happened only a month ago.

Olav had become a good friend to Ingrid over the years, but on a relentlessly cold January day, when a shroud of mist held the city tightly in its grip, something special and magical and extraordinary had happened between them. It had started so badly but ended wonderfully.

Olav had helped Ingrid and her mamma so much over the winter that Ingrid had arranged a special meal of vegetable-and-pork stew for all three of them. But she'd also come to rely on Olav over the years, so when her mamma was suddenly overcome with breathing difficulties early that evening, she panicked, almost stumbling as she put on her biggest boots, then ran across the road and over to Olav's house, where she hammered on the door as if she was never going to stop, oblivious to the falling shafts of snow she was dislodging from the roof, just for once not caring if she attracted the attention of any loitering German soldiers.

The moment the door opened, Ingrid felt the words fall out of her mouth faster than she could control them. "It's Mamma. She's ill, can't breathe. Please. Please help. She can't breathe. Help. Quickly."

Olav said nothing but grabbed his coat and boots.

"She needs the doctor. Can't breathe. She kept complaining, but I thought she'd be all right."

"Calm down, Ingrid. I'm sure it's nothing serious."

"But she's started gasping. And I can't afford a doctor. Please. I don't know what to do. Oh, God, please help me, Olav."

She felt his meaty hands grab her shoulders and give them a gentle shake. "Everything will be all right. Calm down, or you'll do yourself an injury. Take a few deep breaths."

She did as he suggested, but even in her state of anxiety she was aware of something different about him. But that didn't matter now because thoughts of her mamma's suffering took precedence. "Yes," she said. "I'm fine." She took another long calming breath. "But what shall I do?"

Olav thought for a moment, then nodded his head to indicate the thinking was over. "I'll tell you what you'll do. You'll go back to your mamma, make sure her clothing is loose, and open a window to let some fresh air in, but make sure she stays warm. I know someone. Doctor Knudsen. I'll fetch him."

"No, Olav. We can't afford a doctor."

"Don't worry about that. He owes me a favor." He gave Ingrid a kiss on the cheek, shut the door behind him, and started running.

Ingrid watched him go, and at quite a speed for such a large man, a dark block in the endless whiteness, soon fading into the mist. She ran home and did as Olav had suggested, loosening her mamma's collar, opening a window just a little, heaving more blankets on top of her, adding a fresh log to the fire. It was only as she took a moment to relax that she realized what had been grabbing her attention about Olav—what was different about him. His straggly locks were gone. Not exactly neatly cut off, but nevertheless the effect was to make him more presentable. Shaving his beard off was also a big improvement, and by the smell of him he'd also had a bath. It was puzzling but didn't matter just now; she had her mamma to think of.

Soon Olav and the doctor arrived, the urgency preventing them from kicking the snow from their boots. The doctor examined her mamma, nodding agreeably after less than a minute.

"Your mother has a chest infection," he said. "Nothing more."

"What can you do about it?" Ingrid asked.

"Nothing. It will get better of its own accord." He stroked his long beard as he thought. "Although, try this to alleviate the symptoms." He produced a tiny bottle from his bag. "Add a few drops to a bowl of hot water, and get her to inhale it."

Now Ingrid's mamma stirred, coughing but then breathing well enough to thank the doctor and Olav.

"That's no problem," Doctor Knudsen said to her. "One other important thing. Are you eating enough?"

"Is anyone?" she replied, croaking the words out.

"Mamma goes without to make sure I'm well fed," Ingrid said. "I keep telling her she has to look after herself too."

Her mamma shook her head. "As if I'm not upset enough, now my daughter's telling tales."

"It's true, Mamma. You've lost weight. I haven't."

Doctor Knudsen held up an admonishing finger. "If that's true, it must stop."

"It will," Ingrid said firmly.

"I'll write down my address," the doctor said. "Let me know if she doesn't recover."

Ingrid thanked him, and he left, leaving Ingrid's mamma tucked up in bed and Ingrid and Olav alone in the main room of the house.

"Did you run all the way to Doctor Knudsen's house?" Ingrid asked.

"It was only four or five streets away."

"You must be exhausted." She stepped closer to him, now seeing the film of sweat smothering his reddened brow. She lifted her hand and combed her fingers through what remained of his hair. It was short in parts, almost bald in others, obviously cut by his own hand using a rough blade. "What's all this about?" she said. "The hair, the shaving?"

"It's nothing," he muttered. "It doesn't matter now. You've probably forgotten, but you invited me for a meal tonight. I . . . uh . . . thought I might impress you and your mamma, show you I can be neat and tidy when I put my mind to it."

"Oh, Olav. That's so sweet."

He lifted his jacket to reveal large patches of sweat under his arms. "I don't think *sweet* is the right word. I must stink."

"Come here." She reached up again, snaking a hand behind his neck and pulling him down. He seemed reluctant at first, but she insisted, and their lips met. She felt his thick arms enveloping her and gently squeezing her frame. She closed her eyes, her whole mind focused on the warmth of his strong embrace, his smooth chin, his big heart. After what felt like a ride on horseback among the night stars, their lips parted. "You smell beautiful to me," she whispered.

A serious frown drew itself on his forehead. "What was that for? That's to say . . . what does this mean?"

"It means I like you, Olav. I like you a lot. And I couldn't help myself. I'm sorry if you didn't want me to do it."

"Ingrid, I've wanted nothing more, but under the circumstances . . . well, I didn't want to say anything in case you didn't feel the same."

"Well, I do, Olav. I do."

He smiled—the broadest smile she'd seen on his face, those dimples now naked without the beard and reveling in their freedom. Then the smile fell as he regained composure. "Tell your mamma I wish her a speedy recovery."

Ingrid realized that for a few precious minutes, she'd almost forgotten her troubles.

Over the next few weeks they grew even closer, seeing each other every day, Olav helping out even more around the house, Ingrid cooking an evening meal for all three of them on most days.

They managed to keep their affair—or whatever it was—a secret from her mamma, and even when she recovered from her chest infection, it hardly seemed necessary to tell her the truth, instead letting her assume that Olav was still no more than a good friend. After all, much more important things were going on. A little secrecy added spice to an otherwise mundane daily existence, and over the next few days and weeks, the reality became clearer. Olav, the man Ingrid referred to as *our neighbor* or *my friend* in the company of her mamma, had connections—and not only doctors; he knew more than most about what was happening in the war and shared much of it with Ingrid.

Back outside the bakery, Ingrid watched with interest as another woman came out holding not one but two loaves. She held them close to her chest, as though guilty but also protective. A few murmurs of discontent rippled through the people lining up along the street, which seemed very unfair. Ingrid, too, hoped to get two loaves; she made a mental note to hide one of them under her coat before she left the counter. And the people shuffled along one more space. Another few minutes, Ingrid thought, and she would be close enough to the bakery doorway to feel a little of its warmth billowing out.

Until then she could always try stamping her feet some more.

Later, as Ingrid returned to Ostergaten 41 with her two fresh loaves, she glanced at the log store next to the front door. It had been a quarter full when she'd left and was now overflowing, a trail of splinters and bark fragments leading all the way across the street and over to Olav's house. She allowed herself a brief smile. Yes, that would be just like Olav, currying favor with her mamma. And being helpful. Being Olav.

She inhaled the aroma of freshly chopped wood. It was pleasing, but her bones were now feeling the chill, so she opened the door and went inside to find Olav washing the dirt from his hands at the sink and her mamma sitting by the golden fire, darning the elbows of Olav's shirt. They both smiled and greeted her.

She was home, and inside home it was easy to convince herself— if only for a few precious hours—that they were free, that there was no German occupation, no terror on the streets, no fear of saying the wrong thing to the wrong person.

I feel the visions are always around me, lurking, threatening to visit me at any time of the day or night, wherever I am, whenever I dare to close my eyes. You could call them daydreams or tormentors, nightmares or sinister vignettes playing themselves out inside my head. But I call them my visions. I can be resting amid the greenery of the home's backyard, or in my chair in the dayroom, or in my bed but unable to sleep or fully awaken in those desperate early-morning hours. The visions always find me no matter what I do. I've had them for years.

Today, it's late morning, and I'm sitting by the window, a calming sun on my face, the wind safely outside. I'm tired. I close my eyes to rest. Just to rest. But I see a baby in a crib. I immediately know it's Christmas 1915. The baby is me. The crib was previously my mother's and, before that, my grandmother's. It was handmade from willow and leather in the Kingdom of Bavaria. That, of course, was before the creation of the Second Reich, which united the many states of German-speaking peoples into one country. I'm spending the first few months of my life in a country that's struggling to expand its influence in order to compete with its European neighbors. My father, when he's here, is very joyful and proud of the steps our country's leaders are taking to build up our empire.

Of course, as an innocent baby soundly sleeping in that crib, I know nothing. But each of my visions is a hazy half-formed mix of what I witnessed at the time and what I later learned about my country's history. Prussia, Bavaria, and the other Germanic states came together to form the Second Reich. Germany struggled to find its place in a Europe dominated by Britain and France; it pushed to acquire its own empire—one to compete on the world stage—and it desired to build a country all Germanic people could be proud of. As a child I know nothing of any of these, and I have no say whatsoever in the direction of the Great War.

But somehow my vision is not frozen in time, and I know I'll grow up to contend with the aftermath of that war.

Chapter 7

Arnold's sister, Barbara, had come down from Montreal. And not a day too soon. They were all pleased that both of Ingrid's children and both of her grandchildren had been at her bedside when she passed away.

Barbara said she would stay for a few days to talk with her brother and help clear out their mother's apartment, but there was little talk about their mother. Between the two of them, the apartment was soon emptied, and the funeral was arranged—a quiet affair—and also, they found time to catch up on each other's lives and what Rebecca and Natasha were doing with theirs.

They usually ate out, but on the third evening Arnold cooked a meal for his sister and two daughters. Again, there seemed to be little appetite for talk of their mother. So, he was surprised to find them in deep discussion about her when he returned from the kitchen with dessert.

"I'm afraid I don't know," he heard Barbara say. "Mom was always a little mysterious to me."

"You don't know what?" Arnold asked as he sat back down.

"Oh, nothing," Rebecca said.

"Hey, c'mon. This is no time to be secretive, eh?"

Natasha explained it to him. "We were just asking Aunt Barbara whether she knew anything about what Grandma said in the hospital. You know, that kind of cryptic stuff she said just before she . . ."

"You mean the bit about something I shouldn't know about my dad?"

"Right," Barbara said. "Natasha and Rebecca were just telling me. Something you shouldn't know? What did she mean by that?"

"Who knows?" he said. "She wasn't herself in the last few days. She even thought I *was* my dad at one point, called me Olav."

"Really?"

He nodded. "And frankly, who cares? What could it be that I shouldn't tell myself about my own father? None of it makes sense." He smiled sadly. "Look. She was delirious. We all knew that. Most of the stuff she was coming out with made no sense at all. As well as calling me Olav, she even called me Arne—I haven't been called that since I was a kid."

"You don't care?" his sister said, mild admonishment in her tone.

He shrugged. "I don't mean to be disrespectful to her, but why would any of that matter? Our dad died over thirty years ago. What could I possibly not know about him that I need to know?"

"Or, as it were, you definitely *shouldn't* know?" his sister added.

"Absolutely. It's just not something that I think is worth worrying about. Let sleeping dogs lie, especially ones that have been asleep for thirty years."

He saw Rebecca smiling but hiding her amusement by taking a sip of drink.

"What?" he said. "What is it?"

"Oh, nothing."

He looked at Natasha instead.

"Okay," she said. "It's just that . . . for something you don't care about, you've clearly spent a lot of time thinking it through." She finished the sentence with a wry grin on her face, much like her sister.

"Don't listen to them, Arnold," Barbara said. "And you two, why don't you leave your dad alone?"

"Thank you," Arnold said. He pointed his spoon at his sister. "And while you're being nice to me, we need to go through the rest of Mom's stuff."

She looked surprised. "I thought we'd done that already. Her apartment's empty."

"We sorted through everything except a few suitcases stored in the attic." He pointed a finger upward.

"Here? In *your* attic?"

"She gave them to me last year. There wasn't enough room in her place, not once she got all the mobility equipment in there."

"Do you think you need my help to sort it out?"

"I just thought you might want to, but . . ." Arnold peered at his sister, noticing an undercurrent of exhaustion, seeing a stress that was rare for her.

She tried to smile, but it was a flat, polite attempt. "I found it hard sorting out the apartment. The ornaments, the old photos she'd stored away, that floral dress she was keeping for best but never got to wear, the new shoes still in boxes with the packing paper in to keep their shape, newspaper cuttings through the ages. I'm not sure I could face more of that sort of thing."

"Don't think that you have to," Arnold said.

"You wouldn't mind?"

He leaned across and patted her hand. "Hey, don't worry about it."

"Couldn't Rebecca and Natasha help?"

"It's not a problem. Now I think about it, there were only two suitcases. Pretty small ones too."

Rebecca and Natasha exchanged glances. "I'm not sure I'm up to it," Natasha said.

"It might be too upsetting," Rebecca added. "Too early."

"Like I said," their father insisted, "I can manage."

"Or you could ask Merlene to help," Rebecca said.

"*We'll see,*" he replied, now with a firmness they all understood.

"How is Merlene?" Barbara asked him a few silent moments later.

"I think she's quite upset," Arnold replied. "She'd gotten quite close to Mom by the end."

"Dad's been seeing a lot of her too," Rebecca added.

Barbara raised her eyebrows at her brother.

"I think of her as a good friend of the family," he said flatly. "She helped out so much with Mom—well beyond the call of duty. And the two of them became good friends by the end."

"So, she's your friend too," Rebecca said. "I mean, *our* friend."

"Hey, can we just eat?"

They ate.

It took two days and another suggestion from Rebecca for Arnold to call Merlene and ask her if she would be interested in going through the two suitcases of memories that his late mother had given him.

"Because you knew her so well toward the end," he said. "And because I thought you might be interested in keeping one or two of her things as mementos."

"Oh, Arnold. That's very kind of you."

"And also because I can't find anyone else to help me."

After a lengthy pause, she replied, "You know, I've had better offers of dates."

"It's not a date," he said, lacing the words with friendly derision.

She laughed. "I know. But it would be good to see you again. I know I shouldn't get attached to patients, but losing your mom left something of a hole in my life."

Merlene was busy with shift work for the next few evenings, so they arranged for her to come to his place early the next week, where, over a glass of wine, they would tip the contents of the suitcases onto the dining table and sort the various bits of paper into keepers and trash, with Merlene welcome to take something to remember Arnold's mother by.

The two suitcases ended up being even smaller than Arnold recalled, and one contained nothing but a few wooden ornaments created by his father, which Arnold decided to distribute around the house.

The second suitcase was the one full of memories, some Arnold could remember, some from before he was born, but all clearly meaningful to his mother in some way and all now spread out on the table in front of Arnold and Merlene, next to the two glasses of wine. Arnold's was already almost empty, a result of the unease that even he didn't quite understand.

"Your dad looked like a big guy," Merlene said, pointing at a small photo.

"He was. Tall and quite thickset. Was all that manual labor. I take more after my mom, always have been quite slim. I like to think I have his eyes and nose, though."

Merlene looked at the photo and then Arnold a couple of times. "If you say so," she said with a crooked grin.

"Here," Arnold said, picking up a tan-colored leather purse that was coming apart at the edges. He opened it, unraveling just a little more of the stitching, and took out another photo. "I remember Mom showing me this one just after Dad died." He pointed. "Guess who that is."

"Your mom and dad?"

"No. Well, *yes*. But I meant *between* them."

Merlene took the photo and lifted it up, shoving her reading glasses to the end of her nose. "That's you? Really?"

"My first-ever photo shoot. I must have been, I don't know, a few months old."

"This is Oslo?"

He nodded. "Must have been taken at Ostergaten or whatever it was Mom said just before she died. She never liked to talk about her time back in Oslo, but she told me this photo was the one thing she kept from those days."

Merlene handed it back and waited while Arnold stared pensively at his history. Eventually he broke off and carefully placed the photo back in the tiny old purse for safekeeping while Merlene picked up an advertising brochure for a vacation to Norway.

"1965," she said, opening it and letting her fingers scan the promises of pure clean air, majestic fjords, and magical northern lights. Her eyes bobbed up to Arnold. "Did she go back that year?"

"Didn't go back any year as far as I'm aware."

"What? Never? You're kidding me."

He gave her a knowing smile. "Well, I turned twenty that year; I would have remembered. In fact, I would have remembered any year before or after apart from the first few years after the war. And it would have been pretty much impossible then, all that way with little old me and Barbara in tow."

"But . . . *never?* That seems so strange to me. I make sure I go back to Jamaica every couple of years. I couldn't imagine *never* going back."

He sifted through a few more postcards and birthday cards. "It was bad enough getting here in the first place without going back." He stilled his hands and gazed into space pensively. "Mom never talked about the journey. My dad did, but only in his later years, and you could see the stress on his face when he spoke about it. He made it sound like they were going to the moon. So, it wasn't quite the same circumstances as you flying back to Jamaica."

"No, I, uh, guess not. But did you ever suggest it? I mean, like, when you and Barbara were grown up, and they had the time and the money?"

"Oh, I knew they wouldn't go for it. And they always seemed pretty happy in Toronto."

Merlene let out a blast of laughter.

"What?" Arnold said, smiling. "What have you got?"

She showed him the photo, small and yellowing. He took it and screwed up his eyes to focus. "Hell, I must have been . . ." He turned it over to read the scribble on the back. "Summer 1952. I was seven."

"What a cutie."

He laughed again. "If you say so. You can't tell it from this, but I was always tall for my age."

"And here's one of you and Barbara standing next to one another. What is there between you?"

"Not quite a year."

"You're right about being tall. Looks like way more than a year between you."

They sorted through old birthday and Christmas cards, black-and-white photographs, the occasional leaflet or brochure for vacation destinations, even one or two guarantees for products that Arnold knew had been put in the trash can decades ago. It was then that Merlene spotted a bright white envelope and picked it up.

"This seems new," she said, peeking inside. "Uh, it's a handwritten letter. I think you'd better read it."

"Hey, no worries." He took the white envelope and scanned the front, screwing up his eyes to read the postmark. "Saskatoon."

"*Where?*"

"Saskatchewan. Up in the wilds. I'll bet Mom didn't tell you they first moved there when they came from Norway?"

"No." The frown stayed on Merlene's face. "No, she didn't. And I thought—"

"You thought you and her were friends; is that it?"

"Yes."

"Well, let me tell you, she didn't talk about that time to anyone outside of the family."

"Why not? I mean, if you don't mind telling me."

Arnold thought for a moment. "Tell you the truth, I was never really sure why myself. But my dad still has relatives up there. Well, he *did*."

He poked his thumb and forefinger into the white envelope and pulled out a smaller blue one, together with a white piece of paper.

"It's another envelope, addressed to somewhere in Saskatoon."

"Makes sense," Merlene said. "Must have been sent to Saskatoon, and your folks there have forwarded it on."

"It looks like . . ." He squinted once more. "Swedish postmark. Weird."

"What does the first letter say?"

Arnold opened out the single sheet of white paper. "You're right. It's from Dad's relatives. Sons of his cousins, I'm pretty sure. This is from almost two years ago." He read aloud:

> *Dear Ingrid, I hope this letter finds you as well as can be expected. I know you and Olav always insisted that we burn any letters coming from Norway, but that was all a very long time ago, and this one isn't from Norway, so I've taken the liberty of forwarding it to you. I apologize if I'm doing the wrong thing, but you can always burn it yourself if that's what you want.*

His eyes quickly scanned the rest of the letter. "Then there's an update on the health of . . . yeah, Dad's cousin. Not doing so good. That figures. Must be over ninety by now."

"And what about the envelope from Sweden?"

Arnold put down the sheet he'd been reading from and picked up the blue envelope. "It hasn't been opened." He shot a puzzled look in Merlene's direction.

She shrugged. "Perhaps she didn't have time to open it."

"What?"

"I'm only guessing. Why else would she leave it unopened?"

Arnold sighed and shook his head, then stared at the envelope in question. "Could be interesting." He wedged his fingernail under the edge of the flap, and soon the envelope was open, and a single sheet of blue notepaper was in his hand. This time he scanned it but didn't read aloud.

"Well?" Merlene said once his gaze had shifted from the letter. There was no reply. She sat back in her chair. "Hey, I'm sorry, Arnold. Perhaps it's none of my business."

"No, no." He shook his head. "Don't worry about that. Don't ever worry about that. It's just . . . well, why don't you read it for yourself and see what you make of it, eh?"

He handed her the single sheet, and she held it, not taking her eyes off his face. "You sure about this?"

"Go on. Read it."

She did, and her reaction wasn't a million miles from his. "Uh . . . so . . . I guess this doesn't make sense to you?"

He shook his head. She read the letter again, this time summarizing. "It's from a woman called Marit. Says she's trying to trace someone called Ulrich who was born in Oslo in 1944 and came across to Canada with his mother, Ingrid, soon after the war."

They stared at each other for a few seconds. Arnold gave a clueless shrug. "Must be a different Ingrid."

"Was that a common name in Norway?"

"Who knows?"

"But it's addressed to Ingrid Jacobsen, your mom—well, to her old address. This Marit must have gotten that from somewhere."

"And she says this *Ulrich* was born in '44. That's the year before I was born."

Merlene nodded slowly. "I guess it's possible. You sure she didn't tell you about it?"

"I think I might just remember if I had an older brother."

"Well, not if he . . . if something happened to him." She noticed the flush on Arnold's face. "Oh, I'm sorry. Too morbid. A side effect of being a nurse."

"Hey, no worries," Arnold said. "Anyhow, there's something else I just don't get." He picked up the other letter and read it again. "Why did Mom and Dad ask that letters from Norway were burned?"

"Do you think Barbara might know anything about all this?"

Arnold thought for a moment. "Not sure. But more importantly, does all this matter? My mom's not here anymore."

"Depends how keen you are to know more about her."

"Mmm . . . wouldn't do any harm to find out. Let me call Barbara, ask if any of this means anything to her."

He crossed to the coffee table and called her. There was no answer. "I'll try her cell." He called again, but it went straight to her answering machine.

"Won't she be on her way down here for the funeral?"

He clicked his fingers. "Of course. She's driving. I'll mention it when we speak."

"You do that, Arnold. In the meantime . . ." She motioned to the various cards and photos that were still to be dealt with.

"Of course."

Chapter 8

Oslo, July 1943

Despite Ingrid's encouragement, and even after Doctor Knudsen's telling off, her mamma still didn't eat enough in the weeks that followed her diagnosis, so Ingrid didn't want to complicate matters by letting her know that Olav had now become more than just a friend. And that meant keeping their closeness a secret. Olav didn't exactly agree with this but went along with it for Ingrid's sake. She'd assured him she wasn't ashamed in any way but rather didn't want to jeopardize her mamma's improving but still not ideal health by causing her to worry. And even when she did start to recover, it seemed easier to say nothing.

In truth, Ingrid wasn't sure whether she was in love. Olav was a good man—that much she knew from his activities and what he'd done for her and her mamma—but would he ever be her husband? Did she want that? She wasn't quite sure. Not yet. She'd visited his house twice, and that was too many times; it was as filthy as she'd expected a single man's house to be, no more and no less.

But summer crept up on Ingrid, and by July her mamma had made a full recovery and had also returned to a healthy weight. One clear bright day, Ingrid and Olav returned from the park gardens to find the house empty.

"Mamma might be across the road," Ingrid said. "With Laila's mamma."

"Laila?" Olav looked surprised. "How well do you know Laila?"

"Not very well; she's just a neighbor. Why? Do you know her?"

"No, no. Well, I've seen her about. I, uh, was just asking out of interest."

Ingrid stepped toward the door. "I'll go over and check. I want to be sure that's where Mamma is."

"I'll come with you."

Ingrid didn't mention anything else about Laila. Olav clearly knew her—after all, they lived on the same street—but something about his reaction didn't ring true.

Olav and Ingrid went across the road and found Ingrid's mamma chatting with Laila's mamma. Laila was nowhere to be seen, and Ingrid didn't care to ask where she was. After a few minutes of small talk, the unasked question was answered when Laila came in from the street, holding two bulging paper bags in the crook of her arm.

"You must be Laila," Olav said to her.

It seemed an odd—slightly forward—thing to say, but before Ingrid could give the matter more thought, Laila started talking.

"They have spare flour and sugar at the general store." She placed the bags down carefully. "Just arrived today."

"How did you know?" Ingrid asked.

"I, uh, I know a man in the import business. I was just about to let everyone know, including your mamma."

"Were you?"

Laila shrugged. "Well, you know now, don't you?"

"Well, yes, I guess I do," Ingrid said, echoing Laila's false tones. "Thank you very much."

There wasn't much more conversation, the atmosphere soon becoming as thick as an Oslo fog, and then the three of them returned to number 41, where Ingrid grabbed some money and ration coupons before heading for the general store.

She hurried past a group of German soldiers who were laughing and smoking at the end of the street, keeping her head down, avoiding eye contact. Then she had to do exactly the same when faced with another two standing together outside the general store, casting their eyes among the crowds passing back and forth.

She allowed herself a sigh of relief; the line was short, and she reached the counter in less than ten minutes. She felt pleased, knowing that there was a little butter at home and that she could buy an egg or two from another neighbor with no ration coupons and no questions asked. She started salivating at the thought of freshly baked cake— perhaps topped with some ground almonds. She knew that wasn't right, but by now the country had been occupied for over three years, and no other Norwegian would deny her a little harmless self-indulgence.

But as she left the counter, there was just a little guilt, which probably explained why she stumbled and let go of the bag of sugar, falling down to her knees to catch it before it hit the ground.

She checked the bag for splits and heaved a sigh of relief. Her relief was disturbed by the sound of laughter, and after getting up and brushing the dirt from her knees, she looked up to see the faces of those two German soldiers both staring at her as they laughed. The peaked caps, the perfectly pressed gray uniforms adorned with buckles and those symbols all Norwegians had come to despise whenever they dared to look: the swastikas, the SS bolts. These were no ordinary soldiers; these were SS officers.

She should have shown respect, but she couldn't hold back.

"Stop laughing!" she shouted at them.

Their answer was to laugh all the more. Ingrid noticed that by now the taller, older one had lit up a cigarette. He tapped ash from it, then pointed at her. "Very good skill," he said in surprisingly fluent Norwegian. "You must be good at sports, yes?"

Ingrid didn't reply. She'd never played any organized sport in her life, although she remembered beating all the other girls at school when it came to running. Anyway, it was a stupid question.

The officers had now stopped laughing and were muttering to each other in German, both of them looking Ingrid up and down, the smaller one pointing to her legs and nodding approvingly. Ingrid knew what that look on their faces meant. Every young girl in Oslo did, which was one more reason not to even look them in the eye.

Then the taller one stepped forward. "I'm sorry about that," he said, the struggle to control his grin hardly implying sincerity. "Please accept my apologies if you're offended."

"What were you and your friend talking about?"

He took a step back and looked her up and down again, clearly as shocked to hear her words as she herself was. He glanced back at his compatriot before replying, "We were complimenting you on your skill, if you must know. That was a good catch. You're a very athletic woman as well as a very pretty one." His gaze followed the line of her legs, and he leaned to the side to get a better look. "Wide hips, broad yet feminine shoulders, blonde hair." He peered at her face. "Lovely blue eyes too. An excellent specimen all round. Tell me, how tall are you?"

"I . . . I don't measure myself. What's this all about?"

"And would you consider yourself to be in good health?"

"Oh, I'm going." Ingrid shook her head dismissively and turned away, her thumping heart making her immediately regret her insolence.

The soldier stepped in front of her. "I've obviously offended you again. I'm sorry. Let me accompany you home to show you how sorry I am."

It was a cruel trick. It just *had* to be. That level of politeness from an SS officer couldn't be genuine. A nervous fog filled her mind; her throat locked. She knew she was playing with fire but couldn't control herself. She shoved him aside and started walking.

Then she heard a shout: "Papers!"

She also heard the click of a rifle being cocked, which made her legs go weak. She turned around, and he was already right there.

"Could I see your papers, please?" he said more quietly, now a mere question as opposed to an order, intoned as if he were asking whether she thought it was going to rain.

Ingrid fumbled in her handbag and thrust her identification papers into his outstretched hand. While he examined them, she stared at him, noticing how tall he was—noticeably taller than Olav, who wasn't exactly short. Like Ingrid herself, he also had bright blond hair, and when he offered her the papers back, she noticed he had blue eyes, just like her. She snatched the papers back and started walking away again.

"Goodbye, Ingrid Solberg," she heard him shout as she quickened her pace. She'd gone to the general store with thoughts of sweet coffee and sugary almond cake. She was now returning wanting to be sick.

As soon as Ingrid entered Ostergaten 41, Olav stood up from the fireside chair. "Did you get the flour and sugar?"

"Yes, yes. I got the flour and sugar." She knew she sounded annoyed but also knew covering it up would be impossible. She looked across to see her mamma, still sitting in another fireside chair, frowning at her daughter's tone. Then she looked at the floor, not wanting to see either of them, and placed the two small but very full bags down before taking her coat off.

"What's wrong?" Olav asked. "Did they charge extra?"

"No," Ingrid said, rubbing her eyes, a small part of her thinking it might rub out her stress.

"Well, something's wrong," her mamma said.

"Soldiers," she muttered. "SS officers."

Olav nodded. "I see. Arresting another truth teller?"

She looked across to him, at his kind face, its soft features contorting to show sympathy. "Something like that," she said.

"I'm sorry," he said.

"Why? It's not your fault."

"Of course not. But . . ." He let out a slight laugh, shutting it down as soon as he saw the anger on her face wasn't fading.

"No," she said, now determined to force a smile onto her face however bitter that officer had made her feel. "I'm sorry. I'm taking it out on you, and I shouldn't."

Then Olav smiled. Ingrid peered at him, attempting to determine what had changed, because something definitely had. The expression on his face had a hint of naughty child about it.

He stepped toward her with a look of concentration she found unnerving. Then he put a hand on her shoulder and went to kiss her on the lips. She tried to resist, but it was difficult. Olav seemed to calm her nerves the way nothing else could. But no—not with Mamma in the room. She came to her senses and pushed him, the effect being to move herself back more than Olav away. She glanced to the far side of the room—to her mamma, who did nothing but look back at her with a lightly twisted smile.

The crack of a log on the fire punctured the tension.

"She knows," Olav said to Ingrid.

"About us? You told her?"

"I guessed," her mamma said from the other side of the room. "Well, I *knew*."

"Oh," Ingrid said, her mind suddenly engulfed by a relief that overshadowed the surprise and anger she'd expected.

"I know my own daughter. And now I know he's a bad liar." She pointed to Olav and lowered her voice. "Some would say a bad liar makes for a good husband."

"Mamma!"

She shrugged her shoulders. "I said, *some would say*—that's all."

"You don't mind?" Ingrid asked.

"Mind?" Her mamma grimaced. "I want you to be happy. And look at him. Just *look at him*."

They both turned to Olav, who smirked and bobbed his eyebrows up and down.

"And much better since cutting his hair and getting rid of that awful beard."

Olav rubbed his chin self-consciously while Ingrid's mamma continued.

"I mean, if I were fit and well and thirty years younger . . ."

"All right, Mamma. You can stop there. I just . . . I didn't want to risk upsetting you. I thought you wouldn't approve. I know there are more serious things going on."

"Ha!" Her mamma eyed the ceiling and shook her head. "My advice is to grab any piece of happiness you can before the chance gets snatched away from you. None of us knows what God has in store around the corner."

Ingrid sensed Olav's footsteps behind her, then felt the weight of his arm around her shoulders and smiled up to him. It softened her mood. It was calming. She wondered why she'd been so reluctant to let her mamma know, why she'd been so secretive about something there was no need to be ashamed of. Olav was a good man, an honest man, a kind man. And yes, she had to admit that whenever those strong hands of his brushed against her skin, she felt her heart melt with pleasure. Somehow, he managed to calm her and move her at the same time. She hadn't dared admit it to herself before now, but her mamma's words made her think. Olav made her happy and protected her. What more could she want?

With no pressure to keep the secret from her mamma, the next few weeks were the happiest of Ingrid's life. The sun shone more brightly, the early-morning birdsong was louder and sweeter, the backache from digging at the gardens lasted minutes, not hours. And the joy of holding hands with Olav in public gave her a sense of freedom to counteract the ever-present German troops. She was, however, still unsure about Laila, who she suspected was jealous even of her *friendship* with Olav, let alone what it had now turned into.

But it was a price worth paying, and the fact that her mamma both knew about and approved of Olav only deepened her affection for him, and, as Mamma had said, under the current conditions any piece of happiness had to be grasped and held close. Olav's love and affection made the day-to-day realities of life under the Nazi jackboot easier to deal with—easier to forget, if only for a few precious hours.

Chapter 9

Oslo, August 1943

On a Saturday morning that held the promise of bright blue skies for the rest of the day, Olav invited Ingrid out for a meal at a local restaurant that evening. This was a very rare occurrence, but Olav insisted that some remnants of normal life had to continue, regardless of attempts by the occupying forces to control all. It was a matter of defiance. More importantly, he said he knew people who knew people who could get their hands on some beef, and although the meal wouldn't be up to the standard of prewar dining, he wanted to treat her. She joked that she would accept the invitation as long as he didn't cut his hair again, which was still short in patches, although she expected him to shave and put on his best clothes.

So, early that evening, Ingrid made sure her best dress was pressed, and she'd had a bath and washed her hair. She was expecting Olav at seven o'clock, so when there was a rap at the door soon after six, she wondered whether she'd made a mistake—misheard him, perhaps. Then again, it wasn't his distinctive knock—one knock, a pause, then three knocks in quick succession—but five firm knocks. Puzzled, she opened the door and immediately felt her heart turn cold.

"Ah, Ingrid Solberg," the SS officer said. "Good evening." His smile faltered; then he narrowed his bright blue eyes at her. "You *do* remember me, don't you?"

She did. She remembered the eyes, the hair as blond as her own, the height of the man, the uniform most Norwegians had come to dread the sight of, but mostly she remembered the arrogance.

"How did you know where I live?" she said.

"I asked to look at your papers. Don't you remember our last meeting? I thought perhaps I left an impression on—"

"What do you want?"

He laughed off her interruption and said, "Tell me; are you alone?"

"No. What do you mean by coming here? What do you want?"

"In that case, please come for a walk with me."

Ingrid folded her arms tightly. "Why should I?"

He took a moment to gather his thoughts. His demeanor was polite, not unfriendly, but there was nothing she found endearing either. "Ingrid," he said, "my name is Franz. I don't mean you any harm. Please. I only want ten minutes of your time; then I'll leave you in peace."

She stared, weighing him up. She considered quibbling with the word *peace* but held her tongue.

Franz gestured along the street. "Please. Ten minutes. That's all."

She shook her head, then noticed his expression change, a hint of a sneer playing on his lips.

"I'm trying to make this easy for you," he said. "People have been arrested for disobeying orders."

"Does that mean you're *ordering* me?"

He let out an exasperated sigh. "It means I'm trying to be pleasant. Or rather, I'm *choosing* to be pleasant."

She tried to judge him by that subtle expression on his face, but what spoke more loudly was the rifle slung over his shoulder; she knew he could make life difficult for her. Perhaps if she complied, he would leave her alone for good and never return to the house.

At that moment her mamma shouted out, "Who is it, Ingrid?" from the other end of the room.

"It's nobody," Ingrid replied, her glare at Franz deliberate. "But I just need to go out for a few minutes."

Now her mamma appeared at her shoulder and let out a short gasp as she eyed the uniform. "What's happening?" she said, her voice cracking with fear. "What is this?"

"It's nothing, Mamma. I just need to go talk with this man for a few minutes."

Her mamma now looked Franz up and down suspiciously. "Well, I don't believe you do. Go to your room. I'll deal with—"

"Let Ingrid decide for herself," Franz cut her off sharply.

Ingrid noticed the flesh around his eyes twitching in frustration, his lips stiffening just enough to show teeth. Fear shot through her veins. Perhaps there was only one way to settle this. "Please, Mamma," she said, her nerves alight. "I'll go. He won't hurt me."

Ingrid's mamma glared at Franz. "He'd better not."

Franz stepped back farther into the road. "Come," he barked to Ingrid.

"Tell me what you want," Ingrid said a few minutes later when they were walking along the street.

"How are you?" he asked. "Have you had a productive day?"

She narrowed her eyes at him. "Your Norwegian is good. You don't need to boast about it."

"Ah, well, that's because my father spent a lot of time in Norway as a child. Here in Oslo, actually, on the other side of the city. He spoke good Norwegian, and I learned it from him. And then, when I joined the SS and the opportunity arose for me to—"

"I don't want to hear your life story," Ingrid said, stopping and turning to him. "I want you to tell me why you came to my house and what you want of me."

His face was now twitching, and for a moment she regretted her tone, thinking he might even hit her. She was about to apologize for her rudeness when his expression softened just a little. They started walking again.

"I want to improve your life, Ingrid," he said, with more feeling than she expected, certainly more than she thought a man such as him would be capable of.

"I don't understand what you mean."

"You live alone with your mother, don't you?"

"Have you been spying on me?"

"I've been looking up your records. You have an excellent pedigree."

"Pedigree?"

"Excellent physical and mental features—*genes*, if you want the scientific word. I've traced you back three generations. But never mind that. What would you say if I told you I could ensure you and your mother never need to line up in the cold for food again, that you could eat meat twice a week, throw away your ration book, and get the best medical care?"

Ingrid thought for a moment. Something inside of her was willing her to tell the man to go to hell, to shout out to him that she wasn't interested in anything he had to say and never would be. A small part of her was suggesting she just hear him out, if only for the sake of interest, to know what was going on.

"If you asked me that," she eventually said, "I would tell you I wasn't interested. Can I go back home now?"

"But this is a genuine opportunity," Franz said. "I think you should at least listen to what I have to offer you, for the sake of your mother if not for yourself."

"Don't talk about my mamma."

But no sooner had she hissed the words out than a brief image of her mamma at a healthier weight flashed through her mind. Yes, she was recovering from malnutrition but had a long way to go, a lot more food rationing to live through. She threw her arms into a fold. "So, tell me," she said. "Tell me what I'd have to do for this extra food and medical care."

"Well . . . the authorities have set up a program, with clinics to assist. As it happens, many of them are here in Norway, because Norwegians are such good people. And . . . well, there isn't a gentle way of describing this, but . . ."

"Are you going to tell me or not?"

"They say I have good Aryan features. They tell me all I need is a woman with equally good features."

Ingrid's jaw opened and stayed open. She continued to listen, but what she was hearing was the edge of a nightmare.

"There's a program for people like you and me. The authorities are planning the next generation and want children of strong healthy stock."

"But I don't understand. I mean . . . are you seriously suggesting what I think you are?"

He nodded. "Of course I am. But there's nothing to be frightened of. This is nothing personal."

"Nothing personal?"

"No, no. What I mean is that it's merely duty for me—and for you a way of propagating your genes, your *excellent* genes. For both of us it would be our duty to the human race. And on a practical level you would benefit from the very best medical facilities. You'd be able to look after your baby for a short while, after which it would be passed on to a deserving German couple who could give it a far better life than it would otherwise have."

"My God, you're disgusting." Ingrid backed away. "You're *disgusting*. The answer is *no*, and I never want to see you again. Is that a good enough answer?"

"That's a normal reaction."

"*Normal?*" Ingrid screwed her face up at him. "You sound like you've done this before."

"What I mean is that the whole thing sounds worse than it is. It's a purely medical issue. You need to go away and think it through to appreciate the benefits."

She shook her head, sneering. "The answer is *no*, and it always will be."

The last thing she saw before she started running home was his face, which clung onto that impassive, imperious expression.

Ingrid got home and slammed the door behind her. Her mamma, now sitting at the dining table darning socks, asked her what was going on, what she'd been doing with "that man."

"I don't want to talk about it," was Ingrid's reply.

"A German soldier appears at the door, you go away with him, and you expect me to ignore it?"

"He only wanted to check my papers; there was some mix-up."

Ingrid's ingenuity and calm response surprised herself. She watched her mamma nod slowly, as though in agreement, then ready herself to put needle to cloth. Then she stalled and looked up.

"You know people will talk, don't you?"

"I don't care." Ingrid strode over to the fireplace, where her clean dress was hanging. "And I need to get ready now. Olav will be here soon."

"You're still going out for a meal?"

She stifled a nervous gulp. An evening out was the last thing she wanted right now, but she had to maintain at least the impression of normality. "Why not?" she said.

"Because you look upset, and . . ." She sighed and placed the needle down. "Ingrid, I worry. Is that so wrong? Just tell me he didn't hurt you."

"No. He didn't hurt me."

"Or threaten you or . . . or do anything—"

"I'm fine, Mamma. I need to get ready. Olav will be here before I know it."

"All right. You go out for your meal with Olav. I'll just stay here and worry about you."

Ingrid tried to ignore her mamma's words and headed for her bedroom.

But no. It was no good. That kind of talk always worked with Ingrid. She knew those words would follow and haunt her all evening. She turned back, sat down next to her mamma, and put her arms around her, squeezing tightly. "Oh, Mamma. It's nothing for you to worry about. Honestly."

Ingrid knew what was going on. Her mamma accepted she wouldn't be able to force the truth out of her, so she was turning to more subtle means. She gave Ingrid one of those polite but flat smiles Ingrid had seen a hundred times before and plunged her needle into the sock.

"You need to get ready, dear," she said without taking her eyes off the job in hand. A few stitches later she looked up to Ingrid, who was still in front of her, still staring at her. "Oh, ignore me," she said, her tone now more like that of a friend. "If it's important, you'll tell me. I'm sorry."

"Thank you, Mamma."

"Now go. Get ready."

"Yes. I have twenty minutes." Ingrid stood up and approached her best dress. As her fingers absentmindedly caressed the green velvet, a feeling of nausea started to engulf her. The last thing she wanted to do was go out for a meal, but if she said she couldn't go, it would only make both her mamma and Olav worry even more and ask her what had happened, and she couldn't possibly face putting Franz's proposal into words and hearing those words come out of her own mouth.

More importantly, it would mean that Franz—that horrid man—had won, had ruined her evening. She couldn't have that. With her back to her mamma she shut her eyes and tried to breathe away the feeling of creeping nausea. With each long breath she tried to banish memories of the conversation with Franz from her mind.

She managed to pull herself together, gave her face a rare lick of makeup, put on her best dress and shoes, and was starting to brush her hair when there was a knock at the door. She glanced at the clock; she had ten minutes left. It was Olav's knock. He had come early, but that was just like Olav. The thought made her smile and gave her a warm feeling that nothing could change. Olav would make her feel better; he would help her forget the bad things. She drifted across to the door, trying to ignore that devil on her shoulder muttering ill words, telling her that it might not be Olav, that it could be *him* again. But this was Olav's knock, so she tried to keep his image in her mind's eye. She felt faint for a second as she reached for the door, a light-headedness that was as threatening as it was weakening.

And then she opened the door, and Olav was standing there with a neat haircut, a clean-shaven chin, a very smart brown suit, and a bunch of wildflowers clutched incongruously in his fat fist. But most importantly, there was that warm smile between those sharp dimples.

The smile drooped.

"What's wrong?" he said.

"Wrong?" Ingrid tried to hold her artificial smile but could feel her cheeks flushing.

"You look upset."

"No, I just . . ."

And then, just as she was flustered, grasping unsuccessfully for another word, Laila appeared out of her front door on the other side of the street. *Good. That would divert attention.* She didn't consider

Laila a friend, and the feeling appeared to be mutual, but she was an acquaintance.

Ingrid gave her a wave and shouted out, "Hello, Laila!"

It made Olav turn around and do the same, which was even better.

But Laila didn't reply; she just strode across to them. Ingrid squinted to see the expression on her face. It seemed to be a scowl, but Ingrid couldn't remember having said or done anything recently to upset her.

Laila stopped, fists on hips, right in front of Olav. "I don't know what's going on between the two of you," she said to Olav in a conspiratorial tone but so loudly that passersby jerked their heads to see, "but I think you have a right to know that she was with a German soldier just now."

Ingrid held her breath, her tongue paralyzed, while Olav hopped his stark and confused stare between them both.

"Who was?" he replied with a casual laugh.

"Her!" Laila prodded a finger toward Ingrid. "I saw them leave the house together. An SS officer, I think. He came to the house, and they went away together. I don't know what they were talking about, but I doubt it was the weather."

Every vestige of humor vanished from Olav's face and voice. He stared at Ingrid, who opened her mouth, searching for a word that would bring life back to her tongue.

Laila's tongue had no such problem. "You weren't going to tell him, were you? I guess when you're plotting with the enemy, you keep it to yourself."

"Plotting with the enemy?" Olav didn't take his eyes off Ingrid as he spoke, and she could feel the implication in his stare.

"She's talking nonsense," Ingrid said. "I can explain." *Relief. She could talk again.*

"So, tell us what you were doing," Laila said, the anger in her words now not quite so strong.

"It's none of your business. But Olav's parents were taken by the Germans; he has no idea where they are or even whether they're still alive. Do you really think I would betray the man I love?"

"If you could get away with it, yes."

"Perhaps I'm not like you, Laila. Perhaps I have standards."

Laila leaned toward her. "And I would never go off with a German soldier. And it's obvious you're up to something with him."

"And you're nothing but a nasty gossip," Ingrid said, taking a step toward her.

Olav's hulking frame appeared between them, the only thing preventing them from going toe-to-toe. "Stop, stop, stop," he said.

At this, Ingrid turned and went inside, slamming the door behind her. She heard a few mumbles from outside; then Olav joined her inside. He stood by the door, a confused expression on his brow.

"I'm sorry," Ingrid said.

Olav said nothing.

"I've spoiled our meal, haven't I?"

He gave an upside-down smile. "I don't care about the meal. Well, I had plans, but they don't matter now. I'm just a little shocked. It's a side to you I've never seen before. Such anger. I know you don't get along with Laila, but—"

"And with good reason. I knew she didn't like me. Now I know she hates me."

"No, no. She just hates the Germans and anybody who colludes with them; don't you see that?"

Ingrid couldn't think of a retort to that. Half her mind was wondering exactly how well Olav and Laila knew each other. She shaped her mouth to speak, but the reply to Olav's question came from behind her: "Laila hates everybody."

Ingrid turned to see her mamma getting out of the fireside chair.

"I know I shouldn't eavesdrop," she said. "But I couldn't help it, and it was a loud exchange. I don't think I've ever known you so angry, Ingrid, but . . ."

"But what, Mamma?"

"Well, what you did *does* look suspicious."

"Even *you* don't trust me?"

"Don't be childish, Ingrid. I'd trust you with my life. I'm talking about how it *looked*—how it looked to other people."

Again, Ingrid was lost for words.

Olav cleared his throat. "So, does that mean it's true? That you *did* go off with an SS officer?"

Ingrid could only nod, and then it was Olav's turn to be lost for words.

"Olav," Ingrid's mamma said. "I know your evening is now ruined, but I think it would be a good idea if you went home."

"What? Now?"

Two raised eyebrows answered his question.

"Is this what you want?" he asked Ingrid. "For me to leave?"

"I'm the one asking you to leave," Ingrid's mamma insisted.

Ingrid opened her mouth, about to tell her mamma she wanted Olav to stay, but she was headed off by a glare and a sharp headshake. It was a gesture from her mamma that she recognized all too well. So instead she spoke to Olav. "I'm sorry," she said, "but it might be for the best. I'll see you tomorrow."

"If you're sure that's what you want."

"I am."

Hesitantly, he gave her a kiss. "You know where I am if you need me."

"Yes. Thank you."

Olav nodded a goodbye to both women and left.

"What's happening?" Ingrid said to her mamma. "Why did you want Olav to leave?"

"I'm . . ." Her mamma stared at the floor, pensively pursing her lips. "I'm confused—about a number of things."

"Well, perhaps it's for the best. I need time to think before I explain things to him."

"He'll be fine," she said. "He's shocked about what happened, but I think he's also pleasantly surprised."

"Surprised?"

"I don't think he's used to pretty women referring to him as 'the man I love.'"

Ingrid took a moment to think back. "Yes. I guess I did say that, didn't I?" She put on a severe frown. "And so what? It's true."

"Ingrid Solberg."

As always, Ingrid found the mention of her full name by her mamma unsettling. It was her way of getting Ingrid's attention. And it always worked.

"You need to sit down and tell me what this is all about, what you were doing with that German soldier. Laila might have been harsh on you, but she isn't completely wrong."

"But she is, Mamma."

"No. What I mean is, it looks bad."

Ingrid said nothing, just aimed a stare at the far end of the room.

"Come on. It will do you good to tell me. If you can't trust your own mamma, who can you?"

Ingrid closed her eyes and pressed finger and thumb to her eye sockets. "Oh, Mamma. You're right. I need to tell someone."

Ingrid made two cups of coffee—small and weak due to rationing—and they sat down by the fire, where Ingrid relayed in nervous tones exactly what Franz had proposed.

"That's disgusting," her mamma said, although apparently not quite as shocked as Ingrid had expected her to be.

"I could hardly believe my ears," Ingrid said. "But that's what he wanted me to do."

"It's terrible, but . . . but I *have* heard of it."

"What do you mean?"

"I mean, I know it's happened to other women."

"Really? Well, it won't be happening to this one; I can assure you of that."

"Good God, I would expect nothing less of any daughter of mine. You have enough problems as things are."

She gave Ingrid a curious look, pity mixed with concern. It was a look that Ingrid had rarely seen before on her mamma. There was clearly something else going on in her mind.

"What do you mean by that, Mamma? What problems?"

Her mamma took a sip of coffee and paused, her lips nervously twitching as she gathered her thoughts. "That's the other thing that's puzzling me," she eventually said.

"What is?"

"Well, call me a paranoid middle-aged woman if you want to, but under the circumstances I would have expected Olav to ask you—no, to *insist on knowing*—what you were doing with that German soldier."

"I don't think you gave him much opportunity."

"Oh, he had the opportunity. If he really wanted to know, he could have dug his heels in and refused to leave until you told him."

"I don't understand," Ingrid said. "What exactly are you suggesting?"

"I'm not completely sure."

"Perhaps he just trusts me or was going to ask later."

Her mamma nodded slowly. "It could be something like that, but perhaps he didn't want to pry because . . ."

"Because?"

"He behaves like a man who has his own secrets, and perhaps he's a better liar than he's led me to believe. I can't be certain, but age brings a certain intuition. And to give Olav his due, he seems a good and honest man. But in my experience . . ."

"Go on, Mamma. Please."

"Well, perhaps he feels better about his own secrets—that is, he feels less guilty—if he knows you have secrets too. Who knows? There are so many secrets in this city nowadays that anything is believable."

Ingrid thought for a moment, then nodded agreement. "So, what do you suggest I do?"

"Show him he can trust you. He might be hiding something, he might not, but I know he's a good man at heart."

Ingrid was now even more convinced of the sense in her mamma's words. But what else could she do to show Olav she trusted him?

Chapter 10

The morning after Ingrid's meeting with Franz, Olav called round to see her.

"I thought we could walk to the gardens together," he said to Ingrid after exchanging greetings with her and her mamma.

Ingrid looked to her mamma, who offered an approving nod, and moments later the two of them were outside in the clear, almost blinding sunshine.

Ingrid waited for him to ask about the previous day's events, but he seemed more interested in discussing whether to pick carrots today and when the frosts would start.

In the end, her impatience got the better of her. "Aren't you going to ask me about yesterday?" she said, completely ignoring his question on the state of the gardeners' toolshed.

"You mean, about you and the soldier?" He turned his face up to the sky. "As long as you're happy, that's all I care about."

"But you aren't even curious?"

"You obviously don't want to tell me." He harrumphed a laugh. "And I don't think you're passing Resistance secrets to him."

Olav's casual reply took her by surprise, and before she could recover, she was handed a shovel and found herself starting to dig. It seemed he didn't want to discuss the subject further, and Ingrid had to admit that neither did the larger part of her.

Weeks passed without Ingrid's mamma bringing up her suspicions about Olav's behavior, which she knew should have been enough to convince her to let the whole thing pass. Tempting though that was, the more she thought about what her mamma had said—about Olav having a secret—the more unsure she became.

Ingrid knew she should have been happy at that, but a part of her was still concerned, even desperate to broach the subject with him, to find out why he hadn't insisted on knowing what she'd been doing with the soldier. But it was a bright, peaceful Sunday afternoon; there never seemed a good moment to bring the subject up, and it was an awkward question to ask. Moreover, they spent more time lazing together in the sun and chatting with fellow gardeners than working. It was peaceful and enjoyable, two things to be highly valued in the current circumstances. Perhaps, Ingrid thought, her mamma was being unfair.

There was a perverse security in not saying anything but merely just enjoying each sunrise as it came along. The memories of that horrible soldier's repulsive suggestion were fading fast and would soon be as forgotten as the taste of a rotten apple. There was no sign of the war ending, no sign of the end of German occupation, and so no end in sight to rationing or martial law, so Ingrid resigned herself to a fragile happiness of compromises. Such a thing was, after all, better than no happiness at all. And it might have been the case that Olav thought the same, because he still hadn't even referred to the events of that day either, and they both enjoyed the togetherness that seemed much more important.

The middle of September was the time to plant carrots, turnips, and onions, so Olav and Ingrid spent two days clearing their plot of weeds, then seeding and watering the area. Even though Ingrid's mamma helped out, by the end of the second day they were all exhausted, but the job was finished, so they agreed that the next day would be a rest day.

Ingrid got up late—although still earlier than her mamma—and made herself a coffee. It was unusually quiet outside, so she settled down in an armchair with a book on gardening she'd borrowed from the library. She knew Olav would come around sometime later in the morning; there was no good reason to venture out, and she had aching muscles and calloused fingers to rest. So, it was a time to savor.

Within an hour, however, noises started outside. Doors were opened and closed, a few greetings were shouted between neighbors, the Bergen and Tufte children played tag, and a horse neighed as it complained about being taken out for a ride by Nils, the thatcher. Ingrid huffed a few complaints to herself and tried to read on.

She'd read another few pages when there was a knock on the door. It wasn't Olav's distinctive knock, so it was probably some other neighbor. She tutted and went over to open it, moaning to herself about how much her leg muscles ached.

"Hello again, Ingrid," the man said.

She took in a sharp breath, letting the book fall to the floor, to his feet. She'd tried her best to banish all memories of Franz from her mind, and the fact she'd largely succeeded only made her shock as great as it had been the first time he'd visited. Thoughts of aching muscles and sore hands were now forgotten.

"There's no need to be so frightened. Relax." He bent down to pick up the book. "Don't you remember me?"

Ingrid snatched it away and flung it over onto the table. "Oh, I remember. How could I forget? What do you want now?"

"I want to know how you are."

She started shaking her head slowly, glaring at him. "No. Oh, no. I don't believe you."

He smiled with a set of perfect teeth. "Actually, you're right. You see, you're clever as well as pretty. That's good, very good." He glanced behind him at the children screaming as they chased one another. "It's very noisy out here. Aren't you going to invite me in?"

"No."

He looked beyond her. "It looks like you're alone. And the doorstep is hardly a convenient place to conduct a conversation."

Ingrid thought for a few seconds, eyeing that ever-present rifle, then stood aside. "A few minutes only. Don't sit down."

Franz stepped inside and let her close the door. "Excellent," he said. "I didn't even need to cock my rifle."

"What did you say?"

"I'm sorry. That was a bad joke. I apologize."

"Tell me what you want. I haven't much time. My mamma will be up soon."

"And so?"

"She's tired, and seeing you again might upset her."

"That's very caring of you. You're a good person, Ingrid. Tell me, is your mother well?"

"You have a minute to tell me why you're here. After that I'll try my best to throw you out, so help me God."

It was a bluff, and he clearly knew it, but whatever the point of this was, she wanted it over and done with as soon as possible.

Franz laughed. He reduced it to a sickly smile, but that also fell away when he realized Ingrid wasn't joining in. "Well, yes. To business. It's not hard to explain. I just wondered whether you'd had time to give some thought to my suggestion of a few weeks ago."

"The one where you wanted me to breed with you like a mare would with a stallion?"

Beneath the calm facade, his jaw stiffened, and she could make out the action of his teeth grinding behind his pale skin. Up until now there had been a jovial nature to him that made her feel relatively safe. That attitude was changing rapidly, she could tell, being replaced by a threatening sneer. She tried not to look at the rifle, not to tempt him. Instead, she glanced at the door, wishing she hadn't closed it.

"Why do you hate me?" he said.

"What?" Ingrid said. "What do you mean?"

"I know you hate me. You're suspicious and nervous. You keep looking at the door, perhaps afraid of being alone with me. There's no need for that. I can assure you you're perfectly safe in my company."

"I'll judge that for myself, thank you."

"I'm sure you will. You see, I'm just an ordinary man who happened to be born in Germany at the right time. If things had gone differently for my father, if he'd stayed in Oslo and brought my mother across, I could have been your neighbor, perhaps your friend. I don't know what people have told you about SS officers, but I certainly don't wish you any harm."

He stepped forward, so close to her that the smell of the polish used on his buttons and buckles was strong and unavoidable. She retreated, he advanced, and she waited for him to continue, to force himself on her, readying herself to cry out. But he didn't. All he did was speak very slowly and quietly, as though calculating his words.

"This is nothing more than business," he said. "I'm not being personal. It's my duty as an SS officer to look out for suitable women and to try to persuade them of the morality of this. After all, thousands of your countrywomen are taking part in this program. It's nothing to be ashamed of. So please, don't be afraid of me or of what I'm suggesting. Think about it again. That's all I ask."

"I've thought about it, and I'm not interested."

At that, his face was still expressionless, as though he hadn't heard— or was unable to accept—her reply. He reached for his top pocket, unbuttoned it without taking his eyes off hers, and pulled something out.

Ingrid flinched at the action, but he reached across to the table behind her, and then his hands were empty. He stayed there, close but not actually pressing himself against her.

"You're a very beautiful young woman," he said.

He lifted a hand and stroked her cheekbone with the back of his fingers. It was gentle. His tongue flicked out and licked his lips as he performed the action again. Ingrid wanted to push him away—she wanted that more than she'd ever wanted anything—but also was unsure, her whole body in a rictus of some sort, as though restricted by a straitjacket.

Then there was a knock on the door—that familiar one Ingrid was praying for.

"Come in!" she shouted, her voice so strangled it hardly sounded like her own.

The door creaked open, and Olav appeared. Franz stood back from Ingrid, now focusing all his attention on Olav.

"What's going on?" Olav said.

Ingrid, her legs numb, willed herself to move away from Franz. She whimpered and managed to move one leg, then the other, and then hurried over to stand beside Olav. "He was just about to leave," she said, her voice just starting to return to normal. "And he won't be coming here again."

"I hope not," Olav said, glaring at him. "I might not be responsible for my actions." He put his arm around Ingrid and asked whether she was all right.

She let out an exhausted breath and nodded. "I'm . . . I'm fine."

The two men didn't take their eyes off each other. Franz stood tall and leaned back so he could peer down at Olav and took his time stepping over to the front door. "Think about what I asked, Ingrid," were his final words before he left, again making a point of moving slowly. He even took a few moments to stand in the doorway, glancing all around, giving his uniform a quick check, showing he wasn't prepared to be rushed by Olav's presence. But eventually he set off, leaving Olav to firmly shut the door. They listened to his footsteps fade away before either of them spoke.

"So, who was he?" Olav said. "And what's that?" He nodded toward the table.

They stepped over together, not completely sure until Ingrid picked it up. There was no discernible weight to it, but it was something she'd seen a hundred times before lying on the ground and had even held in her hands a few times, usually when she'd been a little girl. She twirled the sharp end between finger and thumb and brought it close to her eyes to examine it.

It didn't have a single filament of color to it.

It was a pure white feather.

I've just eaten lunch. Like most days, I don't eat much, only a few dumplings in bacon soup. I used to enjoy Krustenbraten and Schweinshaxe, but my teeth are no longer up to the task. Nevertheless, my stomach now feels full; the chairs around me are occupied by folk just as quiet and lifeless as me, so I feel sleepy.

I fight against my drooping eyelids but lose that battle very quickly. I almost fall asleep, but not quite. Not just yet. A vision interferes. I see a little boy sitting on the floor, innocently playing with wooden building blocks. It's me, and by now my crib is not even a memory.

I am walking, feeding myself, and managing to put together my first few sentences. I keep hearing that there has been a big war, which is now over, but that there is a heavy price to pay for being on the losing side, with consequences that will affect everyone for years to come. Some people say that will turn out to be an understatement. They say things like "Mark my words" and "Who do they think they're dealing with?" and "We should never have trusted our leaders." When they say such things, they speak with barely contained anger.

Even my father complains; he says that our victors have made us give up our foreign lands while they keep theirs, that Germany has become a new republic, with a new constitution, and we will be under foreign control for many years. He says this is unacceptable, and everyone knows it except our government. Many people come around to our house, and Father always gets angry when they discuss this.

But I am just a small child, warm and happy inside the walls of my cozy house. I understand nothing. I am completely unaware that outside of those walls, those political events are sowing the seeds of a much greater conflict—one that will irreversibly twist my upbringing and my whole life. But although I am oblivious to the politics of the day, I hear and see the anger. And yet, even as an innocent child, I can sense the tension spreading to all people and all corners of society.

Everyone says we are a nation lost, a country unified in defeat, a great people dormant, our pride suppressed but not completely eradicated. They say we are aimless, waiting for someone or something to lead us somewhere. But nobody knows who that might be or where they might lead us.

I continue playing with my building blocks.

Chapter 11

Toronto, 2011

Arnold's mother had kept to herself for most of her life, focusing her attentions on her children and grandchildren and, in her later years, concentrating on keeping her own weakening body in some sort of working order. So, the only people at the funeral were close relatives, neighbors, and no more than half a dozen friends, including Merlene, who Arnold and his daughters had started to think of as an honorary family member due to the close friendship she'd had with Ingrid.

The eulogy, written by Arnold and Barbara from memories of their mother, and spoken by the Lutheran minister, gave a potted history of her life from when she'd first set foot in Canada and nothing from before then because neither of her children knew much about those days. The minister detailed how she'd never held a job, relying instead on her husband's income from his small woodworking business and concentrating on making their home stable and their children honest and industrious. But although she'd never worked, she was keen to encourage first her daughter, Barbara, and then her grandchildren, Rebecca and Natasha, to make careers for themselves. She always told them and, indeed, her husband, that you never knew what changes were just around the corner, lurking in the darkness, waiting for the most inopportune moment to strike. The minister alluded to this and other pieces of wisdom she'd given to her family on all manner of issues.

Arnold and Rebecca held themselves together reasonably well during the proceedings, just wiping away a few tears during the service, although Barbara and Natasha had to sniff their way through it.

There were no tears during the light buffet afterward, only polite and reverent conversation. It was, Arnold didn't tire of telling people, exactly how his mother would have liked it to be.

Arnold promised himself he would speak to everyone who'd come to the funeral and thank them personally. He was halfway through when he overheard his daughters talking about him to his sister. He sidled over to the trio.

"You were saying?" he said.

"I was just telling Aunt Barbara you wanted to speak to her," Natasha said. "You know, something about a letter you found in Grandma's effects?"

"Oh, yes." He turned to his sister. "I was going to say. You remember the two suitcases I mentioned last time you were down?"

"There was something in them?"

Arnold shook his head. "Well, not too much. But there was a letter inside a letter."

"Huh?"

"I mean, there was a letter from Sweden, sent to Saskatoon, where Mom and Dad used to live, and it was forwarded from there to Mom a couple of years ago. Some woman from Sweden is trying to track down someone called Ulrich, born to an Ingrid in Oslo in 1944. I, uh . . . I wondered if you knew anything?"

Barbara looked bewildered. "Why should I know anything?"

"No reason. I just thought, with you being . . ."

"A daughter?"

"Well, I guess so. Perhaps you were closer to Mom than I was."

Barbara shook her head. "Clearly not close enough for her to confide in me about that. That is, if it's true. Could this woman be mistaken?"

"I think that's likely. Probably nothing to do with Mom."

Then Natasha chipped in with, "But you have a contact number, don't you, Dad?"

"For this woman in Sweden?" Barbara said. "So, why not call her?"

"I guess I might. But . . ."

"But what?"

"I was just wondering, how would you feel if—and I know it's a long shot, probably nothing in it—but what if it turns out we have a big brother?"

Barbara's mouth fell open, but nothing came out for a few moments. "Why don't you call her first? I'm pretty sure she's mistaken."

Arnold nodded. "Yeah, you're right. I might call her; I might not. If I get anything, I'll let you know, eh?" He drew a long breath. "Anyhow, did you like the service?"

It was only toward the end of the function, when the neighbors and friends had mostly left, that Arnold got around to talking to Merlene.

"I thought you were avoiding me," she said.

He laughed as he sat down next to her. "I have a lot of people to thank."

"Of course. Inappropriate comment. Excuse me."

"No, no. It's fine. I don't think Mom would have wanted everyone to be upset and tearful. Feel free to crack a joke."

There were a few seconds of awkwardness, Merlene looking down into her glass of lemonade, Arnold looking over her shoulder, scratching his head, nervousness over him like a fast-spreading rash.

"I, uh . . . I have to thank you more than anyone else, Merlene."

She looked up from her glass. "I did my best for her."

"You did. And she really liked you. It meant a lot to us having you there."

"Thank you." She smiled one of her big warm smiles. "It was all a pleasure."

"No, I mean she *really* took a shine to you. She was always talking about you and how you were so helpful."

"Like I told you at the hospital, the feeling was mutual. Ingrid helped me. Just for a year she was like a second mom to me." Her smile now twisted slightly. "I'll really miss her."

"Hey, you're a damn fine nurse," Arnold said. Then he checked himself. "Not that the other nurses aren't good; the whole staff at the hospital were exceptional to Mom. But it means a lot for you to say you'll miss her."

"Truest words I ever spoke. And I guess that's why I'm here." Merlene glanced around the function room. "And it was nice knowing you all—the family—as well as Ingrid."

"Once again, thank you for everything you did." Arnold checked his watch.

"Will I see you again, Arnold?"

"Uh . . ."

"Oh, I'm sorry. Forget I said that."

"No worries," he replied. "I'm sure we'll bump into each other again. That'd be good."

"You could give me a call sometime."

"I will. But hey, now I, uh, have to circulate some more."

"Of course."

Arnold turned to go but checked himself. "Incidentally, you remember that letter? The one from Sweden?"

She thought for a moment, then nodded. "I do. What about it?"

"I, uh, talked to my sister. She's never heard of an Ulrich. Has as much idea as I do what the whole thing was about, which is no idea at all."

"Are you going to follow it up?"

"Follow it up?"

"You know, will you contact the woman who wrote it?"

He gave an upturned smile, considering his reply. Merlene spoke again first.

"If I had a secret brother, I'd like to know about him. Wouldn't you?"

"Guess that would depend on what happened, whether he was still alive."

"Point is, Arnold, you won't find out about him unless you contact this woman. Why not give it a shot? What do you have to lose?"

"Mmm . . . well, maybe."

"Will you let me know if you ever do?"

"Sure." He lifted his glass toward his daughters. "I'd better get back. Bye for now, and, uh, thanks for everything once again. I appreciate what you did. We all do."

Chapter 12

Ingrid and Olav stood at the table of Ostergaten 41, both staring at the feather Ingrid held in her hand, the one Franz had clearly managed to leave without her noticing.

"I suppose I owe you an explanation," Ingrid said, placing the feather back down.

"I'm certainly confused," Olav replied. "Was he the soldier you saw before, the one Laila was telling tales about?"

Ingrid nodded.

"Then yes, of course I'd like to know why you keep meeting him."

"I don't *keep* meeting him, Olav; I . . . listen to me, something else has been troubling me, something I wanted to ask you but . . . didn't have the courage to."

He eyed her suspiciously but spoke warmly. "Ingrid, you don't need courage to ask me a question. Just say it."

"Well, after I saw that soldier, you had every right to ask me what was going on, to insist I tell you. I've spent a long time wondering why you didn't."

He rubbed his freshly shaven chin in thought for a few seconds, then nodded slowly. "You know how much I love you, don't you, Ingrid?"

"As much as I love you, too, Olav. But I don't want secrets between us. I don't think I could cope with that."

"Yes, yes. I agree. I don't like deceit. That's why . . . well . . . you're right. There's something I need to explain to you too." He picked up the feather and started twirling it, stroking its filaments. "Where's your mamma?"

"She's still in bed. But we can talk. I have no secrets from my mamma."

Olav cast a glance toward the bedroom door. "I'm afraid it's not that simple."

"What do you mean?"

"Look, why don't you make your mamma a cup of coffee and tell her we're going for a walk?"

"Can't we sit here and talk?"

He shook his head. "It has to be this way."

"But I don't underst—"

"Please." He held a hand up. "Just trust me."

It was a side to him Ingrid hadn't seen before. There was an ominous edge to his voice, one she wasn't sure she would like the reason for. But this was the man she loved, so she needed to hear what he had to say.

"All right," she said. "If that's the way it has to be."

Ten minutes later they left the house, Ingrid just following Olav, neither of them speaking until they reached the park gardens. Olav scanned the scene, their neighbors all busying themselves watering, digging, or weeding.

"Much too busy here," Olav said and pointed to the far end of the road, a long straight road that led toward the coast.

They walked on, along a few more roads, eventually reaching a hillside where the wind whipped in directly from the sea.

"Good," Olav said. "Luckily for me, people have much better things to do than come here and get blown over."

They leaned on a fence, looking out beyond the rocky landscape to the seas beyond.

"I'm glad it's not a cold wind," Ingrid said, her hair drifting and dancing all over her face.

Olav put his arm around her and hugged her tightly.

"So," Ingrid said, "shall I tell you about Franz first?"

"You'll find I know quite a bit about Franz Wahlberg."

She pulled her head away, slightly shocked. "You know him? How?"

"Please," he said. "Just carry on. I shouldn't have said that."

"There's nothing going on between us, Olav. You have to believe me. You have to trust me."

He glanced around again. A pointless gesture, Ingrid thought; only the mad or the desperate would be nearby. Then she saw fear etched on his face—the frown, the lips pulled back over teeth, the loud eyes. She kept her mouth firmly shut, eager to hear but also unsure.

"Listen to me, Ingrid." He pushed away a few locks of hair that had blown onto her face. "Yes, I know I can trust you." He exhaled loudly, the breeze whisking his breath away. "And if it turns out I can't, then I'm a dead man. For you, I'm prepared to take that risk."

Ingrid heard him sniff. She looked up to see a solitary tear escape from the corner of his eye and run down his cheek. She fumbled to pull a handkerchief from her pocket and absorb the wetness. "I don't know what you're talking about, Olav, but I promise you can trust me with your life. And whatever it is, even if you decide not to tell me, I'll still love you every bit as much."

He let out a sorry sigh, and his eyes ran over her face. "That means a lot to me, Ingrid. Thank you. But it's something I need to tell you. It's too important to hide from you." He held her close, his body shielding her from the wind. "Cast your mind back to that day last month—the day I said I was going to take you for a meal—when you met Franz, and we had that argument in the street with Laila afterward."

"As much as I try, Olav, I can't forget it."

"It was such a shame we didn't go out that evening. I was annoyed because I was going to tell you then. I'd prepared myself, rehearsed it, almost. And after I told you, I was going to . . ."

"To what?"

"Just listen. Let me tell you the truth first. But this has got to go no further—not even your mamma can know what I'm about to tell you."

"Well, of course."

"You're a good, proud Norwegian, aren't you, Ingrid?"

She nodded.

"And you wouldn't do anything to help these occupying forces, would you?"

"What do you mean, Olav? I loathe the German soldiers as much as anyone else. Even more so because they took your parents away."

"Well, that's the thing." He held her hand up to his lips and kissed the back of it. "I'm afraid I haven't been completely honest with you. And I can only apologize for that."

"You lied about your parents? The Germans haven't taken them away?"

"Oh, they were taken away all right, imprisoned, perhaps worse by now. But . . . I told you the Germans arrested them for distributing my uncle's illegal newspaper—the *Norway Light*."

"Yes. But you said they didn't do it, that the Germans got it wrong."

He shook his head. "The Germans got it right. They just got the wrong people. You see, it was me. I was the so-called criminal. I organized the central hub for the distribution of the *Norway Light*. My parents knew about it and turned a blind eye. And yes, they supported me while I did it. But they didn't ever touch any newspapers."

Ingrid turned to him and felt her face chill in the sea breeze, just as her heart chilled at the thought she was in love with a marked man. But she said nothing, just let him continue.

"I feel so bad about it. But what could I do? I was so close to telling them the truth; the words were on my lips, but I pulled back at the last moment. If I spoke up and told them the truth, they wouldn't have let my parents go; they'd only have imprisoned me too. My dear pappa and mamma are stuck in a hellhole somewhere—if they're alive, that is—and it's my fault. I feel terrible."

"It's not your fault, Olav. Don't think that. Please."

"Thank you. But there's very little I can do to get them freed. The authorities won't talk to me about them. It's . . . it's a horrible situation."

Ingrid held his arm more tightly. "Oh, God, Olav. I'm so sorry. This damn occupation. Those damn Germans. I wish the whole thing would go away and leave us alone. We didn't invade any other country. We tried our best not to take sides. And look what this war has done to us."

"I know, Ingrid. And I suppose that's why I got involved with the Resistance . . . and why I'm *still* involved."

Ingrid's jaw fell open in shock; she pulled away and looked up to him. "What did you say?"

"It's true," he said. "I shouldn't be telling you this. But I have a radio transmitter in the house. It's what I do, Ingrid. I work for the Resistance, listening in to foreign broadcasts and transmitting our own Resistance news bulletins here and to our supporters abroad. You remember Doctor Knudsen?"

"Resistance too?"

Olav nodded. "That's why he owed me a favor. We look after one another. There's also Laila."

"Laila? From across the street?"

"I've kept enough secrets from you, Ingrid, but not anymore. So, you need to know about her, too, and how I know her too."

Ingrid felt her chest tighten, perhaps with anger. "Go on," she said.

"When the Germans came to take my parents away, and I said I'd been chopping wood . . ."

"I remember, yes."

"Well, yes, I'd been chopping wood, but before that I'd been with Laila. I was telling her the news I'd heard on the radio. She's the editor of the *Norway Light*. I often meet with her in secret to tell her the news I hear on the radio."

"But . . . *Laila?* I can hardly believe it."

"She doesn't mean anything to me, Ingrid. She's a fellow Resistance worker, nothing more. You have to believe me."

"I do," she said, her body starting to relax on hearing his words.

"Are you all right?" he said. "You don't look too well."

"It's a lot to take in. I wouldn't have guessed that about Laila."

"There's a reason she's the way she is. You see, before the invasion she was in love with a shopkeeper. The Germans took him away soon after they took over."

"For doing Resistance work?"

Olav shook his head. "He had nothing to do with the Resistance. But he was Jewish."

"Oh, yes, I heard that the Germans have taken away all Jews. Poor man. Poor Laila."

"Exactly. That's why she hates the Germans so much and why she works for the Resistance—also why she got so upset with you for talking to that soldier. I'm telling you this because I don't want any secrets between us. I know her well, but I have to pretend we're nothing more than neighbors. So please go easy on her; try not to upset her."

"Of course. I'll try my best."

"And I can't stress enough the importance of secrecy. You can't mention what I've said to *anyone*. Not your friends, not your mamma. *Not anyone.* My life depends upon it."

"Of course, Olav. You know you can trust me. I'm shocked, but . . . oh, God, you're a brave man. And you're not quite the man I thought you were."

"I can only apologize for lying to you all this time. I've hated myself for it."

"No, Olav. You're a better man than I thought—a *better* man. And you don't owe me an apology. I see soldiers every time I walk along any street. I see the beatings, the arrests for no reason, the people who don't come back. I see my city and my country controlled by foreigners for their own benefit. Everyone knows where all our food goes. So, believe me, I understand."

"Thank you. And that night we were going out for a meal, I was going to take you somewhere private beforehand and tell you all this because I can't stand keeping secrets from you, especially if I'm going to be your husband."

"My *what*?"

"Ingrid, I've loved every minute of our time together. You brighten up my life; you keep me going in these, the darkest of our times. And I was going to say . . . well, I guess I *am* saying . . . if you'll marry me, I'm going to give up all of that, stop doing work for the Resistance movement."

"But, Olav. You can't do that. It's like you said—it's what you do. And it's a *good* thing."

He shook his head firmly. "No. My mind is made up. I'm not as committed as people like Laila, and it wouldn't be fair on you or your mamma for me to continue. This war can't last forever, but my love for you will. It's time for someone else to take over my Resistance duties. I want to marry you, and I simply will not endanger the lives of you and your mamma, especially after I saw what happened to my parents."

"But—"

"It's not something I'm negotiating, Ingrid. I love my country, but I love you more. I want you to be my wife. I've worked everything out. It's a bit later than I originally planned, but if you agree, I'll move into your house, supply all the firewood, repair the house, harvest all the crops. The radio transmitter is hidden in my house, of course, but I'll arrange for someone else from the Resistance to take it away. We can marry and live together; that's more important to me. And I really don't mind staying with your mamma; I know she relies on you. What do you say, Ingrid? Will you agree to be my wife?"

Ingrid leaned in toward him. Their windswept faces met. Cracked lips kissed cracked lips. She felt his cold cheek brush against her cold cheek, the contact warming her face just as his words had warmed her heart and soul.

"Oh, Olav. Before I answer, I need to tell you the truth too. Whatever you've heard about Franz, I have to tell you what happened between us."

"Go on."

"It started last month, the day I got the extra flour and sugar at the store. He was hanging around there, began joking with another soldier about me, about how I looked such a good . . . *specimen*, I think was the word he used. He was a horrible man, full of flattery, but none of it the kind a woman wants. I tried to get away, but he insisted on seeing my papers and so got my name and address. He came to see me on that day—when Laila saw me. I wanted him to go away, but he wouldn't, so I agreed to spend a few minutes with him if he left me alone after that. We went for a walk, and he made me a proposition. He . . ." She felt a few tears trickle down her cheeks, the cold salt breeze on them stinging her face. "Oh, Olav, it was horrible," she said. "So horrible."

Olav took a cloth from his pocket and wiped her tears away. "You don't have to tell me," he said. "Not if it upsets you."

She shook her head. "No. I *do* have to. No secrets. It's easy to put into words but hard to say them. He . . . he wanted me to have a baby by him."

"Oh, dear God. I thought so, but I didn't like to say."

"He said it was business, his duty, part of some German program about producing the next generation. He said he would provide food and health care for me and Mamma while I was pregnant, and sometime after the baby was born it would be taken away and . . . Olav? Why are you nodding?"

"I know what this is. *Lebensborn*, the Germans call it. It's a program all over Europe. Many Norwegian women are taking part in it."

"Really? I didn't know that."

"I doubt many of them are proud of their actions. Desperate, more likely. And I asked my contacts about Franz. I was told he was involved with the Lebensborn program. He came today to ask you again, I assume?"

"He did. The man's a pig. So arrogant. He thinks he's doing me a favor. And I have absolutely no idea what the white feather is for."

"He gave you that? Mmm . . . I have no explanation for that either. Perhaps it's some sort of symbol."

"It's just to taunt me, more like."

He held her hands and squeezed. "You don't need to worry about that now, Ingrid. It's over. I don't think he'll bother you again." He stared with a rare intensity into her eyes. "Now, give me an answer, Ingrid Solberg; will you please marry me?"

More tears fell from Ingrid's eyes, but they weren't from the pain of her hair whipping across her face in the wind, and they weren't from the memories of Franz's unwanted attentions; they were exquisite tears born of joy and hope.

"Yes, Olav. Of course I will. I love you. I'll always love you. And I want to be your wife."

They kissed again, and Ingrid sensed a warmth and a feeling of security spreading throughout her body that she'd never known before.

"Did you talk with Olav?" Ingrid's mamma asked when she returned, alone.

"It's fine," Ingrid replied firmly.

"But the man has secrets, Ingrid. I can tell it just to look at him."

"Mamma, it's not important."

"But I'm only interested in the well-being of my daughter. Is that wrong?"

"Everyone has secrets, Mamma. You don't need to know them all."

"Ah . . . *now* I understand." Mamma nodded confidently, a hint of a smile playing on her lips. "He can have secrets from me; I don't care about that, as long as he has none from you."

"Then there's nothing more to be said, is there?"

Mamma's smile came through, one as bright as Ingrid had ever seen on her.

And Ingrid could hold the news in no more. She lunged at her mamma, making her jump in surprise, then told her that she and Olav were to be married. Her mamma started to cry, Ingrid soon joining in.

Tears of joy were rare like the first swallows of spring and so to be savored.

Chapter 13

It had been too late in the year to plan a wedding before the hardness of winter gripped the city, so the following spring was now the chosen time for Ingrid and Olav's new beginning. Ingrid had never been happier, and none of the unpleasantness of the era—the rationing, the armed soldiers on every street corner, the danger of Olav being arrested for Resistance work—could dampen her mood.

October was spent making all the arrangements. It was to be a frugal wedding, using the local church for the ceremony and the adjoining church hall for the reception. The honeymoon was to be at Larvik, just a train ride away along the coast, using a property belonging to one of Ingrid's pappa's old friends, a basic but clean log cabin set back among the beech forests and lakes.

Ingrid was to borrow a dress from a friend of her aunt; the first wildflowers of the year, picked for free from the warmer coastal areas, would provide color; an uncle of Ingrid's promised to play the fiddle as she walked into the church; and Olav knew people who knew people who would get around the food rationing for a price. All these had been taken care of. Olav still lived at the house he used to share with his parents but had assured Ingrid the wireless transmitter and everything else that could incriminate him was long gone.

And that was the one unhappy aspect of the whole event: Olav's parents. He'd tried to contact them yet again via the authorities, even explaining the extenuating circumstances—that they would be missing their only son's wedding. His words were met with blank refusal.

Olav refused to turn down any work that was offered to him, and one day in November, he returned to Oslo from Drammen, where he'd been working for a few days on a carpentry job. It was late, the nights now starting to threaten frost, and he was exhausted and hungry. As usual, his first point of call was Ingrid. But at first, he thought the house was unoccupied, being dark and silent. He went in, tapping the door and asking if anyone was home. But there were no signs of life in the main room. Then he looked to a bedroom door, seeing a dim light around its edges.

He approached, opening it gently. Ingrid was sitting on a chair beside the bed, her mamma in the bed, looking pale, her only movement the slow rhythm of the bedclothes moving up and down. It looked like Ingrid had taken permanent residence in the room, an empty cup and bowl on the floor beside her.

Ingrid would usually jump up and run over to Olav after he'd been away, embracing him and saying how much she missed him. Tonight, she waved him away and silently ushered him back into the main room, quietly shutting the door behind them.

"What's wrong with her?" Olav said in hushed tones. "She seemed well when I left for Drammen."

Ingrid let her eyelids drift down and shook her head. "It's not good. She was ill the night before you left, but I didn't like to trouble you. She's become worse since then, so weak and hardly able to breathe. I don't know what to do."

"What about Doctor Knudsen?"

"I fetched him. He said . . ." Ingrid stopped, took a quivering breath, then started crying.

Olav held her tenderly but closely. "What is it? What did he say?"

"Oh, Olav. It's terrible. She has it. She has the strangling angel."

"Diphtheria? Oh my God. But . . . is he certain?"

She nodded. "He looked in the back of her throat. That was when he knew. He said it might be because she's malnourished, and I know she's been more concerned with the wedding arrangements than looking after herself. She's such a stupid, stubborn woman sometimes. I've been telling her for months she needs to eat more."

"Oh, Ingrid. Your poor mamma. I'm so sorry."

His embrace became tighter; then he drew back and held her head between his hands, his gaze roaming over her face. "But what about you? Do you feel well? What about your throat?"

"It's all right, Olav. Doctor Knudsen checked me out. He said it was unlikely I have it, but that it's essential we both wash our hands after touching and feeding her."

"Do we have soap?"

"Doctor Knudsen left me some."

"He's a good man, Doctor Knudsen." Olav nodded approvingly. "But did he say she would recover?"

"Oh, Olav. That's the worst thing. She needs the serum. The doctor says he can inject it, but I have to buy it from the drugstore."

"I have money, if that's the problem."

"You got paid today?"

"Mmm . . . no, I worked for free to barter for the cost of the wedding. But I have some money saved." He reached for his pockets.

"No, Olav. That's yours."

"It's life or death, Ingrid. Of your *mamma*. So take it. And we'll be married soon; what's mine will be yours." He handed her all the cash he had. "Take it; go on."

She took it and counted it, a sad smile appearing on her lips as she finished.

"What's wrong?" he said.

"This is enough for one day, perhaps two. She needs this regularly."

"Oh." Olav thought for a second. "We could sell some of our vegetables."

"And what would we eat?"

"Then I'll work longer hours. Perhaps go out on a trawler too."

Ingrid gave her head the firmest of shakes. "You're not going out on any trawler, Olav. Definitely not with all those warships on patrol."

"I'm sorry. Of course. Your pappa. In that case I'll find another carpentry job, one that pays well."

"When? Tomorrow? You're exhausted; I can tell." She kissed him full on the lips. "Besides, I've missed you. I don't want you to go away again so soon."

"I'm only trying to help."

"I know. But if you want to help, stay here, just for tonight. I can cook you something while you have a bath. You can sleep here tonight, in one of the armchairs. That way we can both keep checking on Mamma through the night."

He huffed a long breath. "I *do* feel tired. And I could do with something to eat. Are you sure you don't mind?"

"Of course not. But first let me fill the bath for you."

"Oh, there's no need. It's a lot of trouble for you."

"You need a bath, Olav. Believe me."

He stifled a laugh. "Very well. But please take my money. First thing in the morning you go to the drugstore and get as much medicine as it will buy."

"I will. And thank you, Olav."

The next morning Ingrid twice asked Olav whether he was sure he wanted her to spend the money on medicine. Each time he told her to get going, to get in line at the drugstore before it got busy, that he would stay at her mamma's bedside while she was gone.

So she left, still unsure whether she really should be using all of Olav's money, and walked to the closest drugstore she knew of. She eventually reached the counter, where she explained what she needed, asking for ten days' supply. A few minutes later a small bottle was placed on the counter, but when Ingrid was told the price, she halted, unable to speak. She had nowhere near enough money but pictured her mamma, suffering in bed, hardly able to move, struggling to breathe past that leathery growth in her throat. She cursed under her breath at how medicine had become so expensive and wages so low under German occupation.

And the assistant pressed her for payment.

Ingrid eyed the shop doorway, then tried to smile politely, although she knew it must have looked awkward. It was stupid—it was dangerous; she knew that. But this was her *mamma*—the woman who had been her constant companion, her source of life's wisdom, her support through the bad times, even her reason to live on a few occasions.

"Ten days' worth," the assistant said. "Wasn't that right?"

Ingrid said it was and thanked the assistant. She placed half of Olav's money on the counter, letting her hand cover it for as long as possible, then grabbed the bottle, swiftly turning and heading to the door.

She was almost there when she heard the cries. At first it was "Excuse me!" and then it was "Stop that woman!" But as soon as she was outside the shop, she broke into a run, hoping to reach the corner before she was spotted. To her right was a quartet of those wretched German soldiers talking and smoking, so she took a left, but not before she saw the soldiers take an interest in the shouts and the rumble of footsteps coming from behind her. For a few seconds she thought she'd escaped, but soon the voices were everywhere, the shouts relayed. She carried on running, ignoring her shoes pinching her feet with every stride, letting her lungs ache and not caring.

She might have been a fast runner, but within minutes she was cornered, and the crowds gathered around. She fell to her knees, sobbing and hiding her face of shame, while the mouths around her spewed out insults, arguing whether to hand her over to the local police or simply apply a few slaps across her face or even to cut her hair off to shame her. But still she clutched the bottle of medicine close to her chest.

And then there were other voices, still stern but more measured in tone. More importantly, they were German in accent. Ingrid looked up, wiped the tears from her face, and saw four men in those hated uniforms parting the small crowd that had gathered.

"We have local police to deal with petty thieves," an old man complained.

"Go away!" one of the soldiers shouted.

"But this is not your area of responsibility," the man insisted.

The soldier, perhaps lacking the fluency in Norwegian to argue his case, pulled a pistol, which won the argument for him. The man, aged though he was, scuttled off, cursing as he went.

By now Ingrid had locked eyes with one of the German soldiers in particular. It was Franz. There was a brief exchange in German between the four men, accompanied by a few glances at Ingrid and one or two lascivious smiles. Then three of them wandered off, Franz waiting until his comrades were out of earshot before speaking.

"Hello, Ingrid," he said. He held his hand out. "Come on. Get up."

She did so, wordlessly, still gripping the bottle tightly in her other hand.

"They were saying you stole something. Is this true?"

"I need the medicine for my mamma."

"Oh." He gave a flat, unimpressed smile.

"It's serious. The strangling angel."

"It's very common. And you stole medicine for her. Is that true?"

Ingrid sensed the accusation in his glare, then tried to find elsewhere to look. Olav had told her never to incriminate herself where German soldiers were concerned. But perhaps Franz was different. Perhaps.

"It's nothing to be ashamed of," he said. "It's very admirable that you care so much for your mother. It shows you're a good person." He bowed his head a little, trying to place his sympathetic expression in her line of sight. "Did you steal it?" he said softly.

She replied with a sad nod. "But only because I didn't have enough money."

"Mmm . . . so you admit to the charge of theft." His tone had changed, hardening as he delivered the words more as an official statement than a question.

For a second Ingrid felt sick at being duped, but that didn't matter. Nothing mattered right now except being allowed to keep the medicine. "What are you going to do with me?" she said.

At that, Franz laughed quietly to himself. "That's a leading question," he said. A glare from Ingrid straightened his expression. "You need this medicine, don't you?"

"My mamma's weak and in pain. She can hardly breathe. If it were your mamma . . ."

"But it isn't." Franz glanced left, right, and behind. Then Ingrid felt his eyes, like two blue bolts, fasten themselves onto her. "You do realize I could let you take the medicine to your mother and tell the drugstore any number of excuses? Isn't that what you want?"

What Ingrid desperately wanted at that moment was to attack the man in front of her, to make him shut those horrible, uncaring eyes. But again, her head told her to stay calm, to concentrate on appeasing him in order to keep the medicine she'd risked her liberty for. She took a few strong breaths, braced herself, and said, stuttering the words out, "Franz, if you could do that, I would be very grateful."

He slowly nodded, blinking as he weighed up her response. Then he unbuttoned the top pocket of his jacket and dropped two fingers inside. They pulled out a pure white feather, which he held by the bare end of the shaft and offered to Ingrid, brushing the tip against her chin. "Exactly how grateful would you be?" he said. "What are you prepared to do for me in return?"

She focused on the feather in front of her face, its purity now becoming obscene, and then on Franz. "Not that," she said flatly.

"That's a shame," he said. "Guaranteed medical care for your mother. Perhaps you don't love her as much as you claim to."

Ingrid gulped her hatred away. "Please, Franz. Just this once. Let me take this medicine to my mamma. She has diphtheria. You know how horrible that disease is."

He twirled the feather in front of her. "And you know what I want. Are you sure you're going to turn down this offer?"

Ingrid felt her tears pooling on her lower eyelids. She shook her head. "I can't do that, Franz. I just can't."

He huffed, then pursed his lips to one side, his face stricken in a frustrated pose. He reached out and snatched the bottle out of her hand. "In that case I'll take this." He touched a forefinger to his cap. "On your way, then."

"But Franz. This medicine is of no use to you. Let me keep it. Please."

He stared at the bottle for a couple of seconds, then tossed it into the air. It landed on the ground, smashing, its cargo darkening the stone slabs as it seeped away. "I'd say it's no use to anyone," he said, grinding the broken glass with the sole of his boot.

Ingrid pulled her glare away from the remains of the bottle, then back again just to be sure of what she'd seen.

"*On your way,*" he said more sternly. "And please pass on my regards to your mother."

Ingrid could contain herself no more. She jumped up, spat in his face, and thumped his chest a few times. "*I never want to see you again!*"

she shouted, then took a few long breaths while he wiped his face. For a moment she felt better.

"Think yourself lucky you haven't been arrested," he shouted as she fell back down, weeping.

Franz walked away.

Ingrid took a few minutes recovering—that and waiting for Franz to be as far away as possible. Then she got up and staggered home in a trance, trying her best to wipe her face clear of tears before she entered her house.

Inside, it was quiet. She approached the bedroom door and opened it a little. In the bedside chair, Olav stirred from his half sleep and turned around.

"Did you get it?" he asked. "Did you get the—" He shot to his feet, a look of panic on his face, and ushered Ingrid into the main room.

"How's Mamma?"

"She's sleeping well, and she's stable. But never mind her; what happened to you? You look terrible."

"I . . . I can't say."

"Oh, I think you can." He held her head in his hands and tilted her face to the light. "What happened? I thought you were just going to the drugstore."

"I did."

He looked to her empty hands. "So, where's the serum for your mamma?"

She gave her head a sorry shake. "I'm so sorry, Olav. I was in the drugstore. I only had enough money for two or three days' worth of medicine. I . . . I tried to steal a lot more. I got caught."

"*Damn!* What's wrong with them? You were stealing for a worthy cause. Did you get arrested? Charged?"

"Franz was there. He took charge."

"That loathsome creature? What the hell did he want?"

Ingrid tried to answer, but the words wouldn't come. The only words she could find were, "Hold me, Olav. Hold me."

He lifted her up and took her to an armchair, where they sat together for a few minutes, Ingrid lying across him, her head resting on his chest, both of them staring into space.

"Let me guess," Olav said. "He took the medicine back and said he'd arrest you unless you agreed to take part in the Lebensborn program?"

"You know him well, don't you? He didn't arrest me, though. But he did offer to make sure Mamma received the best medical care if I joined the program."

"And you told him what he could do with his proposal?"

"I did. And I told him I never wanted to see him again."

Ingrid felt his fingers gently pulling through her long blonde hair, his fingertips caressing her scalp and neck on the way. She felt a kiss on the top of her head, and they rested in silence for a few minutes.

"What am I going to do about Mamma?" Ingrid said. "She could die without help."

"I wish I knew," Olav said. "I wish I had the answer, but I don't."

Chapter 14

Oslo, November 1943

The next day Ingrid found it hard to drag herself out of bed. It was as if the whole world was against her—not so much conspiring to defeat her as caving in on her.

But she had to get up; there was Mamma to tend to. Doctor Knudsen had said that with the right care, there was a reasonable chance she would recover even without the serum injections. *A reasonable chance.* The phrase kept churning in her mind. What exactly did that mean? The roll of a dice? The toss of a coin? And what were the chances that she *wouldn't* recover?

She dismissed the thought. Her only option was to make sure her mamma was kept warm and well fed. As a side effect, that would also keep Ingrid busy and perhaps even take some of the worry off her mind, so she cast aside fancy notions of a world against her and got on with the job. The previous night she'd waited by her mamma's side until two o'clock in the morning, when both her own body and her mamma had told her to go to bed and get some proper sleep, which she had. Four hours of sleep wasn't nearly enough after the previous day's adventures at the drugstore, but it was about as long as she dared leave her mamma alone. So, the first thing she did in the morning was check her mamma was comfortable. The second thing was make two sweet coffees. She took them into her mamma's bedroom, tried to get her mamma to drink, then settled down in the easy chair to drink hers. She managed a couple of sips before she nodded off again.

She was woken up by Olav. He said he'd repaired Gustav Dahler's cart at the end of the road, so he could spend the rest of the day helping out with Ingrid's mamma, which he did. It was a cold morning, so he made a small fire, heated up some water for everyone to wash in, and at midday boiled some potatoes and a piece of fish he'd taken in payment for repairing the cart.

The rest of the day turned out to be quiet and restful—exactly what Ingrid needed. She spent the evening tending to her mamma, trying not to worry about her illness, and just a little time daring to look forward to marrying Olav.

For the next few days she slept well and one day woke feeling particularly refreshed, a sign that her ordeal with Franz was forgotten, and she could concentrate on getting her mamma better. She made breakfast for them both, then spent a couple of hours washing clothes, wringing them out in the mangle in the backyard, and hanging them above the fire to dry. Then she returned indoors to check on her mamma, who was awake but woozy, telling her she was going to the gardens.

Her mamma looked slightly hurt at the idea.

"I need to go, Mamma. I'll be less than an hour."

She nodded. "Yes. I'm sorry. Life has to go on, and you have to eat. But please, don't be longer than you need to be. I don't want to be alone."

Ingrid gave her mamma her best smile. "I'm sure you'll fall asleep, and you won't know I'm gone."

"Yes. I'm sure. I feel terrible being such a burden."

"Don't say that, Mamma. I'll see if any more vegetables are ready yet. And Olav might even have some more fish today."

"You're a good daughter."

"Well . . . you're a good mamma."

As winter was starting to harden, she went into her own bedroom to pick up her thickest coat, then went to leave the house. At the front door she stopped, one arm in the coat and one arm out, as though stricken. She stared down at the foot of the door. A white feather lay there.

One pure white feather.

For a moment she considered hiding, worried that he might be there on the other side of the door, waiting for her. She stayed silent, listening, but heard only the hubbub of gossip and the shutting of doors outside. Then she realized. Franz had probably visited while she was in the backyard. Slowly, carefully, she reached out and grabbed the doorknob. She huffed out a long breath and pulled.

There was only open space.

She stepped outside, her eyes wildly scanning the street scene. The Bergen and Tufte children were playing tag again. Three women stood together talking, one Ingrid recognized as Elsa Bergen wagging her finger in unbridled disgust at something or other. Herr Bakker was repairing the guttering at the front of his house, a wooden toolbox at his feet. But there was no Franz.

She shut the door and started walking, hurrying to the end of the street and around the corner.

There, she stopped for a second, forcing down a painful gulp.

Soldiers. Six of them. She tried to disguise her gasp of shock, thinking one of them must be . . . but no, he wasn't there. They ignored her as she hurried past and on to the gardens.

Olav had just finished repairing a bench and gave Ingrid a wave as she opened the gate. He used his cap to wipe the sweat from his forehead and motioned for her to sit on the bench.

So, they sat, side by side, Olav thumping the armrest to test the rigidity, admiring his joinery, Ingrid all eyes, staring in every direction and trembling slightly.

"A good job," he said. "Should last years."

She threw her eyes to him. "I'm sure." She watched him smile, a brightness she craved dimmed only by a concern she desperately needed.

His hand covered hers and squeezed it reassuringly. "She'll get better," he said. "With your care she'll recover, and . . ." His smile turned into a puzzled expression. "What's wrong?" he said. "There's something else, isn't there?"

She shook her head.

"Oh, yes there is. Is it your mamma? I haven't missed anything, have I? Did you have to fetch Doctor Knudsen out again?"

She knew she wouldn't be able to fool him for more than a few minutes. "I . . . I got something this morning." She reached into her pocket and pulled out the feather, keeping it half-hidden in her hand, not speaking, as if talking about it would give it some sort of legitimacy.

His reaction surprised her. He didn't ask where it had come from, perhaps because he knew.

"So, you know where I got this from?" she said.

The skin around his eyes wrinkled as he grimaced. There was pity in them. She expected a question about the item at the very least, but he stayed silent.

She was about to ask again when a flat smile drew itself on his lips.

"I . . . uh . . ." He reached into his pocket and pulled out another pure white feather. "This one came yesterday," he said, "while you were asleep. I left for a few minutes to fetch more firewood from my house, and when I got back, it was just inside the door."

Ingrid took the feather from his hands and put it with hers.

"I'm sorry, Ingrid. I thought it best you didn't know, that it was probably an attempt to tease you that would go no further."

"Franz is persistent." She held the feathers together, brushing her fingers up along the edges of the filaments. Two white feathers. In other, better circumstances it could even have symbolized her and Olav.

"Are you angry I didn't tell you?" he said.

She let her eyes drift up to his face and gently shook her head. "How could I be angry with you?"

"Well, I'm sorry. I shouldn't have kept it from you." He put an arm around her shoulder and pulled her closer. "That's twice he's called and missed us. Perhaps he'll give up now."

"You know, Olav, something is driving that man. I don't think he'll give up that easily."

"You think he'll try again?"

"Oh, he'll return. Perhaps tomorrow, perhaps next week. Who knows? But he'll come back again."

Olav nodded firmly. "In that case, I'll be there to meet him. Definitely."

"You don't have to, Olav."

"I'll be there," he said, almost squeezing the life out of her. *I'll be there.*"

"You don't realize how unpleasant he can be. Just promise me that if he comes . . . *when* he comes . . . you'll be careful."

"The man will be armed. I'll have no choice but to be levelheaded."

The next day Olav went to Ingrid's house early in the morning. They sat and ate breakfast. Few words were exchanged. After breakfast, Ingrid washed clothes while Olav attended to the fire and watched over her mamma, and then they both sat in armchairs, neither talking, both listening, both waiting.

When the knock came, it was a lighter one than expected—quieter than when he'd first visited. Perhaps he was more subdued today, if that were possible. Perhaps he'd come to apologize, Ingrid thought for one fleeting second. Or perhaps it was someone else.

Olav got up first.

"No," Ingrid said. "Let me."

He shook his head, then lowered his voice to a whisper. "You go to the bedroom. I'll tell him you're not in. I'll tell him you don't ever want to see him again."

She hesitated to reply, then laid a hand on his shoulder. "Be careful."

"I will." He ushered her away, and when she was gone, he grabbed the doorknob. He thought again and let go, taking a pace back and stretching up to his full height. "Come in!" he shouted.

The door opened. Franz laid eyes on Olav, then peered beyond. There were no greetings. "I need to speak to Ingrid Solberg," he said.

"What about?"

Franz looked him up and down. "That's no concern of yours. Where is she?"

"She isn't here."

Franz now stepped inside, facing Olav squarely, pulling his shoulders back, and in the process appearing to gain another inch in height. "You know I can search the house if I want to, don't you?"

"You don't have the authority."

Franz smiled a sickly smile. "We both know that isn't true, my friend." He took a step to the side to see beyond Olav.

Olav moved with him, knowing his frame was perhaps a little shorter but also stockier. "I told you once. She doesn't want to talk to you."

"Please remember, Olav Jacobsen, that you are in no position to argue with an armed soldier."

"You know my name." Olav shrugged. "So what?"

"Oh, I know a lot about you, my friend."

Olav's expression didn't change. "I don't care what you think you know. Now please leave my house."

"*Your* house?" Franz laughed. "Listen to me. I'll make it easy for you. I'll keep you out of trouble. But I need to talk to Ingrid about a very private matter. Tell her this. Tell her I just need to ask her a simple question, and if the answer is no, then I won't trouble her again. I give you my word."

"I don't want your word. It's worthless, Herr Wahlberg."

Franz's mouth exploded into laughter. "So, you know my name too. I'm impressed. Very impressed. But do you think that somehow makes us equals?"

Olav stepped up closer, raising a finger up to Franz, tapping a finger on his jacket button. "And I'm not passing on any messages."

"If you understand what this uniform means, you'll speak with care, Jacobsen."

"I'll speak how I want to, and if you think you can threaten me—"

"Olav!"

Ingrid came running from the bedroom. "No, Olav. Please." She stood beside the two men, their eyes still locked on each other, neither blinking.

Franz broke off first, turning to Ingrid. "Ah, Ingrid. You were here all the time." He flashed a smirk at Olav. "You were obviously mistaken, my friend. She was here after all."

"The answer's still the same," Olav said. "She doesn't want to talk to you." He put an arm around Ingrid, trying to shepherd her away.

Ingrid resisted, turning to Franz. "Did you mean what you said?"

"You know you can never trust him," Olav said.

"Please," Franz said. "I'll take no more than ten minutes of your time. I have a new suggestion. And I promise you that if the answer is still no, then I'll never talk to you again."

"And the white feathers?"

"No more white feathers. No more visits. And regardless of what your friend here says, I am an officer of the SS and hence a man of my word."

Olav and Ingrid froze for a moment, his arm still around her; then she gently pulled herself free. "I'll be fine, Olav," she muttered.

"All right," Olav said to her. He stabbed a finger at his chest. "But I stay with you."

Franz shook his head. "No. She comes with me for a walk. You stay here."

"You must be joking," Olav said.

Ingrid pushed him away. "Please. I'll be okay."

Olav puffed out his already large chest. "Ten minutes," he said to Franz. "If you harm her or upset her in any way, then all the guns of the entire Third Reich won't stop me coming for you."

Franz widened his eyes and nodded confidently. "As you wish, but . . . I think they just might."

Olav took a step toward him, but Ingrid barked his name, and he stopped. He sneered at Franz and said, "Ten minutes. No more."

Ingrid left the house with Franz, still unsure whether this was a wise move. She made a mental note to avoid alleys or dark corners and kept a discreet distance between them as they walked to the end of the street. With luck, and if Franz was true to his word, all she would need to do was listen to him for ten minutes and turn down any offer or proposal, and she would never see him again.

At the end of the street they turned left and walked some more, neither of them speaking.

"There." Franz pointed to a bench against a wall.

Ingrid walked slowly, but they still got there within a minute and sat facing a weak but pleasantly warming sun.

"I think you know the point of our conversation, Ingrid, so I'll come straight to the point. I like you. You're a fine woman. You're physically perfect, and now I know you have good mental strength too. What can I do to persuade you to be a part of the Lebensborn program?"

"You can't do anything, so please don't waste your time."

"I thought you might say that." He squinted at the sun and leaned back to absorb the full force of it for a few seconds. "You care a lot for your mother, though, don't you?"

"Of course. But please leave her out of this."

"But you do care for her. You care enough even to steal for her."

"Don't remind me of that, Franz. Just say what you need to say, and leave me alone."

"Very well. You already know the program provides health care for the mothers who give birth to Lebensborn babies. What if I could also arrange for your own mother to receive all the serum she requires until she recovers from diphtheria?"

Ingrid looked at him as she considered the question. The sun in his hair made it look more white than blond—almost angelic. "She does need medicine," she said. "You know she does. But not this way."

"It looks like it might be the only way, so I suggest you choose your answer carefully. Consider this lovely sun, and consider how many more sunny days your mother might live to enjoy or . . . or might not live to enjoy."

"You don't give up, do you?"

Franz shook his head and looked her up and down—leered at her, so it felt. But he said nothing else. And there was nothing else for Ingrid to say, and she found her thoughts turning to her mamma, to images of her out of bed and walking, smiling, laughing, shopping, and cooking—perhaps even working at the park gardens or simply enjoying the warming rays of next summer's full sun.

In fright, she cut the thoughts from her mind and stood up. "No," she said. "And I think that's the end of our little talk."

"There's just one other thing," Franz said, still seated.

"And what's that?"

"Sit back down."

Ingrid exhaled slowly, hands on hips.

"Please," he said. "Sit for just two more minutes."

She did, lazily dropping herself into the seat.

Franz took out a packet of cigarettes, tapped it to release one, and reached for his matches. "I don't often do this," he said. "The Führer doesn't approve of tobacco, but now I'm nervous."

"Nervous? Why?"

He lit the cigarette, took a long drag on it, then spewed out smoke, hazing the sunlight. "I didn't want to have to do this," he said.

"Then don't."

"Quiet, Ingrid, please. This is difficult enough." Ingrid noticed a tremor, a tic around his eyes that neither he nor his drug could completely stifle. "The word is that you plan to marry Olav."

Ingrid said nothing, just felt a stirring in her stomach, a lightness in her head.

"You know he's been dealing in illegal newspapers, don't you?"

"No." Ingrid frowned. "He's given all that up."

"'*He's given all that up*,' his wife-to-be stated. A statement of a guilty past is still a statement of guilt."

"I'll deny I ever said it."

"You'll call an SS officer a liar?"

"If I have to."

Franz took another lungful of calming smoke and tapped ash from the end of his cigarette. "I'm only joking, Ingrid. And it doesn't matter anyway. We have proof he was dealing in illegal newspapers and also that he was using a radio transmitter, which, as I'm sure you're aware, is highly illegal."

"He's . . . he's . . ."

"Got rid of it?"

Ingrid resisted the temptation to nod; it would only provide him with another statement of guilt.

"I know he got rid of it," Franz continued. "It's at our intelligence office. But it can be traced back to him. We should, at some stage in the coming week, bring him in for questioning, search his house, probably yours too. You need to realize they'll turn both places upside down, searching in every last corner for any evidence that he's still working for the Resistance."

"They won't find anything."

"And how, exactly, can you be certain of that?"

Ingrid's head hurt. The question was a spit in a tornado. She trembled, trying to reply but unable to free the words from her throat.

"And the people who carry out the searches aren't the most careful of sorts." He took another drag on his cigarette. "Of course, we only have limited resources at our disposal, and we have to choose which cases to investigate and which to forgo." He paused to let his words sink in. "And I'm very well acquainted with people who have the authority to influence such decisions."

Franz smiled at her. It was a confident, knowing smile that only made her headache even worse.

"It's true that he . . . he . . ." *Yes, nearly there.* The words needed to come to defend the man she loved. "It's true that he used to work for the Resistance. But now he's stopped all of that."

Franz's smile widened a fraction, a hint of triumph in his eyes.

"But has he?" he said.

A staff member kindly pushes my wheelchair to the dayroom and positions me in front of the television. I don't know why, but I don't complain. A talk show is on—people I've never heard of but who are apparently famous talking about things I have no interest in—and it's like a sleeping pill. Perhaps that's why I've been placed here. I'm aware of my head lolling forward, so I lean back and rest against the chair. Soon I'm only aware of a vision, my tormentor.

By the mid-1920s I'm starting to tire of playing with my toy train, and I listen more. I sense we are still a nation waiting for someone or something to lead us somewhere. What my father calls "foreign forces" are still controlling our country, interfering with our policies and the way we run our affairs. Now, I am growing up, and the resentment of my people is clear to see, even to a child. I don't understand the details of what is happening, but even as I sit on the floor and play, I somehow know that something momentous is taking place. There are rumblings of a new and progressive political force poised to break the old order, a force that the authorities are doing their damnedest to suppress. But my father says these authorities are grinding our pride into the dirt because they have one eye on those "foreign forces" controlling us. He is adamant they won't succeed.

I often hear my father say that this is the start of the new order, an order we could be truly proud of. He says that now is a time to rejoice at the birth of hope, that the future of our country could be bright and great under this new force. For many there is a view that this new force will bring our country out from the stone it crawled under after the Great War, that in time it will make the rest of Europe—and the world—follow our progressive lead.

But there is a bitter struggle going on; the old guard tries to control the people, to deny average German citizens the right to decide the destiny of their own country. There are peaks and troughs in support for this new force, but many people dream of a new and better Germany, so whenever the old rulers beat off the new political force and have their way on one issue, many people know it won't be forever, that sooner or later the new force will reemerge, and a better, more joyful era for Germany will break through.

Young as I am, I sense changes in myself mirroring these changes in society. But for now, I simply carry on playing with my train.

Chapter 15

For a long time, Arnold's life had been a smorgasbord of hectic seasoned with frantic. There had once been a busy business to run, a family to bring up, and, for a period of time, a divorce to deal with. Soon after that, he'd needed to juggle his daughters' adolescent adventures with visiting his mother's apartment to run errands and fix things. Then, once her health had curved down from poor to dangerous, there had been talks with Merlene to get progress reports and to thank her for doing so much that he should have done but didn't get around to. Soon after that he'd had to wind down the business, after which there had been daily visits to the hospital. Finally, there had been arranging his mother's funeral.

So now, barely a week after that funeral, when his sister had returned to Montreal and his daughters to work, life seemed to consist of a big zero. There was nothing to do but wallow in the quiet reflection that he kept hearing he should do. Just like there was nothing to regret but having too much time on his hands. Even though in her final weeks his mother had had little to say, and in her final days she had been barely conscious, he missed her like he would miss an arm or a leg. For sixty-six years she'd been an ever-present shoulder to cry on, an ear to borrow, a sounding board for life's big decisions and unholy troubles. Now she was simply a never-present. The puzzling thing was that he missed her more than he remembered missing his father when he'd died over thirty years before. But that would probably be due to his own age, due to the fact that concerns about his own mortality were now slowly but surely bubbling to the surface. First your grandparents die; then your parents die. Everybody knew what came next. But that wasn't the kind of thought he wanted to share with his daughters whenever they made those short token visits to his house.

So, he saw a few old friends, watched daytime TV until he could feel his brain slowly wasting away, made himself meals from scratch instead of relying on takeout and the microwave oven, went for walks, and between all these things kept eyeing up the envelope with the Swedish postmark that still lay on the dining room table, where he and Merlene had opened it together and discussed its contents.

He kept thinking back to the day he'd opened the letter, unsure whether the driving force behind his obsession—if that was the correct word—was the letter itself and the search for Ulrich or his memory of Merlene's face across the table, her encouragement, her company. But now, after a week of contemplation, he realized the two were inextricably linked. He had to admit that he needed more on both counts, but which desire was the greater? It was hard to accept, but behind his own back he'd become quite fond of Merlene. Despite her gradually developing into a firm friend of the family, he'd always held her at arm's length but now wished he hadn't. Then again, the purple yearning to know more about this mysterious Swedish woman and her missing Ulrich—whether or not he was Arnold's brother—was now making his head hurt.

And there was more. Lurking in a dark corner of his mind, like jokers that someone was just itching to flick out onto the table and ruin the game, were those bizarre words his mother had spoken from her hospital bed. They turned out to be some of her very last utterances, and Arnold had never forgotten them.

Arne must never know about his father.

Had his father once done something unspeakable? Did it have something to do with Ulrich? Was that why his parents had asked his father's relatives in Saskatchewan to burn any letters coming from Norway?

He washed his face, got dressed, and made and ate breakfast, somehow all on autopilot. He knew he hadn't slept well—never had since the funeral. But why not? The new emptiness of his life? His inquisitiveness about that damn letter? Or his mother's words? Or were they all feeding off one another and turning his mind into a worm's nest every time he turned the lights out at night?

Now he realized that every thought and action over the past few days was funneling his mind toward one unavoidable act. He logged onto his laptop, searched for "time now in Sweden," then laid the letter out in front of him and picked up the phone.

He had no idea what words were coming out of the phone after it was answered. He was thrown partly by the words but also at his own stupidity for expecting anything else. After a few seconds he managed to stutter a reply.

"Do you . . . uh . . . do you speak English by any chance?"

"Yes, I speak English. Hi."

"Oh, thank you. Tell me, are you Marit Fosberg?"

"I am. Could I ask who is asking please?"

"You don't know me directly. You wrote a letter a couple of years back trying to contact my mother, Ingrid Jacobsen."

There was a gasp of breath. "Are you . . . Ulrich?"

Arnold tried a laugh but couldn't. "No, no. I'm sorry. But you remember the letter, yes?"

"For sure I do. So, have you news of Ulrich?"

"No, I don't. Listen, Marit, my mother died a week ago. That's how I got the letter—from dealing with her effects. She was called Ingrid, but I suspect you have the wrong person, although I'd like to be certain. Could we talk now? Is it convenient?"

"Of course. I'm so sorry to hear about your mother. Tell me; why do you think she wasn't the mother of Ulrich?"

"Because . . . uh . . . I guess because if I had a brother, I'm pretty sure I'd know about it."

There was a long pause.

"Marit?" he said.

"I'm sorry. I'm thinking. I'm thinking how to say it. You see, Ulrich wouldn't quite be your brother."

"I'm not sure I follow."

"Your father, is his name Olav?"

"Yes. Well, it was. He died over thirty years ago now."

"Oh, I'm terribly sorry."

"That's okay. But . . . how did you know his name?"

"Because I've been searching records. And this means that your mother is the correct Ingrid. She was the mother of Ulrich."

Arnold detected a tremble in her voice, then heard a few short, sharp breaths. "Are you okay?" he asked.

"I'm sorry. I've been searching for Ulrich for such a long time. I haven't found him, but I feel I'm getting closer. It's a little . . . overwhelming."

Arnold silently cursed himself at his selfishness. It must have been a shock for this woman to even get the call out of the blue two years after she sent the letter, let alone take in what he was saying.

"I'm sure it is," he said. "But . . . I'm still a little confused why this Ulrich wouldn't be my brother."

"Because Olav wasn't his father."

Arnold gulped away the anger climbing his throat, sympathy for Marit fading into the background. "You do realize what you're saying about my mother, don't you?"

"That she . . ."

"You're saying she had a baby by another man the year before I was born."

"I know. I'm sorry. And I'm sure she loved your father."

"You're damn right she did." Arnold took a few calming breaths. "I'm sorry. I know this all happened a long time ago, but it's confusing the hell out of me, and so soon after her funeral."

"Oh, I'm so sorry. Please, I didn't mean to . . . perhaps I should leave you in peace."

"That might be a good idea."

"But is this it, Arnold? Will you call me again when it's more convenient?"

Arnold held the phone away from his mouth for a few seconds, thinking, before bringing it back. "Look, Marit, you've been polite; perhaps I called you at the wrong time. I, uh . . . just tell me one thing I didn't ask. What are you to this Ulrich person?"

"Ulrich and I, we share the same father. He would be your half brother and mine too."

"Right," Arnold said, taking a long pause to process the information. "Look, I'll call you some other time. I promise."

"Thank you."

The rest of the day dragged on for Arnold the way days just seemed to lately, each hour that passed reminding him of those long-gone days, making Marit's words churn around in his head. He could have called his daughters or his sister or even Merlene, but he wasn't sure he wanted to share what he'd learned. And he definitely wasn't sure whether he ever wanted to speak to Marit again. If he never spoke about it again, if he swept the conversation he'd had with her under the rug, life would be simpler. If, that is, he could manage to do that.

The night hours brought no respite from the thoughts Arnold wished he wasn't having. The conversation he'd had that day with Marit was still fresh in his mind—a mind swirling with thoughts of explaining it to his sister or his daughters, of how he would phrase the explanation, of how they would react, and of what they would suggest he do. All of these aspects of his mother's life threw themselves onto him like a suffocating cloak.

And the worst thought, the very worst thought, was of those haunting words his mother spoke just before she'd died: *Arne must never know about his father.* The troublesome creatures that inhabited the darkest corners of his mind kept feeding him the lines. Should he reassess the man he'd looked up to with such pride in his younger days and missed so much even now? Did that kind and generous man have a hand in the disappearance of Ulrich—Arnold's half brother—who was, after all, the result of a liaison between his wife and another man?

He couldn't shake thoughts of the inevitable possibility from his mind.

Did dear old Dad somehow get rid of Ulrich?

As the dawn light hit the curtains, there were other, more pertinent thoughts: Could he afford to ignore Marit? Could he brush the whole thing under the rug and look at himself in the mirror every day? Did he really know his father well enough to dismiss the worries he was having?

And if his parents did "lose" Ulrich, when exactly did that happen? In Oslo? In Canada? En route to Canada?

Arnold suppressed a cold shiver.

There was one avenue he could explore for answers. Arnold himself was only a baby when they all came to Canada all those years ago, so he wouldn't have been aware of any brother only a year or so older than him. But surely the folks in Saskatoon—his father's cousins—would have known. Sure, the place was sparsely populated then as now, but hiding another child wouldn't have been easy.

The last time he'd had contact with Saskatoon, at least one of those old-timers was still alive. Arnold fetched the address book and looked up the phone number for his second cousin in Saskatoon.

Chapter 16

Ingrid stepped out into the street and shut the door, holding herself there, listening to the truck's engine idling behind her, knowing and dreading what that sound meant.

For a moment she wondered if she could be in a dream—even *wished* she was in a dream, a dream where there was no army truck and no Franz, and the sound was a harmless tractor. That self-deceit would make her job easier. And this *was* a job, nothing more.

It was now midwinter, and if she did nothing but stand there, she would freeze. Then again, that notion held some appeal. She heard her name. He was at her shoulder. He asked her if she was ready. She found herself nodding sadly, and moments later she heaved herself up onto the passenger seat of the truck, not looking to her side, not speaking. The truck jerked into action, and in the awkward atmosphere, her mind turned to that day she'd returned home after seeing Franz, fearful of what she was going to say to her mamma, petrified about how she was going to explain it to Olav.

She'd entered her house to find Olav whittling wood away, a mass of shavings at his feet. He dropped the knife and the length of branch into the shavings and stormed over to Ingrid, holding her tightly, lifting her off the ground.

"Thank God you're okay," he said. "I've been so worried. Let's just hope he's true to his word and this is all over."

Ingrid could feel him squeezing, inviting her to do the same. But she couldn't. It was almost as if that could be her way of telling him, a part of her hoping that he would guess, that she wouldn't need to utter the words.

"Ingrid?" he said, letting go of her and stepping back, his eyes scanning her face for the truth. "What's wrong?" He looked her up and down, saw the dour lifelessness in her face. He tried a short laugh. "But . . . it *is* all over, isn't it? Tell me it is. Tell me you refused, and we'll never see him again, yes?"

Then his optimism—the optimism Ingrid had fallen in love with—capitulated to the sorry features in front of him. "Oh, no," he said, his eyes starting to glisten. "Oh, please God, no."

"Olav. I'm sorrier than I've ever been in my life."

"I can't believe you'd do this. Tell me you're not serious."

Ingrid said nothing, just bowed her head.

"But . . . but why?"

"Because I want Mamma to live; that's why."

"But she's living. You saw her yourself. She's recovering."

Ingrid shook her head. "The doctor said without treatment she could easily go one way or the other. She could *die*, Olav; she could *die*. It's my mamma, and I'm not having her life or death decided by the toss of a coin. I have to do something to help her."

Olav turned his back on her and thumped the end of his fist down on the table. Then again and again, and finally a fourth time, splintering a section of the tabletop. He halted, shaking his head, grunting, and huffing.

"Olav, please."

"Please what? Please *what*, exactly?"

"Try to understand. Mamma will get her medicine, you and I can still be married, and when the baby is born, they'll take it away. We can forget it ever happened."

"You think so? Do you think *I'll* be able to forget something like this? And if not me, think of yourself. Do you think your friends and neighbors will take kindly to you doing this?"

"They won't find out about it."

"Oh, God." Olav rubbed his stubby fingertips over his sweaty brow. "You think nobody will find out? Really? You think Laila hasn't got contacts or . . . or . . . won't suspect and start digging until she finds out the truth?"

"I don't care about them; I care about you and Mamma."

"Well, you *should* care about them. You live among them. One day this war will be over, and we'll need to make a living."

He turned, and Ingrid saw his eyes, sad and red rimmed, and she hated herself, knowing he was right, knowing that this whole episode was wrong, very wrong in every way imaginable, but at the same time feeling compelled to defend herself. In panic, tears of her own came freely. "Try to understand me, Olav. Please. I can't think of all those things. I don't want Mamma to die. Whatever happens to me and to us after this wretched war ends, I want Mamma to be a part of it. Don't you see that?"

He stepped toward the door. Ingrid put her arm against it, shielding it from him. "Please, Olav. I love you. I want to marry you. But I have no choice. I know it doesn't seem like it at the moment, but this time next year, and for the rest of our lives—"

"Get out of my way!" He grabbed her by both shoulders, pulling her away from the door. For a second, she thought he was going to pick her up and throw her across the room. He didn't, although a small part of her wished he had. *Perhaps she deserved it.*

Instead he pulled her toward him and held her so tightly she was unable to breathe.

"You might be fine with this," she heard him say, "but I can't go through with it. I can't be a party to this evil."

"I'm not fine with it, Olav. I'm doing it to save my mamma's life."

He said no more but left, leaving the front door open, striding out into the dim daylight.

Ingrid stumbled over to the fireplace and collapsed onto a chair. If Franz had plunged a knife into her heart, Olav's anger had now twisted it, and the possibility of not marrying him—or even not *seeing* him again—cast a black shadow over her thoughts. She knew she had to stay strong, but at the same time she was unable to stop the tears from flowing. Perhaps it would all work out, but also, perhaps she'd made a terrible error of judgment. The longer Olav was gone, however, the more certain she was that she'd made her decision, and there simply was no other way.

A couple of hours later, however, Olav did return. He shut the door and glared across at her. She stayed huddled in her seat, returning the glare. He shuffled over and sat down opposite her.

"I'm sorry, Ingrid. I just had to get out, and . . . and I've done a lot of thinking."

She viewed him anxiously.

"Look, I don't agree with what you're going to do, and a part of me will never be able to forgive you, but I can understand why you have to go through with it."

The words lifted her heart. "You can?"

He nodded. "You obviously have to consider your mamma. It's a matter of life and death, and you have to put her above me. I can understand that."

"Don't say that, Olav."

"But it's true, isn't it?"

"No, it isn't true, not at all." Then there was panic in Ingrid's mind. She had to stop him pressing her on the reasoning of her decision, so she continued talking. "I've agonized enough about Franz, and I've made my decision."

"But—"

"I said I've made my decision, Olav. And . . . and if even one hair on your head isn't going to forgive me, then . . ."

"Then what, Ingrid? Then what?"

"Then I can't marry you."

At that, Olav went very quiet—no shouts, no anger, no piercing gibes at her. That was bad enough, but he didn't even look in her direction, only down at the floor. There was silence between them for what felt like an hour, and then, still not granting her so much as a glance, he turned and left the house once more.

Ingrid felt tears rising to the surface, forced there by a storm of betrayal and confusion. It was hard to accept Olav's reaction, harder still to accept her own disappointment: she expected better from the man she loved.

It was late the next morning, while she was washing clothes, that Olav came round and started talking to her again. He told her to leave the clothes, to sit down, and then he knelt down beside her.

"Yesterday was the most horrible day of my life," he said. "Worse than when they took my parents away."

Ingrid went to speak, but he held up a silencing palm.

"It's made me realize just how much I truly love you. I know why you're doing it, and . . . and if you'll forgive me for what I've said, I'll marry you and stand by you and help as much as I can during your pregnancy. And I will, however hard I have to try, find a way to forgive you. I promise."

She leaned down, kissed him on the forehead, and said, "That's all I need to know, Olav."

As the army truck passed the end of the street, Ingrid resisted the temptation to turn and look across toward the park gardens to where she'd first met Olav. She had to forget him for the next hour. She couldn't, however, forget the efficiency of what had happened next, after she'd met Franz once more and agreed to take part in the Lebensborn program.

Her health checks had been completed. Parents and grandparents had been verified. Documents waiving rights to the child had been signed and witnessed. It would be official state property as soon as it was born and would have to be handed over as soon as it had been weaned. Ingrid's mamma had started getting her regular injections of the antidiphtheritic serum, and the Lebensborn nurses had calculated the best time for Ingrid to conceive. Whether that timing was good for Ingrid didn't matter. Whether Olav cared didn't matter. From now on this was merely a job Ingrid had to do, nothing more than that.

"The hotel is warm," Franz said, his gaze not moving from the road ahead.

She said nothing.

"Warmer than your house, certainly."

Still no words came from Ingrid. But the thought was good; it took her mind off Olav. Perhaps she couldn't bear to talk to Franz, but her thoughts turned to the hotel he was driving her to.

When Ingrid was ten, she'd been taken to see her pappa's family in Kristiansand. There was no mention of where they would be staying, but somehow she'd gotten the idea they would be staying at a grand hotel in a prime position in the city. On the train journey there, she'd imagined climbing a wide carpeted stairway leading up to their suite of rooms, where her own bedroom, brightly lit by a crystal chandelier and heated by a crackling log fire, would contain polished wooden furniture, an intricately embroidered chair, and a bed so thick she would need a small ladder to climb up onto it.

As it turned out, her pappa's parents owned a slightly ramshackle wooden house on the fringes of civilization, and Ingrid had slept on the floor of the living room on a mattress barely big enough for her frame.

In fact, the grandpappa she hardly knew had commented on how she'd grown so much in the two years since he'd visited Oslo, which explained the size of the mattress.

Ingrid had said nothing at the time. How could she complain? There hadn't even been any mention of a hotel, let alone promises—only a child's imagination. But she never forgot the thrill of the mere prospect of staying in a hotel, where a porter would show her to her room, where staff would change the bedclothes and clean the room daily, and where waiters would hand her a menu. With her pappa's death there seemed little real prospect of her staying in a hotel anytime soon, but she always knew it would happen one day. Even her and Olav's honeymoon was going to be very modest—a week in that hillside cottage loaned to them by one of her pappa's old friends, who, with his wife and family, would be spending the week with Ingrid's mamma.

Ingrid had never given up hope that one day she would stay in a hotel, and now that was about to happen. But dear God she didn't want it this way. She told herself whatever happened she wouldn't stay the night there, so it wouldn't count. She didn't even want to read or hear the name of the hotel. That way it would be easier to forget. And as Franz drove her toward the hotel, she willed herself to concentrate on that visit to Kristiansand and her childhood thoughts and what the hotel room might look like and nothing else. Anything that stopped her thinking about the events to come had to be a good thing.

And when Franz accompanied her into the hotel, she found no wide staircase, no carpeted stairs, only a cold dark corridor with distinctly grubby walls. When he opened the door to their room, it was dark inside. He appeared to know exactly where the light switch was and showed her in. There was no crystal chandelier, only a single bare bulb, and there was definitely no fancy chair and no thick, comfortable bed.

The bed was just large enough, with a chipped wooden frame that looked functional and no more. There was an easy chair in the corner, but it was a faded, ragged thing that had clearly supported far too many people over the years. The only other item of note in the room was a pair of patterned curtains, which fluttered in the cold breeze that stole through the gap in the window frame and settled onto the bare wooden floorboards, lurking there.

"There's a bathroom along the corridor," Franz said. "It's very clean."

"You've been here before?" Ingrid asked, not looking at him, just staring at the bed, its sheet neatly but not quite evenly folded back over the two blankets.

"Not often," he replied. "But yes, I have."

"For the same purpose?"

"That doesn't matter."

Ingrid sat on the bed. He locked the door behind them and sat on the chair, in front of her line of sight. Neither of them spoke for a few moments; then Ingrid got up and shut the window, ramming the lever down hard, before sitting back down on the bed.

"Do you want to talk?" Franz said.

"No. I want this to be over as quickly as possible."

He nodded. "As you wish."

"My wishes are not with me at the moment. Just remember our agreement, my conditions. The lights are out. You don't kiss me. You don't touch any part of my body you don't need to. And you leave straight afterward."

He pulled his tie off and placed it in his jacket pocket. "So . . . shall we start?"

Ingrid pointed to the light switch with her eyes.

And then, after a few more ruffles of clothing and some heavy breathing, he was there, as close as only a husband should be. Ingrid tried to push all thoughts of Olav out of her mind. She tried to push every pleasant thought from her mind.

Hold your breath, Ingrid. It will soon be over. No, you are not even Ingrid. And it will soon be over; it will soon be over. Hold your breath. Keep your eyes closed. Don't allow your nose to become infected with his smell. Take shallow, light breaths and hold them with all your might. It will soon be over. Blank against the pain; blot it out. Control, control, control. A few more seconds. Hold on. Hold your breath as much as you can. Don't open your eyes. Don't breathe unless you need to. Take short, shallow breaths. Hold on. It will soon be over. It will soon be over. His breath will soon be far away. The pain will stop, and his body will soon leave you alone. Hold on. Soon, soon, soon.

And then it was over. Franz rested, lifeless for a few moments. A deadweight. Ingrid pushed him, then pushed harder. He revived and moved his body away from her. His mission completed—for now—he got up and switched the light back on. Ingrid used one hand to pull the bedclothes over her body and the other as a shield against the light, which had seemed dim before but now felt harsh. She squinted and saw Franz's bottom poking out underneath his shirttail. He turned to her as he buttoned the shirt. She laid her head back and focused on the ceiling until the clanking of his belt told her his pants were on.

"I didn't hurt you, did I?"

He *had* hurt her, but the casual tone of the question troubled her more than the pain she knew would soon subside.

"Do you care?" she replied.

He buttoned his fly, then took two long paces to stand next to the bed. Now she gripped the bedclothes with both hands and pulled them tightly around her neck. She relaxed slightly when she saw the expression on his face. He looked spent in more ways than one, almost like a schoolboy who'd been caught looking up a teacher's skirt.

"I'm not an animal, you know."

A hundred and one replies to that sped through Ingrid's mind. He was *behaving* like a primitive animal; he was making her *feel* like one. Animals had unfeeling sex; humans made love and cared. And humans didn't "breed." These thoughts and many more went through her mind, but all were quelled before they became words. Her heart hadn't stopped thumping; her body wanted to turn rigid with self-disgust, but she contained the feeling to a tremble, somehow willing her body to hold the moment, to control, to keep those emotions of self-loathing in a heavy-lidded box.

"Do you want me to take you home?"

"I want you to leave."

Franz stilled himself to think for a moment. "You made your choice, Ingrid," he said. "Nobody else. And I don't have any desire to make the experience unpleasant for you." He shot his arms into his jacket and gave her one final look, with perhaps a hint of shame—only a hint—as his eyes flicked to the floor. Then he stepped over and placed a hand on the doorknob. "I'll collect you again tomorrow at the same time, yes?"

Ingrid didn't nod or speak, merely willed the man's hand to push on the handle and his legs to lead him out and far away.

For a few seconds he waited for an answer, his head bowed only slightly. Then he jerked his head up and stood upright, as though suddenly realizing he might have looked subservient, and left the room.

Ingrid concentrated on his footsteps, each quieter than the last, until she could hear nothing. She jumped out of bed and opened the window again, perhaps to let some of the evil in the room escape, then got back in and curled up into a ball, the sheets covering her completely. Her hands were cold, but nervous sweat still lingered on her brow. Her head was hot with temper, her heart cold like a mountain rock.

But now she could relax—collapse, even—the liberation making her body writhe, letting the tears of shame come freely. For a second, she almost dabbed the wetness from her face with the edge of the bedsheet, but no; the sheet was dirty—the sheet was depraved—wicked by association, just like herself. No, the trickle of tears would be as a penance.

She wept freely, letting the tears find their own path.

It was almost an hour before Ingrid left the hotel. After a forty-minute walk she arrived home, prayed that Olav was in his own house, and went inside.

Olav turned from the sink, where he was washing his face. His sour eyes asked the question. She didn't nod her head—she didn't say *yes*—but she knew her stillness would be answer enough. He wiped his hands, letting the towel fall to the floor as he walked toward her. A step to the side, never letting those stark eyes off her face, a dash to the door, and he was gone.

Her husband-to-be was gone.

Chapter 17

The second rendezvous between Ingrid and Franz took place the next night. Again, Franz stopped the army truck outside the house. Again, Ingrid clambered into the cabin without a word, and both of them stared straight ahead as he drove off.

They stopped at a crossroads.

"How is your Herr Jacobsen taking all of this?" Franz said.

At first Ingrid was shocked at the question—so incensed at the man's cheek she couldn't speak. Eventually she came to her senses. "You don't need to know that," she said. "You only need to make sure my mamma gets her medicine."

Only now did he glance at her, his face showing some hurt at his question being batted away. "Your mother's medicine is guaranteed," he said. "I give you my word."

They drove along in silence until Franz had to stop at another junction.

"You don't like it if I mention your husband-to-be. I can understand that. I know it can't be easy for him to—"

"Another rule," Ingrid snapped. "Do what you need to do. No polite conversation."

A few seconds passed before he muttered, "You don't make the rules."

Ingrid had no reply to that; there was, after all, a lot of truth in his words. So, neither of them spoke until they were back in that same hotel room. Ingrid was starting to regret her new rule. She was again taking off her dress; Franz was again unbuttoning his shirt. She felt a shame that one or two polite words might have alleviated. The previous night had been awkward and painful as well as repulsive. Tonight, now Franz's body wasn't quite that of a *complete* stranger, should have felt a little less repulsive.

That was what she kept telling herself as the tuft of hair drooped down from Franz's head, swinging in time like an oily pendulum, as he lazily closed his eyes, as she felt the humid heat of his breath on the side of her face, and even as he grunted his last. No, it should have been easier, but was every bit as disgusting as that first time, somehow feeling even more mechanical. A word—perhaps an apology—might have made her feel less like a heifer chosen for her rearing qualities being serviced in a drafty farmyard shed.

This time he did show a little more humility, albeit only afterward. He sat on the bed, turned to her, and ran his gaze up along her form, resting on her eyes. There was now a softer, less self-assured air about him. He went to rest a hand on her shoulder.

That was too much. She held her own hand up in defense. He desisted, but with no anger or arrogance, just a nod of acceptance, perhaps just a hint of rare acquiescence.

In the end, it was Ingrid who broke the silence.

"I'm sorry," she said. "I can't do this again."

"You signed an agreement," he said, although Ingrid sensed little conviction behind the words.

"I don't care. I just can't do it again."

"Well . . . you won't need to do it tomorrow. I'm busy."

"Another woman?"

His widening eyes provided the guilty reply.

"A Norwegian woman, like me?"

He tried to ignore the question, but her glare wouldn't let it go unanswered. His face twitched, almost a challenge to her.

"And what of it?" he said.

"Nothing of it."

"Then why ask?"

Ingrid hurriedly tried to form the words running around her head into a coherent sentence: mares, stallions, run-down farms, muddy fields, pedigree heifers, best of breed, prize-winning bulls, science, good bloodlines. After all, this was no more than a matter of good breeding. Perhaps she was trying to pierce his conscience. But he spoke first.

"I'm only carrying out my duty," he said.

"You don't . . . enjoy yourself?"

He stood, pulled his pants on, paused to think. "You're a beautiful woman. Of course I enjoyed it. Didn't you? Perhaps just a little?"

Ingrid sneered at him. Now she felt little fear. Somehow there was a strength. She didn't cower and pull the sheets up around her neck as before. Her mouth had the dryness of deep displeasure. But also pity.

As he pulled his shirt on and started to button it, his face took on a solemn, pensive look. He sat, ready to put his shoes on, but instead thought for a moment and then spoke, choosing his words carefully.

"You think I'm a selfish animal, no better than a rapist. I understand that. But you're wrong. It's like I said; I really am doing my duty."

"How can you say that?" she hissed. "And how can you expect me to believe you're not an animal?"

He got up and sat on the bed, at the bottom end, careful to stay some distance away. She pulled her legs up, away from him.

"I don't expect you to believe it. You don't understand the political theory. I have a wife back in Bavaria. Two children. And we bring our children up well. Once a month we all go to the forest. We camp there. I make a fire from fallen branches, and my wife cooks on it. We spend a lot of time watching the birds there. During the day there are whinchats and woodpeckers flitting from tree to tree, buzzards gliding above the clearings. At dusk there are owls. I eat and drink just like you. I have moods—good and bad—the same as anybody. Before I joined the army, I played soccer for my local team—usually as a goalkeeper. I still play with them when I'm on leave, just to keep in practice. I badly hurt my ankle in training last year, and it still hasn't fully recovered. I have friends just like you—enemies, too, in an occupied country such as this. I sleep. I laugh. I cry. Believe me or don't believe me. I'm no animal. So please don't tell me I am."

"So . . . why are you doing all this? Can't you see how wrong it is?"

"I can't expect you to understand. The Führer is trying to achieve something here for Germany, for Europe, even for the whole world if people would only listen. He's trying to make Europe a better place for everyone. More emphasis on healthy lifestyles, increased food production, getting rid of the weak, the undesirable. And yes, making sure the next generation of Europeans as well as Germans is healthier and stronger than the last. I think that's a *good* thing. Can't you understand?"

Ingrid merely stared at him. He was right about one thing: she didn't have the skills to argue, just to know. She could say nothing. He continued.

"And you're helping too—helping to enhance the human race, making a worthwhile contribution. Do you really want a world full of retarded people? Of small, ill people? Of dark-skinned, selfish sorts who would sell their own mothers? You're doing a good thing here, Ingrid. You should be proud of yourself."

The last sentence made Ingrid wince inside. She didn't understand politics, but she was definitely not proud of herself and even less so after listening to the speech Franz had given.

"I don't understand," she said. "But what I do know is that doing this doesn't make me happy or proud."

"Whether you understand or not, it's all true. And I know I'm doing the morally correct thing. I'm doing my duty for my country." He stood and stepped over to the door, picking up his jacket on the way. "I'll pick you up from your house the day after tomorrow, at the same time, yes?"

"I won't be there."

He stood tall, folding his arms. "But you've agreed. In writing. You realize I could have you arrested?"

"Yes."

He strolled over to the window, peered out, took a glance up at the sky. "Do I really disgust you that much?"

She let her silence reply.

"I'll be fair. You might change your mind. I'll come to your house the day after tomorrow. I'll wait a few minutes. If you don't come out of the house—"

"I won't. So, don't bother coming."

He sighed. "Are you really sure about that?"

"I am. If I have to do this again, I'll kill myself."

And then Franz changed once more, his tone softening further, almost sympathetic. "There's no need for that sort of talk. I don't want that. And besides . . ." He waved a finger at her midriff. "We might have already . . ."

"And you wouldn't want me to kill it, would you?"

"No. I wouldn't. And . . . and I wouldn't want you to kill yourself either."

"Are you serious?"

"Have you not been listening to me? This is a matter of duty. I don't wish you any harm. None at all. But now I have to go." He stood next to her, motioned to place his hand on her shoulder, then withdrew it. "I don't understand why you can't accept that what you're doing—what we're doing—is a good thing." He waited for a reply, which didn't come, and shrugged. "Perhaps it's something you simply cannot comprehend."

"That's something we can agree upon."

He gave her a final, doleful look. "Goodbye, Ingrid."

"Goodbye, Franz."

"If I don't see you again, good luck with everything."

Ingrid said nothing, and he left.

She lay back in the bed, too confused to cry.

Was he going to hold her to her agreement and turn up on her doorstep again? She wasn't sure. And she wasn't sure whether she cared. Franz's justification for what he'd done had made her feel sick—sick of Norway, Germans, the hotel room, sick of everything. If he'd simply said he wanted her and enjoyed their physical union, he would somehow have seemed more human. As it was, his justification for his actions only made her feel worse.

She lay on her side, curled up into a ball, and willed the tears to come—anything to make her feel better. When they didn't, she dragged herself out of the bed, got dressed, and headed home on foot.

The walk gave her time to reconsider her actions—time she didn't need or want. If she became pregnant, she would have to leave Ostergaten, to find an excuse to tell the neighbors, to pray they didn't find out the truth, to continue the lie when she returned, when she'd given up her baby. Only now, after the event, was she starting to realize that the lie would follow her around for the rest of her life.

Then again, if she told Franz she didn't want to carry on, and if she wasn't already pregnant, would he do the honorable thing and let her mamma continue with her medicine? More importantly, would his honor stretch to protecting Olav from investigation over his Resistance work?

It seemed that whichever way she turned, whatever decision she made, there was danger, reprisals, a life hardly worth living. The whole thing was a torrid mess, and in the middle of that mess were those two most disgusting experiences of her life in that room with Franz.

She reached a bridge over a fast-flowing river and stopped awhile to relax her mind in its timeless swirling and eddying. For a few minutes she was mesmerized. There was one way out of this mess, and it seemed the only way to avoid the danger, the fear, the impossibility of what to do and what not to do, who to hurt and who to save.

She was disturbed from her daydream by laughter. Along the river she saw a group of men. They spoke German. Soldiers. They were laughing, punching, and shoving each other. Joking, no doubt. Perhaps drunk. They were off duty. Carefree.

She gazed once more into the river. Yes, it was true. That would be one way out of the mess she was in. But that would be letting them win. Her mamma wouldn't want that. Olav wouldn't want that. And Ingrid certainly didn't want it. She huffed a few deep breaths, wiped the tears that she had only just realized were streaming down her face, and started walking again.

When Ingrid got home, Olav was sitting by the fire. He got up and slowly approached her, his hands in his pockets. "Your mamma's definitely getting better," he said. "She's drowsy now with the medication, but earlier she was sitting up, eating well."

"Good."

"I'm . . . I'm sorry about yesterday, about how I behaved."

"It's fine."

"Would you like me to make you something to eat?"

"I just want to go to bed."

"How are you feeling? How did it . . . go?"

She shrugged. "What do you want me to say?"

"I want you to say nothing happened, but I know that isn't the case."

"Then why ask?"

Olav let his mouth fall open but simply sighed. "Don't you want to see your mamma before going to bed?"

"I don't care about my mamma."

Olav said no more but left the house and went home. Ingrid went to bed without even checking on her mamma and slept until the next morning.

The next day, Ingrid pasted a smile onto her face for the sake of her mamma and tried her best to behave normally. She made breakfast for them both, talked awhile with her, and got on with the household chores. Throughout the day, however, one fearful thought never left her: the dread of what would happen when she carried her threat through and didn't go with Franz on the next visit to the hotel. And she was adamant it was a *when* and not an *if.*

Toward the end of the afternoon she chopped up some turnips and potatoes for the evening meal. As she did so, she gave some thought to the meal, guessing her mamma would probably stay in bed all evening. She pictured herself alone, accompanied only by those horrible thoughts of what had happened and what might happen. And then there was the wedding. The dreams and wishes and plans had all been put to one side lately, but despite the troubles of dealing with Franz, she was still in love with Olav and still held dear her heart's desires beyond these wretched times. She needed a sign—however slight—that he still wanted to marry her or even that he still cared for her. It was an impulse, but she headed for Olav's house and knocked on his door.

"I'm making an evening meal," she said. "Would you like to come?"

He shrugged, childlike despite his size.

"Mamma will probably be in bed. Some company would be nice."

He grunted agreement, then nodded slowly, still holding on to a frown.

"Six o'clock," she said and returned home, making sure she stood upright as she strode off.

So, Ingrid didn't eat alone that night, although very few words were spoken over the boiled potatoes and turnips covered in the butter Olav had bought on the black market. But as she stood up and started to clear the plates and cutlery away, Olav spoke.

"Don't you need to get ready?" he asked. "Won't he be here soon?"

It should have been a polite question, but there was a little venom in the word *ready*, a touch of bile over the word *he*.

She let the resentment behind his question slide and answered, "I don't need to go tonight."

Olav's face twitched. "What is it, a night off for good behavior?"

Now he wasn't even trying to disguise the hatred in his words. But still she didn't rise to the bait; her emotional constitution was too fragile for a battle.

"Franz is busy tonight," she said.

Olav nodded. Ingrid noticed his nostrils flexing.

"Is he busy with another . . ."

She waited for him to finish the sentence, her eyes fixed onto his lips, anticipating the word *whore* or *harlot* or worse. Then the word came; it was simply *woman*, and Ingrid felt relieved, even slightly proud of him.

She put down the plates and sat next to him. "Olav, I want to talk to you about something."

"Oh, I'm not sure I want to hear what you have to say. In fact, I'm not sure I can bear to listen."

"Why?" she replied without thinking.

"'*Why?* What's that supposed to mean?"

And now Ingrid—fragile or not—couldn't hold back. Her voice cracked into a frenzied tone. "But you agreed, Olav. You *agreed*, and you promised me you wouldn't hold it against me."

"Well, I was wrong. I can't take you doing this. You must have worked that out. I can't accept it, and I even find it . . . yes, I find it hard to even look at you."

"And your promise?"

"I know, I know. I was wrong to make promises I couldn't keep. I can agree to anything in the world, but I can't help how I feel about something."

"And don't you stop to think how *I* feel about this whole thing?" She hammered a finger to her breast. "It's like a disease eating away at my insides. And all you can do is behave like a petulant teenager, flipping this way and that, being pleasant to me one moment, then ripping my heart out the next. I can't stand it. I hate Franz, but at least I hate him all the time. Don't you see how hard you're making things for me?"

"Oh, stop the sob story, Ingrid. And stop talking about that bastard like that. Or is it that perhaps you secretly enjoy—"

"Don't you *dare*!" Ingrid shouted, standing and lifting a plate as if to throw it at him.

"Calm down," he said. "You'll wake up your mamma."

Ingrid put the plate down but now stood next to him, her finger wagging like the wind had caught it. "And don't you dare talk about my mamma. This is exactly what I mean—you're nice to me one moment; then you treat me like the dirt on your boots."

"Well, perhaps the hat fits. This whole Lebensborn experiment is sick and disgusting, and you're sick and disgusting for going along with it."

"Is that what you really think of me?"

"It's only the truth, nothing more."

"The truth? Ha! Be careful what you say, Olav. You really don't want to know the truth."

Now Olav stood up, too, dipping his head down to meet hers. "And what does that mean?"

"It means . . . it means . . . oh, I've had enough arguing." She slapped his face and flung the same hand toward the door. "Go home, Olav. I can't talk to you. I'm going to bed."

"Aha! So, there *is* something else, isn't there? Something you're not telling me."

"No, Olav. Just go home."

Ingrid turned and headed for the bedroom door, but he grabbed her arm and pulled her back.

"Why won't you tell me the truth?"

"I can't." Ingrid tried and failed to shake her arm free.

"But I thought we agreed—no secrets?"

"Oh, Olav. We agreed on a lot. But you seem to have no problem going back on your word."

Olav positioned her in front of him, then held her by the shoulders and shook her, as if playing with a rag doll. "Tell me the truth, Ingrid. What are you hiding?"

"All right, Olav. You asked. I'll tell you. I'm doing this for two reasons. Yes, I get help for my mamma, but also I have Franz's assurance that you won't be arrested."

"Arrested? Me? Oh, now you're sounding desperate."

"It's true. They traced the radio transmitter back to you."

His grip relaxed to nothing in a second; his face paled a shade. "Wh . . . what?"

"You heard me. They still suspect you of working for the Resistance. They were going to take you in for questioning. They were going to search your house and this house too—turn everything upside down to find more evidence. Franz called all of that off."

Now Olav completely let her go, holding a palm against his forehead, gazing to the floor but focusing on nothing.

"Yes, Olav. Doesn't the truth change things? I didn't want you to feel guilty, so I didn't tell you. But are you happy now you know? Well, *are you?*"

He shook his head, more in disbelief than denial. "So . . ." He took a gulp. "So, you didn't think to call their bluff, to say I had nothing to hide?"

"No, but—"

"You mean you just believed them? You think I lied to you when I said I'd stopped working for the Resistance?"

"That's not the point, Olav. I didn't want them to search our houses, and I certainly didn't want them to take you away for questioning."

"But Ingrid, if they were to search the house—now or then—they wouldn't find a thing."

"Yes, I know that's what you told me, but—"

"You don't believe me even now? Is that what it is?"

"It's not a question of whether I—"

"*Right!*" He grabbed her again and pulled her over to the kitchen area, where his spare hand opened the four kitchen cupboards. "So where do you think I've hidden a transmitter? Here?" A clatter of pots and pans flew onto the floor. Ingrid started crying. "Or what about here?" Plates and earthenware dishes came out of the second cupboard as Olav's arm was plunged into the darkness at the back.

"Stop this, Olav, *please!*"

"Or do you think I've hidden a hundred copies of the *Norway Light* in the bedroom?"

Ingrid shouted his name but found herself being dragged into her bedroom, where the wardrobe door was flung open and a swipe of Olav's arm brought shoes, frocks, a couple of handbags, and some blankets onto the floor.

"Well?" he said.

"Olav! Stop this!"

"Or what about under the floorboards? Shall we look there?"

At this, Ingrid threw her arms around his chest, holding on to him with all her strength. She felt him struggle to shake her off, then struggle some more, then relax. She sensed his body convulse, heard him sobbing on her shoulder.

Their bodies stayed locked together until Ingrid sensed him relax once more. She let go, and they both sat with their backs on the wall.

"I'm sorry," Olav said. "I know I keep saying it, but I'm sorry. I just can't cope with this. I'm not as strong as you. It's eating away at me, destroying me from the inside, and I can't control it."

Ingrid wiped the tears from his cheek, her fingers catching the roughness of his stubble. "It's all right, Olav."

He shook his head. "No, it isn't. It's a long way from all right. I've been horrible to you. Perhaps I should go away. Leave you. Call off the wedding."

"Oh, Olav." She laid her head against the firm flesh of his chest muscles, reached her arm across his belly, and felt him hold her and squeeze her tenderly.

"Olav, I've been trying to decide what to do. I told Franz I couldn't do it again, but I wasn't sure. Now I am. If you can't do this anymore, neither can I. I'm not going again. I'm not letting Franz near me again. If they demand Mamma's medicine back, even if it means they come for you, I'm not seeing that man again."

She felt Olav's strong jaw settle on her head and went ever so slightly weak at the kiss he planted on her crown.

"Thank you," he said, still a whimper in his voice.

"And I swear to you, if I'm already expecting, I'll throw myself down the steps outside parliament to get rid of it."

There was another kiss on her head but no more words.

Chapter 18

Ingrid had made it clear to Franz that she wouldn't go to the hotel with him for their next "appointment," but he'd said he would turn up to collect her anyway, in case she changed her mind, and Ingrid knew his resolve would drive him to keep to that.

And she definitely hadn't changed her mind; if anything she was more certain. So, half an hour before he was due, she went alone to the park gardens and hid in the shed, shivering in the candlelit prison cell of her own making.

Back at Ostergaten 41, Ingrid's mamma was still sleeping, and Olav was waiting with instructions from Ingrid to do no more than talk to Franz and definitely not to provoke him. So, he waited, whittling wood by the fireplace, his nerves as shredded as the growing pile of shavings at his feet, his temper shortening just like the piece of wood he held.

The noise came—a truck engine idling outside—and he slowly got to his feet. He took a few deep breaths and strode to the door and outside.

Franz lowered his window. "Where's Ingrid?"

"She won't be seeing you again."

"And why can't she tell me herself?"

Olav sneered. "You know what you've done to her, and yet you ask stupid questions."

"Olav Jacobsen, be careful what you say to me."

"I'll be as careful as I want to be."

The two men glared at each other.

"Very well," Franz said as he put the truck into gear.

"Stop!" Olav said, laying both hands on the edge of the open window.

Franz left the car in gear. He looked at Olav but didn't speak. The tense breath of both men mingled between them and swirled into nothing.

Olav glanced left and right. "I need to know. Ingrid needs to know. She said you talked. Is this the end?"

The hard expression on Franz's face cracked just a little as he pondered the question.

"I mean, am I safe?" Olav stilled himself, trying to keep his heartbeat in check as he waited for the answer. It felt as if Franz was turning a screw farther and farther in with every second he stayed silent.

"Yes," Franz eventually said. "You're safe."

"How can I be sure?"

"I'm an SS officer. I'm an honorable man, and you have my word." Franz pulled his glare away from Olav, looking around as if to drive off, then stopped for a moment. "Tell Ingrid . . ." He looked ahead, not at Olav. "Tell Ingrid I hope her mother recovers, and pass my thanks on to her. If this all works out, she's done a good thing for her race."

The truck pulled away. Olav knew he should have been relieved. Instead he seethed, the root of every hair on his head tingling with disgust, with relief, with hate, with confusion.

A new year came along; the usual celebrations were muted with the fear of not knowing. But weeks passed without incident, without troops searching the house, without Franz. By then, Ingrid knew she was pregnant. She told Olav. Olav asked how she knew, whether she was absolutely sure. She said she was, that she felt odd, different, that there were signs he need not know about. But she agreed to go with him to the Lebensborn clinic to have the test and then again to get the results, which only confirmed what she already knew. There was then more paperwork to attend to for the Lebensborn records, including signing a declaration that Franz was the baby's father and that she wouldn't do anything to harm it.

As she walked back from the clinic that day with Olav, the German soldiers on every street corner were bitter reminders of Ingrid's predicament, reminders that would not go away until Norway was free again. And each time she saw a soldier, she eyed the nearest flight of steps, her mind flashing back to the time she'd told Olav she would use them to rid herself of the baby growing inside her. As they passed more steps, the thought grew in her mind. She knew that if she went through with that threat, she would leave herself open to action from the authorities—even prosecution. And what might they do to Mamma and Olav in the way of retribution?

And then she stopped—halted at a particularly suitable flight of smooth stone steps with solid flagstones at the bottom. She drew her eyes away to face the opposite direction, no longer able to even contemplate the idea. She was unsure what to do, but that was no answer. There was a baby growing inside her—*a baby*, someone not in any way to blame for those horrible uniforms that colored all public areas with loathing.

"What is it?" Olav said. "What's wrong?"

They began to walk again. "I can't go home yet," Ingrid said as they approached the top of Ostergaten. "I can't face Mamma."

"The gardens?" Olav suggested.

A few minutes later they settled there on a bench, neither talking for a while.

"What am I going to do?" Ingrid said.

"Are you going to keep it?"

"You really want me to throw myself down steps?"

"No. No, I don't. But there are . . . other ways."

"And what if I don't like those other ways?"

Olav shrugged. "Then we both know what will happen."

"Just for now, if we assume I let nature take its course, what do I do?"

"About the wedding? About explaining it to your mamma? About what to tell people when your belly starts to swell? I have absolutely no idea."

They talked more, at first in stilted, abstract remarks, then gathering ideas and discarding them. Eventually they formulated a plan. The wedding would take place in early spring as planned, before Ingrid's pregnancy started to show. After that, she would wear flowing clothes over her bump to hide it from neighbors. By the time it became impossible to hide, she would have to go into the Lebensborn clinic anyway, although they would tell friends and neighbors that she was away looking after a sick relative. The only problem was Ingrid's mamma. Ingrid thanked God that she was now out of bed and making a steady recovery from her illness, but a few months down the line there would be no hiding Ingrid's belly from her or anyone, and if Ingrid decided to get rid of it, that would still be very hard to keep from her.

Moreover, Ingrid *wanted* to tell her mamma. She dreaded the moment of telling, feared her mamma's reaction. But she *wanted* her to know. She loved Olav, but the thinly disguised truth was that she needed her mamma more than at any time in her life. Thoughts of the pregnancy and birth were bad enough, and thoughts of getting rid of her baby were a nightmare, but the idea of going through any or all of those without her mamma knowing was something Ingrid was simply unable to contemplate.

A few days later, Olav and Ingrid sat her mamma down in a fireside chair and said they needed to tell her something.

They knew they could have simply told her Ingrid was expecting a child and left it at that. It would have been the easiest lie in the world. Yes, she would have been shocked and upset about it happening before the marriage, but she would have gotten used to it, would have recovered. Until, of course, Ingrid had to go to the Lebensborn clinic. Or until the baby was born, and she would have to give it away. And as much as Ingrid dreaded telling her the truth now, the dread of how a full explanation a few months down the line would affect her mamma was a hundred times greater.

"We have some news," Ingrid said.

"Really?" Her mamma's lips started to twitch in anticipation. She looked at Olav. He and Ingrid knew what her mamma was thinking. She'd talked a few times of her hopes that Olav might locate his parents in time for the wedding.

"You're not going to like it," Olav said, speaking the words carefully—as carefully as he'd chosen them the previous day.

"Oh, no. You're not calling off the wedding, are you? Please, God, not that. Oh, no."

"It's not that," Ingrid said. "The wedding's going ahead as planned."

"Oh." Ingrid's mamma frowned. "Oh good." The expression of fear froze onto her face as she tried to work out the conundrum.

Ingrid held her hand. "There's not an easy way to break this to you, Mamma."

"So . . . break it to me the hard way."

Ingrid and Olav glanced at each other. Ingrid nodded to him. He drew a stiff breath.

"You see, Ingrid is pregnant, but the baby—"

"You can't be. But . . . you can't be." There was just a little pious disgust in her tone. "Oh, no. Before you're married too."

"Please," Olav said. "Just listen."

172

"Well, all right." She nodded.

"Ingrid is pregnant, but the baby isn't mine."

Now Ingrid's mamma could say nothing, her frown of distaste replaced by a blank, open-mouthed gaze to beyond him. Eventually she shook herself out of the stupor. Her head swiveled to Ingrid, then back to Olav. "Could you . . . could you say that again, please?" she said hesitantly.

He did.

"You're joking." She turned to Ingrid. "Tell me this is a joke, Ingrid. Tell me this is a bad, cruel, disgusting joke."

Ingrid's resolute expression answered her.

Her mamma opened her mouth to speak a couple of times, each time giving up and shaking her head in disbelief.

"Please, Mamma. Before you say or do anything else, let us explain everything."

"I think you need to."

Between them they did. They told her all about what had happened with Franz. The easy part was reminding her of the time the German soldier had turned up on the doorstep and what Ingrid had told her was the reason for his visit. The hard part was telling her the full truth about her expensive medical treatment and about Olav's work for the Resistance and the subsequent threats made by Franz.

"You see our problem," Olav said when they'd finished. "You understand why we wanted you to know as soon as possible."

They waited for an outburst, an expression of disgust or admonishment. None came.

"Mamma? Are you all right?"

She was slow to react. "I'm . . . I'm just trying to take it all in."

"We thought you'd be angry."

"With my baby girl?" She squeezed Ingrid's hand. "No. I'm shocked. Confused. Disappointed. Disappointed you got yourself into such a position. But . . . these are desperate times. And don't think your mamma is so naive, Ingrid. All women have to learn about those sorts of men—the ones whose claws we struggle to escape from."

"And . . . and you did get your medicine."

Ingrid's mamma leaned over and kissed her. "Oh, I could sit here and say I'd have preferred you not to have gone to such extreme lengths. That would be the easiest thing in the world, now I'm well on the way to recovery. But I know I was very, very ill."

"We thought," Olav said, "about the possibility of . . . well, you know . . . getting rid of it."

"Oh, no." Her face wrinkled with disdain. "Oh, you can't do that."

"It would solve a lot of problems," Olav said. "You've almost made a full recovery from diphtheria—they can't take that away, and I've told Ingrid I'm willing to go into hiding in case they come for me." He shifted uncomfortably. "And let's not forget that this will be a baby of a German soldier—a Nazi."

"I understand what you mean, Olav, but . . ." She turned to Ingrid. "What do you think, my girl?"

"That's one of the reasons I wanted to tell you, Mamma. I wanted your advice."

"But Ingrid. It's not my baby. It's not Olav's baby. It's yours. What does *your* heart tell *you* to do?"

"My heart . . ." Ingrid looked to Olav. "I'm sorry, Olav, but my heart tells me that this is a human being I have in my belly."

"You think so?" Olav replied. "I would argue it's only half a human. Let's not forget its father is a monster."

"Oh, Olav," Ingrid's mamma said, "that's not the baby's fault. The baby hasn't done anything wrong and certainly didn't choose Franz as a father."

He turned to Ingrid, his eyes asking her the question, asking for a reaction to what her mamma had just said.

"I agree with Mamma," she said. "I didn't quite know why I thought that way until now, but I agree with Mamma."

"So, you're definitely going to have the baby?"

She nodded.

"I see."

"I'm sorry, Olav. I know I told you if I fell pregnant, I'd get rid of it, but now I have a child growing inside of me; it feels different. And . . . well, we're fighting a war for what's right, aren't we? And if I got rid of my baby, I would spend the rest of my life asking myself what was right about what I did."

Olav nodded his head slowly.

"Olav," Ingrid's mamma said. "This is hard for a man to understand, but any woman would do the same thing. And if it's any consolation, the fact that you're still by my daughter's side shows what a courageous and decent man you are." She leaned across and patted his knee. "You're a good man, Olav. My husband would be proud to have a man like you marry his daughter."

"Well, thank you. And I wish he was here."

"Oh, he's here in spirit, all right. Believe that."

"And I will stand by Ingrid. I love her and want to marry her. My only condition—and Ingrid knows this—is that when the baby is born, she gives it up as soon as possible and never sees it again. After that, we can become a normal couple—hopefully with a normal family."

Ingrid's mamma held hands with both her daughter and Olav. "I can't pretend it's not a shock for me," she said. "And it won't be easy to come to terms with, but at least my daughter has you. I thank God for that."

"I need to lie down," Ingrid said.

I'm in bed, the lights are out, and the only thing I can see is the glow coming under the door. I notice breaks in that glow as people pass along the corridor outside. I don't want to close my eyes because I know what I'll see and feel in that other world. But very quickly I succumb but do not sleep. This time my vision would seem to be one of happier times.

It has been a struggle, but after a lot of hard work, the people have won. They now have what they want and need, and those old stuffy rulers don't have their way. The aspirations of the people take precedence. It's a time to rejoice at the new order.

By the 1930s I think of myself as a young man, and I am starting to understand.

I understand that the dreams of a new Germany are proving to be no desperate fantasy. I know that at last the nation is turning on the traitors who signed away our rights at the end of the Great War, who allowed us to be ruled from abroad, who prevented us from arming our great country or joining with our German-speaking neighbors.

Yes, I now understand because this great new progressive power has educated me and many of my friends about right and wrong, about the new ways of living. Youth groups have seen to that, sharing the hope with younger generations, telling us about the new ways that will eventually benefit the whole of mankind, making us realize that we should salute our glorious new rulers just as one day every human on the planet will.

We are being promised a new beginning, a successful and glorious society, and as a young man I look forward to the social progress that will consign the old Germany to the refuse dump. The older sections of society, still set in their backward ways, continue to resist the waves of new thinking rolling through our country by opposing the new laws. These conservative people simply don't understand that the world is changing and that they will not be allowed to stand in the way of progress.

We are being promised a new beginning. But this is more than a promise; it's actually starting to happen. New laws protect and promote the rights of Gentiles. Taxes on imports to help the German economy and make our country self-sufficient. At last, there are restrictions on the number of Jews entering the civil service, higher education, the arts, the army, and the professions. Wages are finally increasing. There is talk that marriages between Jews and Gentiles will be outlawed. Spending on the military is increasing.

The National Socialist dream is no longer merely a dream. And everyone can see that.

Chapter 19

Toronto, 2011

Arnold's doorbell went off. He glanced across at the wall clock and had to smile.

Five thirty.

Ever since the funeral, either Rebecca or Natasha had been over to see him every day. In fact, they came alternate days on their way home from work.

Yesterday it had been Natasha, so he shouted out a "Hi, Rebecca" even before he opened the door.

"That much of a giveaway, eh?" she said as she came in.

"Let's just say the two of you could mix it up a little," he replied. They embraced. He held her and was secretly annoyed at himself for wanting to hold her for longer. He kissed her on the forehead. "But thanks," he said. "I appreciate it."

A few minutes later a postwork cappuccino was in front of Rebecca. Arnold had a fruit juice.

"We'll mix it up, Dad. I promise."

"Good. I need some variety in life. Adds a little intrigue if I'm not sure who's at the door. It's the closest thing I get to excitement these days."

Rebecca snickered, then said, "Say, how long exactly have you been retired now?"

Arnold had to pause to count back. There had been that horrible eight-month period when he'd tried to balance work with looking after his mother. All else was disregarded. Even his daughters could see that he'd started to lose weight, and they weren't afraid to say it. So, he'd retired—on the face of it to do the shopping errands, to install wall handles and other aids around the house, to help out with her bills and paperwork—but as much as anything to spend more time with her, to keep her company.

"I'll tell you," Rebecca said. "Almost nine months."

"I knew that." He screwed his face up at her.

He also knew exactly what his daughter was getting at. He knew he'd been in a mood of sorts—solemn, somber, more pensive than usual. Even the most ignorant of daughters—which his definitely weren't—wouldn't have failed to notice.

"We know what's going on, Dad. Since Grandma died, it's been hard for you, like your reason to exist has been removed, like a void has suddenly appeared in your life overnight."

"So, you've been reading books on bereavement; is that it, eh?"

She let her eyelids drift down and let out a long sigh.

"Or is it all *online* these days?"

"Da-*ad*. Please!"

"What?" He shrugged. "You think you know it all. I get that."

"Have you thought about getting a job?"

"No."

"Just a part-time one?"

"I don't need the money or the hassle."

"But you need *something* in your life."

"I'm okay. Really."

"What about meeting up with old coworkers?"

"I ran a business. I never had any. You know that."

"Well, have you thought about dating?"

He laughed. "Jesus Christ, Rebecca. You do realize you're talking to your *father* here? You haven't forgotten that, eh?"

"Hey, come on, Dad. Eight years is plenty to get over a divorce."

"Like *you* would know."

"Okay, so perhaps not dating. But you have free time now you're not looking after Grandma."

"Oh, thanks for reminding me of that, Rebecca."

"You know what I mean: you need to find something to do with that time. We all miss her, but we don't want you to be old and lonely."

"One of those I can't do much about."

"Yeah, *one* of those. I mean, have you thought about giving Merlene a call?"

"I have other things on my mind right now."

Arnold continued batting away his daughter's concerns with laughter and sarcasm in equal measures, and she left soon after that.

He had to give it to her; it must have taken a lot of nerve to suggest he give Merlene a call, implying he should ask her out on a date. He'd only met Merlene a couple of times outside of her capacity as a nurse, and despite what could be described as a *professional relationship*, she'd become a friend—a *good* friend, even. But no more than that. And that was why he felt the notion of a date with her—however casual—particularly uncomfortable to deal with.

Rebecca and Arnold had parted amicably, but there was a bitter edge to his daughter's goodbye that made his stomach flutter for a while afterward. Perhaps he'd been too dismissive of her concerns—too heavy on that sarcasm.

He waited twenty minutes for her to get home and called her.

"Rebecca, I'm sorry for what I said."

"What you said?"

"I know you're worried about me, and we both know I'm a grouchy old thing, but . . ."

For a few seconds Arnold could hear only his own heavy breathing distorting the line.

"What is it, Dad?"

"Look. You're right. I *am* lonely."

"Oh, God, Dad. Just hold it there. I'm coming back over to you."

"No, no. Please. Don't come over, Rebecca."

"Are you sure?"

"I am. Just listen to me."

"Whatever you want, Dad."

He took a deep breath. "If I'm honest, when your grandma died, it was a relief. I know that sounds horrible—perhaps that's why I can't say it to your face. Much as I loved her, it was a relief for everyone, including Grandma herself. That's not what was upsetting me. I, uh, I've been thinking about a few things: those strange words she said about me just before she died, that letter from Sweden she was sent. And I, uh, called one of our distant relatives in Saskatoon."

"And?"

"Well, he talked to one of my dad's cousins—the one who looked after us when we first came to Canada. You see, he was adamant that when we arrived, there was only me, my mom and dad, and my own grandma."

"Okay. So . . . it's all nothing to worry about, right?"

"I wish, Rebecca. But, you see, I called this Marit woman too—the one from Sweden who sent the letter. She seemed to be sure Ulrich was born to an Ingrid who was married to Olav, but the thing is . . . well, my father wasn't Ulrich's father."

"I, uh . . . oh."

Arnold gave her a moment to work it all out.

"So, Grandma . . . what? She had a kid before she married Granddad?"

"Guess so. I'm just trying to work out what happened to this Ulrich kid. From what I can tell, he left Oslo but didn't arrive in Canada."

There was a long silence.

"Dad?"

"What?"

"I think you have more important things to worry about."

"But we're talking about my half brother here. I thought you might be interested."

"Oh, I am, sure. But even if you find him, you'll have nothing in common."

"Well . . ." Another long pause. "You really think so?"

"Dad, give some thought to the things I suggested. I mean, get . . . oh, I don't know, get *something* to do with your time."

"Don't you think *this* is something—searching for this Ulrich kid?"

"No. No, I don't. It's what happened almost seventy years ago. It's not what you need. You need to look forward."

"Yeah, I . . . uh, I get what you mean. Maybe I'll give your suggestion some thought, eh?"

"Yes, please, Dad."

Arnold thanked her again for visiting, apologized for calling her, and hung up.

Then he lifted the phone set and almost threw it against the wall.

Why did he ever think his daughter would understand?

Perhaps none of it *should* have mattered. But that had no bearing on whether it *did* matter to Arnold. Somewhere out there he had a half brother, someone his mother had carried and nurtured and given birth to and, at some stage—very early on in the boy's life—had given up. Of course, that was assuming he was still alive. So, what exactly might have happened to him? And how had his mother been affected? However much she'd suffered, one thing was for sure: she'd hidden her feelings well. Arnold's father too. He'd now been gone for over thirty years, but Arnold still remembered him as a great father and a good man. He'd been a stoic man in the traditional mold who'd worked hard for his family with no complaint, had taken Arnold to ice hockey matches and on campout nights, and had driven the family everywhere because Arnold's mother had been too scared to learn to drive. Most importantly, for a big man, he'd often spoken softly to Arnold.

Arnold remembered one occasion in particular when he'd missed the school bus and had to walk home, getting lost and eventually turning up late, disheveled and with cheeks sore from crying and a heart sore from fear. His mother was the harder of his parents, her frustration disguised to an adult but all too transparent to the heightened senses of a frightened child. His sister thought the whole thing funny. His father knelt down to be almost face to face with him, his expression the perfect mix of humor and pity, telling him it happened sometimes, that it was nothing for anyone to worry about, and, when that didn't work, announcing that for Arnold's next day at school he would prepare a rucksack with a milkshake, a sleeping bag, a one-man tent, an emergency flare, and a week's supply of Coffee Crisp bars. The last item on the list was whispered so that Arnold's mother and sister wouldn't hear, a detail of the talk that still brought a smile and a tear to Arnold's face half a century later.

But most importantly, Arnold's father never raised a hand to him or his sister—that, in an era when it was commonplace and only occasionally frowned upon—and never even threatened to, not even as a joke. Arnold heard him shout a few times, usually at other motorists, but not at him or his sister. Never at them.

So no, none of whatever happened with Ulrich all those years ago should have mattered to Arnold. Perhaps his daughter didn't understand, or perhaps she was right, and he should forget the whole thing. He wasn't quite sure.

Either way, there was a thread of anger reaching all the way to his soul that just wouldn't shift, and the question he kept asking himself was whether the "mood" he was in would fade or whether he would still be wondering about his father in five, ten, or even twenty years' time. Yes, he'd recently come into some free time, but he was sixty-six, not ninety-six, and that left a hell of a long time to be ridden with guilt or anxiety or whatever the hell he was feeling.

He needed to talk things over with someone. But not his daughters. He should never have expected Rebecca to understand. His daughters weren't capable of understanding. That wasn't their fault, but it was true. They were normal twentysomethings. Normal twentysomethings would take their parents for granted, would assume they would always be just *there*—a given, a permanently stable hunk of solid rock on which to stand while casting out life's fishing lines.

But Arnold was a generation—perhaps two—away from being twentysomething. In what Arnold's ex-wife had ungraciously termed his "autumn years," thoughts about parents just weren't like that. There was an urge to tie up loose ends, to find out how solid that rock had really been for all those years.

No, his kids would never understand. His sister hadn't shown much interest, and his ex-wife might understand but wouldn't be sympathetic even if she could be bothered to drag herself away from that real estate guy she'd—

And then the obvious hit him.

Merlene.

She would understand. She *always* seemed to understand. And she'd as good as asked him to contact her when they'd talked at the funeral.

"Mmm . . . ," he muttered to himself, "would be good to see her again too."

Then he shook his head, muttering again. "No. It'd sound too much like I was asking her on a date." He laughed briefly, thinking back to Rebecca's suggestion. He dismissed the idea of calling her, then changed his mind and was about to, then stopped and considered tossing a coin to decide.

Jesus, it was like being sixteen all over again.

He told himself to grow the hell up and called her.

"Merlene?"

"Arnold. Good to hear from you again."

"Uh . . . how are you?"

"I'm good. Are you okay? Is something wrong?"

"No, no, no. I, uh . . . well . . ." He was flapping and knew it, which only made him flap even more. He took a deep breath. "I was wondering . . . would you like to come out for a meal sometime?"

"That'd be cool. When would—"

"I mean, not a date or anything."

"Oh, no. No, of course not."

"Tell you the truth, I'm just at a, uh . . . no, I mean, I thought we could stay in touch. If you'd like to, that is."

"Yeah," she replied in a warm tone. "Yeah, I would like to. Thank you."

It was only a few minutes later—after arrangements had been made, and Arnold had put the phone down—that he let out a long, relieving gasp. "At a loose end?" he said aloud. "Did I nearly say that? What the hell was I thinking?"

And then he knew. It was good old nerves.

Jesus. *For sure*, it was like being sixteen all over again.

He shook his insecurities from his head and told himself it still wasn't a date—or a *date date*, as Rebecca would sometimes say. Lord knows he had enough troubles to concern himself with at the moment. He did, however, want to impress Merlene, partly to make amends for his clumsy invitation and partly so she would take him seriously. He made a mental note to get a clean shave, to polish his shoes, and to check out the shirt at the back of the drawer that was brand new and just about fashionable enough without being desperate.

Chapter 20

By now, Ingrid had started feeling sick most mornings, something her mamma had warned her about.

There had also been a more awkward conversation between them, one that Ingrid would find hard to forget. It happened while Olav was working away, and the two women were alone in the house.

"Why don't you come and sit down," her mamma said, in the gentle, calming tone of a parent about to inflict something unpleasant but necessary on their child.

But Ingrid was no child and, aware of an atmosphere between them, did as her mamma asked.

"Something's been troubling me," she said. A sickly smile flashed across her face before falling. "The baby you're carrying . . ."

"Yes," Ingrid said.

"I'm not sure how to ask this." She took a long breath. "But I was thinking . . . are you absolutely certain that Franz is the father?"

"Mamma!" Ingrid felt acid rising in her throat, quelled only slightly by the feeling of her mamma's hand enclosing her own.

"This is important, Ingrid. It's not a time to be polite."

Ingrid could only huff and swallow her dry throat away.

"I'm sorry to ask this question, but you're going to need to be strong to get through this."

Ingrid composed herself. "Yes," she said, nodding. "It's definitely Franz's. I told Olav a long time ago I wanted to wait until we were married."

"Oh, dear. That must hurt the poor man all the more."

"It's not something we talk about."

Her mamma nodded. "And we should talk about it no more. But at least we know Olav is a good man. He wants you for yourself and not just your body, unlike some."

"I know. And that's why I'm going to marry him."

"Of course. That's what I want too. It's not a perfect situation, but I'm sure you'll be happy together." She stood. "Come on. We have a lot of planning to do."

On the run-up to the wedding day they spoke no more of the baby and what Franz had done in the name of the Third Reich. More importantly, Olav's parents were still nowhere to be found, and none of them had any money to speak of. So, the wedding, with all its secretive undertones and shoestring budget, should have been a disaster. It was, in the event, a triumphant celebration of resilience.

The three people who knew of Ingrid's illicit pregnancy put it to the backs of their minds; Olav's acquaintances from his Resistance work provided contacts for him to buy steak, wine, and cream on the black market; and the neighbors kindly donated enough vegetables to fill the guests' stomachs. By the time the church hall was cleared away and everyone had gone home, the newly married couple hardly had one krone left to their names. Olav moved into number 41, and he and Ingrid were, despite the events they could not forget, exquisitely happy for the next few months.

Soon, however, the bump of Ingrid's baby was showing. For a few weeks, loose dresses and coats were disguise enough, but there came a time when she needed to go to the local Lebensborn clinic, as Franz had arranged. Ingrid packed enough clothes for a long stay, and they told neighbors that she was going away for a while to look after an aunt who had become ill and infirm. Whether they believed that or whether they ever discovered the truth didn't matter too much; the story meant that they would keep up the pretense of politeness and not ask questions about how Ingrid was coping.

Olav accompanied her to the clinic, and they were both surprised at the level of care that was provided. Lebensborn mothers were given food far superior to that available to the general population—in terms of both quantity and quality—and Ingrid was told she would stay in the clinic until a few months after giving birth, and while there, her mamma and Olav could visit daily. She settled in well, formed something akin to camaraderie with some of the other mothers, and even found most of the nurses caring and understanding.

One day in midsummer, Ingrid's mamma arrived alone, immediately making her suspicious.

"What's happened? Where's Olav?"

Her mamma seemed surprised at the question, which hardly put Ingrid at ease. "Oh, Olav?" she said. "He's fine. He has a job in Sandvika. He'll be away for a few days." Before Ingrid could reply, she added, "So, tell me how you are; tell me how you're getting on with people here."

Ingrid had already talked about the other mothers—many of whom seemed proud to be a part of the Lebensborn program and openly talked about their situation with friends and neighbors—so she tried a different tack. "Why don't you tell me what's happening at Ostergaten?" she asked. "Have I missed anything? How are things at the gardens? Is Olav managing our plot without me?"

Her mamma took too long to answer, eventually saying, "Well, nothing has happened. The gardens are still hard work; Olav had to get on the roof to repair a leak before he left, but not much else has happened, not much at all."

"But Olav is all right, isn't he? You'd tell me if he wasn't coming back here, wouldn't you, Mamma? You *would* tell me?"

"Ingrid, Ingrid, *calm down*. Olav's fine. You must stop worrying so much about him. He loves you, and he'll be back when his work is finished." She shook her head in dismay.

"I'm sorry. I find I get anxious easily." Ingrid lowered her voice. "And . . . do any of our neighbors know?"

"Know? Know what?"

"You know what: about me being here."

Now her mamma started to give way, unable to answer, eventually merely giving a conceding sigh.

"Tell me the truth, Mamma. Tell me."

She shrugged. "It's nothing. I'm sure it's nothing. When I was leaving the house today . . ."

"Yes?"

"Well, I'd just closed the door and heard a voice. It came from nowhere. She must have been watching me and hurried across as soon as I came out."

"Who, Mamma? Who?"

Her mamma paused, then said despondently, "Laila."

"Oh. I should have guessed. What did she say?"

"She asked how your sick aunt was, and before I could answer, she asked when you were coming back home."

"And what did you say?"

"I was a little flustered. She caught me unawares. I just told her there was very little change."

"What did she say to that?"

"Oh, I didn't wait to find out. I walked off, praying she wouldn't follow. I, uh . . . I didn't want to mention it to you. I didn't want to upset you."

"Do you think she knows?" But before her mamma could answer, she added, "And what do I say when I go home? We haven't thought about that. She'll ask questions about my aunt. What shall I say?"

Ingrid's mamma shook her head, then leaned across and held her hand. "I promise I'll let you know if Laila says anything again, my dear, and we've plenty of time to think about what we do when you return home, but—"

"And what about your strangling angel? Haven't people asked how you got better? How you afforded the medicine?"

"Ingrid, Ingrid. Calm down, dear. I told them I was ill for a time and rested and eventually recovered." She squeezed Ingrid's hand. "Now could we change the subject? What's happening to you here is much more important."

Reluctantly, Ingrid agreed. They both smiled at each other, and their eyes scanned the dayroom for other things to spark conversation. The beds were neat. The floor was clean. The air was warm but fresh. The food was plain but plentiful and nutritious. There was a wholesome ambience that almost embarrassed Ingrid.

"I have to say," her mamma said, "I can see the attraction of Lebensborn for some women. You're kept so warm, well fed, and comfortable here."

"Yes. Sometimes I feel so lucky."

"Well, yes, but . . ."

"What?"

Ingrid's mamma smiled. No, she *forced* a smile onto her face. Ingrid could tell the difference. And it fell away in seconds.

"Mamma, what is it?"

"Nothing, dear."

"It's Olav, isn't it?" Ingrid put her hands on the arms of the chair and readied herself to push herself up. "Something's happened to Olav, and you're not telling me."

"No, no. Stay where you are. Please, Ingrid. Olav's fine."

"Then what is it? You have to tell me, Mamma, you have to."

"Nothing's wrong, Ingrid. You're letting the pregnancy overcome you."

Ingrid relaxed. "Yes. Yes, I'm sorry. I know I feel stressed sometimes, then very sad for no reason."

"Like I keep telling you, it's part of being pregnant. I . . . I know more about it than you perhaps realize."

Ingrid frowned. "What does that mean?"

"Well, now Olav isn't here, I wanted to talk to you, to . . . prepare you."

"There's no need for that, Mamma. They look after us, tell us everything about the birth. It's as if they leave nothing to chance."

Her mamma shook her head. "You don't understand, dear. I need to tell you . . . to warn you that when you bring new life into the world . . ."

"Yes?"

"Oh, Ingrid. I'm only trying to be helpful."

"What are you talking about?"

"Well, have you ever thought about how giving up your baby will affect you, how you'll react?"

"Oh, they've told me about that. I've signed the documentation to agree to it. I'll feed it for around nine months, and then they'll take it away. They'll find a couple in Germany who will give it a better life than it would get here in Oslo, and . . . that's about it."

Her mamma showed another smile that she was clearly struggling to maintain. "Good, dear. Good for you." She took a few breaths. "Tell me, what have you been up to this morning?"

Ingrid told her about how she'd done a few light chores and been for a walk in the gardens, and soon her mamma left and promised to visit again the next day, probably on her own because Olav wasn't due back for a few days.

The conversation puzzled Ingrid, so later that day, when the doctor was carrying out his routine check, Ingrid asked him what would happen after the birth.

"Haven't you been told?" he said.

"Well, I'm not sure," she replied.

He sighed in frustration and reeled the words out as if he was reading them from a script.

"Once the gestation period has expired and the baby is born, it becomes the property of the Lebensborn program but stays with the mother for approximately nine months to gain the full health benefits of breastfeeding—although with the bare minimum of physical contact to avoid bonding between mother and baby. During this time a register of suitable German parents is cross-referenced to find suitable parents, and subsequently it gets given to them to become Germanized and—"

"No, no," Ingrid said. "What happens to the mother? What happens to me?"

He shrugged, puzzled. "That's not really the concern of staff here at the clinic. You go home."

"Oh."

"Does that answer your question?"

"I suppose it does. Yes, thank you."

"My pleasure."

It did, on the face of it, answer Ingrid's question, but for the rest of that night, after all the other women had fallen asleep, with only her little bump for company, something her mamma had said started to play on her mind. She was glad her mamma was due to visit again the next day. Perhaps she would ask more about giving up her baby.

The next day Ingrid's mamma did visit, alone again, which both saddened and pleased Ingrid. She missed Olav but now understood what her mamma meant when she'd said there were some things best kept between mother and daughter.

"I've brought you a present today," her mamma said, reaching into her bag. "I made it myself." She handed Ingrid a straw hat.

"Oh, Mamma. Thank you."

"For the sunny days. I hope you have many."

"I will," Ingrid said. "I can even wear it in the garden here." She paused for breath, a look of concern starting to cover her face. "Mamma, I need to ask you something."

"Of course, dear. Anything."

"Yesterday you said you knew more than I realized about being pregnant."

"Mmm . . ."

Another pregnant woman passed by, and they exchanged pleasantries. As soon as she was out of earshot, Ingrid stared at her mamma and said, "Please, Mamma. If there's something you think I need to know . . ."

"Well . . . I think there is. Yesterday I was trying to make you give a little thought to what might happen when you have to give your baby up, how you might feel about it. Now I suppose I should tell you it will be harder than you think."

Ingrid narrowed her eyes. "How would you know what giving up a baby is like?"

"Because . . . because it happened to me, Ingrid."

"What?"

"Of course, the circumstances were different all those years ago."

"I don't understand, Mamma. The Lebensborn program hasn't been—"

"No, no, no." She shook her head. "Nothing to do with that. It was before you were born. I had to give up a child—not to some program, but to God."

Ingrid's hand flew up to cover her open mouth. Neither of them spoke for a few seconds.

"I had a little boy. We called him Arne. He was perfectly healthy when he was born, with your pappa's beautiful eyes and my mamma's mouth. But there was a terrible disease going around—tuberculosis, they called it. I never had a good ear for scientific words, but I can always remember that one. It attacked his lungs. Your pappa and I decided not to tell you about him. Perhaps that was wrong; who knows?"

"It's all right, Mamma. I understand. And I'm so sorry."

"Thank you. But I remember how I cried my eyes out for weeks. I still think of him now, of what might have become of him. The point is, Ingrid, nobody can explain how a mother feels about her baby. There's an urge to protect—a natural urge that's hard to fight. I just thought you needed to be warned so you can prepare yourself. You're going to miss your little one when they take it away. And when that happens, I would plead with you to put those thoughts aside and concentrate on thoughts of yourself and Olav a few years from now, perhaps with one or two little ones of your own. It won't take away the pain of losing your first baby—nothing will be able to do that—but it will help, Ingrid. *It will help.* Remember that."

"Oh, Mamma. You're worrying me."

"Believe me, Ingrid. It's better I worry you a little now than you think you can give up your baby like . . . like you're handing over a straw hat."

Over the next few days, those words started playing on Ingrid's mind. Yes, perhaps the tiny girl or boy growing inside of her wasn't going to be something she would be able to give away. Then again, there was nothing else she could do. She wouldn't have to *give* the baby away; it would be *taken*. It was in the contract she'd signed.

She felt unable to discuss any of these things with Olav; he'd made it clear he was only waiting for the day the baby—and with it, all memories of Franz—was out of their lives forever. Moreover, she couldn't discuss it with her mamma in his presence. So, the concern slowly slipped from her mind, and she tried her best to concentrate on staying healthy and thinking of life with Olav after Lebensborn.

By September the novelty of Ingrid's pregnancy had well and truly worn off. Her belly was distended so much that she couldn't find a comfortable position whether sitting or lying down. Her appetite was poor, and any food she did eat needed to be washed down with water to avoid heartburn. And walking for more than a few minutes made her back ache as if she'd been kicked by a horse. So yes, she was looking forward to the day when she gave birth and could—as she'd said more than once—have her body back.

The consolation for all these problems was the movement inside of her: the turn in the middle of the night, which was so gentle as though her baby felt the need to move but through politeness was trying not to wake her; the subdued thumps from within, like taps on a taut leather drum; the times she relaxed, hands on belly, only for her fingertips to sense movement, a living undulation of her own skin. All of these should have been disturbing or annoying—mildly unpleasant at the very least. But no; even when on her own she never felt alone, when she felt sad and sorry for herself there was always a kick or turning motion that brought comfort to her heart and a smile to her lips, and when she was too tired to move, there was always a reminder of the reason—a new life, a person who would exist only due to *her* blood and *her* warmth.

It was one afternoon, while she was struggling with all these thoughts—and also struggling to get comfortable after a very tiring ten-minute stroll around the gardens—that he turned up. Ingrid knew he'd been informed of the progress but didn't think he'd have the nerve to come near her. Except, of course, that she could hardly run away, and he knew that.

"Don't worry," were his first words even before the exchange of greetings. He had a concerned expression on his face, one Ingrid wouldn't have thought him capable of unless she'd seen it for herself. "I won't stay long," he said. "The very last thing I want is for you to get upset in any way."

"I can cope," Ingrid replied. "But I don't understand why you're here. Haven't you completed your part of the contract?" She tried to inject some antagonism into the final word but hardly sensed it herself.

"I only wanted to thank you and wish you good luck."

"So, say that and leave."

"How are you?"

"How does it look like I am? Like a dog that's eaten far too much. I can hardly move, eat, or sleep."

"It will all be worth it in the end, Ingrid. You're doing a good thing. A lot of the mothers here suffer as much as you, but afterward they see the benefit to society of what they're doing."

Ingrid couldn't argue with that. Some other mothers were almost rapturous in their praise of the Third Reich in general and the Lebensborn program specifically. Others were more like herself, a little confused as to the whole point.

"I've double-checked all the arrangements," he continued. "Your progress is excellent. A couple in their twenties in Hamburg has been chosen to be parents to our baby. They've already chosen names—Ulrich if it's a boy, Eva for a girl."

Still, Ingrid said nothing, wanting to scold Franz for using the phrase *our baby* but unsure exactly how to object when that was no less than the truth. Instead, she just placed the palm of her hand on her belly, as if trying to protect what lay beneath but also knowing that the act would inevitably be futile.

"They're good people. Our baby will be very well taken care of. I thought you would want to know that." He paused, trying to smile, glancing at her belly, then trying to disguise the fact by looking to the floor.

Then Ingrid spoke, as much to break the pause as anything. "Well . . . I guess that does reassure me a little."

It was a lie. As soon as Ingrid heard her own words, she knew she was only saying what she thought Franz wanted to hear so he would quickly leave. It was a big lie, and the truth was that only now—with Franz's talk of people being "chosen to be parents"—was the reality of her predicament starting to become more than some vague issue to be dealt with some ways down the line. Yes, the truth was that the new life she'd come to think of as a part of her—a baby feeding from her, a singular and unique friend, her constant companion—would at some stage cease to become any of those things and would instead be taken away from her forever.

Franz took a step back, and she felt her heart flutter. Having wanted him to leave a few seconds ago, she now tried to think of any reason to get him to stay. She had no idea why.

To talk to him?

To try to change the plan?

To see if she could show her distaste for him?

She was desperate but unsure what exactly she was desperate for. Perhaps time, perhaps company.

"And how are you?" she said, snapping the words out.

"Oh, I'm fine."

He smiled, and she sensed a genuine warmth in the smile, which she found unsettling. She knew she should hate this man. She told herself she *did* hate him. But she knew there wasn't even a tiny amount of hate in her.

"Anyway," he said when she didn't speak, "I have to go. I have another . . ."

"Another mother to see?"

He nodded, still smiling, now with a little pride. "She gave birth a few weeks ago. A girl. She's progressing very well, I'm told, even putting some weight on already. I thought I should wish her well while I'm here and take a look in case I can't get back before she gets taken away to Germany."

He backed away and half turned, and Ingrid sensed her throat locking and the tears welling up. She felt confusion at her own emotions: she was feeling needy for the company of a man she should despise—*did* despise—and so felt a loathing for her own needs.

"Goodbye, Ingrid," he said. "And good luck. Never forget you're doing a good thing—a good thing for Germany, a good thing for Europe, a good thing for the purity of the human race."

He turned, and he was gone.

Ingrid started to cry but still couldn't understand why.

Chapter 21

Ingrid's moments of melancholy and confusion continued until the end of her pregnancy. The doctors and nurses told her it wasn't that unusual, that changes in her body were the reason for the mood swings, but also told her that she had to try to control the extremes of sadness so as to be in a fit state of mind for the birth itself. "You must put the past behind you," they said, or "The health of your baby is paramount," or even "The mother can always recover, but the baby only gets one chance to be born healthy."

There was an undertone of admonishment to these pieces of advice, which made Ingrid feel that perhaps she shouldn't concern herself with her own feelings. Worries about her neighbors back at Ostergaten—whether any of them had guessed or discovered where she really was—were pushed to the furthest corners of her mind. She didn't ask Olav or her mamma whether anyone had inquired about the health of her "aunt," and they didn't mention any incidents. Her pregnancy, what would happen to the baby, the possibility of more visits from Franz—all of these thoughts overshadowed everything else.

By the time the contractions started, her mind was a carousel of jumbled moods, all vying for attention as they came to the fore and faded, only to return. In the event, what seemed like a small army of doctors and nurses converged on her and gave her little chance to think for herself, a blur of hands and instruments and voices urging her to push and breathe and push again.

She was later told the labor lasted nine hours, and there must have been times of relative peace in that time, but if there were, she didn't remember any of them. And now she lay in bed, with a baby boy in a crib next to her, wondering how it had all happened so quickly.

A day's rest would have been paradise, but any peace didn't last long, what with attentive nurses telling her how to hold and feed the baby, and then feeding her baby only to be told she wasn't *quite* doing it properly, and being woken regularly not only by her own baby but by two more new arrivals in the ward, and being disturbed by doctors and nurses carrying out tests on her baby.

Ingrid asked if her mamma would be visiting but was told there would be no visitors allowed during the first few days.

When her mamma did visit, she had Olav in tow. Olav was second through the door but first at her bedside, looking shocked, repeating her name, holding her head, hugging her as though she were made of porcelain, and seemingly inspecting her face, telling her she looked weary.

"Stop worrying," Ingrid's mamma told him. "It's childbirth, not carpentry. It's exhausting." Then she proceeded to do much as Olav had but also asking how Ingrid was and how much it had hurt. Then she turned back to Olav and said, "You think bringing a life into the world is easy?"

"No, no," he insisted. "But Ingrid, have you eaten?"

"Of course I have," Ingrid replied. "And better food than you, I expect. They make all new mothers eat every last morsel they're given to ensure good-quality milk. And I look tired because I am; I was in labor all day, and I've hardly slept since."

"Believe me," Ingrid's mamma said, "I've seen a lot worse—labors taking thirty hours or more."

Olav widened his eyes in surprise. "Still, it's all done now. A few more weeks, and you'll be out of this damn place."

"Weeks?" Ingrid's mamma laughed at him.

"Uh, well . . . of course," he said. "She'll leave the baby here and come home, won't she?"

"Has my daughter married an idiot?"

"Oh, Olav," Ingrid said. "I need to feed him."

Olav looked just a little angry at this, his teeth showing between twitching lips.

"Did you want to see the baby?" Ingrid said to them both.

"Oh, yes," her mamma said, stepping over to inspect the infant at close quarters, stroking his bulbous cheek.

"So, when exactly will you be allowed home?" Olav asked. "Have they given you a date yet?"

"Ignore your husband," Ingrid's mamma said. "I don't think he cares about the baby."

"And why should I?" he replied hurriedly.

"You haven't even seen him," Ingrid said. "Why not take a look?"

He shrugged. "I care about you. Why should I be interested in a baby that they'll take away from you as soon as you've done your job?"

Ingrid grimaced. She tried to smile but failed, and soon tears started to flow.

"What is it?" Olav said. "What did I say wrong?"

"Go away," Ingrid's mamma told him, leaning across to comfort her daughter as best she could. "Just go away!"

But Ingrid held on to his hand.

"So, stay," Ingrid's mamma said to Olav. "But be a little tactful, can't you?"

"I was only telling the truth."

"The truth is he's Ingrid's baby, her own flesh and blood, and it's bad enough she has to give him up without you upsetting her." She thought for a moment and turned to her daughter. "Has he got a name yet?"

Ingrid drew a few stuttered breaths, recovering from her upset, before saying, "The new parents have chosen one, but I've been told not to use it because it might make me more attached to him."

"So, you just have to keep saying *he* and *him*?"

"I have a name in my mind, for those times I think about him, but I'm not going to say it out loud."

"Whatever you prefer, dear," Ingrid's mamma said. She turned to Olav. "Why not just see the baby, Olav—out of politeness if nothing else?"

He shook his head firmly. "What's the point? It's not my baby, and—"

"The baby is a *him*, Olav. He's not a thing; he's a human being."

"If you say so. Anyway, the sooner Ingrid gets out of this place, the sooner we can forget about it or him and leave this whole episode behind us."

Ingrid's mamma tutted and glared at him. Ingrid tried to ignore his words.

A week after the birth came the christening. It was at a local church, and although Ingrid was allowed to attend as long as she sat near the back, her mamma and Olav were prohibited.

It was a short service, Ingrid's baby behaving himself impeccably as water was poured over his head while prayers were recited. There were flowers, candles, and a few people in their Sunday best clothes. It could have been any other christening if it weren't for the soldiers and the huge banners hung around the font, all intricately embroidered with German phrases and swastikas.

After that, Ingrid continued with the task of feeding her baby every few hours. Her mamma and Olav visited regularly—usually together but occasionally only one of them—and soon the weeks had turned to months, and the long summer days came to an end.

One day in November, Ingrid's mamma was suffering with a heavy cold, so Olav visited alone. It was immediately clear to Ingrid that he had a bounce in his step, a happiness that hadn't been there for some time. They kissed, he gave her an embrace that lasted longer than usual, and he started talking as soon as he sat down.

"I have good news," he said quietly. "No, *great* news."

Ingrid tried to look pleased for him and asked what had happened.

He hunkered down close to her and whispered, "The Germans are losing Finnmark."

"Losing?" Ingrid said, initially confused.

"The Red Army are kicking them out. The Free Norwegian forces are coming from Britain to help. Soon the whole area will be controlled by Norway—the real Norway."

"Are you sure?"

"Absolutely. There were rumors from my Resistance friends a few weeks ago; now it's more than rumor. We have the details. After all these years of German occupation, one part of Norway is no longer under their control."

Thoughts whirled around Ingrid's head of German troops on every street corner, of rationing, of how standards of living had plummeted under the occupation, of the possibility of Franz paying another visit to Ostergaten 41 or them bumping into each other on the streets of Oslo once she'd left the clinic. Perhaps—only perhaps—the end of all these things was in sight. After four and a half years of their living under Hitler's thumb, it took a while to sink in. In fact, she dared not believe it.

"Isn't that good news?"

"Oh, you're right, Olav. Of course it is. I don't know what else to say."

"October, one part of the country; November, another; and by December it will be half the country. And the word is that Germany is on the back foot on many other fronts. Don't you see, Ingrid? Oslo could be free by the break of the new year."

Even though Ingrid had other things on her mind, she sensed a wetness in her eyes and was soon crying freely. Olav embraced her once more, holding her tight, letting her feel the jubilation in his bones but shielding her from any questioning hospital officials.

They continued, still whispering.

"I'm sorry," she said. "I can't take it in. And I seem to cry so easily these past few weeks."

"I know, I know. I can't say I cried when I heard the news, but I couldn't sit still for hours. I wanted to climb onto the highest rooftop and shout the news to everyone. We have so much to look forward to. Once you give up your child, we can be a normal married couple. I can get a regular job, rationing will end, we'll have our freedoms back. It'll be a new start for us."

"Olav, please wait and see how the war progresses before you do anything."

"But, Ingrid. I'm already planning for it. We can both move back into my house. I have ideas for extending the property. No more toiling away at the gardens; we'll have money to buy food instead." He leaned across and kissed her full on the lips, holding on for so long that she had to push him away to take a breath. "And most importantly we could start having our own family."

Ingrid laughed politely and pointed to the crib. "I have this one to deal with first."

He laughed too. "Oh, yes. Of course. I'm sorry. I'm just so excited, Ingrid. Don't you see? For the first time in years we have something to look forward to, a little optimism in our souls. When we get the Germans out, everything will change. We'll be free again."

"I see all that, Olav. All I'm saying is that things can change. I'd be as happy as you if the war ended tomorrow, but it won't."

"I know. I'm sorry." He took a deep breath. "We have to be patient. For the moment, life goes on as it has done for these past few years." He looked around the dayroom, then out into the gardens, to the winds practicing for winter on the tall trees surrounding the gardens. "So, tell me what you've been up to this morning. Have you been outside for some fresh air?"

To stop all thoughts of Olav's plans and the progress of the war from giving her a headache, Ingrid simply answered his question, and the conversation moved on to the latest news from the neighborhood and the gardens. Ingrid was happy with that. The future of her country, like the future of her baby, was something she would deal with when she had to.

As Ingrid suspected, the war kept rolling on, and Olav became more and more frustrated at the grindingly slow progress as far as a free Norway was concerned. Yes, Finnmark had been secured, but the rest of Norway stayed under the iron fist. Olav still didn't bother himself to look at Ingrid's baby, let alone hold him, although he did stop referring to him as *it*. Ingrid told her mamma that it was all right and to stop criticizing him. She also stressed that she *was* going to have to give the baby up whatever any of them said or thought, that it was in the contract she'd signed. But she spoke those words with a lump in her throat and a tremble in her voice. Like the birth itself, she put thoughts of that moment to the back of her mind; it was easier that way, better to avoid the feeling of confusion that engulfed her mind whenever she *did* think of it.

The time came in April 1945. The nurses had helped Ingrid wean her baby. They'd also dropped regular hints about how little Ulrich would be so well looked after in Hamburg and of how Ingrid must be looking forward to going home and getting on with the rest of her life. Eventually she was given a date, and it was marked on the clipboard at the end of the crib so there could be no misunderstanding.

When that day arrived, Ingrid told the nurse that she didn't think the baby was quite ready yet. The nurse held the baby, rocked him for a few moments, then smiled sweetly at Ingrid and told her she was probably right.

The next day, the same nurse came along again, and this time Ingrid held her baby close to her chest, saying she thought he was looking a little ill, suggesting a few more days would probably be needed.

Again, the nurse smiled sweetly, agreed with Ingrid, and left.

The next day two different nurses and a doctor walked into the ward, nodded greetings to the other mothers, and sauntered up to Ingrid.

"Hello," the doctor said cheerily. "I'm Doctor Hummel." He consulted his clipboard. "So, this is baby Ulrich?" he said, standing over the crib.

Both nurses said it was.

"That means you must be Ingrid." He offered her a broad smile. Then he lifted Ingrid's hand, the tips of two fingers resting on the inside of her wrist. He counted, mumbling the numbers. "Mmm . . . ," he said. "I thought so. We . . . uh . . . we need to carry out some tests. Could you follow me, please?"

A nurse motioned for Ingrid to pass her baby over.

Ingrid resisted.

"Oh, please," the doctor said in sympathetic tones. "That's what the nurses are here for—to look after him. Just follow me. You'll be no more than five minutes, I promise."

"But . . ."

"Nurse Ulberg," he said. "Please take care of the baby."

The nurse hesitated. She didn't look Ingrid in the eye but glanced at the doctor, unsure whether to do as she was told.

"Nurse Ulberg," he said, now more firmly, "take the baby from her."

Eventually the nurse stepped over to Ingrid. "It's all right," she said gently, easing the baby from her. "He'll be safe. You can have him back in a few minutes."

The doctor led Ingrid out of the ward, down the corridor, and into a small room.

"You just sit and wait," he said. "I won't be a moment."

He left, shutting the door behind him. Then Ingrid thought she heard a loud click from the door lock. The "moment" that the doctor had mentioned turned out to be a long one, but he did eventually return.

"Right," he said with a self-satisfied grin.

Ingrid, feeling electricity coursing through her muscles, lunged for the door behind him. He held her and called out for assistance, and soon she was completely overwhelmed by uniforms.

Chapter 22

Oslo, May 1945

By the start of May, Ingrid was getting used to living back at Ostergaten, at number 41, with Olav, while he prepared his own house for them to live in. The park gardens, the bed she shared with Olav, having her mamma under the same roof, the crackle and earthy aroma of the log fire—all of those were reassuring. Having to clean and cook, her back aching from digging up vegetables, spending time waiting in line for bread, milk, and the occasional chunk of meat—all of that was not so good, but it was bearable. Even those worries she'd had about how neighbors might react to her return were still firmly lodged in the dark corners of her mind. There was little contact with them—probably, she guessed, because she'd been away so long, and there was nothing to talk about. There were glances in her direction from small huddles of women, a few haughty expressions cast over to her from men, but no words. That suited Ingrid fine. If they knew the truth, they were keeping it to themselves. That suited her fine too.

Life was back to normal, and some days it seemed as if she'd never been away, even down to her mamma and Olav never mentioning that period of her life. There was, she knew, no visible reminder of the time she'd spent in the Lebensborn clinic, only the memories in her own mind, and those memories grew duller with each passing day.

But there came times when she had to pinch herself to remind herself that it *had* all happened. The most vivid memories—apart from her son's cheerful and innocent smile—were of that final day at the clinic. Memories of that day came back to her silently and stealthily, when she was lying in the dark at night unable to sleep, when resting alone next to the fire with only the twisting, elusive flames for company. That day was remembered with a spear in her heart, the images seeming to strengthen and hurt more with every remembering.

It was the last time she'd seen her baby, that morning she was led out of the ward by Doctor Hummel, leaving Nurse Ulberg smiling so sweetly as she rocked the little bundle in her arms.

The next few minutes were ones of creeping concern, the ones that followed of anxiety that threatened to crush her chest. She knew Doctor Hummel had locked the door but didn't dare try it for fear of being proved right. Then the doctor returned, and then Ingrid started crying, shouting, panicking, desperately trying to leave the room. More people in uniforms came in, telling her to calm down. Their uniforms weren't those of soldiers but of people trained to care. But they held her still, held her arms down to her sides. She heard more bawling and desperate shouting, then realized it was coming from her own mouth. People pulled her away; she resisted. She struggled, felt a sharp stab on her upper arm, then tried to struggle but couldn't, then felt weak and faint.

She felt nothing more until she started to wake up in the back of a truck being driven through the backstreets of Oslo. By the time she was fully awake, she was lying in her own bed, and the experience had taken on an ethereal quality, as if the whole episode might have been imagined.

Perhaps that was what led Ingrid to keep pinching herself—to remind herself that it certainly hadn't been imagined. At times she wanted nothing more than to forget but always found something deep inside telling her never to do that.

Her mamma was attentive but polite, as though sensing much of the turmoil in Ingrid's mind, but Olav seemed distant and pensive, as though he either didn't care or had his own mind on other things.

Ingrid went along with the normality. For a time.

One evening, while all three of them sat down to eat, a sensation of emptiness engulfed Ingrid after she'd picked up her knife and fork. She held them but felt unable to do anything with them. There was food—mashed potatoes and carrots, seasoned with freshly picked herbs, streaked with glistening butter. It looked good and smelled good, and she was hungry—or should have been. But there was simply no will to perform the mechanics of picking up the food, let alone inserting it into her mouth. Her mamma and Olav started eating—she telling Ingrid to eat while it was hot, he telling her the carrots tasted particularly sweet. But there was no energy in Ingrid's hands, no impulse for them to move, and the cutlery slowly slipped through her limp hands and onto the table.

"Ingrid?" Olav said.

"I don't feel well," was all Ingrid could say. She stood and slowly stepped away from the table. Olav repeated her name, her mamma, too, but Ingrid walked over to her and Olav's bedroom with the cautious gait of a woman four times her age. She lay on the bed, the door open, the words from the table perfectly clear.

"What did I do?" she heard Olav say to her mamma.

"You didn't do anything. She's upset. You wouldn't understand."

"But I thought everything would be all right now she's finished with that clinic place."

"I know you did. But I think you should go talk to her."

"About what?"

"She's had her baby taken away, Olav."

"Well . . . yes, but much more important things are happening, very strong rumors that are giving me headaches. Soon Ingrid and I . . . well, the country could be—"

"Olav."

"What?"

"I'm not the one you need to talk to."

Then Ingrid heard, in exasperated tones, "I . . . I don't know what to say to her anymore."

She heard a chair being pulled out, then a few footsteps, halting at the bedroom doorway. After a few seconds' silence she heard more footsteps, followed by the sound of that chair again.

Then a manly sigh. "She looks like she's asleep now. I'll leave her in peace, talk to her tomorrow."

Ingrid drifted off to sleep to the tinkling of cutlery on plates.

The next day, Ingrid managed to eat breakfast at a very quiet table; then she and Olav walked to the park gardens together. Again, few words were exchanged as they knelt down and picked weeds from a patch to prepare it for sowing. As they rinsed the dirt from their hands in fresh rainwater, Olav suggested they go for a walk.

"To where?" Ingrid asked.

He smiled and frowned simultaneously. "Please," he said. "Let's just walk."

They walked away from Ostergaten, toward the larger and grander houses of the next neighborhood, which they reached before either of them spoke.

"Your mamma says I should talk to you."

"What?"

"No. I mean, I think I should—"

"Never mind, Olav. Thank you, but you don't need to do this. I'll be fine."

"Please. I've had . . . uh . . . other things on my mind recently— important things. And . . ."

He sighed, then stopped walking and turned to Ingrid. She felt his hands, still damp and fragrant of healthy earth, on her face. She felt his full kiss on her lips, saw his eyes rove over her face as though he were examining every crease and defect. It was the first time in months she'd felt his attentions so directly. It made words difficult, but there was also a silent reassurance that made them unnecessary.

"I'm sorry," he said. "That makes it sound like *you aren't* important." He held her hand, and they walked on, soon reaching a small square with a wooden bench on one side, which they sat on. Olav looked at her again, his eyes lingering, as if trying to see into her soul. "I think I understand," he said. "You miss the baby."

Ingrid let out a long breath. "Of course I miss him, but . . ." It was then that something welled up inside her, taking her by surprise, snatching control of her emotions and refusing to let go. It happened quickly. She collapsed onto him, sobbing and unable to speak. She was aware of Olav's strong arms around her but also aware of a shell of regret that had somehow enveloped her, one Olav would not be able to pierce.

"Oh, God, I miss him," she managed to say after a few minutes, pulsing the words out. "I miss him like I never thought possible." Then she cried some more, unable to tame those emotions for more than a few seconds at a time.

But eventually the tears dried up, and she sat, sighing and sniffing. Olav took a cloth from his pocket and wiped her face dry.

"I'm sorry," he said.

"I just keep thinking of his face. The sparkle of his blue eyes when he used to look up to me. That perfect set of eyelashes. The wisp of blond hair that was so light to touch it was hardly there at all. You know, I used to run my finger down his pudgy little belly, and he gave me a smile that spoke to me of the man he would become. I knew one day it would become a smile to both melt and break the hearts of many a young girl."

Olav held her hand and squeezed it. "You know that by now he's . . . he's probably . . ."

"With some family in Germany. Of course. I hope he's happy. And I hope they're happy with him. Every day I pray they look after him."

"Well . . ." Olav hesitated. "I want the same. I know I said some unpleasant things about him, but I wouldn't wish him any harm. And anyway, we can't change what's happened. Believe me, Ingrid; if I could change it, I would. You have to—"

"I know. I have to accept it. And I will—perhaps later this year, perhaps next. But I will, Olav. I will."

"And I'm sorry if I've been a little preoccupied."

Ingrid leaned up and kissed him. "What have you been preoccupied with? What are these secret *other things* on your mind?"

"It's important, Ingrid. It's big."

"Big?"

"The news from abroad is that Germany is on the brink of defeat."

Ingrid wiped her face, her cheeks itching from tears. "I don't understand," she said. "How can that be true while our streets are still teeming with German troops?"

"You wouldn't know. How can you? Anyone here only sees what they're allowed to see. But it's reliable news. The Soviets have captured Poland. France has been free for some time. German troops in Italy have surrendered."

"Really? Is all of that true?"

"I'm certain it is. Some even say that German troops in Denmark are on the verge of surrendering. Many parts of Germany itself have fallen to foreign forces—British, Soviet, American, even Canadian."

"Canadian?"

Olav nodded. "That word jumped out at me when I heard it. I'm not sure if I ever told you about my cousins."

"Your cousins? No, I don't think you did."

Ray Kingfisher

"Many years ago, one of my uncles couldn't find work here, so he and his wife emigrated to Canada. They had two sons—my cousins. I never met them, but we wrote each other when I was young. And now, of course, I wonder if they're fighting somewhere in Europe. And . . . I worry for their safety." He drew a tired breath and shook his head as if clearing away thoughts of his cousins. "Anyway, there's one more very important rumor—one I have difficulty believing. They say . . . they say Hitler is dead."

Ingrid's mouth opened and stayed open for a few seconds before she managed to speak. She shook her head and grimaced. "Oh, Olav. I feel so . . . so stupid. All of this has been going on, and it's hard to believe, and . . . I know I've been upset, but now I can understand why you've had other things on your mind. I'm so sorry."

"No, no." Olav kissed her on the forehead and pulled her closer. "We all have our own wars to fight, and you're no different."

"But I don't understand. Why isn't Norway free yet?"

Olav shrugged. "My Resistance friends tell me the Germans see this country as a stronghold. Some say they might try to bring their officials here from Germany and dig their heels in, to use our country as a last refuge."

"That sounds terrible."

"It does, but it won't happen. And that brings me to what I need to tell you—why I've brought you somewhere quiet."

"What is it, Olav?"

"Well, I know I promised you I wouldn't carry out any more work for the Resistance, but if taking up arms makes a difference, now Germany is so close to defeat, I'll do it."

"Oh, Olav. I'm scared, but . . ."

"This time it will be different, Ingrid. It will be the fire of me and every other Norwegian man against the dying embers of the German war machine."

214

Images jostled for attention in Ingrid's mind: Franz, the Lebensborn clinic, the arrests, the lack of food, and a baby—the product of her own flesh who had suckled from her breast. She nodded gravely. "I understand the danger, but I want my country back as much as anyone. If you want my blessing to fight, you have it."

"That means a lot to me. But let's wait and see what happens."

Ingrid was on edge for the next few days, not daring to leave Olav alone in case it was the last time she saw him. But although Olav was quiet and pensive, he didn't show any signs of his threat to take up arms. So there came a time when she needed to go out for bread.

She kissed Olav and her mamma goodbye and took her basket and ration books into town.

With each step she realized it was going to be difficult. Ever since coming out of the clinic, she'd been unable to face waiting in line outside *that* bakery—where she'd first met Franz—so she always took a longer route, walking much farther to a different bakery. But today, after Olav's news had sunk in, she decided to put those bad thoughts behind her and confront her fears.

She had no idea where Franz was, whether he was wandering around that same area of the city or had moved on. But she knew if he was there, she would ignore him. Even if he pulled his rifle on her, she would ignore him, because Olav's news of the war had given her strength to deal with her fears.

But something else was now unnerving her. As she walked on, she was aware of a strange unease around her. Everywhere she looked, people were gazing around, puzzled—a whole city, it seemed, glancing left and right and frowning.

And then Ingrid understood.

There had been German troops on street corners for so many years that her eyes had become blind to them. Now there were none. She turned around and peered in every direction, searching. *Not one of those dreaded uniforms.* She dropped her empty basket and walked—soon started to run—to the next street corner and around the corner to a large square. She looked to all sides and could see no German troops there either.

The police station.

She ran to the next street, but people were running toward her, many of their faces glistening with tears of confused half hope. She stopped an elderly man, and before she could speak, she felt his bony arms around her, hugging her as if she were a long-lost daughter.

"It's over," he said. "It's over. It's over."

Then he trotted off as fast as his bowlegs could carry him.

"Over?" Ingrid said aloud, only vaguely conscious of the shiver passing through her body, of her own tears wetting her face. She started running.

But no. *Perhaps this was some joke the Germans were playing.* She rounded another corner.

And there was the police station. There were no troops—at least, no *German* troops. The local Norwegian police side by side with men in civilian clothes, all of them armed with rifles, were talking to passersby. Not shouting. Not ordering. Talking.

She ran up to them, desperate to hear their words.

Other people were asking the questions that were racing through her mind: "What's happening? Can it really be true?"

One of the local police steadied himself and raised his voice. He wasn't barking orders but was broadcasting in perfect, native, beautiful Norwegian. "Let it be known," he said. "Tell your friends and neighbors. The war in Norway is over. Resistance forces have taken over our Royal Palace. We are discussing the handover of government with the occupying forces. But Oslo is free; Norway is free. Rejoice that the war is over."

Ingrid turned and started running. She stopped to catch her breath once or twice. But her pace quickened as she turned the corner into Ostergaten. Her mamma and Olav and most neighbors were on the street, all talking, some gesticulating, some embracing one another. When Olav spotted Ingrid, he ran to meet her.

"Ingrid? Did you hear?"

"It's over!" she shouted. "The war's over! *The occupation's over!*"

Olav lifted her off her feet and swung her around until she felt her shoes coming off, sensed the cooling breeze on her feet. He let her down, and she ran, barefoot, to her mamma, both grinning, both crying. No words were needed.

It was a carnival. Neighbors talked of what part of the occupation they'd resented the most, how life for everyone could now return to normal, but also that they still could hardly believe what was happening.

They talked and embraced and kissed, but eventually there was no more to be said, and people started going about their daily business, returning indoors or walking to the park gardens. But wherever they went, they had new life in their footsteps, a swagger, and a smile to share with anyone who cared to join in.

"Come on," Olav said. "I need to sit down." He headed for number 41. Ingrid and her mamma followed. "Your shoes," her mamma said, pointing to the middle of the road.

Ingrid's mamma and Olav went inside while Ingrid walked across and picked up her shoes. As she straightened up, her eyes caught Laila's. They'd had their differences, but this was a time to rejoice—a rare occasion of late but one to share. It was a time to celebrate peace, freedom, and friendship. Ingrid offered Laila a smile. Laila returned the gesture—albeit with a crooked edge. Perhaps she was embarrassed, Ingrid thought. The two women stepped closer.

"Isn't it good news?" Ingrid said with a glee she could sense faltering as soon as she spoke.

Laila nodded. "A free Norway will be back in charge soon," she said. Then she sneered. "I only hope they don't forgive the traitors."

"What?" Ingrid's smile dropped away. "What do you mean by that?"

Laila threw her head back and spoke freely and loudly. "You understand me very well, *white-feather woman*. Looking after a sick aunt? *Ha!* You really think everybody believed that? Well, not me. I know what you did, and I'll make sure everyone else does too."

"Oh, Laila. Hold on. Before you—"

A flash. A flash of hatred on Laila's face. A reflex flinch from Ingrid, and a splash of spittle landing on her coat. Then Laila was walking back to her house.

Ingrid went to shout across to her, but her throat locked, afraid of the reaction. Then Laila was gone, and the moment was lost. Ingrid wiped the mess from her coat and went indoors.

It's just after the evening meal, and I again find myself in front of the television. Tonight, the volume is turned up high. Nevertheless, I struggle to keep my eyes open. Then I give up the struggle, and another vision railroads its way into my mind. Like all my visions, this one taunts me, poking a sharp stick at the corpse of my wasted existence, making me feel every bit as helpless and foolish as I was all those years ago.

It's now the mid-1930s, and I am a full-grown man and proud to be a part of this new progressive society. The better Germany they promised us is now taking shape. We have a great new leader—one that is making the rest of the world sit up and take notice, a man who fills every true German heart with pride and hope for their beloved country.

We believe what our new rulers tell us, that we all have a crucial part to play in our country's bright future. There will be high standards of living, low illness rates, high intelligence, excellent physical capability, efficient industry, and social harmony. It's all true. We can see that it's happening before our very eyes. In time, once the weaker and undesirable elements of society have been dealt with, every good and honest German will benefit from these new changes. But everybody must commit to these new ways. Even now, many people are still stuck in the past, unable to accept the new progressive ways, so our government has helpfully put together programs to educate them about the benefits of our modern social order.

Everybody has their part to play. Nobody will be allowed to sit on the sidelines and merely watch. All ages have a part to play too. Work and endeavor are to be longed for and enjoyed.

There is talk of celebration days, when civilization will honor and venerate the architects of our social programs. These great rulers of ours will live forever by virtue of the work they are doing to improve the lot of mankind.

Most importantly, everybody has confidence in our rulers. We all know they have a plan; it is up to us to ensure they are allowed to follow it through.

Chapter 23

Arnold thought he'd done his best presentation-wise, but as soon as Merlene walked into the restaurant, he felt utterly overshadowed. For a moment he thought he'd completely misjudged his attire and she'd be offended or, at the very least, laugh at him. In fact, for the very first moment he wasn't even sure if it was her.

The ensemble complemented her ebony skin perfectly. Her hair had been braided and dyed a deep blue. The dress—the same shade—was tied in a bow above each shoulder and clung to her body all the way to the knee. Her eyeshadow, too, was such a perfect match it looked like all three were made of the same material, and subtle pink lipstick with just a hint of glitter added a little magic, as if that were needed. This was a woman Arnold wouldn't in a million years guess was a nurse. In short, this wasn't a nurse; it was a woman.

He wasn't too impolite to give her a subtle embrace and a kiss on the cheek but found it hard to take his eyes off her as they headed for their table.

And she noticed.

"Why do people assume nurses dress like nurses when they're off duty?" she said as they sat down opposite each other at a cozy corner table.

"I, uh, don't know," Arnold said. "Do you always dress like that when you're not working?"

"Only when I'm out on a date," she replied, quickly adding, "or even, out *not* on a date."

"Hey, let's park the date-or-not-date thing, eh? I've had a bellyful of my daughters telling me I should give dating a go."

A bubble of laughter escaped from her lips. "And?"

"And it's ridiculous. I'm sixty-six."

"So what?" she said, a sympathetic frown taking center stage on her face. "You present yourself good, whatever your age."

"Well, thanks." He touched the lapel of his shirt. "D'you like it?"

"My taste isn't the point here."

"Oh, you mean, you don't like it."

"*I like that you've made an effort* is the point." She lowered her voice to a whisper. "I had some internet dates with guys you would not believe."

Arnold felt his eyebrows bob up involuntarily. "You do internet dating?"

"Not anymore, I don't." She shook her head firmly—very firmly. "But I tried, and I got part of what I wanted: it got me some confidence back. And that was all due to Ingrid."

"My mom told you to do internet dating? No! You're kidding me."

"Well, obviously not the internet part. But she told me not to be scared of meeting men if that was what I wanted to do. And it got to the stage where every time I saw her, she asked what I'd done about it. I got so sick of her asking that I tried it, which, I guess, was her idea all along. I always felt like I owed her for it."

"Wow."

"I guess there's a lot about your dear old mom you didn't know."

Arnold nodded, more concerned with what he didn't know about his *dear old dad* but holding his tongue for now. He handed her the menu.

The food was good; the ambience was even better. At Arnold's request they avoided any more talk of his mother. They found they had a shared passion for schlock horror movies and a common guilty pleasure of 1970s disco music. Only as the desserts arrived at the table did Arnold broach the subject he'd arranged the meeting to discuss.

"I, uh . . . I took your advice," he said, finding it easier than he expected to paste a veneer of seriousness on his face.

"Oh?"

"About the letter I got. You remember? Marit and Ulrich?"

"You bet I remember. You called her?"

"Yeah, and it turns out this Ulrich guy isn't my brother but my half brother. That is, if he's still alive."

"And, of course, if he really is anything to do with you."

"Oh, he is. Marit said the Ingrid she's looking for got married to an Olav in March 1944."

"Which is . . ."

Arnold nodded. "Yeah, when my folks married. But it turns out . . . well, if this whole thing isn't some elaborate hoax . . ."

"What?"

"Well, my father wasn't Ulrich's father."

"Oh." Her eyes widened in surprise.

"Marit's been looking for Ulrich for years, and it seems like he's disappeared from the face of the planet."

"Did Ingrid bring him over to Canada with you and Olav?"

Arnold shook his head. "There was only ever the three of us—well, plus Mom's mother—until 1946, when my sister came along."

"Are you certain?"

"As certain as I can be. I contacted the folks in Saskatoon. That's what they said."

"So, what are you going to do?"

"Well, that's why I wanted to talk to you."

"You think I can help?"

"I'd value what you thought, is all."

"You know what I think. You're retired. No strings. I'd want to know. I'd go check out Oslo, meet this Marit woman, find out what happened."

Arnold was slightly stunned. She made it all sound simple. But perhaps she hadn't considered all the angles. The next thing she said shot that one down too.

"Or perhaps you're worried that somehow your dad made your mom get rid of Ulrich?"

The conversation was going too fast for Arnold. Or, worse, the implications were being spelled out too blatantly. His mind halted for a few seconds. His instinct was to tell Merlene that his father wasn't like that, that she didn't know him so shouldn't say such things, but he was old enough to know that there was always that one grain of doubt in a sack of top-grade wheat, that one percent of a person's temperament that only the very closest of people got to witness.

Yes, so Arnold's worst fear about his father had been spelled out, but the antidote came with it. There was only one way he was going to be sure whether his father really was that kindly figure that Arnold remembered him as or whether there was a more sinister side to his nature. For a fraction of a second Arnold's mind cracked and allowed another possibility to squeeze its way in: that his father's exemplary behavior to him had been born out of guilt—guilt of having done something unforgivable.

While Arnold paused, Merlene said nothing, almost drawing the inevitable response from him.

"You think I should just go there?" he said, almost feeling the little boy lost he sounded like. "On my own?"

"You should do what you feel you want to."

Arnold could feel sap rising. This wasn't going to plan. He wanted to talk the difficulties through with her, but she had all the answers immediately to hand. He didn't talk for a few moments, taking time to finish his dessert. Yes, she was making the whole thing seem simple; she even seemed to understand the fear he had: fear of what he might find out. Fear of the truth.

While he dithered, she spoke again.

"Hey, that's probably not helpful, is it? And you wanted me to help. If you want a straighter answer, then yes, I think you should go. You won't know until you go there whether you should have gone there, if that makes sense."

"Thanks," he said. "That, uh . . . that does help."

Arnold's mind turned to the matter he'd considered before: whether his sister or daughters would want to come with him. None of them had shown much interest so far in the whole affair. He considered the logistics of traveling there and doing the detective work on his own. He could do that. Then his mind turned to the reality of finding out about a potential half brother while alone on the other side of the world. He was sixty-six. Very adult. It shouldn't have been a problem. But somehow the idea of being alone in that situation unnerved him. Then he looked across the table at Merlene, who had been as good a friend so far as anyone could have been.

"Cool," she said. "Just go with what you think is right for you."

He thought it over a little more. And what he thought was that he would take that advice.

"Merlene?" he said. "I don't suppose you'd consider . . ."

"What?"

"I mean, you wouldn't think about coming with me, would you? I mean, just as a friend?"

She let out a long sigh, then stared, those saucer eyes apparently examining his face.

"I'm guessing you're probably too busy, and it'll be hard to get time off work."

Still she said nothing, her frown starting to contort in discomfort.

Then he added, "I mean, if you were interested, I'd pay for everything."

"I don't think so, Arnold."

"Oh, okay." He nodded slowly, feeling like . . . well, yes, *jilted*. "I thought not, but . . . is there any particular reason? I mean, we get along, don't we?"

"We do, Arnold. But for one thing, this is perhaps something you need to do on your own."

"Thing is, I'm not sure I want to do it on my own. You know, there's something I've learned in my later years, Merlene. There's nothing wrong with admitting you're lonely."

"And there's the other thing right there. You see, if you're asking me to go on vacation with you because you need someone to hold your hand . . ."

Arnold was about to defend himself. But that would have been hard. Merlene was right. It wasn't a good way to invite someone on vacation.

"Arnold, look at me." When he did, she cast her eyes down at her dress, then lifted her head up, displaying her face. "Do you have any idea what all this is about?"

"What do you mean?"

She gave him a slightly sideways stare, eyebrows stretched up, asking him to try again.

"Uh . . . I know you look . . ."

"Yes?"

"You look beautiful."

"Thank you. Wasn't hard, was it?"

Arnold gulped and took a moment to slow his heartbeat. "So, Merlene, are you, uh . . . I mean, are you seeing anyone, you know, dating anyone?"

She took a breath, but he continued.

"Or perhaps you have someone on the horizon or . . . or have someone . . . someone that, uh . . . listen, Merlene, I'm kinda out of practice where dating and stuff is concerned."

"You're kidding me?" She let out a deep laugh, immediately trying to stifle it.

"Okay, but if I thought someone as good looking as you . . . I mean, if you—"

"I'll be straight with you," Merlene said. "I have friends. I have lots of friends. But if I'm honest, I'm lonely too." She tilted her head slightly to one side and gazed at his face again, this time through him more than at him. The attention made his fingers tremble. "I like you, Arnold. You're smart but not too smart—still on my level. You looked after your mom, which I admire. You're a nice guy, so perhaps I do want to go on vacation with you, but . . . just not as some sort of official envoy or paid accomplice."

"Oh."

"D'you hear what I'm saying?"

"You mean, you'll come with me but . . ."

"But not just as friends. I mean, if that's okay with you—if that's what you want too."

Arnold couldn't speak for a few minutes.

Chapter 24

Oslo, May 1945

Olav stood tall at the far end of the park gardens like a king surveying his lands.

The news of the German surrender had been greeted with a mass jubilation nobody had ever experienced. But when the euphoria faded, there was just a little sadness in Olav's mind. The authorities had announced that the land before him would soon revert to a public place—would become Lyngstad Park once more—because the country's farmland was being rejuvenated, and, more importantly, the produce would go to Norwegians rather than Germans.

But the patchwork of small plots, themselves patterned in rows and dots, held many fine memories for Olav. Building the chicken enclosures and the shed—which would soon be demolished—digging in the rain, sowing seeds in spring's new warmth, weeding with Oslo's clear sun beating down on his bare back, choosing the optimum time to harvest, wondering how the plants could ever survive the biting frosts. But most of all, far more precious than any of these memories were the fond ones of him and Ingrid spending time here together—working, talking, indulging in stolen kisses on the rare occasions they found themselves alone.

So, this land that had provided the community with food for so long was almost a friend—a reliable, ever-present, unquestioning friend.

The end of the war and the end of occupation should have changed everything. And, for many, it did. The whole city rejoiced. Some people didn't sleep for days. The Norwegian Resistance quickly took control and then handed power over to the government as soon as it returned from exile in Britain.

Olav found out that his parents had perished in a prison camp two years before, so he knew that his own personal memories of the end-of-war celebrations would be forever remembered as bittersweet. But others had suffered too—*all* average men and women had suffered. And now it was a new beginning. He would never forget his parents, of course, and whenever he was telling other people to think of the future, he knew he would also be talking to his own uncertain self. Because the country was now free, and the future was as bright as an arctic sun reflecting off a crystalline snowfall. He knew above all else that his parents hadn't died in vain.

And everything was rosy in the garden of Ostergaten 41.

For a week or so.

It was then that Ingrid, after initially accepting her baby had probably been taken to Germany, started mentioning him again, hoping he was healthy and putting on weight, asking Olav whether he thought he was being taken care of. Olav said he didn't even want to hear the question—that this was a new dawn, a break as clean as Norway's break with German occupation. He told her to forget the baby, to try to pretend that it never existed, that thinking otherwise would only cause everyone more pain in the long run. She agreed that that was a good idea and promised to try.

A couple of days later, Olav returned home from the park gardens with what was likely to be their final harvest of cabbages and turnips and found her sobbing by the fire.

"Ingrid?" he said, first with a quiet concern, then repeating it when she didn't react. "What's happened?" He knelt down beside her and pulled her hand from her face. "You've been crying. What's going on?" He held her by the chin, tilting her face to the light. "What's that?" he said as though puzzled. But he wasn't; it was a stupid question. He could see the fresh blood for himself, the graze along her cheekbone shouting the color as it glistened.

He looked her up and down, noticing mud along one side of her coat all the way up to the shoulder, its seam ripped, her frock visible between the gape.

"Did you fall?"

"It's nothing."

"Nothing?"

"Forget it, Olav." Then, as though being pursued, she thrust herself at him, crying freely into his chest, her arms holding on to him with an unnatural tightness, a desperation, almost.

"I want to know what happened," he said.

He waited, but she said nothing for a few minutes, merely continued sobbing. She shook her head, grinding it into his chest. "Please, Olav, just forget it."

Olav gave no reply, thinking that pressing her on the issue might upset her even more, and decided to do as she wished.

Over the next few days Olav took more notice of how people reacted when he and Ingrid were outside together. Some behaved like the friends all good people of Oslo should have been. But one or two immediate neighbors gave Ingrid a sideways flick of the eyes, up and down, then would disguise a sneer—and disguise it badly. He wondered what the reaction of those people might be if he wasn't there. Or, more importantly, *when* he wasn't there—when Ingrid was on her own.

He contacted his old friends from the Resistance movement. Their duties were now redundant, but their acquaintances and their feel for the public mood were habits that refused to subside after five years of intense practice.

They told him that it was true, that some people—and not a tiny number—held grievances against Lebensborn mothers who had, after all, benefitted from what they'd done in the form of better diets and medical care. And there was worse. Some of these people who held grievances were in government office. They had power. In fact, Olav found that many senior members of the Resistance movement were less than sympathetic to women they described as traitors.

Olav spent hours alone at the park gardens or walking along the coastal paths, wondering what to do. Ultimately, what *could* he do? He very soon realized there was one thing he would *have* to do. He would wait until they were alone, and he would ask her—well, *order* her—to tell him whether her injuries had been caused by a fall or something more sinister.

He started striding back home.

Back at Ostergaten 41, Ingrid's mamma was putting her coat on.

"I'm just going across the road to see Elsa Bergen," she said. "One of her children has fever of some sort, and she wants my advice. Do you want to come with me?"

"I'm feeling tired," Ingrid said. "I'll wait here and rest, perhaps chop some potatoes for later."

"Of course."

Ingrid smiled a goodbye to her mamma and watched her leave. Then she heard voices coming from outside—her mamma talking to Olav by the sound of it. She'd started to wonder where he'd been.

Moments later he was giving her a kiss on the cheek. But he seemed nervous, flustered.

"Mamma's gone to see—"

"I know. We just talked."

"Of course."

He drew a long breath, almost spoke, but first took his coat off and pointed to the chairs by the fire. "Ingrid, I need to talk to you," he said with a grave expression on his face.

"About what?"

He raised a hand toward the graze on her cheekbone but fell short of touching it. "I want you to tell me what happened, how you got your injuries."

Energy coursed through Ingrid's veins. She glanced around, trying to think of something, anything. "I was just going out," she said—a little too quickly, she knew.

"Going where?"

"To the store in town."

"What for?"

"I need . . . I need to think about buying some shoes."

He grimaced. "Shoes? But . . . couldn't it wait?"

"No." She bolted for the set of coat hooks by the door and grabbed her coat. "We can talk later, perhaps."

"Well . . . come here."

"Why?"

He looked down, puzzled, then edged over to her. "I want to kiss you goodbye."

"Oh. Oh, yes, of course."

They kissed, bittersweet invading Ingrid's heart, and she quickly left the house, needing a few deep breaths before setting off for town.

Along the way she saw no German soldiers, no guns, no identity checkpoints. But fear was still there—one sort replaced by another. Anyone giving her anything longer than a glance unnerved her. She had done wrong in the eyes of many and had no idea when that feeling would go. More importantly, how long was she going to stay out, and what would she do when she returned and Olav wanted to continue with *that* conversation?

She looked up at the skies, as if asking for guidance, but all she got was a raindrop in the eye. Still, it threw her from her worries. A dark cloud spoiled the blue sky. She knew how it felt.

Then the heavens opened, and she darted for cover into the nearest store, which happened to be a shoe shop, a fact that almost made her smile. She killed a few more minutes looking at the styles—most of which she would never be able to afford—until she became aware of a woman who kept glancing at her. Whenever the woman looked away, Ingrid looked at her. And yes, she'd seen this woman somewhere before. She wasn't a neighbor and was too old for Ingrid to have played with her as a child. Perhaps she was wrong. Perhaps her mind was playing tricks on her.

"Ingrid, isn't it?" the woman said, approaching her.

Ingrid's instinct was to keep a safe distance between them, but this woman smiled sweetly, and they were in a public place. "Yes," she said. "Do I know you?"

"You were in the clinic. I'm a nurse there."

Ingrid's mind turned over and over, searching for a name. That was why she wasn't sure; she'd only ever seen the woman in uniform.

"I'm Kari," she said. "Kari Ulberg."

"Nurse Ulberg. Of course. How could I forget?"

"How are you?"

"It's been hard. I . . . I miss my baby."

Kari smiled sweetly. "I can understand. I see that a lot."

"Have you heard about him? Is he settling in well?"

"Settling in?"

"With his new parents. In Hamburg."

Ingrid saw the woman's lips twitch, noted how she now didn't look her in the eye. "What's wrong?" she said.

"I'm not sure if . . . I'm not sure I should say."

"Has something happened to him?"

"He's fine. He's . . . fit and healthy."

Ingrid didn't need to ask more questions. She knew. "He's still here, isn't he? He never got to Hamburg." She grabbed the woman by the arm, making her wince with discomfort. "Tell me, please, Kari. Is my baby still in that place?"

A nod. A stiff nod as though the woman was disgusted with herself. "He was all set to go. Then they heard that Hamburg was likely to be attacked by British troops. It was too dangerous to take him there."

Ingrid froze, eyes glazed, not even breathing for a few seconds.

"I have to go," the nurse said, taking a few steps back, then turning and heading for the shop door, leaving only the click of her heels on stone for Ingrid to hear.

"He's still here," Ingrid muttered to herself. "All these weeks have passed and . . ." Her mind raced through all those nights she'd hardly slept for worrying about little Ulrich, hoping he was being loved, praying his new parents were taking care of him. And it turned out that on every one of those nights, he had been sleeping in the same city, in that clinic.

In a trance, she stepped outside the store and onto the wet sidewalk. She started heading for home, not sure how Olav and her mamma would take this news. She meandered across the road without looking, and a car horn sounded, making her jump out of its way.

The shock brought her to her senses. Ulrich was in Oslo. It had stopped raining. She could go see Ulrich. Because she was in Oslo, and he was in Oslo. It had stopped raining. She could go home. She could go see Ulrich. *She could go see Ulrich.*

She took a few steps back toward the shoe store and scanned the scene before her. Suits and dresses and skirts and coats and pants and heads and arms and legs all jostled for her attention.

Then she saw her. The sidewalks and roads were wet. In heels, a woman could only walk slowly for fear of slipping. Ingrid set off, dodging passersby, and it wasn't long before she reached her.

"Kari!" she shouted just as her quarry was about to turn a corner. "I have to see him," she said. "I have to see my baby, Ulrich."

"But . . . you can't. I don't think it's allowed."

"Don't say that. It's my baby. You know that, even if others don't."

"But the staff will call the police."

"Kari, I swear I'll break in if you won't help me. Do you have children? Do you know what it's like when they're taken away from you?"

The woman gritted her teeth, staring into space beyond Ingrid. "Are you sure you want to see him?"

"Of course."

"Well . . ."

"Please, Kari. I promise I won't get you into trouble. Just one minute with him, just to see he's safe; then I won't bother you anymore."

"All right, all right." Kari thought for a few moments. "Perhaps I owe you that much. I remember when they took your baby."

"So you'll help me?"

Kari nodded. "Follow me to the clinic—at a distance. Take the path around to the gardens at the very back of the building. I'll go in and open the door. I'll say it's to let some fresh air in. You need to go down the corridor and find ward eleven. Remember, I don't want to see you. And I need my job, so you're not to say a word about this to anyone."

Ingrid flung her arms around her and squeezed. "Thank you so much. I won't forget this."

It was less than ten minutes later that Ingrid, her heart thumping and her legs weak, entered the gardens behind the clinic. She hid behind a hedge, peering out to see someone move on the other side of the glass door. Yes, it was Kari, and yes, she opened the door, briefly looked around, and walked back. Ingrid checked no one was watching, tried to gulp away her fear, and ran to the door, stealing inside without a sound.

She was in a large dining room but saw an open door beyond the long table and could just about see a corridor through the doorway. She stilled herself to listen, but there was nothing, so she crept to the door and tiptoed along the corridor, following the ward numbers on the doors until she reached number eleven. It was a glass door, so she pressed her face against it to look left and right but saw nobody. Then she was inside. She winced, unable to breathe in through her nose but not quite understanding why, more concerned with the names at the bottoms of the cribs. It didn't take long; she headed for the one at the end. She knew her baby. She could have picked him out from thousands.

She wept, holding a hand over her mouth to quiet herself, holding the end of a crib to steady herself. This was Ulrich, little Ulrich who'd been at her breast for months, been by her side, been inside her for nine months. She glanced at the note attached to the crib, merely to see if his name had been changed yet. No, it had his name and also hers on it.

She leaned over and whispered in Ulrich's ear. "Hello, Ulrich. It's your mamma." The reaction was immediate. A smile, a gurgle, a kick of the tiny feet in pure excitement. She held his hand, her joy tempered by the coldness of the flesh.

Then she noticed something else: the state of the crib he was lying in. "When did they last change your sheets?" she whispered. She leaned down, sniffing. "And your diaper too." Then she realized what had stopped her inhaling through her nose: the whole room stank. She also noticed the crustiness around his mouth, his blond hair matted like the mane of a wild pony, the discoloration on the side of his face—dirt or a rash; she wasn't sure.

And then she heard a shout.

"Who are you?"

She turned around and saw a man in a white coat.

"I said, *who are you?* And what are you doing here?"

Now Ingrid cried freely. She reached down to pick Ulrich up.

"Stop that!" he shouted and was by her side a second later, holding her arms, preventing her from even touching her own baby, shoving her away. "Tell me who you are, or I'll call the police."

Ingrid shook him off and ran.

Out of the ward, out of the back door, into the garden, into the street outside, and halfway home. There, she came to her senses. She had to calm herself down, wipe her face dry of tears, and behave as if nothing had happened. She had done a foolish thing. For a moment she wished she hadn't met Kari, hadn't gone to the clinic, hadn't seen Ulrich again. And then she felt wretched for wishing such a thing.

But no. She had to remain calm and behave as if she hadn't seen Ulrich again. Yes, that was it. *Don't mention it to Olav or Mamma,* she told herself. *It will only complicate life.*

Twenty minutes later, Ingrid got to Ostergaten, went inside number 41, and gave Olav her biggest, bravest smile and embraced him.

"Did you buy any shoes?" he asked.

"Shoes? Oh, yes. Uh, no. I didn't see any I liked. Where's Mamma?"

"Still across the road," Olav replied. "And we still need to talk."

"Talk?"

"Sit down, Ingrid."

Now her smile weakened. She told herself the more she talked, the more she might mention what had happened to her. "Not now, Olav," she said. "I don't feel so well."

"It won't take long. Please."

He sat, staring up at her as if he wasn't going to give up. So she sat too.

"I need you to tell me how you got your injuries."

"I already told you. It was nothing."

"Ingrid, neither of us is moving until you tell me the truth. Did you fall? Did you trip on some steps?"

Ingrid went to speak, to tell him they'd already discussed those details, but images of that disgusting dormitory kept forcing their way into her mind, as if the stench of neglect was haunting her.

"And I want the truth," he continued. "Tell me exactly what happened."

She shook thoughts of little Ulrich from her head. "I got into a fight," she said. "That's all."

"A fight? Really?"

She said nothing.

"I know you better than that, Ingrid. I know you don't fight."

"Don't be angry, Olav."

He held her hand. "I won't be angry. Just tell me the truth. Was it more like . . . an assault?"

She bowed her head, thought for a moment, then nodded.

"By who?"

"Three women."

"*What?* Who were they?"

"Just neighbors. But please, Olav. They've had their revenge. It's over."

"Revenge? Revenge for what? What did you do?"

"They know about what I did with Franz."

Olav didn't need to ask how they'd found out; it was, despite their efforts, hardly a secret. People talked. Laila *definitely* talked. And what official records had been kept now lay in the hands of Norwegian authorities.

"Please, Olav. Just forget about it."

Olav used his forefinger to lift her chin, so she looked at his face. "I'll do whatever you want. But no secrets, remember? You have to tell me the truth. Has this happened before?"

"Not as bad as that time," she replied. "A few unpleasant remarks. Two or three times I was . . . spat at."

"Oh, Ingrid," he said. "Why didn't you tell me?"

She shrugged, her gaze low again.

"Look at me, Ingrid. Look at my face."

She did, but blinking and unfocused.

"If this happens again, I want you to tell me."

"I'm not a child, Olav."

He sighed, exasperated. "I know, and I'm sorry. But I need to know. No secrets, yes?"

Ingrid's mind fought with the sounds and sights of Ulrich and Kari and the clinic she'd just run away from. She forced the words from her mouth. "No secrets," she muttered. "I'm sorry. I should have told you."

Olav heard that the government was planning many new laws to gradually unpick the damage done by the occupying forces, and even after a couple of weeks, life in Oslo was already starting to return to normal. But it was a strange kind of normality. He also heard that Lebensborn babies—the ones who hadn't found their way to Germany or had been returned like undelivered parcels—were being held in those same clinics throughout Norway. Some mothers too. Against their will, people said. But he put those thoughts to the back of his mind. It was Ingrid's safety that mattered.

The events of one day late in May brought those thoughts back with a vengeance that threatened to turn his anger into an implacable storm.

Ingrid and her mamma were clearing away the breakfast things while Olav was busy digesting, so he said. There was a knock at the door—four firm knocks, to be precise.

Olav answered it to find three of the city's policemen standing upright and stern.

"Does Ingrid Jacobsen live here?"

"Who wants to know?"

The man took a second to look at his fellow policemen, making a show of his eyes dwelling on their uniforms. "Who do you think wants to know?"

Likewise, Olav made a point of waiting a few moments before calling Ingrid to the door.

"Ingrid Jacobsen?" the man said to her.

She nodded.

"You are charged with collaboration. I have an order to—"

The sentence was never finished. The two other policemen had reached across to hold Ingrid by the upper arms, and Olav had lunged at them. "Hey! Hey!" he said. "What's this? You just get away from her." Those years Olav had spent sawing wood all day now bore fruit, his hands picking the policemen off Ingrid and shoving them away without so much as a grunt of effort from him. "What are you talking about? This is my wife. She's no collaborator."

"To our knowledge she's a Lebensborn mother," the policeman said.

"I don't care about your knowledge. She's done nothing wrong. Go away." He turned and told Ingrid to go to their bedroom, to barricade herself in if necessary. At first she stayed but left at the second telling.

"You must be Olav Jacobsen, the husband," the policeman said, lacing the words with distaste.

"And you must be out of your stupid mind."

The policeman pulled a pistol and aimed it at Olav, whose broad frame was blocking the doorway.

"Olav," came a voice from behind him. "Be careful." It was Ingrid's mamma, silent until now. Her voice was ignored.

"Maybe I am out of my mind," the policeman said. "Or maybe you are committing a grave error of judgment."

Olav stood square. "No, I'm not. This is ridiculous." He grabbed the barrel of the pistol and shoved it to the side. "We haven't lived through five years of German occupation for this nonsense. My wife didn't collaborate. She didn't pass secrets to the Germans. She didn't help them in any way. And she certainly hasn't hurt anyone."

The policeman looked Olav up and down as he paused to think. "If she promises to stay away from the clinic, we could look upon her situation more leniently."

"Stay away?" Olav said. "*Stay away?* She hates that place—detests it. She was forced to take part in that vile program, no better than raped, and forced to give up that . . . that *thing* that was the result. And you should know better than to hold it against her. Now go away—*all of you*—before I make you."

The man looked once more at his fellow policemen, one of whom muttered something about perhaps letting this one instance go unpunished.

"Very well," the first one said to Olav. "We will . . . consider your remarks. Good day."

Olav shut the door without replying and went to see Ingrid.

"They're gone," he said as he knocked on the bedroom door. There was no reply. "Ingrid?" he said sharply. Still, there was nothing, so he opened the door. Ingrid was at the far corner, crouching slightly, rubbing her frightened eyes.

Olav said her name again, but softly this time.

"Oh, Olav. I'm so sorry."

He took a step toward her, and she flinched. "Hey, hey," he said. "You don't need to apologize for that idiot. And now he's gone." He placed an arm around her, coaxing her, and she calmed. Then he saw a sickly expression crawl across her face. "What is it?" he said. "Is there something else?"

"Promise me you won't get angry, Olav."

"Ingrid, please don't say that. You make me sound like an ogre. Just tell me."

She took a long breath. "I think they came because of what I did."

"Go on."

"A few days ago I went back to the Lebensborn clinic."

"Oh, *Ingrid.*" He released her and ran tightening fingers through his hair, pulling at the ends. "Why, Ingrid. *Why?*"

"You know why, Olav. You know why. I went to see my baby."

"But it isn't there. They took it to Germany, didn't they?"

She shook her head wildly. "He never got there."

"Why the hell not?"

"I asked the nurses. They said the British were approaching Hamburg. They canceled the adoption."

"So what? That doesn't mean it's yours."

"He is, Olav. *He is mine!*"

"Oh, for God's sake, Ingrid. It belongs to the authorities. Let them deal with it."

"Don't speak about him like that, Olav." She fell to the floor, kneeling in front of him. Her fists pounded his belly a few times before she gave up and started sobbing. Between her desperate acts she managed to get a few words out. "I miss my baby, Olav. He *is* mine, and I miss him."

Olav stepped back. "I'm going out for a walk," he said, spitting the words out. "A long, long walk. Tonight, I'll sleep alone in one of the chairs."

He left the house, stamping on the grasses sprouting from the cracks in the road, leaving Ingrid's mamma to hold and comfort her daughter.

Chapter 25

Oslo, May 1945

Olav had no idea how long he'd been out walking. It could have been an hour; it could have been two. But now, eventually, he had stopped cursing Ingrid.

Fiery with sweat as well as temper, he sat on a grassy bank overlooking the sea and tried to come to terms with what his wife had done.

Yes, he'd agreed to her having that bastard child by that loathsome SS officer. And yes, perhaps the act had saved him from being taken away by the German authorities, but none of that stopped him hating himself for agreeing to it. And he'd only agreed to it on the understanding that she would forget about the baby afterward, that as far as they were concerned it didn't exist. He'd reiterated that often enough, and she'd agreed every time. And now the . . . he hated himself for even thinking it, but it was true; she was being foolish . . . yes, the *foolish* woman had gone looking for the thing again.

A trawler chugged through the waves in the distance. He thought of the days his pappa had taken him out to sea as a young boy, trying to turn him into a man. His pappa would make it look so easy, pulling the nets away hand over hand to let them drop into the ocean, then winding the winch to pull it all back once he was sure—by the wind direction or the color of the water or God knows what other reason—that the catch was ready. It was effortless for his pappa; it was effortless because he'd started on the trawlers before his sixteenth birthday.

He thought of what his mamma would do with the family's share of the catch, of the different meals she would prepare with it: salted, smoked, boiled, pickled, and baked fish. Olav had eaten them all many times.

He shed a few tears at his own loss. Perhaps it was even worse than Ingrid's loss because it had taken three years of waiting and hoping and praying before he'd found out that his parents had perished thanks to the damn Germans.

Ha! And now Ingrid was talking about how much she missed her baby. And then what? Would he soon be asked to . . . to what, exactly? To adopt? To love? To *love* the offspring of an SS officer who had impregnated his wife? No. Absolutely not.

He shivered at the cool sea breeze drifting into his sweat-ridden shirt, then got up and walked on for another few minutes, during which he made his mind up. The answer was just *no* and always would be. He would go back and tell Ingrid—*insist*—that she had to forget all about that damn baby forever. There would be no compromises; this was something he could not give in to under any circumstances.

He headed back home.

By the time Olav turned the corner into Ostergaten, he was already hot again, so his jacket was open and swinging freely as he strode on. There was noise coming from ahead, probably children playing, but he had more important things to think about. His resolve had, if anything, hardened, and in his mind, he rehearsed what he would say to Ingrid. He loved her and wanted her to be happy, but she was his wife, and he was the man of the house, so his say had to be final. And besides, she would never be happy while the memory of that mongrel baby was still alive.

As he got halfway along the street, his mind jolted, thoughts of Ingrid's baby put away for a moment. The noise from ahead wasn't of children playing. There was aggression in the voices—and not the harmless pretend aggression of children. Because these were no children.

Most were women.

God. It was a fight.

Olav broke into a trot, readying himself to break up a catfight. Then he stopped for a second, the adrenaline choking his throat. He saw blood; he saw a flash of blades. And it was four against one. He started sprinting toward them, shouting for them to stop.

He grabbed one of the women and tossed her away to the ground. For a moment he thought he recognized the one lying on her back on the ground—the one fighting off the other four. But no. The hair was different. Then he realized. *The hair.* "Oh, no," he muttered. "God, no."

The adrenaline boiled. He pulled one of the other women off her, slapping her across the face so hard it knocked her over. He stared for a second at the woman on the ground, the one with blood and dirt splattered all over the side of her face, her hair cut almost to the scalp over most of its area, long only at the back. "Ingrid?" he said, his voice feeble.

But she was too busy dealing with the two women who were holding her down. Now not caring, Olav pulled one of the two remaining women off by her hair, and she shrieked in pain as she fell back. That left only one woman attacking Ingrid.

Olav spotted the glint of a blade approaching his head from the side. He grabbed the offending arm and twisted it, making the scissors fall. A fist hit him on the nose. It might have been a small fist, but it carried the strength of anger and hatred. It hurt. He grabbed the woman by the throat and stood up so her heels floated off the ground. While she pulled and scratched at his arm, he drew his other hand back, tightening it into a fist. Only now did he recognize her. This was Laila, her face reminding him of a snarling lynx cat he'd once come across while out hunting. Except that the lynx had been frightened. Laila wasn't.

He pulled the punch just in time. This was not only a woman, but a woman half his weight. It wouldn't have endeared him to the police. He threw her toward her house, where she stumbled and fell onto her side. She bounced right back up again and didn't run away.

"The war is over, Laila," he shouted at her. "The Resistance is over. We don't owe each other any favors."

Still, she didn't run away. Instead, she took a deep breath and shouted, "That woman's a Nazi whore. She's not welcome in this street, in this city, in this *country*!" She spat toward Ingrid, falling some way short.

"This isn't the sort of free Norway I was fighting for, Laila. Just leave her alone, or next time I won't hold back."

By now, a man—a husband by the look of it—had helped one of the other women to her feet.

"You saw this!" Olav shouted at him. "Why didn't you stop them?"

"It's like Laila said," he replied. "She's a collaborator, a traitor."

"But this?" He pointed at Ingrid as he rushed over to the man, who was the same height as Olav but had the build of an office worker, and grabbed him by the back of the neck. "*Look at her!*" he shouted, pointing the man's face at Ingrid. "You should be ashamed of yourself."

"No," he replied. "*You* should be ashamed of *her*."

Olav shoved the man and gave him a kick to help him on his way, then took another step toward him, which made him run. Olav turned back and knelt down in the mass of dirt, blood, and hair that had once been blonde but was now dark red. He helped Ingrid's battered form get up and cursed. "My *God*, what have they done to you?"

Ingrid stirred but was silent, holding her nose in pain. She got to her feet but limped, one hand shooting to her hip. So, Olav carried her inside, where her mamma gasped at the sight of her daughter—battered, bloody, almost bald.

"And where were you when this was happening?" Olav said to her.

"Well, I heard something . . . something going on outside, but . . ."

"Get some water."

"But . . . I never thought for a moment—"

"I said, *get some water!* And a clean cloth while you're at it."

Twenty minutes later Ingrid's mamma had washed the blood from her face and was assessing the work of the neighbors while Olav paced the room like a man getting used to a new pair of hands.

"Well?" he shouted at Ingrid's mamma, his fists clenching and unclenching.

"A nasty cut and bruise on the temple, a badly bruised hip, a few cuts on the scalp, and . . ."

"And what?" Ingrid said.

"I think your nose is broken."

Olav cursed and set off again, pacing back and forth.

"It just feels big and sore," Ingrid said.

"It will for a while, but not forever. And you'll have to wear a woolen hat until your hair grows back. I'll trim off the few long bits; they look odd."

"Never mind that," Olav said. "Ingrid, what did you do?"

"Do?"

"Did you provoke them?"

"Only by being a whore of the Nazis."

"Ingrid!" her mamma said.

"Well, what do you think I did? Yes, like I already told you, I went back to the Lebensborn clinic, and yes, the police came earlier today. Perhaps the neighbors found that out. But I was coming back from the bakery, and they started calling me names, so I ignored them; then they started spitting at me, so I ignored them. And then they set upon me. Ignoring that was impossible."

"It's terrible," her mamma said. "Just terrible."

"I know, Mamma. But I also know what I have to do now. They've made my mind up for me."

"What are you talking about?" her mamma asked.

Ingrid's face fell, her eyes glistened, and tears ran over her bare cuts. "I'm not going to let them win," she said.

Olav wandered over. "What do you mean?"

She was crying, but her voice was strong. "I know how you feel, Olav, but I can't live like this." She threw a hand toward the door. "If those people out there can't forget my baby, then I swear to God I won't either."

Olav looked her up and down, screwing his face up in disgust. "Oh, no, Ingrid. Not that again. Not him. No, no, no."

"I'm not arguing with you again, Olav. I was so confused when I was in that clinic, thinking of you, trying to please the authorities, worried about what Mamma would think of me, hating Franz but knowing I was carrying a part of him, worried about the neighbors finding out, knowing little Ulrich needed his mamma. All of that made me feel like a horse being pulled in ten different directions. I thought it would stop once I gave up Ulrich, but it hasn't. So, I'm not arguing with you again, just as I'm not giving in to those horrible people outside. I'm going to get my baby back. I'll cry about myself, about my own pain, but I won't cry about him for another second. I've seen him for myself, alone in that place, that second-rate orphanage. I know he isn't being cared for. He's cold, he's lonely, he's not being cared for, and I'll go to hell rather than let him spend the rest of his life rotting there."

"I'm not having this, Ingrid."

"You don't have a choice, Olav. Ulrich is my baby."

"But . . . you can't do this."

"We'll see."

"You think they'll give him up?"

"I don't care what they do. I'm going to get him even if I have to drag him away with my own bare hands."

"You'll steal him?"

She nodded. "Oh, yes."

"But look at you. You can hardly walk."

"I'll walk, Olav. For my baby, I'll walk. I've suffered enough. Damn the neighbors. Damn the authorities. And if you're not on my side, damn you too."

Olav turned to her mamma. "Can you talk some sense into her?"

She shrugged. "She's my daughter, Olav. I know it's hard for you to see, but *she was once my baby*, so I understand what she's saying."

Olav grunted out a meaningless cry of frustration. He turned and rubbed his palms up and down his face. "This is madness," he said. "You're both mad." He paused, let out a long sigh as if it were his last on earth, and shook his head. "I can't stay here," he said. "I'm going for another walk."

It was two hours before Olav returned, exhausted and confused. There were no greetings, and very little talk echoed in the household until late the following day, when Ingrid insisted they all discuss the matter.

I find myself lost in the early hours of the morning. It's been one of those nights when I repeatedly touch sleep with my fingertips but never quite manage to grasp it. So, in my half sleep, to the sounds of the occasional footstep in the corridor outside, my only company is a vision. It's a toxic relationship.

This time it's almost 1940, and the plan our rulers have worked so hard on is now bearing fruit. We are being revered throughout the world as a force to be reckoned with. We are helping our neighbors in Austria, the Sudetenland, and, most recently, Poland, so they, too, can benefit from the changes to society our government is making. One great decade of progress is closing. Another glorious one awaits the might of a new and invigorated Germany.

At home there have been many changes. The rate of progress is truly encouraging. The new laws that were introduced to help Gentiles—for a long time subjugated by Jews—take a greater part in the running of businesses, and the professions are bearing fruit; more Gentiles are now in positions of power and responsibility. There are programs to eradicate human weaknesses—physical and mental—and programs to encourage the production of children with physical characteristics more in keeping with this new progressive society.

We are being encouraged to honor the architects of these great social programs. We are told that people at the vanguard of social progress will be venerated in years to come, that their legacies of the improvement of the human race will live forever in the minds of future generations.

Now, after many years of being downtrodden and controlled from abroad, we feel at peace and comfortable with our nation. We are always being told by the state—the fatherland—that they will take care of all our needs. All we have to do is trust them and do as the laws of our country instruct us to do.

At first, some of those laws felt unfair to me, but it seemed unfriendly to upset people by expressing my views, and now I realize that the needs of society are more important than my own wishes, so I banish such outdated thoughts from my mind. There was a time when many other members of society expressed the same concerns, but they have been silenced. That's for the best, because nothing should be allowed to stand in the way of progress.

Our rulers have done so much for the benefit of our country that I know I have to keep my faith in them and must do my very best to ensure everyone else also complies with our new order.

Chapter 26

Arnold and Merlene arranged a second meal out, neither of them bringing up the topic of whether it constituted a "date."

On that evening, Arnold opened up about his marriage breakdown, Merlene expanded on what she referred to as her "quite frankly embarrassing" internet dating experiences, but over dessert Arnold only thought it fair to bring up the subject of Oslo again, if only to give her another opportunity to decline the offer.

"About this Oslo trip," he said.

But before he could even phrase the question, she hit him with, "Hey, I'm still on for that."

"Are you sure?" he replied. "I honestly wouldn't be offended if you decided . . . I mean, if you've changed your mind and—"

She held up a hand to silence him. "A little advice, Arnold," she said in velvet tones that took his mind away from the firmness of the words. "Please don't take this the wrong way, but have some confidence, both in yourself and in me. If I didn't want to go—trust me—I'd tell you."

With that, she returned her attention to her berry pie and ice cream, and Arnold felt just a little browbeaten despite the gentle delivery. It was probably the nurse in her coming out, but it didn't seem wise to say as such. He resorted to a simple, "Well, thank you."

"Not a problem," she said. "You can't be expected to go all that way without someone to hold your hand now, can you?"

Arnold saw something approaching a wink from those expressive eyes as she said the words, then noticed her shoulders quiver just for a second as she quietly giggled.

"If I could possibly be serious for a moment . . . ," he said.

"We're on a night out, but if you really must."

Arnold let out a groan. "Well, I'm pleased you're coming to Oslo with me, and if it works out . . . I mean, if you enjoy it, then perhaps we could, like . . ."

"I think we're singing from the same hymn sheet, Arnold. Oslo will be very different to my usual choices, but let's agree it's a kind of trial vacation. Let's see how it goes, yeah?"

"Sure," Arnold said. "That's what I was going to say."

"Well, that's cool. Tell me, have you, uh, done much traveling in your life?"

Arnold thought for a moment, trying to remember. The good times had been some way back. "I have to admit, not in recent years, what with looking after Mom and all that, but there are a hundred and one places I'd like to go to."

"Me too." Merlene picked up her glass, just a little wine left in the bottom. "Arnold, I know I want to take this thing one step at a time, but let's raise a glass to our hopes and dreams, yeah?"

"Sounds good to me." He touched her glass with his, and they both took a sip while focusing on each other.

As they waited outside for a taxi at the end of the evening, there was a physical closeness between them there hadn't been on the first night. He leaned toward her, she didn't resist, and there was an awkward kiss—the first kiss of that sort to hit Arnold's lips in many years.

"You want to come over to my apartment next Saturday?" Merlene said.

Arnold looked for signs that it was a joke, but this time she was impassive. Nevertheless, for a few seconds he was stuck for a reply, unsure exactly what she was proposing. "You mean, like, to, uh . . ."

"I mean whatever. I'll cook something up for us. We can chill out. Watch a movie. No pressure."

"No . . . pressure, eh?"

"Course not. Let's just wait and see how it works out between us."

"Good." Arnold nodded slowly. "Think I, uh . . ." He let out a laugh. "Think I might have forgotten what to do after all these years."

She kissed him on the lips again. "Well, I'm a nurse. I'm not allowed to forget."

Arnold's mother had been right. Often in life there was a surprise just around the corner, lurking in the darkness, waiting for the most inopportune moment to strike. He'd been so preoccupied—first by his mother, then his mother's funeral, then the letter from Sweden, not forgetting his doubts about his father—that his feelings had crept up on him. He'd liked Merlene from the first time he'd met her at his mother's place—yes, even in that nurse's uniform. Also she was clearly a caring person. And then he found out that he got on well with her. He hadn't thought much of that at the time; it didn't seem appropriate in that atmosphere to even consider the vaguest notion of it. She just became Merlene. She was *simply there*. But now, after that meal, she was quite a bit more than *simply there*.

By the time they boarded the flight to Oslo three weeks later, they considered themselves an item, and Arnold couldn't have been happier. In fact, only his daughters were happier, which surprised him not one bit. And the more consideration he gave to the trip, the more he looked forward to it. He'd never been back to Oslo and had never particularly wanted to because there'd seemed little point. His mother had always assured him that they had no relatives there. But he and Merlene talked over his concerns some more, and he became even more certain that at his time of life, he needed to confront whatever this thing was. If he found a long-lost half brother, then it would enrich his life; if he found out the person in question had met some tragic or even grisly end, then Merlene would be on hand to help him out, to put the issue in perspective.

They'd arranged to meet Marit there, but the timings weren't perfect. They would have a few days in Oslo on their own before she arrived with some paperwork that she said he might be interested in. The plan was to mix a little sightseeing with some visits to where Arnold's parents grew up. He had two clues as to where this was. One was the little photo of him as a baby with both parents outside their home. It was probably the only photo taken of him in Oslo. The other clue was the place his mother had mentioned just before she died: Ostergaten. They'd checked it out on an internet map. It existed, and although it was hard to judge whether that was the place in the photo, it looked quite possible.

The airport felt much like any other he'd been to—perhaps a little more modern with clean lines to the architecture. The next thing that hit him was relief that many of the signs were in English.

"You feeling okay?" Merlene asked as they waited for a taxi.

He shrugged, peering beyond the covered roadway to the slit of light ahead. "Could be just about anywhere so far."

It was only as the taxi began the half-hour journey to the city itself that Arnold started getting a feel for Oslo. Very soon the spaghetti of roads encircling the airport gave way to the dull freeway, and to the left and right bright sunshine illuminated verdant fields and snowy hills alike, as though bringing life to both.

"I can see why people left here for Canada," Merlene said.

Arnold nodded. "Doesn't look too different so far, does it?"

It was only when the taxi dropped them off in Oslo's city center that Arnold's mind turned back to the past. He walked off in a short circle, wheeling his suitcase behind him, assessing every street corner, every store and building, peering down every road.

Merlene wasn't far behind every step of the way, the rumble of her suitcase wheels starting and stopping a second after his. "You're starting to feel strange now, yeah?" she said after a minute or so of trailing him.

"Does it show?" he said without looking at her.

"Well, you certainly *look* strange."

He looked down at his feet, watching them with each step. "It's odd," he said, lifting his head to gaze into the distance. "On the one hand it could be any city, and I know nothing of it even though I was born here. On the other hand, my mom and dad grew up here, so they could easily have stood where I'm standing, walked these steps, seen all the sights I can see right now."

He took a breath, but as he glanced at Merlene, he noticed her shoulders pulled in tight to her neck, her hands firmly in her pockets, her jaw clenched. "You cold?" he said.

"Freezing."

"Oh, God. I'm sorry. I was preoccupied."

"You're entitled."

"You want to go to the hotel?"

"Yes," she said, showing him a stiff smile.

"Sure. Let's get settled, get a coffee. Then we can talk about exactly what to do."

As it turned out, the flight left them both exhausted and jet lagged. Even though it was early afternoon, and despite the mix of excitement and apprehension swirling around in Arnold's mind, neither of them felt like doing anything other than going to bed. Their first full day in Oslo was better, but not by much. They were also still cold, so they decided that the visit to Ostergaten could wait one more day and did little but eat, rest, and buy a warmer coat each.

But Merlene had decided. The next day there would be no excuses about tiredness or jet lag. They would be visiting Ostergaten.

Ostergaten turned out to be a huge disappointment.

On the approach to the street, the taxi passed Lyngstad Park, and Olav's eyes were drawn to the tidiness, the neat lines, and the colorful borders. By contrast, just a stone's throw beyond, Ostergaten itself looked to be the very opposite. Whatever it had been in the past, now it was nothing but a construction site, the sharp lines of new apartment blocks breaking out of mess and mud, the noises of backhoes, bulldozers, and shouted instructions trying to find their way through air that was heavy with concrete dust.

They got the taxi to drop them at the entrance to the site, next to the many signs and hazard warnings. Merlene gave Arnold a pained smile. "Looks like we're too late," she said. "I reckon the house has been demolished."

"Only recently, I'm guessing," he replied, walking through the gates and onto the construction site. Merlene looked left and right at high-rise buildings stretching six floors up with more to go.

"Is this wise?" Merlene said, following him, starting to raise her voice above the noise of trucks and diggers.

Before Arnold could answer, a woman in a hard hat, heavy boots, and a fluorescent jacket started marching toward them, talking in stern Norwegian. They didn't understand the words, but the meaning was clear from the tone and the gesticulations.

"Do you speak English at all?" Arnold said, standing his ground.

She effortlessly switched tongues. "You must leave. Now. It's dangerous."

"We will," Arnold said. "But we're trying to trace someone who used to live here."

"Away," the woman said, ushering them back through the gates. They did as they were told, and once all three of them were outside the gates, she said, "What do you want to know?"

"I think my parents were brought up in one of these houses." He showed her the photo. "We're looking for anyone who lived here in the 1940s."

The woman checked the photo and very quickly nodded. "That was one of these. Yes. I remember it. It changed over the years, but not too much. We demolished it earlier this year."

"I don't suppose you know who lived there."

"Nobody lived there, not in this one. All but one of those houses were empty and run down for years. Derelict? Is that the word? Anyway, only one was occupied—one stubborn old woman holding the development up for years."

"Do you know her name?" Merlene asked.

"Are you cops?"

"No," Arnold said. "But I'd really like to speak with her." He held the photo up again, pointing at the bundle between the figures. "That baby's me. I was born in that house. I'm just trying to trace my history, to find anyone who had any memories of me or my parents."

The construction woman shrugged. "I just control the site, nothing more."

"But what about the old woman you mentioned?" Merlene said. "The one who held up development. Do you know her name?"

"Everyone around here knows her name," she replied. "Mrs. Karlsen. Lives in a home now. The Aurora, to the east of the city." Then she turned as someone called her name. "I have to go now. Work to do. Good luck."

"Thank you," Arnold shouted after her as she trudged off.

Chapter 27

Oslo, May 1945

Olav had been walking for at least forty minutes and was now eyeing up the former Lebensborn clinic in the darkness. A nearby clock struck three times, startling him, making him run for cover behind an outbuilding.

When the bells stopped, he poked his head out of his cave-black shelter, somehow thinking—a part of him even *wishing*—that someone would appear and force him to abandon his plan. But no. The place was still deserted. He approached the clinic once more, assessing it.

Streetlights illuminated the frontage of the hideously ordinary-looking building, and a half moon threw a dim light upon the right side of it, so he had to head for the left side. He dipped his chin below the turnup lapels of his jacket and pulled his cap lower. Both of these were dark brown. Good. The cap was too large for him, so he seldom wore it. Perfect for today.

He glanced left, right, and behind him, then briskly walked up the grassy bank and to the left of the building, relaxing only when he knew his form was hidden in the darkness.

He sat on the concrete path, his back leaning against the wall of the building, his legs half-bent in front of him. A hint of sweat on his brow brought the cold of the still air onto him, and he wondered how long it would be before the cold reached his bones. There was a flutter from high above. It couldn't have been a bird, not in this darkness. He twisted his head to look up and high above him saw a flag, stretching out as though to catch the moonlight. It was the Norwegian flag. Another fluttering sound from it took Olav's thoughts back to the last time he'd been here, when the form fluttering had been not the blue cross of his homeland but that daggered SS design.

Olav remembered the day the flags had been swapped—when he thought that symbolic act would signal the end of the madness. But no. *This* was madness, and any sane person could see it.

He shook his head, wondering how he'd been dragged into such a stupid game.

He remembered visiting Ingrid at this clinic, her giving birth here, and him visiting her and that *thing*. Well, okay, that baby boy. He remembered finally bringing Ingrid home and hoping to God he'd seen the last of this place. It wasn't to be.

Ingrid had been upset for weeks afterward. He'd dismissed her feelings and told her the thing was the offspring of an SS officer and bound for Germany, that there was no way she would even see it again, let alone keep it. And she'd accepted that, so he thought. But no; she'd persevered like a wolf hunting prey, eventually discovering that it was still in this city.

A light behind him came on, the throw just catching his boots. He pulled his legs back to his body and kept still. He would have to wait here until that light went out, for sure, and for some time afterward to be on the safe side.

And that would give him even more time to torture himself about the ridiculous act he was committing. If he got caught, would he receive a prison sentence? He tried to shake the thought from his head. But it was hard. He'd dug a hole—no, *Ingrid* had dug it for him. All he'd done was climb inside it. He had time to remember the conversation. He had plenty of time.

After the day Ingrid had been attacked, they'd talked further and both had fought hard for their positions. Olav had hoped he could sway Ingrid but very soon realized she still hadn't come to her senses. No. And so they had the same argument again.

"It's theft."

"No, he belongs to me."

"Not in the eyes of the law."

"Then the law is an idiot. He's my baby."

"It's still illegal."

"And I still don't care what you say."

"But . . . if we get him—and I still think we shouldn't—what about taking care of him? Do we hide him from the authorities? Or from the neighbors? Where would he sleep? And what do we—"

"Olav! I don't care about the details. We can sort out where he sleeps and who knows about him later."

Regardless of anything he said, she insisted—painful hip and bashed-up face and all—that she was going to fetch him.

That was when he made the offer. He did that because he knew her well enough to be sure she would go through with her threat or get into trouble trying, and he couldn't bear the thought of her doing . . . well, her doing the mad thing he was now working out exactly how to accomplish.

He told her she was sure to be caught if she went, so he made her a deal: that he would go instead of her, but on one condition. He gave her his word that he would try his best to bring the baby home on the understanding that if he got caught trying, then that would be the end of the matter, and they would both forget about him. At first Ingrid gave a blank refusal; she wouldn't let him risk his liberty for a baby that wasn't his. But he told her again that it would be ridiculous for her to try, that she didn't stand a chance of even *reaching* the baby, let alone stealing it.

Ingrid, now giving the idea some thought, asked her mamma.

"You need to remember," she answered, "that getting the baby— whether you or Olav do that—might turn out to be the easy part. You might have to hide him. You'll certainly need to look after him. One more mouth to feed. Clothes, nappies, another bed. And will Olav really help bring up another man's baby?"

Olav told them both he certainly would if it made Ingrid happy.

"Oh, Olav," Ingrid's mamma replied. "Please don't be offended, but it's easy to say that now, and I'm sure you mean it, but in one, two, even *ten* years' time? How sure are you that you can be a good father to a baby you've never shown a moment's concern for?"

He said nothing to that, uncertain whether she might just be right.

Ingrid's mamma looked at him, taking her time to assess his character. She spoke as if addressing Ingrid too. "Some things are hard, and some things are impossible," she said. "And some things sound impossible but just need a little faith."

Then Ingrid gave him that same look, reading his face, waiting for his pronouncement.

He shook his head in despair. "We can work out the practicalities later. All I know is that Ingrid is my wife, and if she has faith in me . . ."

Ingrid's mamma looked into his eyes, considering the matter. "You know," she said, judgment complete, "I think you can do it, Olav. I really think so."

"Then, yes," Ingrid said. "The answer is *yes*. And I'll never forget what you're doing for me. You know that; don't you, Olav?"

"One thing I do know is that this is still madness." He leaned down and kissed her on the lips, holding her tightly. He tried to let go, but she held on, letting go only when her mamma spoke.

"You were a good man in desperate times, Olav, and you're still a good man. We can only hope that if anything happens, if you get caught—"

"I won't get caught. Not tonight, at least. If I'm spotted, I'll run, and all of this will be over for good. As I've told Ingrid, that's my only condition."

But now, as the light from the clinic window behind Olav was switched off, leaving the scene in front of him dark, he had to wait at least a few more minutes. And the tranquility of the early-morning hours gave him yet more time—time to reflect on the way people deceive themselves. On the journey to the clinic he'd had time to consider Ingrid's mamma's words. Would he really be able to bring that baby up as his own? To teach the thing to eat, to walk, to play, and eventually to be a man? And even that was assuming this ridiculous and ill-thought-out plan would work. He'd lied when he assured Ingrid he would be able to get the baby—when he talked about trying his best. And Ingrid's mamma had been naive in her judgment of him. There was no blood link, and so there was no fathering instinct and never would be. Would he be able to think of this Ulrich person as his son in ten years' time? It was unlikely; that was a long time to commit to. And that was why he'd decided. Yes, he would try to get the baby but perhaps not try his best; if there was even a hint of trouble, he would return empty handed and say he'd tried his best and failed.

And perhaps Olav wasn't the only one lying. Ingrid had agreed that if this didn't work, she would forget about the baby forever. Did she really mean that? She'd promised similar things before and gone back on her word.

But despite all that, there still remained the prospect of Ingrid being unhappy for the rest of her life. He tried telling himself that she would eventually overcome her loss—perhaps in another six months, perhaps in a few years. Yes, he tried telling himself that but deep down remained unconvinced. The thoughts swirled around his head. Eventually he admitted that there was only one way to find out who was lying, who was telling the truth, and who would be happy.

The light from the window behind him had now been off for long enough. It was time to act. He slowly got to his feet, keeping his head low—only high enough to look through the bottom of the window, ready to drop down at a moment's notice. All was quiet, so he peered inside. He saw the darkened outlines of beds and also larger outlines on top of the beds; these were women, not babies.

He dipped his head, crept along some more, and looked through the next window, then the next, until he came across one with a small office of some sort on the other side. He pulled the steel bar from his jacket pocket and started working its sharpened edge into the frame near the hinges. The wood, rotten from disrepair, gave way with little trouble, and so he eased the whole frame out and laid it against the wall. He waited, primed to run, in case anyone had heard the noise and decided to investigate.

Nothing.

A few seconds later he was inside, at one end of a slightly musty-smelling office. At the other end he saw a door, slightly ajar. He approached it silently and peered around to see a wide corridor, austere but for one or two filing cabinets butted up against the side. He entered it and pulled the door behind him just enough to hide the broken window.

A few rooms on one side of the corridor shed a little moonlight through their windows, lighting up rectangles along the side of the corridor. He crept along, checking each room for movement, searching for one in particular. At one point he heard noises and spotted a door right at the end rattling. He darted behind one of the filing cabinets, crouching low as the door opened and closed. Voices, footsteps, another door opening and closing. Then silence. Olav breathed again.

He knew which room to seek out—the nurse had told Ingrid it was ward eleven—and soon Olav found it. He peered through the glass of the door. A few babies stirred, but he could see no adults, asleep or awake. He went in, easing the handle down and holding it there until he grabbed the opposite handle, holding it down while he shut the door, then slowly allowing it to spring back up.

He crouched on the floor and breathed silently.

He was in a ward of government property babies. What the hell was he doing here? Madness? This was beyond *madness.*

Thoughts of what might happen to him if he were caught ran through his mind. *A fight? A chase through the streets back to Ostergaten?* And then thoughts of his agreement with Ingrid followed. His condition had been made clear—at least, in his eyes. If he got caught or was in immediate danger of being caught, he would leave without the baby, and he and Ingrid would live the rest of their lives as if it had never existed. The thoughts melted into one messy headache. He *could* just go. Open the door, go down the corridor into the office, climb back out the window, walk home. And the walk home would give him time enough to concoct a story of how he'd nearly been caught, how there was a nurse permanently on the ward, how it was a hopeless exercise and always would be.

And he would never hear a word about that damn baby again.

He stilled himself and was now aware of two things. For one thing, he was cold. That could have been his sweat. But no; even the corridor was warmer than here. The other thing he couldn't ignore was the stench. It was like a sewer. He glanced around in the half light, looking for a washroom of some sort. There was none. For one thing, there was no room; the cribs had only enough space between them for one person to walk and no more. And there were perhaps thirty or so cribs in the room, fifteen each side. Washroom or not, the smell was repulsive. He got to his feet and trod silently between the two rows. There were notes on clipboards attached to them. He struck a match, and by its light checked the notes of a few. No, no Ulrich yet. But at least the smell of matches masked that disgusting stench.

But now it was stronger. He looked more closely at one or two babies and then the others. Each was naked but for a single thin blanket. It wasn't fully clear in the darkness, but the mattresses had an unusual patterning. He tentatively reached a hand out to feel a mattress. It felt wet. He lifted his hand to his nose, but didn't need to lift it far. He grimaced at the smell. And the patterning. The mattress was soaked in urine, smeared with excrement. Then he realized that the baby was too. He cursed under his breath. He checked another crib. The same. He looked along the rows. They all told the same story, although some worse than others.

Now, more than ever, Olav wondered what the hell he was doing here. It was disgusting. But no matter. He shook those thoughts from his head, because the conditions were no fault of his, and lit another match.

And there it was. The last bed. In a corner. In a corner, just like Olav.

Given name: Ulrich Becker

Lebensborn mother: Ingrid Jacobsen

Olav moved the match forward, and by its dying light his eyes fell upon the creature that was the cause of so much trouble. And now was the moment of truth. Was he going to take the thing back to Ingrid?

He had time to see the blond hair, now long enough to be matted and messy, and the mouth, caked in food or vomit—it wasn't clear which. Then the match fizzled out.

He took a long, deep breath and crept over to the windows. A moment to work it out. The only opening window was opposite the door. And it was a sliding window. No trouble. The clips clicked loudly, and Olav froze to wait for a reaction. Nothing. He lifted the window by the handle, pulling it up a fraction at a time, until there was room for him to step out.

A creep back to the far corner. A hand under little Ulrich's body. A shiver when he felt how cold the little thing's flesh was. Never mind. How should he hold a baby? He had no idea. But he lifted it with one hand, and the thing's head lolled back, saved only by his other hand supporting it. But it was enough to awaken it.

The screams made Olav curse aloud. Soon there were more screams from the other babies. The damn things were like a chain reaction.

And that was when Olav made his mind up. This was ridiculous. He would go back and say he'd failed, that he'd tried and failed and that as far as they were concerned, the baby never existed. He eyed the open window and went to put the screaming thing back down.

That was it.

Finished.

Except that the baby clung on to his jacket, to his shirt, to his fingers. The screaming, stinking creature wouldn't let him go. The more he pushed the baby away, the more it held on, and the more it screamed.

Footsteps. Voices from the corridor.

Olav looked over to the open window again. The open window opposite the door. That was when he saw the doorknob move.

He mouthed a curse and looked around. There was only one place. He dropped and slid his body under Ulrich's crib, only realizing then that Ulrich was still with him. And still crying. And he was still a mess. And now Olav's coat and shirt were covered in filth. Olav put a hand over Ulrich's mouth and felt crustiness around it.

"Shut up! Shut up!" came a jaundiced voice from the other side of the room.

There was another voice: "The window's open. Who left the window open?"

Olav, curled up under the crib with his head against the floor, had a good vantage point. Two men. Two pairs of shoes.

"You shut the window. I'll check the rats."

The sound of the window being slammed shut.

"What's the matter with them?"

"I don't know. They can scream as much as they like as long as I don't have to hear it. Let's get back to the card game."

"What about the far one?"

"What?"

"The crib in the far corner. It's empty."

"That's odd. Let me check."

And still little Ulrich screamed. Olav held him closer so the head and the chubby little arms pressed against his chest. His screaming settled just a little. But not enough.

More footsteps coming toward him. Ulrich still crying. No escape. Olav shuffled back as far as he could, pressing his shoulder to the back wall, trying to make his shape as small as possible. But still Ulrich cried. He could simply slide the baby out for the men to find and put back into the crib. But the baby still wouldn't let go of his jacket.

"You're right," came the voice above. "There's one missing."

It was then that Olav dipped his little finger into the baby's mouth, and the crying stopped. He whimpered for a few seconds as he accustomed himself to chewing the tip of Olav's little finger, but after that there was no sound from him, and his eyelids fell shut. Olav felt gums softly gnawing his flesh, squeezing his fingernail. The little man was a mess; he'd made Olav filthy, and Olav's eardrums had only just stopped hurting. But then again . . .

"I can't see it."

"How about under the crib?"

"What?"

"Perhaps it's fallen onto the floor, rolled underneath."

"Well . . . perhaps. But I can't be bothered. Little Nazi rat."

A laugh. "And I can't stand the stink. It's like a pigsty in here."

"We can check it in the morning. Let's go. I have a card game to win."

"Ha! We'll see about that."

Footsteps, more hurried this time. The door closing. Olav let out a sigh of relief. Perhaps he should stay where he was until the other babies settled down, until the two members of the staff had restarted their card game. Little Ulrich still suckled his finger, occasionally letting out a strange purring growl. Olav stroked his dank hair away from his face and simply watched for a few minutes.

When the ward had fallen silent again, Olav shuffled himself out from underneath the crib and sat on a window ledge, wrenching Ulrich from his little finger and sitting him on his knee. "Well, well, little fellow," he whispered. "What should I do with you?"

Ulrich smiled. Olav smiled back. Ulrich's smile quickly turned into a wide and innocent grin, and his eyes seemed to sparkle in what little light there was. Olav looked behind him to the bare, cold crib. He smelled the stale ammonia. Then he looked once more at Ulrich's smile.

"Perhaps we . . . uh . . . we should get you to your mamma." He unbuttoned his jacket and clasped the naked little boy to his shirt, folding the jacket over and buttoning it up again so Ulrich's face was still visible between the lapels. He stood, slowly and carefully, still supporting baby Ulrich with one arm. He eyed the window—the window he would need two hands to open.

Ulrich gurgled from beneath the folds of his jacket.

"Mmm . . . ," Olav muttered. "I could always get out the same way I came in."

Two minutes later Olav was on his way home, one hand swinging by his side as he walked, the other keeping his stolen goods safe.

Chapter 28

The moment Ingrid saw Olav standing in the doorway in the early hours of that morning, little Ulrich buttoned up inside his coat, she knew the image would stay in her mind for a long time—would probably be etched there forever like a first kiss from a first love or even the final goodbye of a pappa lost out to sea.

Ingrid and her mamma, initially shocked to tears at the baby's condition, got on with the job of bathing him and feeding him. Olav simply went to bed. Ingrid managed to ask him if he was hungry before he disappeared into the bedroom, but he shook his head. She thought that unusual but said nothing, just busied herself putting her baby to bed; she'd kept an old wooden fruit crate used at the gardens and given it a thorough clean, and when lined with newspapers and a blanket, it was just about big enough.

After those initial moments of shock, Ingrid had hardly stopped smiling—her mamma, too, as if none of the troubles had ever happened. She knew, of course, that that wasn't the case, that a strident rap on the door might come at any time of the day or night, so on that first night she and her mamma between them managed to shove the table against the door, barricading it against unwanted guests.

She went to bed, careful not to disturb Olav but also aware he was still awake. She told him she loved him, kissed him good night, but he said nothing. She slept soundly with her arm clasped around his chest, her baby by her bedside.

The next day called for more measured action in case the authorities came, so Olav went out to buy locks and spent the day fitting them to the doors and windows. It was a necessary measure—they all knew that—but unfortunately whenever hammering was required, the noise would wake little Ulrich, and once or twice he bawled his lungs out, requiring the combined efforts of Ingrid and her mamma to calm him down.

But eventually the hammering stopped, so Olav tidied his tools and sat by the fireside, soon to be joined by Ingrid.

"It looks a good job," she said. "As secure as a bank." She forced a laugh, but all Olav did was glance at her and return his gaze to the small fire burning in front of them.

"It is secure, isn't it?" she asked.

Olav nodded. "Should be."

"Did, uh, did everything go well?"

Olav nodded again.

"I was worried someone might have heard Ulrich crying."

Olav's face twitched at the suggestion.

"What is it?" Ingrid said, leaning toward him. "What happened? Did someone hear?"

"It's possible," he said. "When I went outside to check things, I could hear him."

"Oh, I see."

"It's nothing to worry about."

"I'm sure." She turned her head briefly to the doors and windows. "Your handiwork has seen to that."

They waited, usually with one eye on the door, but there were no unwelcome visitors, no shouts from outside, no aggressive thumps on the door. That was a relief to Ingrid. But still, there had been very few words from Olav. That puzzled Ingrid, but he didn't appear angry, so she decided to let it pass. He would tell her in his own time what was wrong.

That afternoon, Olav dug up the last of the potatoes and carrots from the park gardens, and they all ate them with a little fried fish. Ingrid asked Olav what he thought of the meal. He merely nodded and said it was nice. Afterward, Ingrid and her mamma gave little Ulrich another feed, with Olav watching silently from the sidelines as though it were a circus act. Afterward, Olav said he was going out for a walk.

"Where to?" Ingrid asked.

He just shrugged. "Anywhere."

"Well, we need the bath over by the fireside before you go," she replied.

Without a word, he brought the tin bath, a little lukewarm water in the bottom, from the sink to the fireside, and stood by while they dropped Ulrich into the water, bit by bit, lifting and dropping, teasing him until the looks of fright on his face turned to giggles of delight.

"It's hard to believe," Ingrid's mamma said as she ran a soapy cloth over the boy's chest and belly, "that some people in power—even religious people—are calling for little boys like him to be sterilized."

"Sterilized?" Olav said quietly from behind her. "What does that mean?"

She frowned at him, then briefly lifted Ulrich from the water to display his full naked form. "What do you think it means?" she said.

"Dear God," Olav hissed, and he hurried out of the house without another word.

Olav was gone a long time—long enough for Ingrid and her mamma to feed Ulrich, do a little darning, clean the kitchen, restock the fire with logs, and feed Ulrich once more before putting him to bed. When Olav finally did return, he said he was tired and needed to sleep.

Ingrid asked him whether he wanted to eat, saying that she still had some bread and butter. He just shook his head and went to the bedroom.

Ingrid gave her mamma a worried look.

"Don't worry about him," she said. "He's probably still exhausted after what he's done, and he needs to come to terms with no longer being the most important man in the house."

Ingrid didn't believe that and didn't think her mamma did either.

The next morning Olav was still distant and quiet. He watched Ulrich giggle and gurgle as Ingrid and her mamma ran tickle fingers over his paunchy belly, then said he needed a walk.

"Are you going to the gardens?" Ingrid asked.

He shrugged. "I'm . . . I'm not sure."

"Did you hear the news about them?" she said.

He nodded. "They're going to clear the vegetable plots away and turn the place back to a park."

"Very soon," she said. "I think we should go there and look."

"Why?"

"You know, for old times' sake."

"Just you and me?" He glanced at her mamma. "What about Ulrich?"

"He'll be fine with me," Ingrid's mamma said.

Olav nodded. "Well, all right. Just be sure you lock the doors and the windows."

"I will."

"Right." He went over to fetch his boots, which were drying by the fire.

While he sat down and put them on, Ingrid's mamma leaned in to her and whispered, "By God, he made you work hard for that."

"I'm not sure what to do," Ingrid replied. "I mean, is he feeling left out? He's always made it clear how he feels about Ulrich."

Her mamma frowned. "Mmm . . . who knows? Men can be very strange creatures."

"What's all the whispering about?" Olav said from the other side of the room.

"Never mind," Ingrid's mamma replied. "Are you ready yet?"

"Of course." He stood.

"Now you two go. Take as long as you need."

A few minutes later they were walking to the park gardens.

"It's a special place," Ingrid said as they turned the corner at the end of the road. "In a way it's a shame they're turning it back into Lyngstad Park."

"You really think so? It's funny. I was thinking that too."

"So, we agree on that." She laughed.

He didn't, simply replying, "We've certainly had many memorable times here."

"It's where you proposed to me."

Olav said nothing to that, but his face reddened with embarrassment.

"The bench. Don't you remember?"

He just nodded and said nothing else, leaving Ingrid to mention the weeds and wildflowers that had already started to take over where there had once been neat rows of vegetables. Even when they sat together on the bench, he was still silent.

"It makes you wonder why they're doing it," she said.

"Well . . . I guess it's symbolic to them. It means the war is over; things can get back to normal." He turned and smiled at her.

"Olav, I'll never forget what you've done for me—what you're *doing* for me. You know that, don't you?"

"You're my wife. I want you to be happy."

"Thank you. And I still don't really expect you to understand how I feel about Ulrich."

Olav's only reply was a boyish, uncertain stare punctuated by nervous blinks.

Ingrid put both arms around his arm and hugged it. There was little reaction from him, so she lifted her face up to his, tentatively at first, until their lips met. Now she felt a response from him. She moved her hands to the back of his head and held him, pressing their lips together.

"Thank you," he said once she'd released him.

"Olav, you have nothing to thank me for. But . . ." She let out a frustrated sigh.

"What?" he said. "What is it?"

"Well . . . if you want to do something for me . . ."

He shrugged. "Of course. Just say it."

"Tell me what's wrong, Olav? You've hardly said a word since you brought Ulrich back."

He opened his mouth as if to speak but merely shook his head.

"I know you're not angry. But what is it? Is it something I've done? You can tell me, Olav. Please."

"It's not you. But I'm not sure how to explain it."

Ingrid resisted the temptation to say more but kissed him on the lips once more and looked him in the eye, waiting.

"I . . . I think I made a terrible mistake," he said. "I feel bad."

Again, questions danced on Ingrid's tongue, but she kept them at bay.

"You know when you think you're right about something—when you *know* you're right—and then something happens, and you realize you were blind to it all, perhaps intentionally?"

Ingrid gave him an encouraging nod.

"I lied to you when I left to get Ulrich—that is, when I said I would try my best. A large part of me just wanted to come back and say I'd tried and failed. I could easily have done that; I had every chance. Even as he was in my arms there was still that fleeting thought. But the more his little fingers gripped onto my jacket, the more I understood, and the more I pictured him alone in that horrible, cold place—perhaps for years. At one point he started crying. Somehow, I had to make him quiet down, so I held him close to my chest, and for a reason I'll never understand, I just put my little finger in his mouth . . . and then he settled, closing his eyes. He seemed so contented. He clung to me, to my warmth, as if I was his mamma—or pappa, even."

Ingrid nodded, almost biting her tongue.

"And I realized your mamma was right all that time ago, when we were arguing about the baby, when I was . . . unable to see clearly. Ulrich has done nothing wrong. He didn't choose his father. He's a baby, nothing more." Olav wiped a tear from his eye and tried to sniff more away. "And so, I feel bad about the things I said—and the things I thought."

"No, no, Olav. Please don't say that. I still don't think you really understand what you've done for me."

"And there's something else I have to tell you," Olav continued. "I've been thinking about it over the past couple of days. There's something about him—about his face—that I didn't notice when he was in the clinic because I never really looked at him, something that I see now. His eyes are the same shape as yours, and whenever I look at him, I see something of you. Now I realize that he's going to grow up with some of your features, and I think . . . no, I'm sure . . . that in time I could be the boy's father—his pappa in every way except blood. That is, if you want me to."

"I want nothing more—*nothing more*."

Ingrid waited for more words, but her husband seemed empty of them. She kissed him once more on the lips. "Olav Jacobsen," she said. "I love you."

"And I have some dust in my eye," he said, a wry smirk on his face. "Excuse me."

"Do you think they'll come looking for him?" Ingrid asked Olav on the walk back home a few minutes later. She'd asked the question before, while he'd been fitting the locks, but didn't get much in the way of a reply. Now, she figured he might have more to say.

At first, he said nothing, his face holding a disappointed, almost disgusted expression. "I feel sad to say it, but something tells me those people just don't care enough to even notice. You told me that he wasn't being looked after very well, but I wasn't quite prepared for the state of the place. It reminded me of a cowshed I once had to repair."

"So, we can relax?"

Olav shook his head. "Not yet, I wouldn't say. Keep the doors and windows locked. Never take the little one outside."

They turned the corner into Ostergaten hand in hand.

"But you can still be happy," Olav said, now with a little more joy in his voice.

"I *am* happy." She giggled, then stopped. "But are *you*?"

Olav said nothing, but his nod was worth a thousand words to Ingrid. As she walked on, it was as if clouds were under her feet. The war had ended. Now, perhaps, Ingrid's own battles had ended too.

Then Olav stopped walking, jerking her back by the arm. She looked at him. If he was happy, he wasn't showing it now, his jaw sagging with shock. Ingrid became aware of banging noises, but the source of them didn't register with her at first.

Olav, staring straight ahead, muttered, "What in the name of . . ."

Ingrid followed his gaze to the front of their house, to the two policemen hammering on the door.

"Go back to the gardens," he said. "Hide in the shed. I'll come for you when I've sorted out what they want."

She shook her head.

"*Go*, I said."

"No, Olav. I need to know my baby's safe, and I'm not running away from anyone."

"But . . . oh, if you want." Olav sighed and quickened his pace. Soon he was shouting at the policemen, so they stopped hammering on the door and turned their attention to him.

Ingrid noted that this time the police seemed to have been warned about Olav and his intimidating personality, because both men were as large as him.

"We've been told there's a baby in this house," one of them said.

"Not your concern," Olav shouted back.

"So you admit it? Could it possibly be the same baby that was taken from the old Lebensborn clinic in the early hours of yesterday morning? The baby whose mother happens to live here?"

"Go away!" Olav shouted, standing square and pushing his shoulders back. "Any baby is better here than in that pigsty."

"And here we have the mother in question," the other policeman said, approaching Ingrid. Ingrid jumped backward a step—not at the policeman's action but at Olav's punch thrown at the man's head, at his shout for the man to stay where he was and leave her alone.

She cowered, lost for words or actions as first one and then both policemen tried to restrain Olav. One of them drew a pistol, but Olav grabbed his arm and twisted it to the side. The other grabbed Olav from behind, one arm around his neck, one frantically trying to hold back an arm. Olav tried to shrug the man off and swung a wild kick out at the other, who evaded the kick, stepped forward, and gave Olav two punches to the head in quick succession. This had little effect, and Olav twisted his torso in an attempt to throw the man off his back, but the weight was too much. Three more solid punches to the head subdued him, and he collapsed onto the ground, one arm now curled behind his back, his fist forced up between his shoulder blades.

"Olav!" Ingrid shouted, kneeling down, seeing the blood pouring from his nose and mouth. She looked up, drawing breath to shout, but was met with a pistol being waved in her face.

"Get away!" the policeman shouted at her.

"Leave him alone!" she screamed back.

"We'll leave him alone if he leaves us alone."

"What do you want?" Olav blurted out, the side of his face still being ground into the dirt.

"First, we want to get inside this house."

Olav heaved his shoulders, twisting himself out from underneath the hold of the other policeman. He stayed on the ground, panting, then looked up to the other and spat out a mouthful of blood. "You'll have to kill me before you take that baby away," he hissed.

Ingrid did her best to shove the policeman away from Olav and cradled his bloody head in her arms. "That goes for me too," she shouted.

"So now we have three offenses. Collaborating with the enemy, theft of government property, and assaulting a policeman."

Olav got to his feet, holding his hands up to assure the policemen he was no immediate threat. "It's a baby, not property. And he belongs to my wife, not the government."

"Nevertheless, we—"

"Do you ever stop to think what you're doing?" Olav interrupted.

"We're trying to uphold the law."

"Up until recently the Nazis made the laws. Did you uphold those laws so happily?"

The policemen glanced at each other, neither willing to speak.

"We're all Norwegians," Olav continued, wiping blood from his face. "Surely we can behave like friends. Remember the Resistance, how every Norwegian prayed for their success, for the triumph of good. Now that they've succeeded, do we really need to tear each other apart?"

"But . . . uh . . . you're forgetting something." The policeman looked at Olav, then Ingrid, then the door of their house. "The baby in that house is half Nazi."

Olav held his hands on his hips and shook his head as he laughed. "That baby can't walk, talk, or even feed himself. How can you say such a thing?"

"We're only doing as we're told," the other policeman offered.

"Well, don't. Let's all try to rebuild this country—*our* country. We're doing no harm, just bringing up an innocent baby as best we can. Why not let us be?"

Once again, all the men could do was glance at each other.

"I don't want to make enemies of you two or any other officials, but what I said earlier still stands. If you try to take my wife or her baby away, I'll fight you every inch of the way. Even if you come back with more guns or a hundred men, I'll fight you."

One of the policemen turned to the other. "Perhaps we should report back."

The other man looked at Olav, then at the small crowd of neighbors who had gathered around, assessing both. He nodded to the other policeman, and they walked off without another word.

Olav glanced at the neighbors. "If they didn't know before, I expect they've guessed now."

Ingrid stared across the street at people she used to trust but now couldn't be so sure about: the Bergens, the Tuftes, the Bakkers, Nils the thatcher, and especially Laila. "I'm not hiding Ulrich anymore, Olav. I don't care whether people know."

"Are you sure?"

She nodded. "Oh, yes. Positive."

Olav faced the crowd and took in a large lungful of air. "Yes, we have a baby!" he hollered across to them. "He's our baby, and as long as I breathe, he stays here with us! Do you hear me?"

Words were spoken between them, that much was clear, but seconds later they started to quietly disperse. Olav and Ingrid stood tall, watching every last one of them return to their homes before themselves going indoors to Ulrich. To their baby.

I'm in my bed again, wondering whether I should try to sleep. I'm aware that, as always, many lonely and pointless hours lie ahead of me. I try to read but can't concentrate, perhaps because it's so quiet and warm, perhaps because my mind is stricken. I decide I need sleep, but as soon as I switch my lamp out and close my eyes, a vision invades my mind.

It's now the early 1940s, and we are doing so much good in the world, in spite of those foreign forces that want to ram their heels onto our throats, that prefer to halt the progress we are making and return to the old, outdated ways.

An important part of the social progress we are making is forging a new morality. For instance, until the Third Reich, unmarried motherhood was seen as something to discourage, and children born out of wedlock were often looked down upon. Even now, for instance, all other European countries despise the idea, calling the children illegitimate, thinking that somehow they degrade or threaten marriage as an institution. But our new morality has swept that attitude away. On the orders of the Führer himself, these children are treated as equals of those born to married mothers. As long as a child is of good stock—healthy and preferably tall, blond, and with eyes of either blue or green—the National Socialist government rejoices at another worthy citizen joining the fatherland.

To encourage mothers to give birth to these babies, our rulers initiated the Lebensborn program in the 1930s, and it has quickly expanded and gained support from all areas of the German establishment. Europe has been scoured for children who meet the correct physical criteria, and such children are subsequently being distributed to German parents who will bring them up in the more progressive ways of the fatherland. Also, suitable women are actively being encouraged to become mothers. Tall healthy blondes with no Semitic genes are chosen and matched with equally suitable German officers.

Some people are uncertain—even worried—about this program, but this is social progress, and dissident voices should not be allowed to stand in the way of social progress.

Again, our great and good National Socialist government rejoices at the prospect of more healthy Aryan stock to facilitate our plans for human advancement.

Chapter 29

Oslo, 2011

Arnold and Merlene waited in the foyer of the Aurora care home, a complex that looked more like a modest hotel. The place had been easy to find, and the plan was to talk to this woman about Arnold and his parents, and then, if she remembered them, to ask if she knew about anyone called Ulrich.

They had initially been refused entry, told that although they weren't considered suspicious, the unpleasant fact was that occasionally tricksters would get to the residents. The home contacted Mrs. Karlsen's grandson, who agreed to come over as soon as he could, and the visitors were allowed to wait inside until then.

"You okay?" Merlene said.

"Sure, sure." He nodded once. "Well, I, uh, think so. It's a bit weird. Surreal."

"I wish my history in Jamaica was half as interesting as yours is here."

"Ah, no you don't, Merlene. You definitely don't."

She returned his smile. "Well, perhaps not. But would you like to come over and see my folks sometime?"

"Oh, for sure. Kingston, wasn't it?"

"My dad and Herbie's parents are from there. Mom was born in Montego Bay."

"You still miss Herbie, don't you?"

"I'm sorry. Does it show?"

Arnold shrugged. "It's not a bad thing. I don't mind." Just then his phone went off. "Hello?" He took the phone from his ear and checked the screen. "No reception," he said to Merlene and hurried back out of the building.

"Dad?"

"Hi, Rebecca."

"You didn't call to say you'd gotten there safely. You didn't call me or Natasha."

Arnold noted the tremor of anxiety in her voice, the way she shot the words out.

"I'm sorry," he said. "It was thoughtless of me. I'm really sorry, Rebecca." Then he heard a long sigh. She was relaxing, which was a relief to him. "I had other things on my mind," he added.

"Yeah, of course. I know I shouldn't worry. So, how's Oslo?"

"We haven't seen much of it. But it feels weird to think I was born in this place."

"I can get that. And Merlene?"

"She's good. Cold, but good."

"Dad, you know we're all happy that you and Merlene are . . . like . . ."

"Well, don't be. That's not why I'm here. Like I said, I have other things on my mind."

"I'm sorry, Dad. Forget I mentioned it. Everybody just wants you to be happy."

"I know, sweetheart. And . . . uh . . . well, between you and me . . ."

"Yes?"

"It's not the kind of thing I like to talk about, but I've learned something over the past few weeks I never thought I would."

"What's that?"

"Well, being . . . it's hard for me to say I'm *in love*, but . . . well, whatever it is, it's different when you're older. It creeps up on you. It's slower, less frenetic, less intense. Well, no, just as intense, you still get that . . . I don't know, a glow, I guess, but it's less energetic, and . . . and also sweeter. Much sweeter. I don't know why, but it is. I'm sorry. I'm rambling."

"No, you're not, Dad. I promise I won't mention it again, but I'm pleased for you." A sniff distorted the line. "And as long as you're safe and well, uh, I have to go now, right?"

"Sure, sweetheart. Thanks for calling."

A few minutes later, after managing to get back through the security door and into the foyer, Arnold was faced with Merlene and a nurse.

"They say Mrs. Karlsen's ready to see us now," Merlene said.

Arnold took a few enlivening deep breaths and nodded. "Lead the way," he said to the nurse.

He gave Merlene's hand a quick squeeze on the way, and they were escorted along a wide corridor and past a dayroom that was much like the rest of the place: clean, functional, and somehow nowhere near as soulless as it had every right to be. Eventually, they were shown into a bedroom. A man—probably late twenties—with long blond hair and a slim face stood up and shook hands with them both, introducing himself as Bjorn.

"And you must be Mrs. Karlsen," Arnold said, sitting down next to the woman in the armchair. She was even slimmer than her grandson, white haired, very much looking as though she'd witnessed those ninety years or more, with a pair of glasses dangling from a beaded necklace.

"She speaks no English," Bjorn said. "But I can translate."

"Of course," Arnold said. "Tell her I was born in a house in Ostergaten in 1945, and I'm trying to find out more about my parents."

Bjorn talked to his grandmother in Norwegian, gesturing to Arnold as he did so. The woman's face lit up as he spoke, making her look ten years younger, and as he continued, she looked even more animated, talking back to him, questioning him.

Then he spoke in English. "She's excited to know more."

"Of course," Arnold answered. "What does she want to know?"

"She asked me what your parents' names were."

Arnold spoke slowly and clearly directly to the woman. "The Jacobsens," he said. "Ingrid and Olav."

"Ingrid Jacobsen?" she asked, her furrowed brow showing how much her memories were being tipped upside down and shaken.

Arnold nodded. "She was my mother. Did you know her?"

The woman's frown deepened, and she spoke again, repeating the names to herself.

"Here," Arnold said, showing her the tiny photo. "This is me with them."

She lifted her glasses onto her nose, then gasped at what she saw. She looked at Arnold and back at the photo a couple of times, unblinking, her nostrils twitching, her wiry eyebrows drooping to concentrate her glare. "Jacobsen," she said weakly, her eyes widening.

"What is it?" Arnold said. He turned to Bjorn. "Could you ask her, please?"

Before Bjorn could answer, Mrs. Karlsen started talking, almost pleading, spittle flying from her mouth as she threw a stream of words out.

"What's she saying?" Arnold said. "Tell me what she's saying."

But Bjorn seemed just as confused. And the storm coming from the woman's mouth continued, her voice trembling and threatening to give up completely. She grasped Arnold's sleeve, tears now breaking out over her reddened eyelids.

"I'm sorry," Bjorn said. "You'll have to leave."

"I want to know what she's saying," Arnold insisted.

"No," Bjorn said firmly. "She's getting upset. Please leave."

Merlene stepped forward. "Bjorn's right," she said to Arnold. "We should leave."

Arnold took a moment to look the woman in the eye, and as he did so she stopped talking fast and loose, took a deep breath to compose herself, and said just a few words, but with a considered clarity.

Arnold thanked her and stood up to leave the room, whereupon she said the same few words again and then a third time.

All Arnold felt able to do was smile and thank her again, and a few seconds later the three of them stood outside the bedroom door.

"I'm sure you understand," Bjorn said. "I won't allow her to get upset. Not at her age."

"We understand," Merlene said.

"Sure, we do," Arnold added. "And I'm sorry. But just tell me, Bjorn; what was she talking about?"

"I, uh . . . I'm not sure. It was confusing, didn't make sense."

"And at the end? She said something to me clearly. The same few words three times, as I recall."

"Yes, that part was clear. She was saying, 'Tell her I'm sorry.'"

"Just that?"

Bjorn nodded. "I don't know what she means, but that's definitely what she said."

"Well . . ." Arnold paused, knowing he was leaving Mrs. Karlsen with none of his original questions answered and yet more conundrums to confuse him further. "Well, thank you for your time, anyway. And please thank Mrs. Karlsen again for me. It was very kind of her to see us."

"I will," Bjorn said.

Merlene added, "And we both hope she's well after getting so upset. We didn't mean any harm."

"I know," Bjorn said. "And thank you, but she'll be fine. She's a tough old woman."

"By the way," Merlene said. "What's your grandmother's name?"

"Laila," he replied. "Her name's Laila."

"That's a pretty name."

He smiled. "I always thought so."

A few minutes later Arnold and Merlene were in a taxi on the way back to their hotel.

Merlene broke the somber silence. "So, I guess we're no closer to finding out who Ulrich was or what's happened to him?"

"I guess you're right," Arnold said, still staring out of the taxi window.

Merlene gave his hand a gentle squeeze; he turned to her, and she kissed him on the lips. Arnold gave her a grateful smile, but no more words were spoken.

Chapter 30

Ingrid had now been looking after her baby for two months. And despite the fear of further hostile visits from the police, despite the locked doors and windows, despite the sleepless nights and the disdain of neighbors, they had been special months.

There had been the occasion Ingrid's mamma had told Olav to hold the boy's naked form close to his equally naked chest. He said he'd rather not. She replied that it wasn't for his benefit but for Ulrich's, to keep him warm. Ingrid walked into the room just as Olav was trying to stop Ulrich's little fingers pulling at his chest hairs, yelping sharply whenever Ulrich got the better of him.

There was the wooden crib Olav had built for Ulrich to go at the end of their bed. He'd worked on it in secret to surprise Ingrid and brought tears to her eyes when he unveiled it.

Ingrid quite often found Olav with his little finger in Ulrich's mouth, soothing him, and she had to tell him off once or twice for not washing the finger first.

There was the time Ingrid had silently stolen into the bedroom because she thought Olav was sleeping off a long night's work, only to find him tickling Ulrich's belly and talking nonsense to him. Olav, of course, was red faced at being caught but laughed off the episode.

It was late in that same month when the policeman knocked on the door.

He was full of "due consideration" and "special circumstances" and "best interests," but the outcome was clear: all and any charges against Ingrid and Olav were dropped, and the authorities felt it was in the best interests of everyone for Ingrid to keep her baby. Olav couldn't resist a barbed comment about how it had taken so long for them to come to what should have been an obvious conclusion. Likewise, the man couldn't resist a riposte: "Better the mongrel bastard your problem than a burden on the state."

It took every ounce of Ingrid's and her mamma's strength to hold Olav back as the man left, walking briskly with regular glances over his shoulder.

By September they assumed that the unwanted attentions of neighbors—who up until now had merely called them names—would cease or, at least, ease off, that people would have more constructive things to do with their time, such as rebuilding their country. However, despite winter being some time away, a bitter wind often whipped through Ostergaten, and the long-held bad memories only sharpened its sting.

Olav and Ingrid always told each other that at some stage, life would have to return to normal, and for Olav that meant occasional carpentry jobs where he had to stay away from Oslo. One such morning, Olav kissed Ingrid's mamma goodbye, gave Ulrich's tummy a farewell tickle, then turned to Ingrid.

"Come back the moment you can," she said.

"The very moment," he replied. "And remember, always lock up every time you're in the house, and always check who's there before you open the front door."

"Of course."

They embraced. Olav pulled away, but Ingrid held on and held on. Olav laughed. "I have to go."

"Can I come too?"

"You wouldn't like it. I'm sleeping on the floor, and I stink after the first day." He pushed her away, and she stepped back with a groan. He picked up his toolbox and reached for the door. Then he stopped and lifted his nose up, sniffing. "Can you smell something?" he said, immediately adding, "Never mind. I'll see you in three or four days."

He opened the door, and they both stepped outside. Ingrid, her gaze locked onto him, went to take a final embrace, but he resisted, pushing her away. There was a look of repulsion on his face. She turned to follow his stare.

"Go back inside," he said.

"But . . ."

"Go inside. And don't tell your mamma about this. I'll clean it up."

Tears swelled in Ingrid's eyes, soon breaking out and wetting her cheeks. "Who would do this?"

"We both know who: the same woman who told the authorities about Ulrich being here."

Ingrid peered across the street, focusing on one door in particular. "Laila," she hissed.

"She'll stop her games in time," Olav said. "For now, go inside; get me soap and a brush in a bucket of water. Forget this. Forget you saw it."

Ingrid knew that would be impossible, but she grabbed the doorknob, giving her eyes one last chance to linger on the words daubed across the door, below a hastily painted swastika: NAZI SPAWN LIVES HERE.

A few white feathers drifted in the breeze as though a footnote.

The abuse was sporadic, and Olav and Ingrid gave up trying to hide the worst of it from her mamma. Physical attacks were rare. Finding their home pelted with rotten eggs or excrement was less rare. Returning home to find obscene messages painted on the house or one of those damn white feathers pinned to the door were regular occurrences. The longest time Ingrid had gone without being spat at in the street was nine days. And in all the time since he'd been home, little Ulrich had never been out of the house without being escorted by Olav, who felt the need to strut his imposing figure around wherever they went. Likewise, windows and doors stayed locked unless Olav was around.

On many occasions, Olav, Ingrid, and her mamma discussed the possibility of complaining to the police about the intimidation and the blatant criminal damage. Olav made inquiries via his old Resistance contacts, who told him the attitudes of the people in power varied from genuine concern to willful disinterest, and that although details would always be noted down on record, the outcome would probably be the same: nothing would be done because it had been their choice to take the baby back, and they should be grateful they still had their freedom. So the idea was left to one side.

Whenever they played with little Ulrich, the stress seemed a small price to pay, and they often felt like a normal, happy family. Most importantly, Olav and Ingrid made sure that what stress there was stopped with them. Ingrid's mamma knew what was going on, but there were never any arguments or discussion of the troubles when Ulrich was awake, just in case voices became raised.

One or two of Olav's regular customers declined to provide work for him when they found out about Ulrich, and a few tradesmen refused to work with him on the larger projects, which ultimately lost him a little more work. These were rare, if upsetting, experiences but forced Olav to work farther away from home than he would have liked, and their financial situation was never more than barely comfortable. They ate better than they had done in previous years, but otherwise the waves of postwar economic revival seemed to pass right over them, and they had to make do with mere dreams of a better future. The hope that the intimidation would tail off and cease at some point—a faith in the basic decency of their people—never deserted them.

The event that proved the final straw wasn't even one of the most dangerous or extreme episodes. It came in the silent heart of one cold night.

A crash, then shouts from the street outside. More crashes. Olav running out of the bedroom, then telling the others to stay where they were. Ulrich crying. Olav cursing, opening the front door, and shouting defiantly to nobody. The perpetrators had gone; they were well practiced by now. The immediate panic now over, Olav realized he had some unpleasant cuts on his feet from the broken glass. Stones had been thrown through every window of the main room, leaving the floor strewn with a carpet of piercing fragments.

By the time he'd fetched a broom, tidied up, nailed some old slats of wood across the holes, and picked the glass fragments from his bloody feet, he was in no mood to go back to sleep. Ingrid and her mamma felt much the same, so they lit a fire and sat huddled together in front of it, waiting for the sun to rise. Only Ulrich slept.

"I've had enough," Ingrid said after a particularly long period of silence.

"Haven't we all?" her mamma added.

"It will get better," Olav insisted. "We've said it before. You need to have a little faith in people, or else . . . your humanity is gone."

"We all used to believe that," Ingrid said, "but now even *you* don't sound convinced."

He shrugged. "Well, yes. It's my own country, my own people. I risked my life for our freedom, so I can't say I'm not disappointed, but—"

"But what? You'll lose your faith in our people when one of us is killed?"

"It won't come to that."

Ingrid let out a humorless laugh. "Well, I'm not waiting to find that out. Not with . . ."

A sharp glower from Olav told her not to finish the sentence.

"But what else can we do?" Ingrid's mamma asked her.

"We can . . . we can *leave*," Ingrid replied.

A frown of pain descended onto her mamma's face. "You mean to . . . Bergen or Kristiansand?"

Ingrid shook her head. "Even farther away."

"Oh, Ingrid, no."

"Mamma, there's something you should know."

Olav groaned. "No, Ingrid. This isn't the time."

"It's not how we planned to tell her, but . . . perhaps it's the best time." She turned to her mamma. "We were going to break the news to you in happier times, Mamma, but . . . I'm going to have another baby."

Her mamma gulped and glanced at Olav.

He smiled. "I'm sorry you had to find out like this, but . . ."

"But nothing," she said. She stood up and grabbed him, kissing him in the middle of the forehead. Then she hugged Ingrid, all the while muttering congratulations. They waited a few minutes while she dried her eyes and recovered some composure.

"Perhaps now you understand a little more," Ingrid said to her. "And you, too, Olav."

He went to speak, but she held a hand up to silence him.

"It's been worrying me ever since I fell pregnant. And I've decided. All the trouble around here—I'm not putting up with that while I'm coping with Ulrich and another baby. Absolutely not."

"But we'll support you," Olav said. "You'll have two people here to help you."

"One person most of the time," Ingrid said. "You spend more and more of your time traveling farther to get work because of Ulrich— because of what people think of him." She sighed. "I'm sorry, Olav. That sounds ungrateful. I know you work hard. But it's not good enough. It's not your fault, but it's not good enough. And there's something else neither of you is considering."

"And what's that?" her mamma asked.

"I've been thinking a lot. And it's played on my mind. If this is what we're suffering now, almost six months after the war, what happens to Ulrich when he grows up? We can protect him now, but we won't be able to protect him every day of his life."

Olav scratched the day-old stubble on his chin thoughtfully. "I'm not as pessimistic as you," he said. "I still have hope that somehow—"

"Well, I don't. I've given up that sort of hoping. And I'm the one who has to deal with that rabble out there while you're away. Me, the one carrying your baby." She scowled. "I'm sorry, Olav. But I've spent enough time just hoping things will improve. I've decided."

"Oh," Olav said, looking down. "Well, if that's what you really want . . ."

"What I want is a better life—a better life for Ulrich and a better life for this one too." She patted her still slim belly. "But also for us, the three of us. I want to leave Norway. And the sooner the better."

"*What?*" he said. "But . . . for where? And how?"

She shook her head despairingly. "Oh, I don't know. I'm not saying I have all the answers. But the answers don't lie here, I'm sure of that."

There was more rasping of Olav's fingernails on his stubble. "I . . . I understand what you mean."

"You do?"

"I've been thinking much the same myself; I just didn't want to say it."

"That's good, Olav. You *should* have said it."

"I . . . I didn't know *how* to. My, uh, reasons are different from yours."

"Oh. What do you mean?"

"I haven't mentioned it. I keep it inside. Well, I *try* to. You see, I still feel bad about my parents, how I betrayed them when they were taken away. I'm sure they wouldn't want me to wallow in guilt for the rest of my life, and I was thinking a fresh start might help me feel better.

But then I always thought it would be impractical, because of . . ." He looked at Ingrid's mamma and raised an eyebrow.

"If you want me to be completely honest," the object of his attentions said, "I don't want to leave." She gulped, clearly trying to stop the tears. "Oslo is my home. I was born here. My friends and my family are here, and I've known nothing else." She glanced over at Ingrid, where she saw steely resolve. After a long silence she let out a tired sigh. "Then again, I guess . . . I *could* live without them. Many of the people I thought of as friends have turned their backs on me lately. And I'd much prefer to stay close by my only daughter."

"Thank you, Mamma. I promise you, whatever happens, we'll look after you." She looked to Olav for agreement.

"Of course," he said. "Wherever we go, you'll have us—and, of course, your grandchildren."

The three of them sat in a heavy silence for a minute or so.

"What about Sweden?" Olav suggested.

Ingrid and her mamma pondered the suggestion for a few seconds.

"We don't know anyone there," Ingrid's mamma said. "But I'm sure in time, if we settled there, we could make friends."

Ingrid shook her head. "I'm not so sure. It's too close. I don't think I'd feel safe."

"We might as well go anywhere," her mamma said. "We don't know anyone outside Norway."

"I do," Olav said. "I have relatives in Canada."

Ingrid's mamma screwed her eyes up. "Canada? Where's that?"

"North America," Ingrid said. She turned to Olav. "Are you serious? Is that a serious suggestion?"

"It wasn't a suggestion." Olav glanced at Ingrid, then her mamma; then his eyes fell upon the hastily repaired windows. "But it could be. They live in an area called Saskatchewan, where the weather is similar to here. There are lots of well-paid jobs too. And a lot of Norwegians have gone out there over the years. But . . ." He stood up and started pacing, scratching his bowed head. "No, no," he said. "Let's just stop and think for a moment. Could we really leave Oslo? Just like that?"

"We're not talking about going today," Ingrid said. "But soon. Do we have enough money to get us all there?"

He shrugged. "I have no idea how much it would cost, but probably more than we have. What I *do* know is that I can work more and save, perhaps sell a few things."

"And I have some savings," Ingrid's mamma said. "Not much, but it will help."

"So, it's possible," Ingrid said.

Olav stopped pacing and nodded. "It's possible," he said. "It's certainly *possible*. But I suppose I have to ask you the same question you asked me." He crouched down and faced his wife. "Are you serious?"

"Oh, yes." Ingrid nodded confidently. "Serious with all my heart."

Chapter 31

In the small and close-knit community of Hagansberg, not too far from Saskatoon, Ingrid opened the door of the log cabin and peered to the side. To the mailbox. Ah, yes. She thought she'd spied the colorful figure of Smiling John, the postman, flash along the drive a few minutes ago, and she was right. She and John would have a short conversation most mornings, she keen to hear and practice English, he only too happy to oblige. Today he must have been running late.

She stepped over to the mailbox with a confidence she was now only occasionally conscious of, head high, shoulders back, allowing herself a brief grin. She'd caught that from Smiling John. She took in a few gasps of air, no longer ice cold but somehow still ice fresh, and stopped to admire the scenery. Everything was so still that she could have been in a gallery, admiring a painting. A beautiful painting. A faint squawk from above drew her eyes to a vee of geese traversing the blue sheet of sky. Then she noticed other things: Smoke rising vertically from a few cabins across the road. A pair of curtains jerked open in the cabin right in front of her. She waved, and the wave was returned. Good old Susan, yet another local who had befriended her when she'd first arrived in Hagansberg with her husband, mamma, and, of course, little Ulrich in tow. It had been clear to all how reluctant she was to mix with neighbors back in those days, when her levels of anxiety were as high as those geese. But every last one of the locals had been so friendly and welcoming and understanding of her complete lack of English. It had been like an eerie paradise in comparison with . . .

No, forget those days, Ingrid, she told herself. *Those days are gone forever.*

Despite the morning sun there was still a chill this time in the morning that caused her to shiver. She hurriedly lifted out the single slim letter from the mailbox and headed back indoors. As she did so, she noted the Norwegian stamp lying askew on the corner as though stuck on in a hurry. The fact that it was a Norwegian stamp wasn't so odd; it could have been from a relative in Oslo. But in the past, they'd usually been from her aunt and always addressed to her mamma. This one was addressed to Ingrid.

Never mind. But it also felt empty. She ran her fingertips along it. No, it wasn't quite empty. There was something inside. Not much, but something.

She heard little Barbara crying and placed the envelope down on the cabinet by the front door for later. In contrast to Ulrich, who had always been a contented baby despite the circumstances of his birth and the situation he'd found himself in soon afterward, his baby sister, Barbara, would cry at the drop of a fur-lined trapper hat.

Ingrid picked her up and rocked her in her arms, and soon the cries turned to groans, and then there was nothing but very quiet, rhythmic gurgling. Ingrid decided—as she always had to with Barbara—to sit and hold her for a few minutes after she'd apparently gone to sleep. But that gave her time to think.

Olav had gone to the lumberyard early. Well, he went early *every* day. But it was worth it for the extra money. Also, Ingrid's mamma had insisted on paying her way, so she worked a part-time shift at the settlement's only store, and if they added that money to the equation, they had enough to survive, save, and also enjoy a very occasional luxury.

Life was good. Simple but good. Yes, Olav had to work six days a week to meet the bills and occasionally—well, *very* occasionally—complained about the work, that it was unskilled labor, and he preferred to think of himself as a craftsman. But in the next breath he would always insist he was happy. The five of them were happy. And the neighbors didn't spit at her or throw eggs at the house or hurl stones through the window. And nobody painted horrible messages on the house. Thoughts of that day when she'd had her hair cropped and her nose broken might just as well have been left on that other continent.

She put little Barbara down, checked on Ulrich—yes, still sleeping—and went back to the cabinet by the front door. She picked up the envelope and went over to the kitchen table, where she sat, stared at the envelope for a few seconds, then opened it and dropped its contents in front of her.

And then the thoughts of all those horrible times in Oslo flooded back into her mind like a long-forgotten childhood nightmare. She might as well have been back at Ostergaten 41, deep in that cruel morning when they'd had that fateful discussion.

The wind was whistling through gaps in the hastily repaired windows, the sound taunting them almost as much as the people who had caused the damage. Likewise, small mounds of glass fragments dotted the floor here and there, where they'd been swept, bitter reminders of how a neighborhood could turn.

"So, we're all agreed?" Olav said to Ingrid and her mamma. "We go to Canada as soon as we can?"

Ingrid thought no reply was needed from her but looked at her mamma, who gave the matter three seconds' thought, then nodded.

"Then I'll make plans," Olav continued. "I'll write my cousins in Hagansberg, explaining, uh . . . that we want to make a new start over there and asking for help. He speaks reasonable Norwegian, so he'll be useful until we can learn English."

"Good," Ingrid said. "Just be careful what you tell them about Ulrich."

"What do you mean?"

Ingrid spoke with uncharacteristic intensity. "Never forget the main reason we're doing this." She pointed at the broken windows and mounds of broken glass. "Even if the three of us for some reason are unhappy there, if we never truly settle, at least Ulrich will grow up in a different country; he won't know the circumstances of his birth, and he definitely won't ever get to know the identity of his father. Do you understand?"

Olav stood, swiped his boot to clear a few more glass fragments, and knelt down next to her. "Ingrid, my darling wife, I promise that as long as I live, I will never mention how he came to be in this world. He will always be my son; do you hear me?" He paused, wiping a tear from Ingrid's cheek with his meaty thumb. "But more than that, we *will* make a new life over there, and we *will* be happy, all of us, or I will spend the rest of my days trying to achieve that. It won't be easy; we'll all have to learn English, and we'll have to leave behind everything we've ever known except each other. But we'll be happy; I feel it in my heart."

Olav stroked Ingrid's hair, inviting her head closer. Seconds later they kissed.

"I can't pretend not to be scared," Ingrid said. "But I'm more determined and, yes, more hopeful than I've ever been about anything."

Three weeks later, Ingrid felt that her fear had dulled, that her hope had stolen the ascendancy, that a bright light was growing in her mind day by day as the plan had come together one element at a time. Olav's discreet inquiries among his Resistance friends had shown that many were still bitter about everything and anything to do with the German occupation but also yielded one man sympathetic to the plight of Lebensborn mothers, who said that the war was over, that what was done was done, and that reconciliation should always triumph over revenge. His name was Magnus, and before long Olav confided in him about Franz, Ulrich, and the neighbors. Magnus admitted he'd heard such stories but never firsthand. He said he was almost ashamed to call himself a Norwegian and would be pleased to help.

Olav worked day and night, they tried to sell everything they wouldn't be taking with them, and the family left Oslo just after the close of a bright October day. Everything essential for Ingrid, her mamma, her husband, and her son to survive the next few days had been crammed into three suitcases. Everything they hadn't sold— furniture, household utensils, most of their clothes, the few ornaments Ingrid and her mamma had collected over the years—all of these were left behind. Selling Ulrich's crib—the one Olav had made for him—was a particularly sad moment. Ingrid did, however, take one sentimental possession: the only photo she had of herself and Olav with baby Ulrich, taken outside the front of the house by a traveling photographer who'd passed through their neighborhood a few weeks before they'd left. She kept the photo safe in a tiny old tan-colored leather purse, placed in the center of her suitcase, cushioned by clothes on either side.

Magnus took them all in the back of a borrowed farm truck to the more northerly wilderness of their country's backyard, through mountain passes, along deep valleys smattered with pine trees poking the sky, along a river that seemed as keen to escape as they were, and eventually to a strip of barren lowland. From there, a little-known track led them to the uncontrolled—and uncontrollable, according to Magnus—border with Sweden.

They passed through more wild terrain, reaching a remote fishing village late the next day, where they ate and stopped overnight. The next morning, they had to say goodbye to Magnus. He wished them luck and told Olav it was wrong that they needed to do what they were doing and that one day the authorities would recognize that fact.

They traveled in a small fishing boat to the port of Stockholm, from where a cruise ship took them via the British port of Southampton across the Atlantic Ocean to Quebec City. Their home for the following couple of days was a series of railroad carriages traveling out into the wilds of Saskatchewan.

It had been a marathon journey, and the two hours they waited for Olav's cousin to pick them up and drive them to Hagansberg went by as if it were only a few minutes. And then, finally, they reached home, which, for now, was a room in his cousin's timber-framed house. Ingrid was hardly in a state to take anything in, but it seemed darker, quieter, and far more remote than anything she'd experienced in Norway.

They were all shown to the room and all thanked Olav's cousin for the lift and his generosity. He replied that it was fine, that getting their own place wouldn't be hard, and asked if they were hungry.

"I just need to be still for a while," Ingrid replied, her mamma nodding in agreement.

"Thank you once again," Olav said. "But we need rest more than food."

"I'm sure. I remember when my parents and I came over many years ago. I slept for a week."

"Well, I won't. Be sure to take me into the lumberyard with you tomorrow morning."

Ingrid was wearier than she ever thought possible after the journey, her mamma even more so by the look of her, but Ingrid wasn't too weak to let that idea go unchallenged. "No, Olav. Please stay with us for a few days. You must. We all need to settle in here, and you need rest as much as anyone."

"I can't." Olav looked around, his face pleading for support. "We need to pay our way."

"I think they're right," his cousin said to him. "It's dangerous work. You need to be alert. Why don't you rest, and I'll tell them you can start next Monday?"

"Well . . ." Olav let out a few frustrated breaths. "All right then."

Little Ulrich seemed to have suffered the least from the journey, perhaps the various motions of transport settling him down. The rest of them settled onto thick woolen blankets laid on the floor and soon joined Ulrich in deep and undisturbed sleep.

"Your cousin," Ingrid said to Olav over breakfast the next morning. "What did he mean by *dangerous work*?"

"It's just feeding timber into the machinery. I'll be fine."

"But they know you can do better, surely? You're a carpenter, not a laborer."

Olav smiled at Ingrid's mamma and used a napkin to wipe the oatmeal from Ulrich's chin. "Perhaps in time," he said. "But I have to start at the bottom. And the money is good."

"Of course. I'm sorry. Let's just enjoy these few days before you have to start."

After breakfast they all ventured outside, Ulrich riding on Olav's shoulders, his legs dangling out front, his hands grasping at the straggles of Olav's long hair. The dirt road was wide and deserted, edged on either side by timber single-story houses much like Olav's cousin's, all with wide plots and neat verdant gardens out front. The sun ahead of them reflected brightly on the road surface, making it hard to look anywhere but the houses. They walked on until they reached a main road. Olav pointed left, to road signs in the distance. "Signs of civilization," he said, leading them there.

A few minutes along the main road Ingrid's mamma shivered. Ingrid noticed.

"Do you want to turn back, Mamma?"

She shook her head. "Let's explore a little more."

A man walked past them and said something they didn't understand, but a smile and a nod was universal, so that was their reply, and the man smiled back and sent a few more pointless words in their direction.

"That reminds me," Ingrid said. "We all have to make the effort to learn English."

Her mamma and Olav agreed but were more interested in where they were headed. Eventually they reached the crossroads. A store of some sort nestled some way back from the road at the intersection.

"This looks like the center of town," Olav said, peering along four roads in turn, each as straight and featureless as the next. "Even with only four roads I could imagine getting lost here."

"Could we go into the store?" Ingrid said. "Mamma's getting colder."

"Mmm . . . that's one thing we need to buy first—or rather, four things."

They went into the store, which had a few shelves of fruit and vegetables and a glass-covered selection of meat and fish. The sole customer was speaking with the man behind the counter in that same English language they all knew they would just have to get used to.

"Don't they sell clothing?" Ingrid asked Olav.

"If I could speak English, I could ask," he replied.

Ingrid's mamma pointed at some apples in a basket on the counter. "They look delicious. We could have one each for lunch."

Olav laughed. "We could if we had some money."

"Oh, yes. Of course."

The customer left the shop, and the man behind the counter beamed a smile so wide it looked like it was trying to break out of his face. He spoke a few words, then paused, waiting. Olav looked at Ingrid, who looked at her mamma. The man's expansive smile faltered. He said another few words but still got no reply. He pointed at them all, pulling his finger back as though it was rude. "Norsk?" he said.

Olav, Ingrid, and her mamma all started nodding and telling him they were exactly that. But the man shrugged. He did hold up that finger again, backing out the door leading to the storage area, speaking words that he must have realized were wasted.

There were muffled voices; then the man returned with a woman in tow, wiping her hands on her apron, giving off a strong smell of fish. "My husband tells me you're Norwegian?" she said in competent but clearly rusty Norwegian.

"Arrived yesterday and hoping to stay here for a long time," Olav said. "And you?"

"Oh, I arrived here thirteen years ago. I didn't intend to stay long but . . ." She threw a glance at her husband. "You'll like it here. We all get along well with each other, all help each other. You have to in a place like this."

"I'm sure."

"So . . . can I help you?"

Olav glanced around at the meat, the fresh bread, the basket of apples. "I wish you could. We have no money."

"Oh."

Ingrid stepped forward. "But he has a job, starts Monday at the lumberyard."

"So, what would you like?" she said, positioning herself behind the counter.

A few confused glances were exchanged.

"Don't worry about paying," the woman said. "We can sort that out when you get paid."

Five minutes later they left the shop with some bread, sliced beef, and four of those apples. But they were all relieved to get back to the warmth of the house.

Olav offered his first wage packet to his cousin, but it was refused. "Buy what you need first, which I would say is coats for you all. I'll drive you down to the next town, where there's a clothes store." Olav accepted, saying that the second, third, and fourth wage packets would be handed over in their entirety—minus a few dollars for treats—for rent and food, and he wouldn't argue the point.

Ingrid mentioned the menial nature of Olav's job only once again. "Have you told them about your carpentry skills?" she said.

He just shrugged those square shoulders and said, "A job is a job, and we need stability." Then he pointed to her growing belly, adding, "And I need to put money aside for child number two."

A month flew by, during which they'd bought heavy boots as well as warm coats, and English lessons had been arranged. Ingrid's mamma got part-time work in the stockroom of Hagansberg's only store, which brought in some extra money, and Olav's cousin insisted that just a quarter of Olav's wages would easily cover the cost of the family staying there. So another month on, they'd saved enough to rent a modest log cabin not far away that Ingrid felt she could call home.

They moved in before the end of the year and spent the next few weeks furnishing the place. Ingrid's mamma often mentioned how some of the old chairs and rugs and beds from Ostergaten 41 would have been useful, but each time she did, Ingrid told her the past was the past, and they simply had to cope. Acquaintances gradually became friends— especially Smiling John the postman and Susan across the road—and Hagansberg was fast becoming home.

When winter's first onslaught steamrollered in, it was harsh even for a family used to the Norwegian climate; the snow was deeper, and there was no ghosting sea wind to bring in milder air. Blizzards often pinned them indoors—except for Olav, who was picked up and taken to work by his cousin in some contraption that looked like a cross between a tank and a tractor.

But they were all assured summer would bring warmer weather than back in Oslo, which Ingrid's mamma found very confusing.

A pregnancy in such conditions was a pregnancy squared, but as spring brought new life to the Hagansberg countryside, it did the same to the Jacobsens—a baby girl they decided to call Barbara. The winter months had been hard going, but Ingrid had so much to show for those difficult times. As well as a husband she loved, a healthy little son, and a mamma close at hand, she now also had a new home and a new daughter who had strong lungs and liked to prove it. To add a cherry to the icing, she also had the benefit of neighbors whom she counted as friends. And it helped that the many dark winter hours had given the family plenty of time to learn English.

The negatives of living in a remote town didn't seem to matter. Life was good. Life was *really* good, better than she'd dared hoped for. The tiny town, the house, the neighbors, Olav's relatives. In fact, the whole place had already started to feel like home.

But now Ingrid sat at the rough-edged table in their rented cabin, staring at the contents of that envelope with the crooked Norwegian stamp on it. She felt like ripping up and burning what lay in front of her but knew that wouldn't help. Nothing would help. She felt the burn of her breakfast crawling back up her throat.

That tortuous trek halfway across the world, getting to know a whole new country, struggling to learn a new language. Getting to know all these wonderful people. Had all of those been for nothing? Was that *really good life* they'd sacrificed so much for and traveled so far for about to unravel?

Ingrid had a lot of thinking to do.

It's a sunny day, something to be joyful about. I ask to be taken out into the backyard, for my wheelchair to be placed on the lawn in the sun. A member of the staff tells me it's colder than it looks. I tell him I like that because it might keep me awake. He laughs. I don't. I tell him I still want to go outside.

Soon I'm on the lawn, a blanket around me. It keeps me warm, which feels nice at first, but after a few minutes of staring at the scenery, I start to nod off, and before I know it, a vision is before me—a vision of myself in full uniform, in a cold city.

We are now four years into the war, and the rest of the world is in awe of the power of Germany. It really is something that I and every honest German can feel truly proud of. The rump of Europe has lain down before our great armies, and I am now stationed in Norway.

For me it has always been an honor and a pleasure to serve my country, so when the opportunity arose to take part in the Lebensborn program, I obviously saw it as my duty to serve the fatherland, so I am currently searching Oslo for suitable females to provide our rulers with the progeny they require for the new Europe.

Many of these women need persuasion, because unlike me they haven't had the benefit of education in the new ways and are afraid of concepts they don't understand. Even I find it difficult to reason with such women—the ones who might serve as my partners in this program—and yes, I feel pity for them. But I have a duty to carry out and know that together we are doing this for the benefit of the whole of the human race.

Yes, I have sympathy for these women because they don't understand the wider social benefits of the program, but we need to be vigilant, because recently the course of the war has started to turn against us. We must keep faith and consider what sort of a backward and horrible world it would be without our great government—without the Führer. We must all keep fighting, because if we lose the war, we will forever regret it and spend the rest of our lives wondering how great the world would have become had Germany been allowed to continue with its groundbreaking plans for social progress.

A chilly gust of wind cuts my cheekbone, taking me away from my vision. I should ask to go back inside, but I know all I have to look forward to is another lonely day, another sleepless night, and the prospect of waking up to go through another dreadful day. And those visions.

Chapter 32

The day after the apparently pointless meeting with Mrs. Karlsen, Marit called Arnold to say she was now in Oslo, too, and the three of them arranged to meet up in the hotel restaurant over lunch.

When they met Marit, the first thing that struck Arnold was how much she resembled his own mother in her earlier days—slender and long limbed with white-blonde hair. And because of that similarity, Arnold himself wasn't so different from her, having clearly inherited his body shape from his mother more than his heavyset father. For a confused moment he considered the possibility that his mother was also Marit's mother, and he told himself to be serious. Marit also looked around the same age as Arnold, probably a few years younger, although the makeup and the years of clean Scandinavian living might have been responsible for that.

As they sat down, they introduced themselves, and as they started eating, they made small talk, eventually getting around to how clean and efficient the city was.

"I take it you've been to Oslo before?" Merlene said.

Marit nodded. "Oh, many times. Many, many times, mainly for carrying out my research, but I've done my fair share of sightseeing too."

"I'm sure," Merlene replied. "How far away are you from Oslo?"

"About two hours if you include getting to Stockholm."

"Not too far at all," Arnold said.

"And, of course," Marit added, "it was a long, long time ago, but I was born here."

"You were born in Oslo?" Arnold asked. "Any particular reason you left?"

At that question, Marit's features sagged slightly, and her skin blushed. "It's best I tell you later," she said.

Arnold and Merlene talked about life in Toronto, Merlene about her childhood in Jamaica, and Marit seemed keener to eat and listen rather than talk.

So it was Marit who finished eating first. "We need to go somewhere quiet to talk," she said, glancing around.

Arnold did likewise, and it was true that the restaurant was getting busy, customers and waiting staff passing their table every minute or so.

"Would you be happy to talk in our room?" Arnold asked.

"Of course." Marit spat the words out and now sat, tight lipped, arms tightly folded, shoulders hunched.

Arnold assessed her stern image for a few moments. "Would you prefer it if we went right now?" he said.

Marit shook her head while unfolding her arms, her hands now fidgeting. "Oh, no. I'm sorry. I must seem so rude."

"It's not a problem," Merlene interjected.

"No, finish your meals," Marit said. "And excuse my impatience. I've waited so long for this."

"Of course," Arnold said.

Merlene leaned across to Marit and added, "Don't worry. We have all the time we'll need, however long it takes."

So, Arnold and Merlene finished their food, and fifteen minutes later all three of them were sitting around the desk in the hotel room.

Arnold felt the need to take in a deep breath as Marit took a folder out of her bag and placed it onto the table. She opened it, and a dozen or so scraps of paper—a variety of colors, sizes, and ages—fell onto the table in front of them.

"This represents everything I have researched over the last seventeen years," Marit said with a gravity that Arnold suddenly found unsettling. "I'll be as open as possible with you concerning what I've discovered about Ulrich."

Arnold cleared his throat. "Uh . . . do you mind if I ask . . . well, why the secrecy?"

"Ulrich has to be the first to know the truth. Unless, of course, I find out he has died."

"Which is quite possible," Merlene said, "bearing in mind he was born in '44."

"And the fact that he seems to have completely disappeared," Arnold added.

"Let's start with his birth certificate," Marit said, spreading the pieces of paper out. "Well, a photocopy of it."

"This looks like it," Merlene said, picking up the sheet of paper closest to her, its bright white border contrasting with the cream-and-black image inside. "Could you translate it?"

Marit did, reading the details out loud.

"What did you say?" Arnold said, alarm breaking through his words.

She repeated the information.

"That can't be right." He grabbed the piece of paper and read for himself. "I can just about work this out; it says the mother was Ingrid Jacobsen, née Solberg. That's correct. But . . ." He showed it to Marit, his forefinger underlining one section. "Is this the date of birth?"

"September 28," Marit confirmed.

"But . . . that can't be right. It's only . . ." He paused, looking up as he counted in his mind. "That's less than eight months before I was born."

"Are you sure?" Marit said, frowning.

"Of my own birthday? Hey, I like to think so. It's on my passport."

"And that matches your birth certificate?"

"I don't carry it around with me," Arnold snapped. "I, uh, I have it at home—at least, my Canadian one."

"You were born in Canada? But I thought . . ."

"No, no. I was born in Oslo, but when we all emigrated, my certificate got left behind. They couldn't bring too much over, and I guess . . ." He hesitated, a sickly smile betraying a little embarrassment. "Well, some things were lost. They got a new one made up once they moved to Toronto."

Marit nodded slowly. "I see."

"It was soon after the war. Everyone accepted that things got lost. My father contacted the authorities in Oslo and tried to get a copy of my original certificate, but apparently lots of official records from that time got lost."

"And the Canadian authorities checked the details with Oslo?"

"I . . . I . . ." Arnold shrugged as though he was shrugging for his life. "I guess so."

Marit gave an upturned smile, unimpressed. "And this birth certificate definitely names you as Arnold?"

"Well, it says 'Arne.' When I was growing up everyone called me Arnold, and I got tired of correcting them. It kind of stuck."

Marit took a few seconds to drag her gaze away from Arnold and spent a few more seconds deep in thought. For a moment Arnold thought she was going to cry.

"What's wrong?" Merlene asked her. "What are you getting at?"

"Oh, it's nothing." Marit dismissed her thoughts with a shake of the head and pointed to the other pieces of paper. "But I'd like you to continue looking at these pieces of paper to find out if anything more occurs to you about your mother and Ulrich." Then she froze for a moment. "On second thought . . ." She reached back into her bag and pulled out a plastic pouch, inside which was a small booklet. "I got hold of this. I probably shouldn't be showing it to you, but there's one thing troubling me and . . . well, I have an idea."

"Sure," Arnold said. "I'm as keen as you are to find our long-lost brother."

And then Marit gave him a strange, pitying look. He was about to ask her whether she was all right when she opened the small booklet. "This is the Lebensborn record for Ulrich," she said.

"The *what?*" Arnold said.

"The Lebensborn program was set up to produce babies with what the Nazis saw as the correct genetic features. Ulrich was a Lebensborn baby."

"You mean, like . . . what's that thing? Eugenics?"

"That's right."

"You're *kidding* me." Arnold took a sharp breath. "My mother took part in that? *My mother?*"

Marit smiled politely. "I know it's hard to accept, but please, just . . . just let me read this to you."

Arnold nodded for her to go ahead, and she read out a list of events. There was the date Ingrid had applied to be a member of the program, verification of the racial purity of her parents and grandparents, the date she'd been accepted, recommended dates for conception, the estimated date of actual conception. Then there were details of the monthly checks carried out during pregnancy and progress of the baby's weight and general health. Then she said there was a point in time after the war when entries changed from German to Norwegian, followed by details of the occasion when, in the early hours of one morning, baby Ulrich was removed from care by Ingrid Jacobsen and/or an accomplice.

At that point Arnold interrupted. "No, no, no," he said. "Double-check that date."

She repeated it.

"But that can't be. May 26, 1945. That's . . ." He paused for a few moments, as though a spurious thought had stopped him in his tracks.

He threw the thought to one side with a shake of his head. "That's the exact date of my birth."

"Are you certain?"

"It's the date on my birth certificate." He saw Marit stare down at the floor, shoulders hunched, so he continued, "Surely that's too much of a coincidence. I mean, if she'd just given birth, or was still in labor, how could she . . ."

Marit started to gasp and then cry.

"What's wrong?" Arnold said. "I'm sorry if I . . ."

Marit stuttered words out. "No, Arnold. I'm wondering. Could that be the date she deliberately had put on your Canadian birth certificate?"

"I'm not sure I follow." Arnold could feel the flesh on his face getting heavier by the second. "I mean, they gave that date when they registered my birth in Toronto. Why would they deliberately put down a different date? Unless they wanted to . . . no, no. They wouldn't have . . . I mean . . ." All he could finish with was, "I'm confused."

"I was confused," Marit said. "But I don't think I am now." She looked across to him, her eyes bright and glinting like two watery blue gemstones. "You know what I think? I think, as far as she was concerned, that was the date you truly became hers." Arnold froze as Marit reached over and held his hand. "It could be," she said, "that after seventeen years I've finally found my half brother."

Arnold shook his head. "No," he hissed. "No way." He cursed under his breath, and again, and in a few frantic seconds his mind reeled with memories of how as a boy he was always tall for his age, how he didn't seem to physically resemble the man he always assumed was his father, the new birth certificate his mother had made up in Toronto, and of course, the more recent memory of the words his mother told him while she lay dying in the hospital: *Arne must never know about his father.*

He stared at Marit's face, now trying to convince himself that it didn't resemble his own at all but failing. He snatched his hand away from hers. "I can't handle this," he said. "I just . . . I can't believe it. This isn't true. None of this is true. You're lying."

Merlene put an arm around his shoulder. "Take it easy, Arnold."

"Okay, okay." He took a few heavy breaths, a palm holding his chest, then turned his head to face Merlene. "So, what do you make of all this?"

"You want my honest opinion?" Her face held the crooked smile of bad news. "The whole thing looks pretty convincing."

"But I . . . I don't know. It's like I'm not sure who I am anymore." He looked at Merlene and Marit in turn. "Does that sound stupid?"

"I know who you are," Marit said. "And there's nothing to be ashamed of or worried about, Arnold. You're my half brother. *You are Ulrich.* You might not like it. I can understand that. But think about it. There can be no other explanation." Her eyes roamed over his face for a few seconds. "It's funny," she said, sorrow more than humor controlling her own face. "As soon as I saw you, I thought we looked alike."

Arnold took another deep breath and let it out slowly.

Merlene gave the back of his neck a squeeze, caressing it. "Come on, Arnold. It's a shock."

"A *shock*? Jesus."

There were a few moments of silence, both women waiting for Arnold's next word.

He addressed Marit. "So, *if* this is all true . . ." He noticed the two women exchange a knowing glance at his stress on the *if*. "Hey, don't look at each other like that. This isn't certain . . . well, okay, we'll see, but . . . who is my real father? That's to say, *our* father?"

"Oh, Arnold," Marit muttered, her face creasing with pity. "I'm not sure I should say. It might be better for you to sleep on this news and—"

"Tell me who the hell my father is," Arnold said. "Just tell me."

Marit now looked more intently at his face, assessing him. "Okay," she said, nodding. She opened the booklet from the war years, then showed it to Arnold and pointed to a name.

"Franz Wahlberg?" he said. "My father is called *Franz*?"

She pointed to the word in front of the name.

"*Oberscharführer*?"

Marit nodded.

"What does that mean?"

"Look at me, Arnold," Merlene said from the side. He did as asked, his mind a fog of turmoil. "Whatever it means, it doesn't change who you are. Not to me. Not to anyone."

"She's right," Marit said. "Don't take any of this to heart."

"Never mind that. Tell me what that word means. Just *who* is my father, Marit?"

"He's a man who has been searching for you for a long time. Seventeen years ago, he tracked me down and told me who I was, and together we've been searching for you ever since then. And now I've found you, he . . . well, he wants to meet you."

"And?"

"He lives in Germany, in a care home in Munich. Arnold, your father was an SS officer during the war."

"An *SS officer*? I . . . but . . . isn't that a *Nazi* officer?"

Marit didn't nod or shake her head. It was all the answer Arnold needed. He held his head in his hands. Nobody spoke for a minute or two.

"Let me get this right," Arnold then said, wiping the film of sweat that had greased his brow. "You're saying a Nazi soldier . . . what . . . he *raped* my mother, and I'm the result?"

Marit opened her mouth but paused to fully consider her reply before speaking. "I guess in these times it might possibly be considered that, yes, but . . . well, your mother signed the papers." She flicked through the booklet and pointed to a signature. "She agreed to the whole thing. It was very common back then."

"I'm not sure I really care whether it was common. We're not exactly talking love-child scenario here, are we? It all sounds so mechanical, so . . ."

"Formal?" Marit suggested.

"Yeah."

"Well, Lebensborn was an official government program. It was very formal by its nature."

"Excuse me, Marit," Merlene said softly from the side. "Is that what happened to you too? I mean, to your mother?"

In a second the wrinkles around her eyes deepened. "Exactly the same. Franz is my father too."

"Dear God," Arnold muttered, shaking his head.

"She went through hell," Marit said. "I know, because I was lucky enough to talk with her about it before she died. Times were hard; the officers could be very persuasive. Persuasion is easy when you have power. But even when the war was over, and the baby was handed back to my mother, when she thought the nightmare was over, she suffered terribly."

"Even when the war was over?" Merlene asked. "Could you tell us why?"

"The neighbors and authorities saw me as a half Nazi, a reminder of the Germans. My mother was beaten, her home attacked—eventually she couldn't take any more and fled to Sweden."

"It fits," Arnold said. "Your mother fled to Sweden, mine to Canada, where my father had relatives. Except, of course, he wasn't my biological father."

Marit took a breath to speak, but Arnold's head jerked as he convulsed in tears, head in hands. Merlene got out a few tissues and handed them to him, holding him, resting his head on her shoulder.

The two women waited in silence until he recovered.

"I'm sorry," he said, sniffling. "I just had an image appear in my head of my father—I mean, the man I thought of as my father." His hand shot up in front of him. "No, no, no. He *was* my father. This son-of-a-bitch SS guy was no father of mine. My real father—he was so good to me, even though I wasn't really his. I can't believe I'm only finding this out thirty years after I said goodbye to him. And in all that time he didn't let on."

"I know how you feel," Marit said. "My father—my father in Sweden—was such a good man. I was lucky. I wouldn't have guessed the truth, not unless Franz tracked me down. They fled the country, like yours, but your parents went one step further. They must have changed your name after they got to Canada so you wouldn't ever find out about your biological father and Lebensborn."

"It all must have been so horrible for them," Merlene said. "For all four of your parents equally."

Marit nodded. "Of course, I've researched the subject. It's only very recently that people in Norway have come to terms with how unpleasant many local people were to Lebensborn mothers and how the authorities colluded in their mistreatment."

"I guess it does all fit together," Arnold said. "Emigrating to Canada. Changing my name. Telling the folks in Saskatoon not to forward letters. Cutting herself off from Oslo. I can understand my mom doing that. So, not only did those German soldiers get to screw lots of pretty girls, no strings, but the mothers had to go into hiding after the war. Sounds like a woman's worst nightmare. And now you're telling me the slimy creature that did this to my mom wants to meet me? You have to be kidding. I'm likely to break the guy's neck."

"He's ninety-five and very frail."

"Like that should make a difference? Wrong is wrong, for Christ's sake."

"Hey, Arnold," Merlene said from the sidelines. "You should take it easy."

"Don't tell me to take it easy. I've just found I'm the bastard son of a . . ." His words trailed off to curses. "I'm sorry, Merlene. I'm sorry."

"It's okay."

Arnold stood up and paced the room for a few minutes, took a drink of water thrown into the back of his throat as if he was putting out a fire there, and eventually settled back down, facing Marit. He let out a long breath. "I guess I . . . I could calm down and meet the guy. Is that really what he wants? Seriously?"

"He speaks good English, and he wants to talk to you."

"About what?"

"It's probably best coming from him. Does this mean you are prepared to meet him?"

"Oh, yeah." Arnold nodded. "I'll be on my best behavior. I know I won't hurt the guy, but I'd like to meet him. I have quite a few questions I want answered."

They all booked themselves onto a flight leaving for Munich early the next morning, after which Merlene and a silent Arnold accompanied Marit onto the street outside, where she caught a taxi to her hotel.

"You go back in," Arnold said as the cab drove off. "I'll only be a few minutes." He grabbed his phone from his jacket pocket.

"Your daughters?"

"Oh, I can't face them just now. I have to call my sister."

"You're gonna tell her?"

"You don't think I should?" He motioned to put his phone away.

She gave him a discreet peck on the lips. "I *do* think you should. Take whatever time you need."

Arnold watched her walk to the door, where she threw a smile over her shoulder at him. He felt his heart get just a little lighter, then hit *Barb* on his phone.

"Arnold?"

"Hi, sis."

"Sis?" She laughed. "Since when did you call me that? Is everything all right?"

"Everything's fine, but there's something I need to tell you."

"Have you found Ulrich?"

Arnold took a gulp. "Listen to me, Barbara. About Ulrich. It's . . . it's me."

"What? I don't understand. I think you were breaking up."

"It's me, Barbara. It's me. I mean, *he's* me. I'm Ulrich."

"I don't understand."

"The person I was looking for, my half brother, the baby Mom had by another man. That baby was me."

"What? Are you certain? How can you be—"

"It's certain. It's . . . certain."

Silence.

"Barbara? You okay?"

"Me? I'm fine. A little shocked, but what about *you*? You must feel so confused."

"Oh, to say the least."

"So, who was your real father?"

"Listen, Barbara. There's more to tell, but I had to call you. I'll let that sink in with you, and . . . God, it's still sinking in with me . . . look, I'll come see you as soon as I get back."

"I'd like that, Arnold."

"We should see more of each other. Stay in touch more."

"I hope so. And yeah, I need a while for it to sink in."

"Okay."

"You know something, Arnold?"

"What?"

"Whatever you tell me, I'll still think of Dad as your father."

"Me too, Barbara. Nothing changes that. Look, now I've got more free time, I should make a plan to come up to Montreal to see you once a month or so."

"And I'll call you every weekend."

"Sure. I gotta go."

"Arnold, just tell me one thing. Did Dad know about this?"

"He did. All the way along. Right from before I was born."

"Oh, God." Arnold heard her voice crack. "He must have loved Mom a hell of a lot, eh?"

"More than we could imagine, I'd say."

"You know, somehow I always had Dad down as one of the good guys. Always."

"He was. He really was. I really need to go now."

"Wait." Arnold heard her sniffing. "Could I ask you one more favor, Arnold?"

"Sure."

"When we meet, whenever we talk, and for always, please, let's not get into any of this half brother and half sister crap. You'll always be my brother, no matter what you say."

"You . . . uh . . . you don't know what it's like to hear that, Barbara. Listen, I'll be in touch. And soon."

"Bye, brother."

"Yeah. Bye, sister."

Arnold closed the call and headed for the hotel entrance. "One of the good guys, for sure," he muttered to himself as he went inside.

Chapter 33

Saskatchewan, 1946

Ingrid sat at the kitchen table of their log cabin, the envelope with the crooked Norwegian stamp and its contents in front of her, and tried to stem the trickle of tears.

"Oh, no," she muttered to herself. "No, no, no." She gasped, fighting for regular breaths.

"Who are you talking to?" came a voice behind her.

Ingrid quickly covered the envelope and its contents with a newspaper and wiped the tears from her face.

"Are you all right?"

Ingrid nodded, perhaps a little too frantically. "Yes, Mamma. I'm just . . ."

"Tired?"

"Yes. Just a bad night with little Barbara. You know what she's like."

Ingrid's mamma smiled and gave her a kiss on the temple. "Aren't they odd, children? You think of everything little Ulrich's been through in his life, and he's good as gold. But Barbara? Well, she looks like she's going to grow up to be the awkward one."

"There's nothing wrong with Barbara."

Her mamma stilled herself at Ingrid's tone.

"I'm sorry, Mamma. I didn't mean it like that."

"Of course, dear. I was only . . . are you sure you're all right?"

"Like you said, I'm tired. That's all."

"It's fine, Ingrid. I know what babies can be like."

Ingrid half expected her mamma to add that she knew twice over what babies were like, but she didn't, and Ingrid understood it was something best left unsaid. Ingrid had often wanted to ask more about Arne, the brother she never knew. Now she felt an urge to just say the name, because the name had been on her mind ever since she'd been in that horrible Lebensborn clinic. But her mamma spoke first.

"Look, Ingrid. I was going to fix myself some breakfast and get off to work, but if you'd prefer me to look after the children while you sleep in, I don't think they'd miss me. You *do* look awfully tired."

Ingrid shook her head. "I'll be fine, Mamma."

She watched her mamma mix a breakfast of salmon, cheese, and eggs, all the time pretending to read the newspaper, and as she sat down at the table to eat, Ingrid spoke.

"Could I ask you a question, Mamma?"

"Of course, dear."

"You're still in touch with your sister in Oslo, aren't you?"

"We were never what you might call *close*, but I like to keep in touch, to hear what's going on back home, and they like to hear what's happening with us."

"Did you . . . did you tell them not to give our address to anyone?"

Her mamma had started eating but now stopped and screwed her face up with suspicion. "What do you mean?" she said. "What's wrong?"

Ingrid took a gulp. "Oh, it's . . . it's nothing. I just wondered."

"Well, of course I told them that. I can't remember exactly what I said. Does it matter now?"

"No," Ingrid said, making herself smile. "No, it doesn't matter. You get to work. I have to get Ulrich up and feed him."

Ingrid spent all day alone with her son and daughter, which gave her a lot of time to think. And to read the newspaper. And to read a few older ones too. It was the only option. By the time her mamma and Olav returned home, she still hadn't decided for certain but knew she would tell them what was going to happen and assess their reaction.

"What are you cooking?" Olav said, kissing her even before he'd taken off his jacket. He sniffed the air. "I can't smell anything."

"I haven't had time to cook anything yet," Ingrid replied.

He frowned, puzzled, but said nothing as he took off his jacket and boots. When he realized Ingrid was still standing next to him, and when she asked both him and her mamma over to the table, it only made him eye her up more suspiciously.

Her mamma asked her what was happening, but they all sat down, Ingrid next to the small pile of newspapers she'd been perusing off and on all day.

"How do you both feel about moving to Toronto?" she said.

Her mamma and Olav exchanged a look that questioned her sanity, but a smile quickly appeared on Olav's face, and he started laughing. He quickly stopped when Ingrid's face didn't join in. "What?" he said. "I don't understand."

"I received something in the mail today," Ingrid said. She moved the newspapers to one side, revealing the envelope. She opened it and took out the two objects she'd been thinking about all day but had hardly looked at after first seeing them.

One was a slip of paper with the words YOU CAN'T HIDE, WHITE-FEATHER WOMAN scribbled thickly on it in Norwegian. The other object was yet another pure white feather.

"Oh, dear God," Olav muttered, holding his head in his hands.

Ingrid's mamma burst into tears.

"Someone knows?" Olav said. "But who? And how?"

"The letter stinks of Laila, but that doesn't matter now. I've had a lot of time to think."

"Oh, no," Olav muttered.

"*Just hear what I have to say*," Ingrid told him.

"Of course. I'm sorry. Go on."

"Olav, I know your cousin's here, and he and his family have been so good to us that we'll never be able to repay them. But your talents are wasted at that lumberyard; we both know it's not even *close* to what you can achieve. You're a carpenter. You have a skill that could earn more money." She prodded the newspapers. "Look in there. A big city like Toronto. Lots of jobs. Skilled jobs. Well-paid work."

At first, all Olav could manage was a sigh. But Ingrid waited, and the words eventually came. "You don't think you're being a little . . . paranoid?" he said.

She firmly shook her head. "I'm not having this, Olav. Not for my son."

"For *our* son."

"I'm sorry, *our* son." She smiled politely. "But we can all speak a little English now. We shouldn't be afraid of new opportunities."

"But that isn't why you want to go, is it?"

"No, but—"

"And what happens when whoever sent that finds out our new address?"

"They won't. I'll make sure of it." She turned to her mamma, now dry eyed but blowing her nose. "Mamma? How do you feel about going to Toronto?"

She shrugged. "You're my family. I go where you go."

"Are you sure?" Olav said to her. "We're all settled here, you with your job at the store and—"

"Olav," she snapped. "*You* are the one with family ties here. You should understand that *I* go where *my* family goes."

"Thank you, Mamma," Ingrid said. She stared blankly at Olav. "Well?"

The reply was immediate. "Well, of course. If that's what you want. We'll do it."

She reached across and held his hand. "Good," she said. "That leaves just one more thing I have to tell you."

"What's that?" Olav said. "Another surprise?"

"Little Ulrich," she said. "We're doing this for him more than ourselves. I've decided it must be a clean break. When we move there, nobody must know . . . well, *you know what.*"

"Whatever happened to *no secrets?*" Olav asked.

"No secrets? Think about it, Olav. Do you really want to tell the truth to that boy when he can speak and understand? Or when he grows up to be a man? You want to tell him who his real father is? You think he could live a happy and normal life knowing that?" She gave her head a stiff shake. "Some secrets are secrets for a good reason. I want him to grow up thinking *you* are his pappa and knowing nothing more. And so help me, Olav, big as you are, I'll fight you all the way on this issue."

"No, no." Now he grabbed her hand and squeezed it. "You don't need to argue with me, Ingrid. I understand, and I . . . I agree with you."

Ingrid took a swallow to recover. "Good," she said. "That boy must never know about his blood father, and as long as I live, I'll pray for that. And that's why, when we get to Toronto, he isn't going to be *Ulrich*; he's going to be *Arne.*"

"Arne?" Olav said. "Why Arne?"

"Aah," Ingrid's mamma said softly, tears pooling in her eyes again. "Your brother."

"Brother?" Olav said. "What brother?"

"I'll tell you later. But one last thing. You know we never had his birth certificate? We could register his birth in Toronto. I've checked."

"Register him as *Arne?*"

"Yes. And if we're all careful, he'll never know his original name and so never have the shame. What do you think?"

Olav exhaled loudly, went to speak once or twice before giving up, but eventually said, "Yes, of course. If that's what you really want. If that's what will make you happy."

Ingrid leaned to the side and held him close, kissing him on the lips. "I love you, Olav," she said.

Chapter 34

Munich, Germany, 2011

Arnold and Merlene were waiting for a taxi outside the airport while Marit was getting some euros. Both were silent, Arnold gazing ahead to nothingness, Merlene keeping one eye on him as if he were a toddler about to run off.

"You okay?" she said.

"Sure," he replied. "Still feeling a little stupid for not working out the obvious. I mean, why didn't it occur to me that this might be a possible explanation?"

Merlene stepped closer to him, their shoulders touching. "I guess you try to ignore some possibilities."

"I guess you're right. And I'm still not sure I'm doing the right thing here."

"The right thing? You're meeting your father. How can that be not right?"

"I'm meeting *a stranger*. And I'm wondering . . . well, I just get the feeling what I'm doing isn't fair on my father—that is, my, uh, *Norwegian* father, Mom's husband. God, it feels so weird to even *say* that. I'll never get used to that."

"I can't see he'd mind. You're going to *meet* Franz; that's all. It was Olav who had your best years—years nobody can take away from either of you. I think he'd be happy with that."

Arnold glanced at her. It was a glance of uncertainty. "Something else has been troubling me."

"Hey, I'm not surprised."

"Well, I was wondering how *you* feel about it."

"Me?" Merlene shrugged. "How I feel about what, exactly?"

"About who my father is. About *what* he was."

"I . . . I don't know what you expect me to say."

"Surely it bothers you, the fact I'm descended from him?"

"Oh, now I see what you're getting at." She narrowed her eyes at him. "And you really think I care about that?"

"So, you don't?"

"You're still the same guy you were yesterday or last week, aren't you?"

Arnold felt his body relax, as though poison was draining out of his veins. "Thank you," he said breathlessly. "It's a hell of a relief to hear you say that."

"Just don't let me down when you meet him. And don't let yourself down. He's an old man."

"Well, actually, the guy's a Nazi."

"To me, he's an old man. That means he's a human being."

Arnold thought about that for a moment. "I'll try my best to take that into account."

They were joined by Marit, who immediately asked Arnold if he was okay.

"I think so," he replied with as much calmness as he could muster.

"There's one more thing I should have told you," she said, so slowly and clearly it unnerved him. "Franz might talk about you being his son, but you don't have to call him Father or Dad. I don't, and he doesn't seem to mind."

"Good," Arnold said. "And will you two please stop asking me if I'm okay?"

The taxi took them through the backstreets of Munich to a rather dilapidated slab-fronted block of a building. The glass door was reinforced with heavy wire mesh, the plastic cover on the handle taped up by way of repair. It was a stone's throw from a railway bridge across the road, and just as Marit pressed the security intercom button, a train whistled past, camouflaging the sound of any bell or buzzer that might have sounded.

It took almost a minute for the call to be answered. Marit explained to the intercom in German who she was and who she'd come to see, and the heavy solenoid clunked to unlock the door.

Inside, the home was functional, if only just about clean enough, with a stickiness to every handle and surface, fire doors wedged open with scraps of paper, and a musty smell permeating the whole building. But eventually they signed in and were shown to a dayroom where most of the patients were asleep in front of the television.

Marit took the lead, and the three of them were soon sitting with a figure in the far corner—a painfully slim man with just a few tufts of hair on either side of a bald pate covered in lesions, and eyes so red they looked like they'd been sandpapered.

Marit spoke slowly and loudly.

"Franz," she said, "it's Marit."

He frowned and peered at her for a moment. "Marit, my daughter. How are you?"

Arnold was thrown. It seemed such an ordinary greeting for a meeting that was so surreal and, to him, momentous.

"I'm fine," Marit replied. "And I, uh . . . well, I have some important news for you."

The man gulped and looked in puzzlement at the two other strangers, and it took him a few seconds to follow it up with, "Have you found Ulrich?"

She turned to Arnold and whispered, "He always says that. Every time I've seen him, he asks about you." She turned back to Franz. "Prepare yourself for a shock, Franz." She pointed to Arnold. "Say hello to this man. He is your other Lebensborn child, my half brother."

The man's eyes now fully opened; his jaw gaped.

"This is the man you know as Ulrich."

He coughed and spluttered a few times, not taking his scared eyes off Arnold; then his face became edged with a steely suspicion. "Is this true?" he said to Arnold. "You are Ulrich, my son?"

Arnold found it hard to nod, as though it would be giving in, almost betraying his mother. "My name is Arnold," he said. "At least, I've been known by that name for most of my life. I was brought up in Canada and still live there, but the evidence would appear to prove I was born to Ingrid Jacobsen and Franz Wahlberg in Oslo in September 1944 and was christened Ulrich."

A weak groan escaped from the old man's lips, and his hand, a row of walnuts for knuckles, shook wildly as it covered his face.

"Are you okay, Franz?" Marit asked.

He took his time but nodded in reply. "I should be happy. I've waited for so many years to meet my son, but . . . it upsets me to hear the name *Ingrid*. I remember her well." He peered at Arnold. "You know, your mother was a beautiful woman."

"I do know," Arnold replied.

"Of course you do. She was tall and slim with just about the right amount of curves. She was beautiful, and I was horrible to her."

"I know that too."

"And I remember the man she married. Olav was his name. A very brave man. Fearless."

"My father. Well, technically not so, as it turns out."

The old man shook his head, slab-of-steak jowls not hurrying to keep up. "No, no. Please don't think of me as your father."

"I don't." Arnold could feel the thumping of his heart fading rapidly. He'd prepared himself for this, rehearsed in his mind how he would give the bastard the third degree, regardless of his age. He had an arsenal of questions he would demand answers to from the man who had done such a disgusting thing to his mother. There was anger when he'd first become aware of his history, anger on the flight to Munich, anger even as he'd walked to the man's room. But now, faced with a figure about as dangerous as a warm marshmallow, there was only a little bitterness and a lot of desire to find out the man's motivations all those years ago.

"Mister," he said. "I'm not here for your benefit; I have my own reasons. Tell me; did you ever think of my mother as a person—someone with a heart and feelings?"

"It was a long time ago." Franz shifted in his seat, his face showing pain as he did so. "I have to confess that at first I didn't. But very quickly I realized that your mother was a caring person, putting the interests of her mother and Olav before herself. You could say she sold herself to me to save them."

"Oh, yes?"

"Her mother was ill; Olav had worked for the Norwegian Resistance. She agreed to do what I wanted in return for medicine for her mother and a guarantee of protection for Olav. Her crime was to care for them too much, which, to my own eternal disgust, I saw as a sign of weakness and took advantage of."

"So, why the hell did you do what you did?"

"At the time I was doing my duty, nothing more, nothing less. I was doing what my government asked of me."

"But you realize how bad that sounds now? Do you think you deserve mercy or forgiveness for what you did?"

"Please be careful," Marit said to him. "He's very frail."

"Don't listen to her," Franz said. "Shout at me if you want to. Strike me if it makes you feel better. It's what I deserve, what I want."

"It's what you want? In that case I won't."

"Hey, go easy," Merlene whispered.

"Easy? This guy might be old and frail—he might be my biological father—but do you know what? I don't think I can forgive him."

"Perhaps *this guy* doesn't want forgiveness," Franz said, silencing them for a moment. "But I can tell you what happened to me after the war. If you'd like to listen, that is."

Arnold looked at Merlene and Marit, who both nodded. "Okay," he said to Franz.

"Well, the first thing you should know is that I was poisoned from the start, born into a bitter country. In the 1920s Germany was a void, nothing more. And then, in the 1930s, there were promises. We had dreams, we were given hope of a better world that our government was shaping for us, and I was carried along in the tide of fashion. I can't go into those details, but when I close my eyes, the visions come to me."

"You have visions?" Arnold said.

The old man's head nodded just a few degrees. "They tell me of those promises, dreams, and hopes of what we thought would be a better world. The visions stop me sleeping with their message of a new beginning to come. But the most upsetting thing—the thing that keeps me awake—is not the words, but the fact that every one of those visions contains the same person: me—that is, my younger self. The visions won't let go of me, and they tell me of a poor soul that only sees what it was told to see for so many years. No, I can't talk of the visions I have; they haunt me enough as it is. But I can tell you about my feelings during and after the war, about how I felt about Lebensborn."

"I think I'd like to hear that," Arnold said. "How you might try to justify what you did."

"Oh, I often ask myself that. I often asked myself at the time what my motivation was, whether it really was a desire to help the fatherland or whether it was pure desire to have your mother and Marit's mother—to possess them, in a sense. And every time, I convinced myself my motives were social and political, not personal."

"So what happened after the war? Did you come to your senses?"

"What's hard for anyone now to understand is that when the war ended, it was hard to cope."

"What? Are you after sympathy?"

"Hey, Arnold," Merlene interjected. "Go easy."

Arnold let out a sigh. "Okay. You were saying?"

Franz continued. "I'm most definitely not seeking sympathy. I'm just telling it as it is—or *as it was*. You see, everything we had been brought up to believe—all those promises, hopes and dreams of a better world—were being broken up by the victors, just because they had won the war. It seemed so unfair. I was still adamant that the Third Reich, in some form or other, would soon rise again. Loyalty to the fatherland was the calcium in my bones. I refused to believe it was the end. The Lebensborn program was social responsibility, the solving of the Jewish problem was essential for the progress of humanity, and expansion of the Germanic Empire was for the good of the world. I had been brought up to believe in all of that, and now that progress was being taken away in a few months."

"Mmm . . . well, I guess I can see that. You must have changed, though?"

Franz's face creased up in pain. "Not at first. After a year or so I was impatient, wondering why the new government had given up on the National Socialist dreams of my better years. Also, my marriage was in serious trouble, partly because of my obsession with the war—with losing it—and partly because my wife found out what I'd done in Norway. But none of that seemed important to me. I joined an underground organization dedicated to resurrecting the aims of the Third Reich."

"You mean you carried on?"

"We tried to. It was my state of mind at the time. My wife said I was mad, but I didn't listen. I lived in the woods, preparing for the first assault on the occupying United States forces. That didn't last long, so I returned home. I argued with my wife, could hardly bear to look at my children because they reminded me of my other children, and I drank heavily. I said and did things to my wife and children I am ashamed of. It took me three more years to accept that those promises of the 1930s would come to nothing, that the dreams were nightmares, that the hopes were unfounded. By then my wife had disowned me and wouldn't let me near my children. Such was the shock that I starved myself for six months and nearly died. I think nowadays they would call it a breakdown. As I recovered, I started to learn more of the concentration camps, of my fellow Germans who had used live Jewish bodies for experiments, scavenged dead ones for hair and gold. I learned of how they considered the blind and the infirm to be a burden on society that needed to be eradicated. It was about then that I started to have my visions."

"These are the visions you still get now?"

"Unfortunately, yes. And it was at that moment that I started to see the Lebensborn program in a new light—the children dragged away from their loving parents, the treatment shown to those considered to have inferior physical traits through no fault of their own. I was shocked, unable to function, because I could finally see the faults in everything I had been led to believe was right. I became institutionalized, only coming out when I was nearly forty to a world that resembled nothing I recognized. I did the only thing I felt able to do: I talked about those years and my experiences. I talked to children, to adults, to anyone who would listen, just explaining how I had been misled in my younger years."

"And did any of that help?"

"I'm not sure, but I know those visions in my head continued. As much as I tried to bury all thoughts of my two Lebensborn children, I kept thinking of them and read about how they were so badly treated in their own countries, by their own people, often with the collusion or even the instruction of governments that should have been protecting them. These innocent children were not one thing nor the other, half-good but also half-bad, mongrels of the worst kind, disowned by societies that should have been caring for them, unwanted by all but their own mothers. I felt a need that I couldn't fight—the need to do something about my own Lebensborn children, to find them and help them. I knew that in my mental state I couldn't do that, but the thought of never meeting them and never finding out how their lives had turned out simply wouldn't leave me, and the strain of suppressing those thoughts was too much for me. I . . . I went into a home, and I haven't been able to care for myself since then. And that's a long time."

There was silence for a few moments, Arnold simply staring at Franz, at his withered form. He was on the verge of telling Franz that he could now see what a rough life he'd had but held his tongue, confused in his own mind about his feelings toward such a frail old man.

"But I persevered," Franz said. "There is some goodness in everybody, and my goodness was that I didn't give up. When I entered my seventies, I decided that if I only did one useful thing with my life, it would be to trace my two Lebensborn children. I knew it would be too late to help them, but I wanted them to know that I never forgot them and always wished them and their mothers the best in life. Marit was easy to trace. You, not so easy."

"I guess my mother covered her tracks well."

"She didn't have much choice. She had a lot to put up with in Oslo."

"I know. Marit told me the people of Oslo showed little mercy to Lebensborn mothers."

"That's putting it mildly. Your mother didn't deserve that, just like she didn't deserve what I put her through. Even people who should have been her friends turned on her. There was one woman in particular, I remember, a neighbor of theirs who coordinated the attacks."

"Attacks?" Arnold said, the word adding even more sourness to the picture unfolding in his mind.

Franz nodded. "Physical attacks. This woman worked for the Resistance during the occupation, hated us Germans, and hated any Norwegian who had anything to do with us."

"But how do you know what happened after the war? You must have left Oslo, surely?"

"I did, but that was where Marit helped."

They all turned to Marit, who spoke quietly in a sad, regretful tone.

"When Franz tracked me down all those years ago, he also wanted to know what happened to his other Lebensborn child, and, of course, when I found out I had a half brother, I wanted to find him too. Franz told me about this woman—the unpleasant neighbor—and she turned out to be a major clue. I went to Ostergaten while a few of that generation still lived there and talked to them. I found out that after the war this woman was absolutely determined to drive your mother out of her home, out of Oslo. And she succeeded, as it happens, driving her out of Norway."

"And only now do we know where to," Franz said. "She was such a nasty woman." He shook his head in disgust.

"This woman," Merlene interrupted, "do you happen to remember her name?"

"Oh, I've never forgotten her name. It was Laila."

"Laila?" Arnold said, shooting a glance to Merlene.

"That explains a lot," Merlene said.

"Anyhow," Franz said, "all I can say is that I hope your mother enjoyed her life."

"She did."

Franz looked Arnold in the eye. "I'm pleased. She deserved happiness. And tell me, Arnold; do you have any regrets in life?"

Arnold thought for a moment. "Uh, one or two, I guess. Nothing major."

"I know I don't deserve any happiness, but that gives me a warm feeling, and I'm pleased for you, not for myself. I think you should know that my life has been one long regret. Those visions whenever I close my eyes—visions of myself in situations my madness prevents me from describing—keep me awake every night. Only belligerence and cowardice—fear of what awaits me—keep me alive. Sometimes I think the only thing that kept me going until now was the desire to know that my children were happy in life. Have you been happy in life, Arnold?"

"I have. Very."

"Good. We both have Ingrid to thank for that. She sheltered you well. She was a good mother, as I'm sure you know."

"She was the best I could have had. I think I understand that more now than I ever did before."

"Arnold, I don't want forgiveness, but will you do one thing for me after you leave here?"

"What's that?"

"Will you visit her grave and tell her I said I'm sorry?"

"I, uh . . ." Arnold gave a heavy sigh. "You know, Franz, I think I will do that for you."

"Thank you," Franz said, his already rheumy eyes now overflowing with tears. "And feel free to visit me again. I mean, only if you want to."

"We'll see."

"How are you feeling?" Merlene asked Arnold, who hadn't spoken since the taxi left the care home for the airport.

"Oh, still confused," he replied, his weighty frown starting to wane just a little. "I never thought I'd be able to feel sorry for someone like that."

"It's clear he's had an awful life," Marit said. "If you consider everyone involved, the people who had foreign troops on every street corner, the people like our parents who were forced to flee their own countries, people like Franz, even you and me a little bit. There were no winners. Everyone ended up with scars of one sort or another."

"And you?" Arnold said. "Did you have an unhappy life?"

"No. Not at all. I was lucky that my mother was a strong woman."

"I guess I was lucky that way too." Arnold nodded. "They appear to have cleared up a whole lot of trouble, your mother and mine."

Merlene curled her arm around his and held his hand, squeezing. "It was a mess," she said, "but it's history. We should be grateful it's all over."

Arnold and Marit caught each other nodding in agreement at that. They smiled at the coincidence, a bit like brother and sister might.

"Tell me," Marit said. "Would you please stay in touch with me?"

"Funny. I was, uh . . . I was about to ask you the very same thing."

Marit smiled, the flesh around her eyes wrinkling as she did so, and Arnold realized it was the first time he'd seen such contentment on her face.

"I was worried you wouldn't want to," she said. "I never had any brothers and sisters, and my parents both died some time ago."

"Oh, I'm sorry. So, are you on your own? I feel a fool for not asking before, but do you have any other relatives other than myself and Franz?"

"I have a husband of almost forty years."

"Oh, good."

"And four daughters and nine grandchildren."

Arnold let loose with a husky laugh. He held his spare hand out. She took it. "You'd like Toronto," he said. "All of you."

Arnold and Marit talked all the way back to the airport and for most of the flight back to Oslo. Merlene just let them get on with it.

Late that evening, back in Oslo, Arnold and Merlene said farewell to Marit, saying they would arrange to meet first in Toronto, then in Stockholm, and returned to their hotel room.

Arnold immediately collapsed onto the bed, staring up at the ceiling. Merlene lay next to him, her chin resting on his shoulder.

"Thank you for coming with me," he said quietly.

"I enjoy your company," she said, her voice as soft and smooth as melted caramel. "Minibar or coffee?"

"I know what I *need*," he said. "And plenty of it too."

"I'll put the kettle on."

"Probably a good idea."

She got up, emptied two sachets into mugs, switched the kettle on, then lay back down next to him. He said nothing for a few moments, still gazing at the ceiling.

"You still thinking about Franz?" she said.

"You think I should see him again?"

"Well, do you want to?"

"He did some horrible things."

"There were a lot worse. From where I stand, he wasn't much more than a dumb foot soldier. And he's an old guy. You have to show a little mercy to an old guy. I'd keep in touch."

"Guess you're right. I'll be an old guy myself someday—well, an old*er* guy."

"Hey, shut up with that. You got plenty of time left."

"Yeah, yeah." A half smile twitched his lips. "Anyway, I wasn't thinking about him. I was thinking about . . ."

"About Olav? I mean, about your dad. Should I still call him that?"

"You should. And yes, ten out of ten for being perceptive; I was thinking about him."

"And what were you thinking?"

Arnold went to speak but shook his head instead.

"I'm not sure I can help you with that," she said. "I only knew him from what Ingrid told me, but he seemed a decent, honest man. And, I guess, after today I know he was exactly that." She lifted her head up to look at Arnold, at the pain on his face. "You okay?"

"Mmm . . ."

"What is it?"

"I feel bad about him."

"Bad? Why?"

Arnold sighed. "All my life I thought of him as . . . as just a great, great dad. Period. Well, I thought that up until a few weeks ago. And then, just for a while, I thought he was . . . oh, it doesn't matter what I thought, but it was bad; it wasn't nice. And now I find out he was actually more of a hero than I could ever have imagined."

"And so?"

"And I wish I could tell him I'm sorry for thinking something horrible about him. And also, I . . . I miss him. Thirty years. Thirty years, and I still miss him."

Arnold was in a trance for a few moments, until he noticed that Merlene had started to cry. He pulled out a handkerchief and handed it to her. "I'm sorry; I'm sorry."

"Don't apologize."

"You mentioned us visiting your folks in Jamaica."

"You still on for that?"

"One hundred percent. If you'll let me, that is."

She gave his shoulder a playful slap. "Good. But I'm warning you; I can't promise to match your family for intrigue and drama."

"Ah, that kinda stuff's overrated. Take it from me."

She dried the last of her tears, kissed him, then got up and made coffees. The flights had taken their toll. Neither Arnold nor Merlene felt like doing much but couldn't sleep either. Neither of them mentioned watching the TV. They talked for a couple of hours about their parents, their children, and themselves, both saying they'd like to get to know each other better. Then they made love slowly, as if they had all the time in the world for each other. And then they talked some more—this time about Merlene retiring and perhaps them taking some vacations together. Finally, their relaxed bodies entwined, they fell asleep within minutes of each other.

The next morning, Arnold was stirred by bright yellow dawn light leaking around the curtains. After a quick rub of his eyes he felt awake, refreshed. Against his expectations he'd slept well. His eyes fell upon Merlene's restful form, and he wondered how he'd gotten lucky enough to find such a beautiful and smart woman.

He immediately realized exactly how. He was indebted to his mother for inadvertently getting them together. He glanced upward and thanked her.

Then he thought he heard her voice.

As he took a few enlivening breaths, he thought some more about his mother, about what she'd gone through all those years ago, and what, perhaps, she might be trying to tell him.

And somehow he knew.

It takes courage and a lot of effort to make a fresh start in life. But more often than not, if you're with the right person, it's well worth the effort.

Epilogue

The farmhouse was modest and ramshackle, and the nearby chicken enclosures dotted over the yard were long past their best. There was, however, a distinct air of fastidiousness; all tools were labeled and placed in order from largest to smallest along the back wall, the borders and lawns had clearly been regularly weeded, and each chicken enclosure had been allotted a code number, which was displayed high up at one end, the sign dead center and perfectly level.

Two men approached one of the chicken enclosures. The uniformed one was slender, studious in appearance, and stood bolt upright. The one wearing dirty work clothes was taller and round shouldered, slouching as though trying to appear as small as the other man out of sympathy.

"Now these," the studious man said, "these have been of tremendous importance to me."

"What have? The chickens?"

"Of course."

"But they're just chickens. How can chickens be so important?"

"You didn't listen. I said they *were* important, but not any longer."

"So, why were they important? What did you do with them?"

"My wife took care of the feeding and the cleaning, I paid someone to look after the maintenance of the enclosure, and, most importantly, I tried my best to manage the breeding program."

"Breeding program? Don't you just put them in the same enclosure and let nature take its course?"

"Not if I want the best chickens possible."

"I don't understand."

The uniformed man sighed and spoke slowly and clearly. "My work is coming to a halt here. It hardly matters whether a person such as yourself is capable of understanding."

"But I'm interested. Could you please tell me what you were doing?"

"Very well." The uniformed man nodded. "You see, for some years it's been my desire to eliminate all traces of color from my stock. You see that one, for instance?"

A chicken stopped midstrut and flashed an eye toward them. The uniformed man crouched down to be closer to the bird and pointed at it. "Yes, I'm talking about you."

The comical routine forced a smile from the other man. "What about it?" he said.

"It has quite a lot of brown and black feathers on its back and tail; do you see?"

"Yes, I do."

"That one is for the pot. But the ones with only a few flecks of color here and there—those are the ones I would keep for breeding."

"Why didn't you just let them breed with whichever ones they are happiest to breed with?"

"Because I was trying to create pure white chickens."

"Why? Do the white ones taste better?"

"No."

"Well, do they behave themselves better? Or have more meat on them?"

The uniformed man suppressed a hint of a snarl. "Of course they don't."

"So, is the color of feathers really that important?"

"Of course it is!" He took a few breaths. "I'm sorry, but you obviously don't appreciate how much hard work I've carried out on this project. I kept records of the lineage; I can trace each one of these birds back generations. I've been trying for a few years to produce pure white specimens by breeding out unwanted genes, and I've made significant progress."

"Really? You've been working with these chickens for many years?"

"Oh, yes. Although I've spent a lot of that time studying genetics. It's more complicated than you might think, with a variety of dominant and recessive genes playing their part."

"I'm . . . not sure I know what you mean."

"I wouldn't expect a man like you to understand the science, but the basic practical aspects aren't hard to grasp. You only let the whiter ones breed. But it's complicated. For instance, the albinos—the white ones with bright red eyes—are not really pure white as such but are genetic defects, so they get killed straightaway. There's not even any point wasting food on them. Like I say, it's been hard work. I still think it could be done if I only had the spare time. Some people disagree, but I know it's possible for selective breeding to eradicate the nonwhite feathers completely and produce a breed that is both perfectly healthy and pure white. It's only genetics."

"I see. And now?"

"Well, now I'm finding I have less and less spare time due to other commitments of extreme national importance, which is why my wife and I are selling the place."

The other man nodded and opened his mouth to speak.

"Heinrich!"

The shout coming from the farmhouse made both men turn.

"Excuse me," the uniformed man said. "That's my wife calling. I'd better see what she wants." He gave the wire netting a pat. "Anyway, my beloved chickens are not important now. It's such a shame I haven't been able to complete the breeding program, but my country's need is far greater."

"And, I suppose, it's a shame you've wasted time on chickens."

"Oh, no. On the contrary." The man puffed his chest out and straightened his jacket. "I've learned so much. The theories I've developed in breeding chickens can be put to good use in other ways. Biology is biology, and genetics are genetics, regardless of the species." He took a step back toward the farmhouse. "And now I need to go. The future of this place is up to you, so take a look around. When I return, I'll expect you to decide whether you want to buy. Do you understand?"

"Oh, yes, Herr Himmler."

The uniformed man's final words were shouted as he walked off: "I will make history; believe me. And you could be buying a piece of that history."

The man in dirty work clothes turned back to the chickens and shook his head. He crouched down and picked up a feather—white but for a few flecks of black. He twirled it between his thumb and finger.

Just then a brown-and-white chicken strutted toward him, clucking and squawking.

"What a strange man your owner is," he said to the chicken. "Perfectly harmless, but very strange."

AUTHOR'S AFTERWORD

Like most of my historical fiction, this story is one that I believe could have happened. In other words, the historical facts are accurate, and the situations the characters found themselves in (and their reactions to those situations) are typical of the era.

The prologue and epilogue paint my own picture of how the seeds of Lebensborn were sown. Some of the historical facts are disputed, but it's generally accepted that while Heinrich Himmler headed up the SS from 1929 and held many responsibilities at the top of the Nazi government until his death in 1945, he was also trained in the science of agriculture and owned a poultry farm in Waldtrudering, where he experimented with selective breeding in a quest for pure white chickens. He sold his farm to give his full attention to his "other job" in politics and soon spearheaded the Lebensborn program, attempting to apply the theories of genetics he'd learned during chicken farming to the human population.

The symbology of pure white feathers and their use by the SS to represent Lebensborn is the result of my imagination and artistic license.

It's also generally accepted that the Nazi government saw Norwegians as having very desirable genetic traits, so much so that about half of the Lebensborn clinics outside of Germany were in Norway. Aside from the all-encompassing horror inflicted by the Nazi regime, perhaps the saddest feature of the Lebensborn program in Norway was the fate of the children and mothers once Norway had been liberated. In a country still recovering from the occupation, any reminder of those lost years was always going to be undesirable. But the people and government of Norway didn't cover themselves in glory with their treatment of these human "reminders." Most Lebensborn children were ridiculed and mistreated and went on to experience horrid lives at the hands of both the state and their fellow Norwegians—painfully ironic for people designed from their very conception to be the master race and the future of mankind. It took the Norwegian state seventy years to apologize for how Lebensborn mothers and their completely innocent children were treated after the war.

One particular victim of Lebensborn was a baby girl taken by her mother and grandmother to the safety of Sweden soon after the war who subsequently found fame and hopefully peace. There isn't really a park in Oslo named after her family; it's just my slightly clumsy way of bestowing a little honor on her true-life story. It's not a bad idea, though, if any Norwegians are reading this.

ACKNOWLEDGMENTS

I owe huge thanks to the following people for this story: Sammia Hamer, for advising me on what was wrong with the initial version; Celine Kelly, for her usual expert eye, which helped me kick the clunky bits into shape; Mindi Machart, for her excellent copyediting work; Stephanie Chou, for her eagle-eyed proofreading; and my wife, Maria, for putting up with me ignoring her for a few months while my head was in Toronto and Oslo.

ABOUT THE AUTHOR

Ray Kingfisher was born and bred in the Black Country in the United Kingdom, and he now lives in Hampshire. He has published novels under various pen names: Ray Backley, Ray Fripp, and most notably Rachel Quinn.

For more information on the author, please visit www.raykingfisher.com.